BEYOND

Born above a shoe shop in the mid-1960s, Neil spent most of his childhood in Wakefield in West Yorkshire as his father pursued a career in the shoe trade. This took Neil to Bridlington in his teens, where he failed all his exams and discovered that doing nothing soon turns into long-term unemployment. Re-inventing himself, Neil returned to education in his 20s, qualified as a solicitor when he was 30, and now spends his days in the courtroom and his evenings writing crime fiction.

To find out more about Neil go to www.neilwhite.net

By the same author:

Fallen Idols
Lost Souls
Last Rites
Dead Silent
Cold Kill

NEIL WHITE

Beyond Evil

AVON

AVON
A division of HarperCollins*Publishers*
77–85 Fulham Palace Road,
London W6 8JB

www.harpercollins.co.uk

A Paperback Original 2012
1

A catalogue record for this book is
available from the British Library

ISBN 978-1-84756-130-5

Set in Minion by Palimpsest Book Production Limited,
Falkirk, Stirlingshire

Printed and bound in Great Britain by
Clays Ltd, St Ives plc

Acknowledgements

My name appears on the cover of this book but that doesn't go anywhere close to telling the full story.

My editors at Avon have been fantastic, as always, pointing out the flaws without being too brutal, and so I will always be grateful to Caroline Hogg and Helen Bolton for their input and help. My thanks also go to Keshini Naidoo, an editor with whom I have enjoyed a great relationship from the very beginning. Of course, I would never have had the opportunity to work with the people at Avon had it not been for my wonderful agent, Sonia Land at Sheil Land Associates Ltd, and so I thank her once again for working so hard on my behalf.

Away from my publisher, I would like to thank Angela Melhuish for setting up my Facebook fanpage, and Luca Veste for maintaining it with such enthusiasm.

To everyone else, thank you for the emails and for attending the author events. It's been great to hear from you.

To everyone at Avon

Chapter One

The blue flickers of the police lights dominated the view as Sheldon Brown looked out of his windscreen. He'd had the call thirty minutes earlier, and so had scrambled out of bed, the fatigue chased away by adrenaline. That had faded, replaced by the rhythm of his heartbeat, like flutters in his chest.

Sheldon reached into his trouser pocket and pulled out his bottle of diazepam, small blue wonders. He washed two down with a bottle of water. They wouldn't take effect straight away, he knew that, but just the act of taking them made his fingers tremble less. He checked his reflection in the car mirror, that his tie was straight, his shirt not too creased. He didn't look too bad. It was the middle of the night. That would give him some latitude.

He stepped out of his car and pulled at his shirt cuffs. The cold hit him straight away. It was summer, but the night air never stayed warm in Oulton, the Lancashire town that had become the hub of his police career. He had started out in the town as a young cadet, a few years spent sorting out the fights that spilled out from the pubs, the licensing hours just a guide, not a rule. His rise through the detective ranks took him to the larger towns in the county, but eventually he made his way back.

Oulton was the last stop before the moors, where the roads out of the valleys snaked upwards and towards Yorkshire, where there were few trees to stop the howl of the wind, just coarse grasses that grew wild. The town didn't offer much for tourists other than a starting point to go somewhere else. There was a small maze of shops, once family-run businesses turned into charity shops and nail salons, but most of the pubs were boarded up now, victims of supermarket booze and the smoking ban. Weather-beaten terraced streets ran up the hills to empty patches of land where factories used to dominate. Some of the houses were rendered and painted in pastel shades, except that exhaust fumes and cold winters had turned them shabby, so that they were just dirty breaks in the lines of grey stone.

There were some elegant spots though, where the mill-owners had lived, grand stone gestures set in their own grounds, with curving gravel drives and wide lawns, nymph statues spraying water into lily ponds. The mills were gone, and so they made for large country hotels, used for weddings and by those walkers who liked to start their hikes as near to the top of the hills as they could.

Sheldon was in front of one of these hotels, the drive lined by marked police cars, headlights illuminating a huddle of people in uniform slacks and shirts. Ivy spread over dark grey walls and around white lattice windows, with wide glass conservatories along both sides. He took his suit jacket from the hook in the back of his car, and once buttoned up, he took a deep breath and set off walking. Just take command, was his thought, as he got closer. He tugged at his cuffs again. The gravel crunched under his feet, like loud cracks in the night. There were people looking out of their bedroom windows, curiosity beating sleep.

A uniformed officer walked towards him, his fluorescent

jacket bright green in the darkness, bouncing back the weak light from the faux Victorian lamps that lined the driveway. His arms were outstretched, ready to turn him away. Sheldon pulled out his identification and said, 'What time did the call come in?'

The constable held his hand up in apology and said, 'Just after one, sir.'

'Who's supervising the scene?' Sheldon said.

'Sergeant Peters.'

Sheldon knew her. Tracey Peters, smart and ambitious, but normally on the burglary team.

'You're the first inspector to arrive, sir.'

Sheldon nodded, just to stop the panic rising. This could become his case, but he had to control it.

'So what have you heard?' Sheldon said.

'You won't like it, sir.'

'I don't expect to like it,' Sheldon said, the words coming out clipped and precise. 'I said what have we got?'

A blush crept up the constable's cheeks. 'A male, dead, in there,' and he pointed towards the hotel. 'There was a complaint about noise, and when the duty manager went to the room, he found a body.'

'Any word on who it is?'

'The room was booked in the name of John Bull, so I heard, but that sounds like, well . . .'

'Bullshit?'

'That's the one.'

Sheldon set off for the front of the hotel. He went to a plastic crate filled with forensic suits, hooded paper jumpsuits packed into plastic wrappers. He ripped at the polythene and slipped one on over his clothes. Once he had snapped on the face mask, he set off to join the small huddle of white paper suits just outside the hotel doors.

The crowd turned to look at him as he joined, and when they realised who it was, Sheldon spotted the exchange of glances, the raised eyebrows.

'How bad is it?' Sheldon asked.

'As bad as anything I've ever seen,' someone said. He recognised the voice, and the long dark lashes blinking over the mask. Tracey Peters.

Sheldon nodded, and tried a smile. 'A bit different to looking at overturned furniture,' he said, and then, 'how much of a mess have the staff made?'

'No one stayed long enough to get near the body. As soon as they looked inside, they backed away, screaming.'

Sheldon looked towards the building but didn't say anything for a while. He looked up at the bedrooms. Someone was taking photographs with a phone. A tale for the dinner party.

'Let's take a look,' he said, and walked around the small huddle. He heard the boots of Tracey Peters behind him.

He climbed the hotel steps quickly and went through the revolving door. His footsteps echoed in the marble lobby, a walnut reception desk in front of him, a brass plaque reminding him of the hotel name. Sweeping stairways curled upwards behind it, lined in plush wine-coloured carpets.

Tracey stepped in front. 'It's at the back,' she said, and led him away from reception and through a long room filled with high-backed chairs and a large stone fireplace.

They turned into a long corridor lined by doors. There were plates outside some, remnants of room service. Neither said anything. All he could hear was the rustle of their paper suits. His eyes scanned the walls for any blood smears that might have been missed, but it looked clean. At the end of the corridor, by an open fire door, he saw the bright glare of arc lights coming from one of the rooms and the bustle of more white forensic suits.

The crime scene investigators stepped aside as he got near. One was dusting the glass on the fire door, hoping for a print. Another was swabbing the doorframe for DNA, in case someone grabbed the door on the way out.

'Anything yet?' Sheldon said.

The dusting stopped for a moment and the tired eyes of a middle-aged man turned to him. 'Nothing much, sir. All the blood is on the bed. No footprints in the room. There were handprints, but they were smears, and so no good for getting any prints.'

'I'll need to speak to everyone who was using rooms along this corridor, and the night manager,' Sheldon said.

'He's been trying to get in the way since we got here, worried about his business,' Tracey said.

'He'll have to keep worrying,' Sheldon said, and then went into the room. He shielded his eyes as they became used to the glare of the lights, and once he was able to take in the scene, sweat prickled across his forehead and his mouth filled with acid. He looked away for a moment and took a deep breath. Once he knew that he was able to look again, he slowly raised his head.

There was a man in front of them, lying spread-eagled on a bed, his arms and legs pulled to the corners and tied to the bed legs.

'That's some extreme sex game,' Tracey said, and she pointed to a ball gag that was discarded in the corner of the room, a leather strap with a plastic ball in the centre. Sheldon thought he could see teeth marks in it.

Sheldon let out a long breath. 'I don't think he was enjoying it,' he said, and took a step closer, leaving Tracey nearer the door.

The man was naked. He didn't look old, the Maori tattoos that swirled down from his shoulders giving that away, but it was what was above his shoulders that made Sheldon wonder if he'd sleep again that night.

There was a shock of black hair on the pillow, slick with blood, because where the face had once been there was just the bright white of cheek and jawbones, streaked red by blood and remnants of torn flesh and muscle. The eyes were still in place, and teeth seemed set in some final grimace. The face had been cut away in a neat shield, as if a stencil had been used.

'Why would someone do that?' Tracey said.

'It makes him harder to identify, but that can't be the reason,' Sheldon said, his voice quieter than before. 'Is the face still here somewhere?'

Tracey shook her head. 'Not in this room.'

Sheldon closed his eyes.

'There is a bit more to this,' he heard Tracey say.

Sheldon opened his eyes and looked at her. 'In what way?'

'I spoke to the police doctor when he left,' she said, and then raised her eyebrows. 'He thought that the victim had been alive when it started.'

Sheldon looked back to the body on the bed and shook his head. The constable outside was right. This was going to be a bad one.

Chapter Two

The noise started in his dream. There was a bird on a branch, bright red and blue feathers, chirruping at him, but then the bird faded and the room came into view.

He was in bed and the chirrups were still there, except that they were now electronic. He groaned and put his head under the pillow. It was the telephone. He could ignore it, just wait for the answer machine, but then he realised that he couldn't let it do that. He might need the call.

He threw the pillow to one side and stumbled out of bed. The floor swayed under his feet. He tasted the booze as he exhaled, stale and unpleasant, and then he pulled the discarded T-shirt from the front of the clock radio. Eight o'clock. Later than he thought.

The phone was still ringing.

'All right, all right,' he shouted, and made his way through his apartment, wiping his eyes. The answer machine beat him to it.

'Charlie. It's Julie. I can't make it this afternoon. There's been a murder. It was supposed to be my day off, but they've cancelled my leave to cover for those drafted in to help. We'll do it another time, but we need to sort it out. And Charlie, you called again Saturday night. Don't do it again, I told you. Andrew is getting sick of it.'

Then it clicked off.

Charlie sat down. This afternoon? Then he remembered. They were supposed to be sorting out their things, the break-up routine.

He put his head back and closed his eyes. He was glad he had avoided it. The apartment would need cleaning, and he didn't need to look to know that there were the remains of a late night Sunday film session on the floor: a pizza box and a line of empty beer bottles. He would get a life-lecture from Julie if she saw it, and he didn't need it. They'd been together for just a year, and he hadn't changed. He was almost forty and was drinking too much when they got together. He was just the same a year on. He guessed she was supposed to change him. Was it his problem she hadn't succeeded?

It was his own fault for getting involved with police officers, he knew that, but Julie hadn't been the first. He was a defence lawyer, and the police had an expectation that he would be some successful go-getter, all about sports cars and the best restaurants. It had never taken them long to find out that it wasn't like that, because some lawyers are just courtroom shouters and part-time ambulance chasers.

Julie had been one of the longer relationships, but that was only because of his reluctance to let her leave. She was attractive, tall and elegant and blonde, like a tick-list on a dating site, and they had got together during one of those long chats at the custody desk. He hadn't fought as hard that day, and spent most of the interview watching her. They went out for a meal, and she moved in two months later. She moved out ten months after that, when she realised that they had nothing in common, and that Charlie wasn't interested in finding anything they might share.

And then he remembered she mentioned a call. He sighed. He had done it before when drunk, just a call to see if she wanted to give it another try. It wasn't that he even thought that way when sober, but bad ideas are sometimes crafted on the long weave home from a pub. Julie was with someone else now. Perhaps that was what rankled.

Charlie opened his eyes and stumbled to his feet, groaning at his reflection in the mirror. His dark hair was now streaked with grey and too long for his age, gathered in greasy curls around his collar. His beard was unkempt, more like he'd forgotten how to shave rather than he'd decided to grow one.

It wasn't a good start to the week. His mother had always said that he would amount to nothing, and he thought he had won the argument by qualifying as a lawyer. Except that he had spent the next fifteen years slowly proving her right.

He looked away and went to the window instead.

His flat was on the top floor of a four-storey apartment block overlooking Oulton, blocking the view to the open moorland, the bricks clad in fake stone to make it blend in with the growing town. He got the sun as it set in the evening, and the views gave him something to look at when he was on his own, even the grey sprawl of Manchester, although the city buzz never got as far as the town.

The phone rang again, and he thought about not answering, but he didn't think it would be Julie again. It could be a client, or the police.

It was one of the drawbacks of being a defence lawyer, that he had to be available when the clients needed him, but most calls meant nothing. Like relatives letting him know that their cousin or brother had been arrested, only to find out that the prisoner had chosen a different lawyer. But there is always the prospect that the next call will be the big one, the case that keeps the practice ticking over for another year. The large frauds are the best, where the volume of paperwork creates plenty of billable hours, but not many came in like that. Anyway, he wasn't the sort who liked to spend his time scouring through paperwork. He knew what he was: a tub-thumper, defending on emotion, shouting for his clients in a small northern town. He had the guile and legal brain for trading blows with barristers in the Crown Court, and he had thought about going down that route, but he didn't have the temperament. He might enjoy the arguments, but sometimes he fought too hard when finesse would be better, and he struggled to control his hackles when he heard the sniggers of the country-set.

And he'd have to shave more often.

He clicked the answer button, and it took him a few seconds to recognise the greeting as Amelia's, his business partner.

'Amelia? This is early.'

'You've got a change of schedule today, Charlie,' she said, her voice curt. 'We've been burgled.'

The day was getting worse. 'Anything taken?'

'Not as far as I can tell, but there's a broken window and they've been through the files.'

Charlie didn't like the sound of that. Some of the town's worst secrets were in those files, the real stories behind the crimes, not the excuses the defendants spill to their friends. 'I'll be there as soon as I can.'

'No, I need you to go to court and deal with my cases. I'll sort things out here. And there's been a murder.'

'Yes, I know. People are rushing to tell me.'

'From the whispers I'm getting, it's a bad one. You need to get to the police station.'

'We've got the suspect?'

There was a pause, and then, 'I don't know if there is one, but I want you to find out what you can, in case they bring him in and he hasn't got a lawyer. Your name might just tumble out of the custody sergeant's mouth. You know how it works.'

'I think I'm right out of all charm,' he said.

'My cases are quick, and I've checked your diary,' Amelia said, not listening. 'You haven't got much on. Just try and get the gossip.'

Charlie wiped his eyes. He did know how it worked, but he wasn't in the mood for a Monday morning schmooze at the custody desk. It wasn't the sergeant who was important, but Amelia had never learnt that. She thought that a flick of her hair with a sergeant brought her work. Unlikely. Custody sergeants are immune to charm. No, the people who pass your name to the prisoners are the civilian jailers. Make friends with those people, and it is your name that gets mentioned through the hatch of the cell door.

'How will I get access?' he said.

'I'm sure you'll find a way,' she said, and then there was a click.

Charlie stared at the phone as Amelia hung up. That was her way. No unnecessary politeness. Just get the job done. He was tired and feeling rough, but he had learnt not to question her methods. His name might be higher on the brass plaque outside the office, but she ran the practice because she had saved it.

He struggled to the bathroom, and was about to wipe the condensation from the mirror, but decided against it. He knew that he wouldn't like what he saw. The beginnings of broken veins and purple skin under his eyes. He was thirty-nine years old, and looked already like the milestone birthday was a long way behind him.

When he came out of the shower, his eyes caught the empty side of the bed again. He still slept to one side, not used to the fact that Julie was no longer there, her tangle of blonde hair almost lost in the soft white pillow. A year-long habit was hard to break.

He looked in the wardrobe for his suit, but swore when he realised that it had been lying crumpled in the corner since Friday night. He pulled his emergency suit out of the wardrobe, all threadbare cuffs and shiny elbows. As he pulled on the clothes, tightening the tie around his neck and threading his cufflinks into his shirt, he started to feel like a lawyer again. It was always the same. Weekends in scruffs, weekdays in pinstripes, and the tightness of the shirt collar seemed to squeeze out the weekend.

He just needed a coffee and then he would be ready for the world.

Chapter Three

Sheldon Brown's eyes were closed. There was sweat on his top lip and his fingers were clenched into a tight fist to stop the shakes. He breathed through his nose and began the countdown from ten.

He got to one and opened his eyes. His reflection in the mirror in the police station toilets gave nothing away. His dark hair lacked some shine, and there were purple rings under his eyes, but he had looked worse. He had got used to not sleeping.

He splashed some water onto his face and dried it off with a paper towel. He nodded at his reflection and then headed for the door.

As Sheldon came back onto the corridor, he became aware of the sound of men laughing and joking, waiting for the day to start. The squad was padded out with officers from other teams, drafted in to help with the routine stuff. The door-to-doors, fingertip searches. The door to the Incident Room was ahead, and he strode towards it. A voice from behind stopped him. 'Sir?'

Sheldon turned round. It was Tracey Peters, the sergeant from the night before. Tall and brunette, with deep brown eyes, elegant in a fitted grey suit, she looked like she had caught the sleep Sheldon had missed.

'Sergeant Peters, good morning.'

'It's Detective Sergeant, actually, although I prefer Tracey.' She smiled. 'I hope you don't mind, but I have spoken to my inspector, and he says that if you want one more, then you've got me.' When Sheldon didn't respond, she added, 'I was there last night, and so I want to see it through.'

Sheldon swallowed and nodded. People would be watching him. He would need all the help he could get. 'Yes, thank you,' and then, 'it's been hard getting the numbers in.'

Tracey grimaced. 'I know how it is.'

Every team was the same. Budget cuts had decimated the force, and so every squad was running at its leanest. Sheldon had assembled a unit from whoever could be spared, with some drafted in from the nearest towns. They had taken over the small Oulton station, a stone block in the middle of the town next to the Magistrates Court, with old wooden windows and a genteel blue lamp hanging over the door.

There was supposed to be a detective chief inspector coming over from the Force Major Investigation Team, to see whether they should take over the case, but there had been a double murder on the other side of the county. Sheldon had been instructed to keep things afloat until he got there.

Sheldon stopped at the doorway of the Incident Room and looked in. The station wasn't used to so much activity, and the squad looked crammed in. Condensation was building up on the windows and officers lined the walls, the few available chairs taken by the keen ones who had arrived first. He recognised all the detectives in there, testament to the twenty-five years he had put in, the eager young cadet turned into a jowly man in his fifties. As people saw him, the sounds of conversation died away, and they exchanged glances, some of disappointment, some of surprise.

Sheldon smiled, but it came out like a twitch, and then he walked in, his head up. All the eyes in the room followed him as he took a place at the front. The only sound in the room was the rustle of an envelope as he pulled out a set of photographs, and then the rip of sticky tape as he pasted them to the whiteboard at the front of the room. They were the pictures from the night before, the body on the hotel bed, strapped to the corners, the face sliced off.

Murmurs went around the room as they took in the images. Sheldon guessed that word of the body had gone round the station, but photographs made things more real.

Sheldon cleared his throat and then turned round to look at the squad. His hands went into fists again. 'Last night was grim,' he said. 'I was there. I know how it was. We need to catch whoever did this.' He tried to make it sound like a rallying call, but he was met by stares and silence. His tongue flicked across his bottom lip, waiting for someone to ask a question, just to fill the gap.

'Do we know who the victim is yet?' a voice said at the back. Sheldon recognised him. Duncan Lowther, the poster boy for the local CID. He was a hobby copper, inherited wealth funding his life, not the job. His was the Porsche on the car park, to match the expensive cologne, and the weekends spent in the wine bars of Manchester. He talked of great literature and art-house cinema, and didn't wear the usual uniform of pastel shirts and chain store suits, preferring tight grey V-necks and silk ties.

Sheldon had seen too many coppers like him. All glory, no graft.

'That's the first thing we need to work out,' Sheldon said. 'Always start with the victim. And someone needs to go through the incident logs for the county for the last twelve hours, just to check if someone didn't come home.'

'Extra-marital?' someone else said. 'Maybe a jealous husband?'

Sheldon nodded. 'Maybe. That is one angle. It was cruel, and so revenge seems a motive.' He looked at the photographs again. 'The face was removed and wasn't left in the hotel room. We need to find where it went, because someone took it away for a reason, and so we need to know why.'

'It could just be a random sick murder,' Lowther said. 'These things do happen. And does it matter why? It's the *who* that's important.'

Sheldon felt the smile grow on his face, although it felt tight and unnatural, and he knew it hadn't reached his eyes. 'Thank you for your wisdom, but if you get the *why*, you've got yourself a suspect list. And you've just got yourself the CCTV job.' When Lowther looked confused, he added, 'Go to the hotel and watch the camera footage. Account for everyone staying there. If someone comes in who you can't put in a room, there's your first suspect. Then go through the town cameras. Someone running, or a car going too fast.' He looked around the rest of the room. 'The rest of you. Divide yourself up into twos. It's time to knock on doors. You know the routines. Get the paperwork in, look for the unusual, and let's hope for a forensic hit.'

'How long have we got the job in Oulton?' a voice said at the back. 'FMIT are coming over.'

'I want to keep it with us,' Sheldon said. 'The people in this town know us and trust us. You know how it is around here, that they don't like outsiders. If we let FMIT take over, people might clam up and we will lose that local contact.'

There were some murmurs of agreement, before everyone looked to the front, startled, as a uniformed officer burst into the room. He looked at the photographs, and then at Sheldon.

'Yes?' Sheldon said, irritated.

'We've just had a call, sir, from the paper, the *Lancashire Express*,' and he pointed to the photographs taped up at the front. 'It's about your case. They said they've got something you have to see.'

Chapter Four

Charlie walked to his office, as usual. Even though there had been a burglary, getting there earlier would only make a bad start come sooner.

The stroll shook off most of the booze from the night before, although he couldn't get over the slump as quickly as he could a few years earlier. Managing a hangover was just about patience though, and so he knew he would be over the worst by lunchtime.

His apartment was at the top of the town, just so that they could sell it by the views. It wasn't a long walk; just past the entrance to a council estate, where the street signs were obscured by graffiti, and then along a row of terraced cottages whose views across barren hills had been stolen by the march of progress.

As he walked past the Eagleton, the best greasy spoon in town, with large windows that were permanently steamed up, he heard someone ride alongside him on a bike, the tyres crunching on the small stones in the gutter. Charlie's pupils were still sluggish, but he recognised him as Tony, one of his regulars. This was the part of the day when Tony made sense, before he stocked up on bargain vodka and watched the day dissolve into a blur of survival, every day just an attempt to get through to the next one. Sometimes he got into fights, just messy brawls most of the time, and that's when he turned up at Charlie's office.

'Tony. How are you doing?'

'Have you seen up by the Grange?' he said, pointing over his shoulder, towards the moors. 'There's police everywhere.'

'There's been a murder,' Charlie said. 'It's probably to do with that.'

'Who is it?'

Charlie shrugged. 'I don't know.'

'It must be someone important. I've never seen so many police.'

Charlie smiled. 'We're all important, Tony, even you.'

He was about to set off walking again when Tony said, 'I've just had a summons, for threatening behaviour. I'm up next Thursday. I was on my way to your office.'

'You won't get legal aid.'

Tony scowled.

Charlie stopped walking and sighed. He knew the scowl. If Charlie wouldn't do it for the goodwill, then someone else would. He remembered refusing to turn out for someone on a freebie, and the client killed someone two months later. The one who did the freebie got the murder.

'Guilty plea?' Charlie said.

Tony nodded.

'Okay, I'll see you there, but if something else comes up, you're on your own. I'm yours if I'm available.'

Tony smiled. 'Thanks Charlie.'

Charlie didn't say anything as Tony set off riding again. People like Tony kept the work flowing. Sometimes he got paid, and sometimes he didn't, but Charlie had to look after him for those days when he did, because he had chosen criminal law, the budget end of the trade. He remembered the brochures for high-earning corporate firms that littered the career racks at his university, attracting those with polished accents. The only child from his family to go to university, Charlie guessed at his limitations and aimed low. At least he achieved his aim, and it didn't seem like failure.

As Tony rode away down the hill, Charlie noticed a group of people on the other side of the street. Six of them, all in black clothes, and Charlie thought they were looking straight at him. They were near the office, and even as Tony went past them, they didn't change their focus.

That made him pause. For every client he had to defend, it usually meant upsetting someone else, like a victim or a police officer. Charlie paused for a moment, made some pretence about checking his phone, but when he looked up again, the group were no longer there.

Charlie frowned. Perhaps he had misread it. He shrugged and set off walking the last hundred yards to his office, above a kebab shop and accessed by a door squeezed between it and a tattoo parlour.

Charlie had set up his own practice five years earlier, when the firm he trained with started to replace the lawyers with paralegals. He had known that he was next in line, and so he went on his own. The dream of building an empire soon soured, with long hours just to make the practice break even, with too much time spent on practice management, just to prove that he was fit to do legal aid work. He had been on the brink of walking away from it all, knowing that he wasn't cut out for it and that a job behind a bar might make him happier, when Amelia had approached him and said that she wanted to buy in.

Amelia Diaz. He had seen her a few times around court before then, and her appearance was hard to forget, with long dark hair and an olive-tanned cleavage that she flaunted at men to get what she wanted, and at women just to show that she had it. Her father was from Barcelona and had married an Englishwoman, except a northern upbringing had given her more brashness than Catalan swagger. Charlie hadn't wanted a partner, but he was too desperate to turn her away, because it let him carry on being the only thing he knew he was good at – a Magistrates Court legal hack.

As he climbed the stairs, he could hear the coffee machine bubbling.

'Amelia?'

She popped her head around the door of her office and scowled. 'Glad you could make it. Come in.'

Charlie rolled his eyes at Linda, who had been his receptionist and secretary and office manager since he started, a woman with the stature of a bowling ball with hair cropped close to her head.

He grabbed a coffee from the machine before going into Amelia's room. There was someone else in reception, a skinny teenager, late teens, in a blue skirt and jacket. Mixed race, her teeth white as she smiled, bright against her caramel skin and the loose frizz of her hair. Charlie raised a hand in greeting and fought the urge to smooth down his hair. Then he caught his reflection in a picture frame, grey streaks and messy whiskers, and looked away. He was a generation too old, and he wore every year of it.

Amelia's office was minimalist, with a coat of white paint and a glass desk in one corner. The carpet had been taken away and the floorboards stripped and stained white to match the walls, the old curtains replaced with modern office blinds. A computer hummed on the corner of the desk.

Except that it wasn't in its usual tidy state. There were files strewn on the floor.

'How did they get in?' Charlie said.

'They smashed the glass in the fire escape and climbed in through there.'

'What about the alarm?'

'It needs fixing, you know that.'

Charlie leant against the doorframe. 'Did they take anything?'

'I don't think so,' Amelia said. 'It was more like a search. The monitors are still here. Even the petty cash tin and the television.'

Charlie frowned. 'That worries me more,' he said. 'If they wanted something from the files, one of our clients might be in danger, if it's important enough for a break-in. Have you called the police?'

Amelia thought about that and then shook her head. 'If they want something from the files, the police will want to know what we think it is, and I'm not breaching a client's confidence.'

He knew she was right. He represented burglars. He couldn't get too worked up about one of them coming to visit.

'Leave it, Charlie, I'll sort it out,' she said. 'These are your files for court,' and she handed over two blue folders.

'And what did you say you were doing?' he said.

She looked at him for a moment, as if she was about to tell him something, but then she sighed. 'Sorting this out, and then some admin stuff; you know, like keeping the accounts up to date, and some bills. And I've got a private payer coming in to see me.'

He waved it away. 'You can keep that one,' he said. 'They expect too much for their money.'

'You should learn to love them, because they pay three times more than legal aid, and they won't go through your handbag when they're alone in the room.'

Charlie didn't need Amelia's take on the business. He had been doing the job longer than she had, and all Amelia could offer was something that he knew already but just didn't want to hear.

He watched her as she sat at the desk. Charlie thought she seemed distracted, her scowls interrupted by the occasional faraway gaze.

'You all right?' he said.

She looked up at him, and Charlie saw vulnerability. It didn't surface often with Amelia. A couple of times after too much booze, and when they'd talked money. Or the lack of it. Amelia was business-like, brisk, and could even be fun, when the wine flowed and the music was right. But today her eyes seemed a little wider than usual, more searching. It was just for a moment though. She shook her head, and then smiled. 'I'm fine,' she said.

'Who's the girl in reception?'

'Donia. She wants some work experience, is about to go away to university. I thought you could show her round the court.'

Charlie rolled his eyes. Great. Now he had to babysit someone all day. This was Amelia's idea of making business pay, getting students to work for nothing, all of them hopeful of some job opportunity that would never materialise.

'She's come a long way, from Leeds,' Amelia whispered, her door open. 'Even rented somewhere for the week. Be nice to her.'

He walked away and went to his own room. As he went past Donia, she looked up again, as if she expected him to stop, but he didn't. There was no point in getting friendly. If she hoped for a training contract, she would be disappointed.

As Charlie went into his room, he was surprised. It was

untidy, but that's how he had left it. He put his head back out of the door. 'Why just your room?' he shouted towards Amelia.

'You can ask them if we ever find out who did it.'

Charlie shrugged and closed his door. He threw his files onto the desk, before he let his feet join them as he slumped into his chair, an old burgundy recliner with coffee stains on the arms.

Charlie's room was at the front of the building, because it came with a view of the street. It wasn't much, just the curve of a cobbled street, but it gave him something to look at. It was the comfort to Amelia's austere. The desk was old and scarred and faced the window, so that the sun had bleached out the varnish. There were some dirty coffee cups that had never made it back to the kitchen and a pile of files that needed work.

Amelia hated the premises, but Charlie refused to move.

So this was it, he thought, as he stared out of the window. The week was about to start. Just another grind through routine court cases. The week will end, and then it will be the same again. A lost weekend, and then Sunday spent wondering what he had said the night before. He watched an old woman walk up the hill, her back bent, as if she had spent most of her life walking up hills that were too steep to live on. That's how it seemed in Oulton. Too steep, too cold, too isolated. The town didn't grow or reinvent itself. It just crumbled a slow death, every closure bringing more boarded-up windows, and one more reason for people to head down into the valley and not come back.

As he looked out, he saw something further along the street.

There was the same group of young people he had seen outside the café, all around twenty years old, all in black, their hair long and dyed black to match, their faces pale. There were glints of metal in their faces. One of them had a guitar. He looked older than the rest, with wild dark hair and lighter clothes. Dirty denim rather than black. The others seemed to encircle him as they walked, and most seemed to be smiling.

They must have seen Charlie staring, because they glanced up as they passed below his window. The older one nodded, and Charlie thought he saw him smile.

Chapter Five

John Abbott squinted as he opened his eyes. It wasn't a bright day, he could tell that from the greyness on the other side of the glass, and there were no curtains or blinds at the window. It was later than the usual waking time, because they woke with nature, but the night before had been a late one.

He waited a few seconds for his eyes to adjust, and then looked towards the window again. There were other people moving elsewhere in the house, but he wasn't ready to get up.

He felt Gemma stir against him, her skin warm, her arm across his chest. His thoughts went back to the night before and he grimaced. It wasn't supposed to happen like that. She'd been more excitable than normal and had chosen him again. He could have said no, that it wasn't right, made up some excuse, but he didn't. He gave in every time. It was the way she smiled at him, cute, coy, with large appealing eyes, and how she covered her mouth when she giggled.

It was more than just her appeal though. He had needed the warmth and the closeness, although in the harsh light of morning he knew he shouldn't have done it.

Her leg moved across him and he pushed it away. The noises were getting louder in the house, and so he knew he had to get up. He moved her arm and slid out of bed, although that was a generous description for a mattress on the floor covered in blankets. Only a rug stopped his feet from hitting the cold wooden floor. He looked down. The covers had slipped from her. He shook his head. Gemma was too young, her shoulders thin and bony, her skin pale and mottled. Her face was too innocent for what had happened the night before, her nose small and dappled by freckles, wisps of mousy hair across her cheeks.

He padded over to the window and looked out. He was naked, but it didn't seem to matter whether anyone could see him outside. The view calmed him. They were on the top of a long slope, with mist in the deep valley below, just bracken and gorse for the most part, but clusters of trees broke up the hills and sheep dotted the slope on the other side. John liked the isolation, the countryside the same as it had been for hundreds of years, the chimneys and terraced streets in a different valley he couldn't see. He looked down at the Seven Sisters, remnants of a stone circle in the field in front of the cottage, just seven stone fingers rising out of the ground in a grey crescent.

They were in an old stone farmhouse, where everyone slept in cramped quarters, five to a room. The room he was in with Gemma was the exception, the party room, apart from Henry's room, where he slept alone. The farmhouse owner slept in a room downstairs. John didn't like to think of that, because he was neglected, too infirm to look after himself.

There was a noise behind him. He turned round. Gemma was sitting up, smiling. He went as if to cover himself, but she laughed.

'Too late to be embarrassed now,' she said, her voice light and soft. 'Nothing is wrong that is beautiful, you know that. Henry said that.'

'I know that, but, well,' and he shrugged.

She reached over to the side of the bed and rummaged in a bag. She pulled out a spliff and lit the paper twist at its tip. That warm, cloying smell of cannabis drifted towards him. She took a hard pull and held it in, before letting it out with a cough and a smile. The first one of the day was always the worst. She leaned forward to offer it to him. 'You're free, babe. Leave your hang-ups behind.'

He was reluctant, but she thrust it again and said, 'Come on, it's okay.'

John went to her to take it from her and rolled it between his fingers, watching as the glowing tip turned soot-grey. He took a small drag and then hacked out a cough when he took in the smoke.

She laughed. 'I thought you were getting used to it,' she said, and then flopped back onto the bed.

'How old are you?' John asked, his eyes watering from his coughs.

Gemma wagged a finger. 'I've told you before, details spoil a good time.'

'It's important though.'

'But why?'

'Because of what we did last night.'

'You've so much to learn,' she said, shaking her head, smiling. 'You're not bound by the old rules anymore. Freedom. Remember that word, John. It's the whole point of us. Don't you listen to Henry? The law is just what society says we cannot do, but we are not part of that society anymore. We are our own selves, free people, living human beings.' She turned over and propped herself on her elbows, her chin in her hands. 'Didn't you enjoy it?'

John looked at the naked stretch of her body. Her smooth back, her pert backside, and his mind went back to the night before. 'Yes, I enjoyed it,' he said, and a flush crept up his cheeks.

She giggled. 'I can tell,' she said, looking at his groin.

He took another drag on the spliff and then bent down to pass it back to her. She smiled as she took it, her features lost in a pall of sweet smoke, and there it was again, that disquiet that there was something too childlike about her.

As Gemma took a hard pull, John asked, 'Where did Henry go last night?'

There was a pause as she held the smoke in her lungs. She smiled as she let it out again, and then said, 'Why?'

'Henry went out again, and he goes out a lot. I'm confused, that's all. He wants me to give everything up for him, for the group, but does he give everything up for me?'

Gemma sat up, her face more serious now. 'You know things are happening. He has to arrange things, and so he has to meet people.'

'But he could phone, or email or something.'

'Haven't you noticed yet, that we have nothing like that? They can trace where you are and intercept what you are saying. He told you that. Didn't you understand?'

'Of course I did. I just thought there must be a better way to organise things.'

Gemma frowned. 'You ask a lot of questions.'

John paused before he answered. 'Just curious, that's all.'

Gemma looked at him, her head cocked, serious for a moment, and then she asked, 'So how old are you? Thirty?'

'Twenty-five,' he said. 'I've got an old face, that's all.'

'I like your face,' she said, her voice softer. 'Come here.'

He shook his head. 'I don't think we should. I can hear people moving around.'

'Henry told me to make you happy,' she said, and then she giggled, her hand over her mouth. 'I can see that you are happy.' Gemma parted her legs. Her hips were bony and thin.

John closed his eyes for a moment and tried not to think of how she had been.

'Is Henry always going to approve everything?' he said, and opened his eyes again. 'How can we be free if we need Henry's approval?'

'Are you questioning Henry?'

John shook his head. 'I wouldn't do that, you know that.'

'We have to fight for our freedom,' Gemma said. 'You do believe that, don't you? We are building for something big that will make everyone take notice, and if you don't believe that, well, there's no point.'

John nodded, and took a deep breath. 'I believe in us, you know that.'

'So come back to bed, because if Henry decides that this shouldn't happen anymore, it will stop, and I don't want that, because I want to please you. And you want to please Henry, don't you?'

He nodded. 'Yes, I want to please Henry.' His voice sounded weak.

John went to the bed again. Gemma's arms went around his neck and he felt her body begin to press against his. He closed his eyes as his resolve weakened, as she guided him towards her.

Chapter Six

Sheldon's heartbeat was drumming fast again as he skipped up the stone steps to the *Lancashire Express* offices. Tracey Peters was behind him, walking with a crime scene investigator. There was a uniformed officer in a fluorescent green jacket by the corner of the building, someone's arm around her. Further along, on a low stone wall, there were people gathered in a huddle.

The newspaper was produced from a large millstone building on the road that sloped down into the valley. It reported on the towns and villages along the Yorkshire border, with courtroom stories and council meetings, road crashes and summer fetes, its articles padded out by items pulled from the internet. Whenever they got a story that was big in Oulton, its base, the paper ran it for as long as people were still interested, and sometimes even beyond.

As Sheldon got near to the large double wooden doors at the top of the steps, someone stepped in front of him. Sheldon recognised him as Jim Kelly, the newsdesk editor, a man in his fifties who smelled of cigarettes and dressed like a journalist cliché, from the grubby blazer to his crumpled cords.

'Inspector Brown, I was hoping it would be you,' Kelly said, sweeping his greasy flick of hair over his head.

Sheldon stopped. He'd had press attention in the past, not much of it supportive, with the *Express* at the heart of it. 'I hope this isn't some kind of trick to get a quote,' he said.

Kelly smiled. 'It's better than that, follow me,' and he headed into the building, Sheldon walking quickly to keep up.

'Seeing as though you're here, Inspector,' Kelly said, over his shoulder, 'have you got anything I can print?'

Sheldon didn't answer. Kelly had never been kind to the police in his reporting, and so he wasn't going to get any special favours.

Kelly shrugged and just kept on walking. Sheldon thought he could see the trace of a smirk.

There were no people left inside, just small clusters of desks and computer monitors, the walls lined with framed front pages. The chairs were pulled untidily away from desks, as if people had left quickly. Their footsteps echoed as they walked, the ceiling high and arched, the building an old Methodist chapel converted fifty years earlier.

Kelly must have seen Sheldon looking at the empty office, because he said, 'We thought they ought to wait outside until you'd finished.' He pointed towards a desk at the end of the room, facing out so that it looked over all the others and towards the door. Kelly's desk. There was a white cardboard box on it, like a cake box. 'It was handed in at the front desk, in a plastic bag.'

'Who delivered it?'

'I don't know. We don't have someone at the front all the time. It was left on the desk, that's all I know.'

Tracey went to the box first, but then let the investigator get in front so that he could take some photographs. Once he had finished, he stepped aside to let Tracey get a proper view.

'There's something written on it,' she said

Sheldon looked at Kelly, who nodded and said, '*The face of greed.* Has a certain sort of message to it, don't you think? A great headline.'

'Did you open the box?' Sheldon said, his mouth dry, starting to guess what might be inside.

'I didn't know what was in there,' Kelly said, defensively.

The crime scene investigator passed Sheldon a paper mask and a bonnet to put over his hair. Sheldon snapped them on and then went over to the box, pulling on latex gloves, Tracey moving to one side. He took hold of the box by the corners. A trickle of sweat made his eye sting as he started to lift off the lid slowly.

As the lid came off, revealing the contents, Sheldon had to take deep breaths in and out, to calm himself. He gagged but clenched his teeth and forced himself to stay in control. He glanced at Kelly over his paper mask, who said, 'I spent the first ten years of my career taking photographs of road accidents. These things don't bother me.'

Sheldon scowled and then closed his eyes to ready himself for what he would see when he looked in the box again. His forehead was moist. He counted to three and then opened his eyes.

There was white tissue, but most of it was smeared dark red. In the middle, nestling in the paper, was a face, except that it looked more like a grotesque mask. The edges of the skin were smooth, as if it had been cut away with a very sharp knife, but Sheldon could make out the more ragged pieces of flesh and muscle stuck to the underside, where someone had reached into the cuts with their fingers and pulled the face away.

But it wasn't just the sight of the face that made Sheldon's pulse quicken and a flash of sweat cover his cheeks. It was the feeling that he recognised the person, even though the face had no form, torn away from the bones that had once made the features unique.

He thought back to the body tied to the bed. It had been hard to guess the age. There were tattoos that made him look younger, Maori swirls on the upper arms and onto the shoulders, but the body looked older, pale and flabby.

The face in the box answered that question, the skin soft, a small dark goatee on his chin.

Sheldon's knees weakened. It couldn't be him. Jim Kelly was saying something, but the words were indistinct mumbles.

Memories rushed back at him. A dead woman, a large house, the floor wet with spilled booze, but there were no glasses lying around. The dishwasher was running but there was no one there. He had moved through the rooms, looking for an answer to the call that had come in, that a young woman was dead. Then he had found her, floating underwater in the swimming pool, almost at the bottom, naked.

Jim Kelly's voice became louder. Sheldon opened his eyes and apologised. 'Sorry, what did you say?'

'Do I get a quote now?' Kelly repeated. 'Is it who I think it is? Billy Privett?'

Tracey said, 'Shit,' behind him, but Sheldon shook his head. 'This does *not* make the paper yet.'

Kelly smiled. Sheldon guessed that he had already taken photographs, ready for syndication when the time was right, and he had the exclusive.

Sheldon turned away and headed for the exit, not bothering to say goodbye, knowing that the day ahead had got a whole lot more complicated.

Chapter Seven

Charlie walked to the courthouse most days. It was when he got his day together, when he worked out how long each case would take, what he was going to say to his client, what excuses he would spin to the Magistrates. This time, he had Donia with him and his routine was disrupted. All he could hear were the click-click of her heels, like little jabs in his head shaking the last remnants of his hangover.

'You don't say much,' Donia said, when they were almost at the court building. There was a slight tremor to her voice.

He considered her for a moment. She was staring at him, expectantly. He stopped. At least it made the heels go quiet.

'I have my routines,' he said. 'I've been doing this job too long to care too much, and so don't expect me to gush about it. One of my habits is a quiet walk to court. I was just sticking with it.'

'Okay, I'm sorry,' she said, and then he felt a stab of guilt when he saw a deep flush to her cheeks 'Do you think the police will catch whoever broke into your office?'

Her naivety made him smile. 'We haven't called the police,' he said. 'And they won't care anyway, particularly when there's been a murder in town. A defence lawyer has had his office burgled – I wouldn't figure in their priorities much, and what if it's one of my own clients? Siding with the police would not be good for business.'

'So you just ignore it?'

'No point in trying to change things,' he said, and set off walking again. When he heard her heels fall into step with his, he asked, 'What are you expecting from this week?'

She seemed to take a long time to think about that. 'Just to learn more about the law,' she said.

'Why law? Have you got a university place?'

'At Manchester,' Donia said. 'I want to experience it first though.'

'And so you thought my little practice would give you a taste of what it's all about,' Charlie said, and then he laughed. 'Think of it like this; whatever your legal career has in store for you, this week will be just like real life.'

'What do you mean?'

'No money and no fun.'

'Did you always think like that?'

He looked at her, and his mood darkened just for a moment. No, he hadn't always thought like that, but things hadn't turned out like he had hoped.

Then Charlie saw something in her eyes. Resentment? He was being dismissive of her career before it had started, when he had made the same decision as her too many years earlier.

'I'm sorry,' he said, and then he smiled. 'Try and enjoy your week. Maybe you'll make a better job of your career than I have.'

Donia seemed pleased with that, although her joy lost some of its sheen when they arrived at the court and had to make their way through the pall of smoke that hung around the entrance, the nervous defendants taking a cigarette as they waited for their cases to be heard. Some of the more experienced nodded at Charlie, and someone shouted his name. He waved a greeting and tried to recall the client's name, but he couldn't. He was just another face from years of hopelessness. Society cast them aside, but this was Charlie's kingdom, his role as champion of the oppressed and dispossessed. Or so the poster might say. The reality was different. He was where they were, at the bottom of his profession, except that amongst these people, he was still king.

Charlie heard a whistle, a long, drawn out sound that told him someone had spotted Donia. He couldn't help smiling when a skinny man in a tracksuit and missing teeth leered at her. The whistler's best years were a long way behind him, and Charlie thought they had probably never been that good, but he didn't seem to realise how many leagues below her he was.

The court served all the towns in the valley, although it was always at the point of closure. The paint around the doors was peeling, and cracks were appearing in the plastered walls. Charlie remembered being distracted during a trial once as a mouse ran across the well of the court. The open doors were the only things that kept things bright, because once they creaked to a close, the inside was all gloom, brightened only by yellow strip lighting, so that everyone took on a jaundiced look.

Charlie paused for a while and looked towards the activity outside the police station, the road filled with cars and police officers grouped outside. People watched what was going on, and from the buzz of conversation he knew that the murder acted like a magnet for the whispers and the gossip. It looked like some were going to make a day of it, red eyes flicking between the bustle of people and the bottle of sherry being handed around.

As he went in through the wooden doors, he had to step

to one side to avoid a little girl running through the crowd giggling, her blonde hair in curls, all smiles as she sang to herself.

'Cute,' Donia said.

'That's the worst part, the children,' Charlie replied. 'They laugh and play like most kids, but their parents will mess it all up for them eventually. Drugs, booze, violence.'

'Booze,' she said, and she smiled. 'Bad stuff.'

'What?'

She blushed, embarrassed now.

'What do you mean?' he said.

Donia pointed to his mouth. 'The mints, well, they don't work as well as you think.'

Charlie smiled at her bluntness. 'It's better than nothing,' he said, and then popped another mint into his mouth. He pulled the first blue file out of his bag and shouted out the name. A tall man with a stoop came towards him. A shoplifter. No profession for a small town, where everyone knows you.

Charlie pointed towards an interview room at one side of the waiting area, and as they all went inside, his client said, 'I'm pleading not guilty.'

This was the part Charlie was most bored with, pretending like he cared. He'd heard mostly crap over the years. The innocents were pretty rare. 'Go on then, Shaun, let's play the game. If you go not guilty, the court will want to know what bullshit excuse you've got this time.'

'That's your job, to come up with the defence.'

Charlie closed his eyes for a moment. When he opened them again, he saw that Shaun was still staring at him, waiting for an answer.

'No, it isn't,' Charlie said. 'You come up with the lies. I just repeat them and pretend I believe them.' When Shaun scowled, Charlie added, 'You're just not very good at your job, as a shoplifter.'

'What do you mean?'

'Shaun, every video I've watched of you shoplifting, you look around so much that even little old ladies know what you're doing. Here's a tip; if the cameras watch you from the minute you walk in, you're going to get caught.'

'I didn't think your job was telling me how to be a better crook.'

'Perhaps I'm just telling you to pick a different career, because you're not good at the one you've chosen.'

'Or go to a different town?'

Charlie shook his head and laughed. 'If you think that will help.'

Shaun shrugged and then said, 'I saw you Friday night.'

'Oh yes?'

'In the Gloves. You were fucking wasted.'

That wasn't news, but he didn't want to hear it. 'Let me go speak to the prosecutor,' Charlie said, and left the room, Donia behind him.

As they walked into the courtroom, the prosecutor was in his usual place, at the front desk, next to a large pile of files. Tall and greying, he was the slow and steady type, who had learned quicker than Charlie that calm and precise got further than bluster and adrenaline. He was flicking through his papers, just a refresher. Charlie knew that he'd already been through them once, but it beat staring at the wall, waiting for the court to start.

'I've got Shaun Prescott,' Charlie said, as he leaned over him.

He turned round and looked surprised. 'Amelia not here? Or is she getting ready for the cameras?'

'Cameras? You've lost me.'

'The murder,' he said.

'I've heard about it.'

'Between me and you, I was speaking to the court reporter before. He got a text from someone at the *Express*. The rumour is that the victim is Billy Privett.'

That was a surprise. 'Billy Privett? You're joking, right?'

'That's what I was told,' the prosecutor said. He glanced up at Donia, and then leaned into Charlie so that he could whisper. 'Tied up and face sliced off, so I heard, with his features posted to the local paper. They've got themselves really excited, because the scoop will keep the paper afloat for another year.' Then he smiled. 'So a bad day for you, because the killer won't be coming your way, even when they catch him. Conflict of interest.'

'I'll worry about my ethics,' Charlie said, even though his brain was still trying to take in what had been said.

Billy Privett had been all over the press for the last year, public enemy number one, the lottery winner with no class versus the poor but noble dead girl's father.

Billy had played up to his image, knew that people were jealous of his money, and so he wanted to make sure everyone knew how much he had. Parties, cars, gold chains around his neck, diamonds in his teeth. The press loved him, even though they painted him as a hate figure, because someone to hate sells newspapers.

He'd been heading for a life of crime before the big win. Charlie had represented him before he made it rich with those magic six numbers. Billy had collected his winner's cheque with an electronic tag on his leg, and he'd had to race back to Oulton before the curfew kicked in. Once the money arrived, Amelia represented him, because she was more ruthless with her billing, and looked better than Charlie whenever she spoke to the press.

But it was the girl that defined him. Alice Kenyon. Going places, from a good family, but ended up as the victim of a brutal sexual assault and found drowned in Billy's pool at the end of another wild party. Alice's father kept her name in the paper, campaigned for those who were at the party to speak out, but no one did.

Alice's father found out the downside to fame, that a small moment of stupidity makes the front pages. Caught with a young woman in a car, he went from sympathy figure to pervert, and so the public clamour for answers about Alice died down.

Charlie was still thinking about Billy Privett when he realised that the prosecutor was still talking. 'Amelia will get some publicity though, and so it all works out. Except for Billy, that is.'

Charlie nodded, just to get himself back into the conversation. 'People like to go to a name they recognise.' He lifted up his files. 'And I could do with some better clientele.'

'Doesn't Amelia bring it in? Some of the rough trade we get in here must like a touch of glamour.' He looked down at Charlie's clothes. 'No offence, Charlie, but you're breaking mirrors these days.'

'None taken,' Charlie said, and the wrinkle of the prosecutor's nose told him that Donia was right, that the mints weren't working. 'Amelia brings the work in that I can't. Most of my punters don't win, know that they have no chance against the system, and so they might as well look at someone nice before they lose.'

'And how do you find it? Distracting?'

'Not my type,' he said, lying. He didn't fall for Amelia's tease, but he had looked at her body for too long and too often when she didn't realise he was staring. Or maybe she did but didn't mind. Someone told him once that women always notice men looking. That hadn't stopped him looking. It just made him stop apologising. 'Are you sure it's Billy Privett?'

'No, but that's just what I've heard.'

Charlie sighed. 'Murder cases are hassle anyway. If you foul it up, your name is dragged through the Court of Appeal. I don't want that. Let someone else have it.' And then he stepped away, knowing that there was no need to spend time in the police station. He would be back at the office in an hour, with just Amelia's disapproving glances to get him through the day.

Chapter Eight

John emerged from the bedroom and made his way downstairs to the kitchen. He had slept better for sharing a mattress with Gemma, rather than the bunks in the other rooms.

The stairs descended into the hallway by the front door, with the living room in the middle of the house. The floor was still strewn with spilled ashtrays and empty vodka bottles from the night before. There was a large capital *A* in a circle spray-painted onto the wall, the universal symbol for anarchy, along with photographs from demonstrations and camps the group had been on just pinned around the room. In all of the photographs, there was the same image, a group dressed in black but made distinctive by the now infamous plain white masks they wore, their faces expressionless.

He went through the living room and into the kitchen. There was a long wooden table alongside an old porcelain sink that was cracked and veined with age. He was surprised that there were so few people there. They cooked and ate as a group. Thirteen people lived at the house, including Henry, but there were only five others in the room, and Gemma just behind him. They were standing at the window, looking into a small courtyard.

John looked to the table, scattered in crumbs, left over

from an earlier sitting, with chipped white plates and glasses of water in front of them. There were loaves of bread piled up at one end, with blunt-looking knives next to them. Everyone turned towards him, and then Gemma.

He blushed and then he looked to the end of the table. Henry's seat. He wasn't there.

'What's going on?' John said.

'There are people here,' someone said. It was Dawn, a woman in her early twenties, dressed like the rest of the women in a long black skirt and T-shirt, with round glasses and eyes that flitted around the room nervously.

'Who is it?'

'They're from another group. They used to come and drink with us, but not anymore. They just speak to Arni or Henry and then go.'

John looked towards the window. Arni was outside, a large Danish man, with broad shoulders and muscled arms that bulged with veins. His hair was long and light, pulled into a ponytail, his goatee board twisted to a point, beads on the end. Large black rings made holes out of his earlobes and silver hoops cut through his eyebrows. Arni was speaking to someone in a white van, the window wound down, parked in a small courtyard with farm outbuildings on the other side, just low stone barns accessed by large sliding wooden doors.

'So what are they doing here?'

'I don't know, but they have been coming for a few weeks now.'

John watched as Arni lifted down a barrel from the back of the van and started to roll it towards one of the barns. He spoke to the other people in the van, and then the engine started again, spluttering and belching smoke.

Arni turned to look at him, and so John stepped back

quickly from the window. He looked round at everyone and smiled nervously. He sat down and was conscious of the silence. He looked at the plate of bread in front of him. It was dry and unappetising. Gemma sat opposite. As she reached forward for some bread, her T-shirt gaped open, too big for her, showing her bony cleavage. She smiled at him.

The group was mostly made up of young people, teenagers, but they had a look of maturity that he didn't see in many people of their age, as if they had found what they wanted from their lives and so had no reason to kick back against it anymore. The people left at the table were the quieter ones. There was Dawn, along with a couple in their forties, the Elams, Jennifer and Peter, ageing hippies whose communal living lifestyle had drawn them to Henry. Jennifer was the curious one, with wide, bird-like eyes and grey roots showing through the dry ponytail of jet-black hair. Peter was quiet, with a paunch and lost hair.

It was to Dawn that John's eyes were drawn. She seemed unhappy compared to the rest, and he couldn't work it out. No, that wasn't right. It wasn't unhappiness. It was reluctance. Always the last to join in with cooking or cleaning, and she said little when Henry was there.

John felt something on his leg, and as he looked, he saw Gemma's half-smile, her foot running slowly up his calf.

Arni came back into the house. Gemma's foot dropped and she looked downwards. Arni looked at John, his eyes narrowed.

John pushed the bread away. He knew what that look was for. Sex was allowed, but they weren't supposed to form bonds.

'Where's Henry?' John said.

'He's gone out, with some of the others. There are things that have to be done.'

'What like?' John said. The rest of the group looked at one another.

It was Gemma who spoke. 'Don't question, you know that,' she said, her tone light, but John spotted the hint that he had already said too much.

There was a moan from a room along the hallway, on the other side of the living room. Everyone ignored it, except for Dawn, who shuffled uncomfortably.

Another moan.

John looked at Gemma, who shook her head, almost invisibly, but John caught the warning. Don't go in there.

The moans were from the farmer who owned the house. A man in his seventies, he spent his time bedridden, looked after by whoever could face going into his room, provided that Henry agreed.

More moans, except that they were more pleading this time.

Dawn went to the table quickly and grabbed some bread, filled a cup with water, and started walking towards the door.

There was a crash. Plates banged. People jumped. Arni held out his stick, a gnarled cane made from polished oak, a brass gargoyle for a handle.

'Don't go in there,' he shouted at her.

Dawn stopped. People looked at Arni, and then back at Dawn.

'He's hungry, and thirsty,' Dawn said, her voice trembling.

Arni pointed the stick at a chair and shook his head. 'Sit.'

Dawn looked back towards the doorway and then at the stick. She bowed her head and then sat down. As John looked, he saw that tears were running down Dawn's cheeks. She pulled at some bread, but didn't look like she was going to eat again.

Arni put the stick under her chin, the cold metal of the gargoyle against her skin. 'We need more food. Worry about the old man later. Understand?'

Dawn nodded slowly.

Arni didn't move the stick.

'Take John with you.'

John was surprised. He had been with the group for three weeks now, and he hadn't been allowed out of the compound. It had been that way ever since they had turned up at his house.

His mind went back to that night, when it had seemed like just another talk. They had spoken to him a few times, but on that night they wanted him to go with them and leave everything behind.

They had made him wear a blindfold at first, made from a torn-up hessian sack that scratched at his eyelids and made him itch. Except that he couldn't scratch it, because his hands were tied behind him, sitting against the side of the van, his head up, trying to work out where everyone was as they prodded him, just for a bit of fun. There had been giggles all the way from the young women, and he had tried to laugh along with them, making out like it was a game, but had been worried that perhaps he had misread them.

It had been stop and start as they made their way out of town, but then the curves and tight bends of the countryside had taken over, throwing him around the van, making everyone laugh louder. The jolts and bumps as they drove along a rutted farm track were the final part of the journey, and then he felt the rush of cool air as the van doors flew open. Gentle hands guided him out of the van, and then he was taken inside, pushed along a short corridor into what he now called home.

The smell of cannabis had hit him straight away, sweet

and strong, and he was put into a wooden chair. There were voices around him, whispers, giggles, murmurs of conversation, but all he had been able to see was the inside of the blindfold. The bindings around his wrists were loosened and then tied to the chair, so that he was exposed, vulnerable, unsure as to how many people were there.

'John?'

It was Gemma, bringing him back to the present.

'So are you coming with us?' she said.

He smiled and nodded. 'Yes, I will.'

John stepped out from behind the table and went towards some hooks on the wall. When he found his jacket, a plain black zip-up, he waited by the door as Gemma and Dawn got up to follow him.

Chapter Nine

Sheldon's hands gripped the wheel as he drove towards Billy Privett's house. The tight streets of the town centre turned into winding lanes that headed towards the moors. Drystone walls lined the way ahead, although they were down to untidy piles of rock in places, so that the roads opened straight onto open moorland, bleak and wild, with sheep grazing up to the tarmac, the grey dots of stone farmhouses peppering the views.

He had left Jim Kelly, the reporter, at the station, giving a statement about how Billy Privett's face was delivered to him, although it was really to keep him out of the way.

Sheldon turned into a narrow lane and felt his tyres slide on some mud thrown up by a tractor. The road bumped and dropped towards a small cluster of houses hidden deep in a valley. Except that one of the houses stood out from the rest.

'Is that Billy's house ahead?' Tracey said

Sheldon nodded. 'Yes,' was all he said. His jaw clenched when he got a good view of it.

The house was a large block of red brick that sprawled over two plots that had once been home to two bungalows. The house was double-fronted, with large pillars between them that supported a tiled porch, reached by the long stretch of the driveway.

Billy Privett had bought the house when his lottery numbers came in, and since then he had put his own mark on it, with games rooms and a bar, although Sheldon didn't see them as any kind of improvement.

Tracey looked at the house as Sheldon pulled up at the kerb.

'I was just thinking that he was a lucky bastard, but then I remembered that he is now in the mortuary,' Tracey said.

Sheldon climbed out of the car. 'He still had more luck than he deserved,' he said, and then set off for the gate, Tracey catching up with him. He pressed the intercom. No one answered for a while, and Tracey eyed up the fence, as if seeing whether she could scale it. Sheldon touched her on the arm.

'Privett has dogs,' he said. 'And they'll be hungry by now.'

Tracey rolled her eyes. 'I should have guessed that.'

Sheldon jabbed at the button, more impatient this time. He was about to turn back to his car when a voice came through the speaker.

'Hello?' It was a woman's voice, timid and quiet.

'It's the police,' he said. 'We need to come in.'

There was a pause, and then, 'Billy isn't here.'

'I know. That's why we need to come in. Could you open the gates please.'

Another pause followed, and then there was a buzz as the gates began to creep open. They exchanged glances and then began the slow walk along the driveway, as the house loomed ahead of them.

'Who was that, his sister?' Tracey said.

'He didn't have one.'

'But what about his family?' Tracey said. 'Shouldn't we be speaking to them first?'

Sheldon shook his head. 'His mother died ten years ago.

His father fell out with him when Billy wouldn't spend the money on him. The family liaison officer is trying to find him. We'll leave the hand-holding to her.'

The door opened before they got there and a woman appeared, no older than twenty, with her hair light and short, swept behind her ears. Her arms were folded across her chest, although her tight blue shorts and a cropped vest top took away any pretence at modesty. Her breasts jutted out, her nipples visible through the cloth.

'I'm Christina,' she said. 'I'm Billy's housekeeper.'

Sheldon guessed that it wasn't her skills with a duster that got her the job.

'Is there anyone else here?' Sheldon asked.

'No, just me,' she said. 'There was supposed to be a party last night, but when Billy didn't come home, everyone went.'

'How long have you been working for Billy?'

She paused, as if she had to work it out, and then said, 'Around a year now.'

Since just after Alice Kenyon died, Sheldon thought, although he was surprised he didn't know this. He hadn't seen her before, even though he had done surveillance on Billy Privett after Alice's death.

'I'm sorry,' Sheldon said, his voice soft. 'We need to come inside.' Christina didn't look much older than his own daughter, and he didn't know what hardships had made her decide that cleaning up for Billy Privett was an improvement in her life. And he knew that she was about to become jobless.

'Is it Billy? What's he done? Is he okay?'

Sheldon looked at Tracey, and then sighed. 'We do need to come in. Please.'

'No, tell me now,' she said. Tears had appeared in her eyes.

Sheldon wondered how much he could say. He was confident that it was Billy's body in a mortuary drawer, but confirming that to some young housekeeper seemed a step too far.

'We're worried about Billy,' Sheldon said.

'How worried?' Christina said. She gripped the edge of the door and glanced back into the house, as if she knew what she was about to lose.

'I just want you to let us have a look around, and then come with us, to tell us where Billy went last night.'

Christina stepped aside, and Sheldon walked into the house.

There was a grand entrance hallway, dominated by curving stairs that swept upwards, the carpet lush and deep red, a chandelier dropping down from the ceiling. Corridors went either way, with light streaming across from the open doorways.

Christina sat on the stairs, her face filled with confusion. 'So is Billy hurt, or worse?'

'We're trying to establish that,' Sheldon said, not wanting to get drawn into disclosing anything. 'Did Billy say where he was going last night?'

Christina didn't answer at first, but then she looked up and shook her head. 'He said he had to go out, that's all. We thought that maybe he was getting something for the party.'

'Drugs?'

Christina shrugged, non-committal. 'But then he didn't come home, and so everyone went home. Even the girls.'

'What girls?'

Christina snorted a laugh. 'There are always girls. Money is better than good aftershave for drawing them in. They don't like Billy, but they let him play because he buys them things.'

'Did any of them have boyfriends?' Sheldon said.

Christina nodded. 'Some did. But the boyfriends didn't

mind, because Billy bought booze and took them on holidays. He even let them race his cars.'

'And what about you?'

Christina shook her head, her lip curled. 'No, never. That's why he doesn't sack me, because he hasn't got bored of me. He gets tired of the girls he fucks, because there are always more. Me, I'm like a target for him, but I'm better than that.'

Sheldon smiled. He liked Christina, because she had been playing Billy, although the investigation was growing with every question. Jealous boyfriends, young women who gave too much of themselves for a taste of the high life. Maybe drugs too.

'We're going to look round the house now,' Sheldon said. 'Just wait here.'

'Why?'

'Because we need to search everywhere.' He moved away, but then something occurred to him. 'No, you can help us,' he said, turning back to Christina. 'Try and remember who was here last night. I want a list when we come back.'

Christina frowned and sat down on the stairs. 'Is Billy hurt?' she said. 'Why can't you tell me?'

'Just stay there,' Sheldon said, and then he set off along one of the corridors. As he looked ahead, he felt the tingle of his nerves again, the tightness in his chest. He reached into his pocket for the diazepam, but stopped himself. He had to confront this.

Sheldon turned to head for the room at the end. As he walked, his mind flashed back to one year earlier, when he had walked along the same hallway, the first detective at Billy's house. It didn't look much different. Memories flickered and imposed themselves on the scene. The large window looming at one end, the once-white carpet covered in dirty footprints and spilled wine stains. There was a bar on one side, with lager pumps on the granite surface and optics for spirits pinned to the wall. The television seemed to dominate the room, and there were beanbags strewn around. This was the party room. Just like last time, except that it had acquired more grime. And like last time, once the party ended, when Alice was found, everyone left.

Sheldon closed his eyes for a moment as he saw the tell-tale blue shimmer on the wall. The door that led to the pool room.

He opened his eyes and walked slowly towards it. The memories of a year earlier came faster this time. As he approached the door, the light from the pool shining through the glass, he saw his hand reaching for the handle as if he was looking through a haze, his clothes different, the sleeve of his jacket navy blue, not the grey suit he was wearing. He had gripped the chrome handle sharply, really just expecting another room, but instead he had seen Alice.

She was in the water, close to the bottom, her arms out, flaccid, distorted as he looked down on her, her hair fanned out. She reminded him instantly of his own daughter. Her hair was the same colour, her build similar. His stomach rolled as he saw that it was someone just like Hannah. Except that Alice was naked.

He opened the door again. The pool was still there. It ran the length of a brick extension, with large windows all around. There was a large tiled area at one end, with a jacuzzi. The pool was tiled in bright white, except for the six numbers that were set out large in dark blue on the bottom. Billy's winning numbers, his life defined by six balls that rolled out of a machine one Saturday evening. It didn't look quite as clean though. The jacuzzi was empty and there were some broken tiles along one side of the pool.

The gentle shimmer of the water transfixed Sheldon as he thought once more about Alice.

Alice Kenyon had been a nineteen-year-old economics student, part of a group of young women with high prospects, but like most young people, they wanted to enjoy themselves. Billy Privett's parties had become the talk of the area, with private security paid to keep out the uninvited. The guests were Billy's friends, plus any hangers-on that Billy picked up during the evening, along with any pretty young woman who wanted to have free booze and drugs.

The rumours quickly became legends, with nude pool parties, orgies in the bedrooms, and drunken stock car races in the back garden. The police were called often in relation to noise; mainly from the cars he raced and crashed in the field he owned at the back. Sheldon once heard about a young female officer who went to the house because of a noise complaint, and when she walked into the pool room, she was the only person wearing clothes. It was only her pepper spray and baton that kept it that way.

Then one night changed everything.

Someone had called the police anonymously, said that something had gone wrong at the party. Sheldon went with a young cadet. The house had been insecure; the gate unlocked, the front door open, and when they'd crept through the house, it had been deserted. There had been a clean-up though. The dishwasher had been full of glasses, and if there had been DNA on them to establish who was there, it evaporated with the steam that rushed for the ceiling as Sheldon opened it to check.

And in the pool, there had been Alice, her body just brushing the numbers etched into the tiles.

Sheldon had dived in to pull her out, but his attempts to resuscitate had been futile. Alice was dead. It wasn't the body that had fuelled his anger though. It was how the investigation floundered that had got to him. He had started to lose sleep, waking up in the middle of the night, sweating, clutching at his chest.

He was dragged back to the present as Tracey appeared behind him.

'It's too warm in here,' she said.

Sheldon agreed and nodded, his forehead moist, his shirt stuck to his chest. 'I think it's supposed to make everyone get naked.'

He backed out of the pool room to make his way to the stairs, edging past Christina, who was still on the bottom step, her chin resting on her hand.

Sheldon remembered which was Billy's room. He glanced into some of the others on the way, and they were pretty much unchanged. Some were set out with soft chairs and large screens, while others were party rooms, with floor cushions and red cloth covering the window. Christina's was different. It was tidy, with cosmetics and perfumes lined up in front of a mirror.

Billy's room was just the same as it was a year earlier. There was a large round bed in the middle of the room, with a mirror attached to the ceiling above it, the bed covered in red silk sheets. It was a cliché of luxury, more sleaze than style. The computer was on a desk next to the bed, and when he gave the mouse a nudge, the screen came to life.

He sat down to start browsing as Tracey went through his drawers.

He went to the emails first, but as he scrolled through, he saw nothing of interest. It was mainly racist jokes circulated amongst friends and confirmations of purchases. There was nothing to help in the documents folder either, just invoices that had once been received as attachments and a few manuals for the gadgets he had around the house.

Sheldon was just about to go to the pictures folder when he heard Tracey whistle. As he turned round, she was holding a piece of paper.

'It seems that Billy wasn't all heart,' she said.

'What do you mean?'

Tracey showed him a piece of paper that was ragged along the edge, as if it had been torn out of a notebook, with a list of names with numbers alongside. 'It looks like a dealer list.'

As Sheldon looked, what he saw was all too familiar, because a list of names and numbers usually meant one thing: a list of drug debts.

'So Billy was charging for whatever people were taking on party nights,' Sheldon said. 'No longer the generous millionaire.'

Tracey nodded. 'It looks that way. He might have put pressure on the wrong person.'

Sheldon sighed. 'We'll have so many lines of enquiries that we'll need a road map soon.'

He turned back to the pictures folder. When he clicked on it, he saw that it was organised into party dates. He clicked on one, and it was what he expected. Men leering at the camera, drinks in their hand, some women giggling, and as Sheldon scrolled through, the women ended up naked. The men became more exuberant as the photographs progressed, the women more vacant, with the latter ones being the most graphic. It seemed that Billy was more interested in taking pictures than he was in taking part.

Sheldon scrolled backwards, wondering if Billy had got blasé as the months wore on, that whatever he had removed from the computer a year earlier, when they were investigating Alice's death, had made its way back onto it. It was just the same. There was no folder for the night of Alice's death, or for the few weeks before then. It had made it hard to find out who had been going to Billy's parties just before Alice died. A young woman had died, and all Billy could think of was to remove evidence.

There was a noise behind him, a slight cough. When he looked round, he saw that Christina was watching him.

She leant back against the doorjamb. 'I've remembered some of the names.'

'Tell me at the station,' Sheldon said, and as he walked towards her, she held out her wrists mockingly, as if she was about to be arrested.

Sheldon ignored her and brushed straight past. He wasn't in the mood for games, and there was something about Christina that troubled him, except that he couldn't quite work out why.

Chapter Ten

Charlie's hangover started to clear as he walked back to the office with Donia. He had been too harsh on her. She was just a kid, and he had been like her once, filled with eagerness about a legal career. It was the way his life had turned out that had killed the dream, which wasn't her fault. And he could tell from the occasional grimace that she just wanted to sit down and take off her shoes. They looked brand new, and her heels were probably shredded. There was a time when work experience was just that, a taster. Now, the kids treated it like a job interview, and got themselves the clothes to match.

'So why the law?' he said, turning to her.

She perked up, seemed surprised by the attention. 'It looks interesting.'

'It can be, depending on what you do. Although that's one of the problems, because it seems like the more you can earn, the more boring it gets. The worthy stuff is the best, and you get to keep your conscience, but you'll be poorer than your clients. Get a nice suit and a bright smile and flaunt yourself around the big city money pits, and then maybe you'll have a decent life.'

'I'm from Leeds. Will I have to move away?'

Charlie smiled. 'No, Leeds is good. I went to university there.'

'I know.'

'Do you? How?'

Donia looked flustered. 'I saw it on a profile somewhere. I researched you before I arrived.'

Charlie thought about that, and couldn't remember when he had ever put his university in a profile, but he let it go. The internet can tell you anything now.

'So why are you here?' Charlie said.

Donia seemed to think about that, but then said, 'I need the work experience.'

'But you're a long way from home.'

'The placements in Leeds were all taken up.'

Charlie shrugged. It was her summer, and all law students need work experience. The colleges keep taking the money, but there are no jobs anymore, not unless you know an uncle or aunt with a law firm. So they write to him, begging for some experience. And he lets them come, because it's free labour. Sit them behind a barrister in the Crown Court or interview witnesses, and they can even make the firm money.

'What have you made of it so far?' he said.

'What I expected, although can I say something?'

'Yeah, sure.'

'Well, I've been wondering how you would be, and I thought you would seem happier.' When Charlie looked surprised, she added quickly, 'I'm sorry, that's rude of me, but this is going to be my career too, and so I want to know whether it will make me happy.'

Charlie smiled. Donia knew nothing of his past, or how he lived his life. She was looking at the superficial. She saw his name on a sign, the status as a lawyer. She didn't see the panic about the bills being paid when the legal aid money arrived late, or the nerve-shredding fatigue of a night at the police station after a long day in court, with paperwork still to do.

'Your career will be what you make it,' he said.

They were on the street that led to his office, past the charity shops, and the newsagent who had abuse yelled at him most weeks and had to replace his window a couple of times a year, the price of being the first Asian shopkeeper in the town. Charlie tried to make excuses for the ones who had done it when they were taken to court but the newsagent was still friendly to him.

As they got closer to the office, Charlie saw the group he had seen before, with the dyed black hair and black clothes. The older man was in the doorway of an empty bingo hall, the neon letters fixed to the wall now dark and dirty. The rest of the group were sitting on the pavement, listening to him talk.

The older man seemed to watch Charlie as he went past, and so he and Donia slowed down as they got near, to listen to what they were saying. The older man stopped talking when he saw that Charlie was watching.

'Don't stop on my behalf,' Charlie said. 'I'm curious.'

The ones sitting on the floor looked at the standing man, who pulled his hair back before saying, 'You ready to hear the story?' His voice was low and slow.

'What story is that?'

He smiled at Charlie, and everyone else smiled when he did so. 'You're not ready.'

'Try me. Or try this – why are you hanging around here?'

'You sound nervous. You've no need. You're part of the law machine that ties everyone together.'

'So you know who I am?'

'Everyone knows who you are.'

‘It feels like you are watching me,’ Charlie said.

The man frowned. ‘Everyone gets watched. You’ve bought into it all, so the government knows everything about you. Where you shop, what you buy, what you think. Your legal system? It is built on lies. You know that though, that there is no search for truth, not ever.’

‘So what do you offer?’

A pause. ‘Something new, a fresh beginning, where we can look after ourselves, make our own rules. A new morality, that’s what we are.’

Charlie rolled his eyes. ‘I thought maybe you were different.’

‘From what?’

‘Some hippy set thinking you can change society. We’ve been here before, but human nature ruins it every time.’

‘Not this time.’

‘Who says?’

The man looked at Donia, who smiled politely, and then turned back to Charlie. ‘Look at you, man. Dark suit. Tie. Shirt. You wear your hair long, but it’s a small protest, because you still follow the crowd. You’re scared. I can smell it, your fear. Of getting older, of your life. We have no fear. We are free.’

Charlie stepped closer. ‘Bullshit. You’ve been hanging around here all morning. We were burgled last night. Was that you?’

‘There are no boundaries.’

‘There are when I lock my office door. Do you want me to get the police?’

The man’s smile disappeared. ‘They mean nothing to me, because they don’t rule me. This society rules by consent. I’ve withdrawn mine, and so I’m not bound anymore.’

‘I’m sure they will find a way to bind you somehow.’

The man shook his head, his eyes narrowing. 'Not this man. I'm free. Not ruled by you or those like you. But look at you, Mister Lawyer. You are all about the rules.'

Charlie looked at him, and then down at the group again. 'I'll leave you to your way, and you leave me to mine. That's real freedom, isn't it?'

He turned away, Donia alongside him, questioning why he had bothered to get involved, and carried on towards the office. He heard the group laugh as they moved away.

Charlie climbed the office stairs to the reception. Someone was coming out. Two men, both in trim dark suits, shirt and tie. He stepped to one side as they came towards him. They looked like money, but there was steel in their eyes. He knew that look. It was hardened criminality, not some professional caught on a speed camera.

Amelia was picking up clients like that, whereas Charlie's congregation was filled with drunks and petty thieves, or the Saturday night fighters. The real criminals made demands he didn't have the interest to meet.

He went to his own room first and dumped the files on his desk. Donia hovered near the door.

'What now?' she said.

He looked down at his files. There were letters to dictate, to confirm the outcome of the court hearings, but they could wait. The clock was working its way round to lunchtime, and so a quiet half hour would do no harm.

'A coffee would be good,' he said, pointing towards the kitchen.

Donia smiled, some disappointment in her eyes, but she went anyway.

Charlie fell back into the old armchair in the corner of the room. As he put his head back, he let the stresses of the morning wash over him. Someone had been into the office during the night and made an untidy search. What had they wanted? And the news about Billy Privett.

He didn't open his eyes when heard the door to his office open. He knew it would be Amelia.

'The glazier has been,' Amelia said. 'We need to get better security.'

'If we keep netting clients like that, a bit of broken glass won't be a problem.'

'What do you mean?'

'The two men who just left. The big hitters. Dark suits. Bad attitude.'

Amelia faltered, and then said, 'Just clients.'

'Empires are built on people like them,' Charlie said. 'I salute you, and let God make Oulton a less safe place.'

Amelia didn't respond, but she stayed in the room.

Charlie opened his eyes. 'I've got some bad news on the murder as well,' he said.

'Murder?' she said, and then, 'Oh yes, that. What about it?'

'We won't get the suspect, if he's caught,' Charlie said. 'The rumours are that the corpse is Billy Privett.'

She nodded but didn't respond.

'You don't sound surprised,' he said.

'Rumours travel quickly,' she said, although she sounded distracted. 'Are there any suspects?'

'I don't know. I didn't get further than the courtroom.'

She turned and walked out of the room. No pleasantries. He looked out of the window instead. The view was the same as always. Slate rooftops. Telephone wires. He got to his feet and strolled to the glass. The cobbles were worn and streaked with engine oil, the street curving downhill. Charlie looked past all of that and watched the drift of the clouds. He could ignore the files for a moment.

Then something caught his attention. It was a white van

further along the street, a logo on the side. It looked like it had just arrived, with two men behind it, one holding a camera.

He groaned to himself. The police had become less keen on passing information to the press since all the phone hacking stories, but the reporter at court had said the rumours came from the local paper, and so they were bound to spread. He left his room, almost knocking the coffee cup out of Donia's hand as she brought it to him.

Charlie took it from her and went to Amelia's room. She was standing at the rear window as he went in, looking out. She didn't have the view that Charlie had, just the yard behind the kebab shop and a row of houses. She went to sit down at her desk.

'So how do you feel about Billy Privett?' he said.

'Why should I feel anything?' she said, although her tone was unconvincing.

'Because there is some faint warmth to your blood, that he was a human being you came to know? Or maybe just because he can't pay you any more money.'

'He was a client,' she said. 'And that's always been your problem, that you see them as friends, all these wasters.'

'They are, a lot of them. I grew up in this town. I'm no better than them.'

'Save your working class guilt, Charlie, because none of them give a damn about you. They would drop you in it quicker than they'd have your wallet.'

'You're all heart,' he said. 'You better get your sympathetic face ready though. You became Billy's spokeswoman once he came into the money, and the press are outside.'

'What, now?'

Charlie nodded. 'Come on, take a deep breath and think like a real life person. Use words like "regret" and "sorrow". Good soundbites.'

She scowled. 'You know I can't say anything, not without Billy's consent.'

'I don't think he'll complain too much,' Charlie said. 'Billy was good for you, although there is some irony in that someone involved in a high-profile death should end up dying prematurely.'

'What, like karma?' Amelia said, and then shook her head. 'There are things you don't know. He died an innocent man, you need to remember that.'

'I'm a lawyer. You don't need to feed me the line. Not being guilty is a long way from being innocent. A young woman died and he stayed quiet. He could have said something to help the police, even if he had no part in her death. His silence just made him look guilty.'

A look of irritation flashed across her face, but it was fleeting.

'I'll say it again,' she said. 'He died an innocent man.'

'If that is going to be his epitaph, *they* need to hear it,' and Charlie pointed towards her doorway, meaning the people on the street. He started to walk back to his own room, and Amelia followed him. He could hear the sway of her hips in the way her heels made loud taps on the hardwood floor. The scent of perfume drifted towards him as she got close, soft musk, delicate and expensive. When they both got into Charlie's room, he pointed to the van that had pulled over at the side of the road. There was someone on the pavement with a boom microphone in one hand, talking to a cameraman and looking around. Charlie raised an eyebrow at Amelia as the cameraman pointed up at the window.

'Oh shit,' she said, although it seemed like a whisper to herself, rather than any comment Charlie was meant to hear.

Then he saw someone just further along the street, a face he recognised. Amelia hadn't spotted him.

'Got to go,' he said to her, and as Amelia shot him a frosty look, he added, 'Cheer up. You'll look great on the news.' Charlie went towards the door, leaving Amelia gazing out of the window, one hand just flicking at her hair.

Chapter Eleven

John stepped out of the door that led into a stone courtyard, Dawn next to him. They were going to find food, on Arni's order.

He hadn't gone more than two paces before Gemma fell into step alongside him, heavy black boots on her feet. John looked down, and for a moment he wanted to put his arm around Gemma, to enjoy the walk in the countryside, but Dawn was with them. Instead he said, 'How far is it?'

'A couple of miles.' Gemma smiled. 'How does it feel, to be leaving the farm?'

He thought about that for a moment. 'Strange,' he said eventually.

'It's all still out there, babe, just remember that,' she said. 'That's why it's been so long, to let you shake off your old life, but it's still there somewhere, ready to suck you back.'

'I think I can fight it,' he said. 'I've listened to Henry. I understand his message now.'

'We're creating our own world here, where none of all that crap matters. We're free people, but it isn't easy, because people are weak. That's right, isn't it, Dawn?'

Dawn looked like she was going to stay silent again, but then she looked at Gemma, then at John, and nodded. 'We have to stay together, to avoid temptation.'

John watched Dawn look away. He leaned into Gemma. 'Is Dawn weak?' he whispered.

'From time to time, we all are,' she said, and then Gemma let go of him and skipped ahead, her long skirt swirling around her ankles, along the muddy path at the side of the house, past the outbuilding that housed two quad bikes and the barrel that Arni had brought in earlier. There was a small square enclosure against the wall, fashioned out of chicken wire, with wooden shelters at one end, housing the hens that provided them with eggs. The peace was broken by the hum of a generator that powered the lights in one of the barns, where they grew cannabis.

As they emerged from the shadows they started to cross a field, the ground bumpy and pitted from tractor tracks and the root clumps of meadow grasses. In the middle were the Seven Sisters, the stone circle, although it was just a crescent really, some stones taller than others, with one slab in the middle.

Dawn waited for John to catch up, Gemma running ahead. When he reached her, he said, 'I didn't know there was a stone circle near Oulton before I joined the group.'

Dawn looked at it, and then down again. John thought he saw a tear run down her cheek.

'Dawn?'

She wiped her eyes with the heel of her hand and then tried out a watery smile. 'It's our legacy, so that it will be there long after we're gone and people will know that we were here. And why.'

He was surprised. 'I didn't know it was a new thing, that we had put the rocks there.'

'You haven't been here long enough. You'll find out soon enough.'

John nodded to himself, curious, and then said, 'You can trust me, Dawn.'

She shook her head. 'No, I can't.'

'Why not?'

Dawn looked towards Gemma, who was heading for a tumbledown part of the drystone wall and to a path that cut through the northerly woods opposite, which kept the coldest winds away from the house.

'Things are not what they seem,' she said. 'You need to get out.'

'What do you mean?'

Dawn wiped her eyes and then said, 'Tell me what you think of Henry.'

John thought about what to say. 'He's a strong leader, delivers a good message, and I believe it, like we all do.'

Dawn laughed, but it was bitter and hollow. 'So we've no need to talk.'

'What do you mean?'

'I thought we weren't about leaders.'

'We always need leaders.'

'I thought we were about freedom,' she said and then walked quickly ahead, to catch up with Gemma.

John followed them, curious, wanting to find out more, but Dawn was with Gemma now, and he knew the moment had gone.

He looked around as he walked, at the roll of the fields and clusters of trees that dotted the green hills. He stepped over the fallen down rocks by the wall and into the shadows of trees, where the soft swish of the grass was replaced by the echo and snap of the woodland path. Patches of bluebells glimmered in the shafts of sun and he caught the scratches of grey squirrels clambering up the bark. The path would take them lower down the hill, to the stream that trickled and gathered pace until it ran between the stone sides of the Oulton buildings.

As he emerged back into the daylight, Dawn and Gemma were ahead, but apart from each other, Gemma turning as she walked, playful, young. Dawn looked down, her step leaden.

'How far now?' he shouted.

'Not far,' Gemma yelled back. 'More of the men should do this. If it wasn't for the women, you'd all starve.'

John laughed. 'Hasn't that always been the way?'

He turned to look back towards the house, and saw that it was hidden now. Two rabbits chased each other in the long grass on the other side of a low wall. The sun felt warm, the blush of early summer on his cheeks. It felt good, free and easy. John felt the same surge of happiness he had felt when he first arrived, the simple contentment of belonging.

The path followed the line of a wall and then reached the top of a small rise, where the view changed. He looked ahead and saw Oulton. The buildings in the centre were tight together, the grey stone rising higher than the others around, with tall windows and ornate facades, boasts of Victorian wealth long since gone. A disused railway line ran away from the town and down the hill, towards the towns in the valley, now part of the commuter spill over from Manchester, driving up the house prices and sending the locals further north.

The town fanned out like a flower, with the closed-in centre, and then the swirls and curves of the newer housing estates on the edges. The peace of the countryside was replaced by the sounds of lorries rumbling along the roads or straining up the steep hills.

'There,' Gemma said, and pointed. He looked and saw the corrugated metal roof and tarmac car park just below them, the first part of the town they reached. A supermarket.

'We're going shopping?' John said, confused.

Gemma giggled. 'Not exactly.'

They followed a path that was long and steep, curving down the side of the hill until it ended by a high wooden fence made up of strong horizontal laths with gaps in between, perfect for footholds.

Gemma turned to Dawn. 'Have you got your bag ready?'

Dawn held up her rucksack.

'Come on then,' she said, and the two women scrambled over the fence, their long skirts riding high on their legs, Gemma's bare, Dawn's clad in torn black leggings.

John peered through the fence to the rear of the supermarket and saw large open doors, through which he could see high shelves of stock. A forklift truck lay dormant just inside.

'Wait,' he said. 'Are you going to steal?'

Gemma turned around. 'It's not stealing,' she said. 'We are not taking things from inside the shop. They throw too much food away, even though there's nothing wrong with it.' She shrugged. 'It's crazy. I mean, we grow food to feed ourselves, but then throw it away because the fruit looks less fresh or the bread too hard. So we are taking it back, so that it does what it is meant to do. Bread, milk, cheese, butter, and jars and tins. Coffee, tea, cereal. It is all fine to be eaten, and so we should take it, because it is the right thing to do. It has been thrown away and so they don't want it anymore. How can it be wrong?'

'What does the shop say?'

'This shop?' Gemma said, and pointed. 'Nothing. There is a bigger one a few miles down the road, and they spray the food blue so that we can't take it. Where is the morality in that, that it is better to throw it away than allow people to eat?' Then she grinned. 'We come at night sometimes, because the security man lets us look without any problems. We know how to make him happy.'

John felt a bite of jealousy, and his eyes must have given him away, because Gemma said, 'We get fed, he gets satisfied. What's the problem? Except that he isn't working this week, he's away with his wife, so we have to do it this way.'

'Are you sure you'll be all right?' John said, looking towards the large open doors.

'We'll be fine. If we get caught, we'll just smile and flirt, and no one really cares.'

John watched through the gaps in the fence as the two women scurried through the yard and clambered into a large blue skip. They were in there for just a couple of minutes, and then they scrambled back out again and ran across the yard. They threw their bags over the fence and clambered over to join him.

Gemma showed John the contents of her rucksack, and seemed pleased when he nodded his approval.

'We will eat well today,' he said.

Gemma set off walking back, Dawn more slowly again, quiet and still, and so John followed. The sun was on his face and his head was filled with bird whistles and the swish of the grass and Gemma's giggles. And he felt it again. Happiness. It was the simplicity of it all. It was joyous, with no troubles, no worries, with just the scents of the fields and the pleasure of his companions to fill the day.

Gemma turned round to him and blew him a kiss. When he returned it, he was smiling, couldn't stop himself, his heart skipping like a teenager.

He felt it at that moment. A certainty, a resolve that he had left his old life behind, and it felt good.

Chapter Twelve

Charlie walked quickly down the stairs from his office, popping a couple of mints into his mouth. He knew who he had seen outside and wanted to catch him up. The sight of the television people had reminded him of how big the Alice Kenyon story had become.

Billy Privett had been everyone's favourite hate figure even before Alice Kenyon died. He'd got his money too easily and flaunted it too much. Billy knew that it got his face in the paper and so he played up to it. Once Alice died, face down in Billy's pool, a horrible end to just another party, the publicity became less fun. It became about the questions he wouldn't answer. Who had given her the drugs? Who had brutalised her sexually? Who else was there?

The good times for Billy waned after Alice died. No one knew if Billy had killed her, but everyone guessed that he had stopped the killer from being caught. The press highlighted every new thing he bought, every party he still held, as if he was mocking Alice's death. Time passed though, and Alice would have been forgotten, except that her father, Ted, wouldn't let that happen. He learned the lesson pretty quickly that the media can help if you harness it correctly. He became the victim's champion, and campaigned about the right to silence, about drug laws being too relaxed, about an individual's responsibility to help.

Except that by putting himself in the public glare, he became a target for the media. When Ted was caught in a car with a girl who looked younger than Alice had been, a blurred photograph showing them in an embrace, the public view turned from sympathy to dislike.

Ted was outside Charlie's office, his hands thrust into his coat pockets, staring up at the office window.

The camera crew wasn't ready yet. The reporter was adjusting his tie and checking his hair in the van mirror, and the cameraman was looking at the floor, waiting. Ted Kenyon had once been a good source for a quote, but it didn't look like he had been spotted. Or more importantly, Ted seemed keen on keeping away from the lenses.

Charlie walked slowly towards him, looking for a sign that all wasn't well. Ted knew that over the years Charlie had been Billy's lawyer from time to time, and that Amelia had dealt with the fallout from his daughter's death, but what was he doing outside his office? As Charlie got closer, Ted looked at him, a flicker to his eyelids showing that he had recognised him, and then he nodded a greeting.

Charlie popped another mint into his mouth before saying, 'How are you, Mr Kenyon?'

Ted stared at Charlie for a few moments. Ted wasn't tall, but the broadness of his shoulders and the faded cuts and nicks on his hands showed off his years in the building trade. He had built up a successful business, and the money it had brought in had given his daughter the confidence to think that she could leave Oulton and make something of herself. Until one night back in her hometown had brought it all to an end, and Ted Kenyon realised that although sheer determination could bring him the good things in life, it didn't do much to keep away the horrors.

'I'm not sure,' Ted said, his voice quiet. He was smartly dressed, although Charlie had never seen him any other way, in trousers with a sharp crease and a V-neck jumper, a shirt and tie just visible. He was not even fifty, but everyone who knew him said that Alice's death had aged him. Whatever energy he'd had left, he had channelled into Billy Privett. What would he do now?

'So you know that Billy Privett has been killed?' Charlie said.

He nodded. His jaw was clenched, and he was looking past Charlie, towards the office.

'Is that why you're down here, to give a quote?' and Charlie pointed towards the television van.

Ted paused for a moment and then shook his head. 'No, not today.'

'I don't want any trouble, Mr Kenyon. I'm sorry for your daughter, I always have been, but I was just doing my job whenever I helped him. So was Amelia.'

His look darkened for a moment. 'She did more than that.'

Charlie was confused for a moment. 'What do you mean?'

'People like you turn *doing my job* into an excuse, as if it makes everything all right,' Ted said, his mouth set into a snarl. 'It doesn't though, does it?'

Charlie didn't try and respond. He'd tried to justify his job to enough people in the past, but not many had agreed with him, that everyone deserves someone to speak up for them.

Ted looked up towards the office window. Charlie followed his gaze, and saw Amelia there, speaking into a telephone.

'So what do you think about Billy dying?' Charlie said.

'Nothing will bring Alice back,' Ted said, after thinking about the question for a few seconds. 'I thought of myself as a tough man. It's the way I was brought up, that it's a tough world, and so you've got to be tough with it. Alice being murdered made me realise that I wasn't as strong as I thought, and so I went with my feelings more, instead of trying to hide them. Now?' and he shook his head. 'I don't feel anything. No pity, no sympathy, no anger. I know that it sounds cruel, because Billy was also someone's child, but that is how I feel.'

'People will understand,' Charlie said 'Your daughter died.'

'No, they won't,' he snapped. 'I know what people think of me now. It's not about Alice anymore.'

Charlie didn't answer that. Don't get frisky with girls barely out of their teens, was his thought, but he didn't voice it.

'Why have you come here, Mr Kenyon?' Charlie said, and when Ted looked confused for a moment, he added, 'Amelia's office. Of all the places to come, you've chosen here.'

Ted paused, and then he said, 'I was passing that's all.'

As he said that, Charlie saw a flash of Ted's ordinariness for a moment. That was why his message had once been so powerful, because he was an ordinary man with a heart-breaking message. He was hard working, had provided for his daughter, an outgoing bubbly teenager. No one had a bad word for her. She was popular, the boys liked her, good at sport, did well at school. She was everyone's favourite daughter. Then she was found face down in Billy Privett's pool, and Ted Kenyon was the voice for every victim who felt like they got lost in the system. But for all of the media skills he had been forced to learn, he looked lost, as if he didn't know what to do now that the source of all his hatred had gone.

Charlie didn't know why he did it, but he held out his hand. 'I know you'll think it's hollow, but now that Billy has gone, I can say what I always wanted to say, that I'm sorry about your daughter, and I hope one day you get all the answers.'

Ted looked down at the outstretched hand, and then shook his head. 'Not today,' he said.

'So what now?' Charlie said, pulling his hand away, embarrassed. 'We don't want any trouble here.'

Ted looked up at the office again, and said, 'I'm going home to what's left of my family,' and then he walked away, his head down.

As Charlie watched him go, he saw the two men in suits who had been to see Amelia moments before. They were watching him and quietly talking to each other.

As Sheldon got closer to the police station, he saw that journalists were already gathering outside.

Billy's housekeeper, Christina, leaned forward from her seat in the back to look at the reporters. She had agreed to provide a statement about what Billy had told her he was doing.

'Billy's dead, isn't he?' she said.

Tracey exchanged glances with Sheldon, who gave a small shrug.

'Yes, we think he is,' Tracey said, her voice soft. 'I'm sorry.'

Christina stared out of the window for a few seconds, and then said, 'They soon found out, the reporters. Are the police still selling secrets?'

Sheldon drummed his fingers on the steering wheel as he thought of it. He remembered the press outcry about

Alice Kenyon. They had turned on Billy Privett at first, and hounded him for not telling anyone what had happened, but he had been a caricature before Alice, the lottery winner with no class. Once they got bored of Billy's infamy, they turned on the police for not finding the answers.

'We don't sell secrets,' Sheldon said, although he knew that he didn't sound convincing. There had always been coppers ready to pass on information for the right price.

'Or you just got better at hiding it,' Christina said.

Sheldon's car rumbled up the cobbled slope that led to the station, and some of the reporters turned towards his car and took an interest.

'You need to get into the middle of the seat, put your head down, unless you want to be all over the press,' Sheldon said to Christina.

Christina flicked at her hair and smiled out of the window instead.

He pulled into a space in the far corner of the car park, into what used to be an enclosed yard where prisoners were allowed to take cigarette breaks. It meant he could enter through the door at the other end of the corridor though, away from the public entrance. As they walked from the car, Christina in front, Sheldon detected a sway to her hips that was not there when they had been at Billy's house. He glanced upwards, to the white-framed windows that ran the length of the station, and he realised that she was playing to whatever audience there might be. Tracey raised her eyebrows at him.

Sheldon took the lead as they went inside, through two sets of doors and into the long corridor that led to the front entrance, the Incident Room further along. Some male officers passed them as Sheldon walked to an interview room, Christina alongside him, and he noticed the second glances that went her way. As he looked at Christina, he saw that she was smiling still, enjoying her moment as the centre of attention. She knew the secrets of the man found dead in the town the night before, and the look on her face told Sheldon that she would relish telling the story.

Duncan Lowther came towards him along the corridor, bursting out of the Incident Room. He did the second glance at Christina, the look to her breasts that he presumed she wouldn't spot, and then gave a tilt to his head that told Sheldon that he needed a quiet word.

Sheldon turned to Christina and smiled an *excuse me*, before going to the wall on the opposite side of the corridor. Lowther kept his eye on Christina for a while longer and then leaned in.

'The buzz about it being Billy Privett has reached headquarters,' Lowther said.

'What do headquarters say?'

'They want to send FMIT over today.'

Sheldon closed his eyes for a moment. The Force Major Incident Team had taken over the Alice Kenyon investigation. Some people had said that he'd become too involved in the case, but he shouldn't have been punished for it. He could have caught her killer, if he had just been given more time. *They* hadn't caught the killer either, but that didn't seem to matter. It had been Sheldon who'd had the case taken away from him.

'I thought they were too busy?' Sheldon said, after a few seconds. Sweat popped onto his lip.

'They are, but it looks like they have spotted the press exposure on this one and want the limelight.'

Sheldon raised an eyebrow. He knew how it went, that FMIT would take over all the murder investigations in Lancashire if it was possible, but they had limited resources, like every department. So they picked the bigger cases, the ones that were the most complex, or attracted the most attention. When the Alice Kenyon case had first started, it was just a student found drowned in a pool, and at the wrong end of the county. Oulton was left to fend for itself in most things, and the local chiefs liked it that way, but sometimes things got a little too big, and in Alice's case, the press clamour made them ask for more help. The big city boys had been glad to help out.

'I can do this,' Sheldon said, although he surprised himself that he had voiced his thoughts.

Lowther nodded, uncertain. 'It's not always up to us, sir.'

A door opened further along, and Chief Inspector Dixon appeared in the corridor. She was once the rising star of the force, but she was pushed out to Oulton and her career stalled as she got used to the quieter life. Perhaps that had been the intention of the top brass.

She was going outside for a cigarette, the lighter and the gold of the packet visible in her hand, but then she faltered when she saw Christina.

Sheldon glanced across to Christina, whose smile had turned into a smirk. The Chief stopped in the corridor for a few seconds, her eyes towards the floor, and then she turned away and went back into her office, the door clicking closed behind her.

'And I got a message from the reporter, Jim Kelly,' Lowther said. 'He's gone back to work, but he said that he's going to write his story about,' and then he paused as he noticed Christina listening. He leaned forward and whispered, 'About what was delivered to his office this morning.'

Sheldon closed his eyes. It was the same old problem, that there wasn't much they can do to stop press reporting until they had a suspect charged and before the court. They got agreements sometimes to hold things back, but Sheldon guessed that Jim Kelly wanted to squeeze every bit of publicity out of the case. Sheldon's fingers trembled and so he clenched his fist to stop it.

'Sir?' It was Lowther.

Sheldon opened his eyes. A bead of sweat trickled down his nose. 'I'll speak to Kelly,' he said, and then took Christina into a side room.

Chapter Thirteen

As they crossed the field in front of the cottage, their bags bulging with food, Arni was waiting nonchalantly in the doorway, leaning against the doorjamb. John knew it was an act. Arni's jaw was clenched and the veins in his arms showed his tension.

Arni stepped forward as they got closer and held out his arms. Gemma and Dawn passed over their rucksacks, and Arni's lips were pursed as he looked through them. Dawn was trembling next to John, and so he turned to nod and smile, but she didn't respond.

Arni pointed at John and then towards the van. 'It needs cleaning out,' he said. 'And there is some mesh near the barn. Cover the cottage windows with it. We need to be ready.'

'What for?' John said.

Arni glowered. 'You'll find out soon enough. Until then, you don't need to know.' And then he went back into the house.

Once Arni was out of earshot, Gemma said, 'I'll help you with the van.'

John smiled. 'Thank you.' He knew the rhythm of the group now. Arni was the enforcer, Henry the inspiration. 'I'll sort out the mesh.'

He went to the side of the house to find what he needed

as Gemma went to get a bucket. He approached one of the farm outbuildings where he had seen the wire mesh rolled up earlier, leaning against a wall. John picked up the roll but then stopped to peer into the shadows of the outbuilding. There was a large sliding door that ran on rusty rollers, and it had been left ajar. As he looked, he saw a metal barrel, just like the one Arni had unloaded earlier.

John looked around to check that no one was watching, and then stepped inside.

It was cold and dark and smelled of oil and old machinery. His shoes scraped on grit, and so he walked slowly, anxious not to betray his presence.

John looked at the barrel. There was nothing written on the outside, but as he got closer he saw that it wasn't welded shut but had a lid.

He looked around to check that he was still alone, and then he lifted it slowly and peered inside. It contained white crystals, the barrel half full.

He heard voices, and so he dropped the lid and went back outside. It was the Elams collecting eggs. Jennifer looked up and waved. He waved back, and then went to pick up the mesh. Gemma appeared behind him, dragging a hosepipe to the van. He smiled at her as she filled the bucket with water and then clambered into the back.

Dawn was sitting down outside, watching them, absent-mindedly throwing stones like a bored child.

John thought about the barrel as he watched Gemma spray at the floor of the van, her boots loud in the confined space as they scraped on the dirt and the grit. Water started to stream out, like dark rust, staining the courtyard.

Gemma had been there on the first night, when he'd been brought blindfolded to the farmhouse. Someone had sat him in a chair and then tied his hands to the back. John remembered his nerves, his breaths fast, his tongue flicking over his lips to remove the sweat, the creaks of his chair audible above the sounds of people around him.

He had seen the light come on, bright even through the blindfold, so that he had moved his head around, more nervous as he tried to work out what was going on. There had been hands on him. Soft hands, feminine hands, running up his chest, his legs, his groin, touching him. People were laughing, young women giggling. It was a tease, a joke, but the powerlessness turned him on.

Then fingers had tugged at the small knots at the back of his head and the blindfold was loosened.

The glare from the light had been bright, and so he squinted and turned away. As the room had come slowly into view, all he could see were smiling faces. It had been carefree, but mixed with the flush of arousal, the glint of excitement that something new was happening. He thought then that there didn't seem to be many men, that it had been mainly young women, some little more than late teens. His eyes had moved frantically from one to the other, checking for hostility, or hatred or danger, some sign that he had read everything wrong, but there were none. They wore the same look of contentment they had worn when they had visited him at his own house.

Then he had seen him for the first time. Henry.

John heard him before he saw him. There was a rustle behind the lamp, the crossing of legs, a cough. Then Henry commanded everyone to sit down, his voice quiet, but it had held everyone's attention, because they all did just that, sitting cross-legged on the floor. John had known that Henry was their leader, because everyone else had talked about him so much, but that was the moment when John knew exactly how much Henry led, and how much they followed.

Henry had leaned forward into the beam from the lamp, so that it cast a halo around his hair. It was wild, long and unkempt, and dark strands against the brightness of the light made it fan out.

'I'm Henry,' he said.

John had looked down at first and licked his lips, like a nervous twitch. When he looked up again, his voice was strong. 'I've heard of you.'

There had been silence at first, everyone waiting on Henry's response, but then his laugh started as a low rumble, a deep chuckle, and everyone else joined in, laughing at John's innocence, his impudence. Everyone remembered the first time they met Henry, John knew that now.

Henry had leaned into him, and John got a scent of sweat and oil and dirty hair. Henry was unwashed, grubby, with dirt around the collar of his denim shirt, but John knew that he shouldn't turn away from it.

That was the first time John saw Henry's eyes.

Everyone talked about Henry's eyes. They were bright, excited, piercing, but searching and compassionate. They could be everything to everybody, and back then his eyes looked joyful, wide, to match the grin that gleamed through the dark shadow of his beard.

'There's no going back, John, you know that,' Henry had said, but it hadn't come out like a threat. It was more a statement of fact.

Henry had clicked his fingers, and then he had seen her. Gemma. She had been the one he had been drawn to when they had visited his house. There had been a connection with her, and she had felt it too, he was sure, but it had been impossible to speak to her on her own, because she was never alone. He remembered the flutters of excitement when he saw her, her body young and lithe.

John's focus had been entirely on Gemma as she went to her knees in front of him, flutters of excitement in his chest as her hands ran along his legs. Her eyes never left his, a half smile on her face, flirting. As her hand went slowly between his thighs, just brushing him over the cloth of his trousers, it had seemed unreal, almost hazy, because he knew that people were watching, but in that moment it was just Gemma, the soft movement of her fingers on him. He had tried to fight his arousal, but his hands were still tied, and so all he could do was go with the sensations.

Then it was just a blur of images, of sounds. The pop of his trouser button, the cloth sliding down his legs, Gemma warm on him, soft moans, flashes of bodies in the candlelight, other people naked, all the time Henry's quiet laughter in the background. He had felt the rope slip from his wrists and Gemma led him to the bedroom. Once in there, he had let Gemma take charge.

John took a deep breath. That had been just three weeks earlier. He had relived that memory on those nights when Gemma wasn't there, and he had waited for it to happen again. And it had, whenever Henry allowed it.

'You're daydreaming again.'

'Uh-huh?' John said, and then he realised that Gemma was talking to him. He laughed and splashed some water towards her. She giggled and squeezed on the hose, sending a jet of water towards the stains on the floor from whatever had been in the van, before flicking it upwards, laughing with him, sending an arc of water towards him. John threw some more water at her, dunking his cloth and splashing her, her pink skin visible through the wet cloth.

Gemma jumped down from the van and put her hand on her hips, as she mocked up a stern look. John flicked some more water towards her, making her shriek out, laughing.

She must have heard the voices first, because her laughter disappeared, and as she turned around, John followed her gaze, and then he heard them too, excited laughter and shouts. There were other people in the house. They must have arrived when they were at the shop.

There were people coming out of the house, shaking hands with Arni and walking towards two old cars parked further along the farm track. John hadn't noticed them before. John counted nine of them, and they looked like the type of people in the photographs that adorned the walls. Mohican haircuts, long scruffy jumpers, hobnailed boots. White boys in dread-locks and small wispy beards.

'What's going on?' John said.

'Probably a planning meeting,' Gemma said.

'What for?'

Gemma looked at him and blushed. She glanced over at Arni and then shook her head. 'I can't tell you.'

'Why not?'

'Because not everyone knows,' she said, and then smiled. 'It's going to be a big surprise when it happens though.'

John looked back towards the group. As they got nearer to their cars, Arni turned towards him.

John waved. Arni stared back, and even though he was a distance away, the coldness of his eyes made John lower his hand and turn away.

Chapter Fourteen

Sheldon cricked his neck as he got closer to the Incident Room. He had left Christina, Billy's housekeeper, with Tracey. A woman-to-woman talk might elicit more information.

He had spoken to Jim Kelly to try and get him to delay the story, but Kelly hadn't been interested. He had a failing paper to keep in business, and so the sensitivities around Billy Privett's death didn't matter to him.

Billy Privett's story was inextricably mixed up with Alice Kenyon's, and her murder hung around the local police like a stain on the uniform. Now that Billy was dead, all the mystery surrounding Alice Kenyon's murder would burst to the fore again, and with Jim Kelly ready to write his story for the paper, he expected it to be on the front page.

For Sheldon, though, it had never gone away.

He saw Alice's dead body when he least expected it, during his quieter moments and when he thought he was a long way from his job. Reading the newspaper, sitting in the park. And it wasn't just Alice. He remembered all of them. Young women murdered by random strangers. Men punched and stamped to death outside nightclubs, just because they looked at someone the wrong way. Victims of domestic abuse who endured years of beatings until finally he went too far, and all those lost chances to get away came to nothing. Or old men battered in their homes for the contents of their dead wives' jewellery boxes. Lives ended by violence, all leaving extra victims. The grieving mothers, and husbands and wives, or children who grow up never knowing their mother or father. The injustices stayed with Sheldon, and his memories seemed like a film on fast forward, speeding glimpses of limp flesh or blood-soaked clothing, except that with every year, with every new case, the film just got faster, so that he couldn't make out the faces anymore. It was just a stream of images, like a flicker book. Pink. Brown. Fat. Thin. But at the end of all of it was Alice Kenyon.

He looked up and realised that he had stopped walking. He was standing in the corridor, his fists clenched so hard that his fingernails dug into his palms, making small crescent cuts in the skin.

He scrambled in his pocket for his pills, his blue saviours. He popped one into his mouth and swallowed. It seemed to catch in his throat, but he kept on gulping to force it down. Tugging at his cuffs, he told himself that he was ready to do this, and then walked into the Incident Room.

People watched him as he went in. The corpse had been confirmed as Billy Privett by fingerprints, and the mood seemed different to earlier in the day, as if everyone had felt the spotlight turn on them, making them more earnest.

Duncan Lowther was at the other end of the room.

'CCTV?' Sheldon shouted.

Lowther looked up and then pointed towards his computer monitor. 'I'm going through the footage now. I've got it on here, if you want to see it.'

Sheldon nodded that he did and went to stand behind Lowther's shoulder, other detectives crowding round.

'The hotel only records the lobby,' Lowther said. 'It gets used a lot for conferences, and not many people will want to stay in a hotel that might film them room hopping.' He moved the footage back quickly, so that the woman behind the reception desk seemed to vibrate. 'This is Billy checking in,' and he let it play at normal speed.

Sheldon watched as Billy moved into shot. He looked like he was trying to hide his appearance. He was wearing a baseball cap low onto his brow and sunglasses, so that he just drew attention to himself in the opulent surroundings of the lobby.

'Why were you there, Billy?' Sheldon said to the screen.

'It's more about why he was keeping it such a secret,' Lowther said.

'What about later on, nearer the time when he was murdered? Is there anyone unusual coming into the hotel?'

'I haven't gone through all of it. I've got a list of every guest and their checking-in time, and so I'm looking at that to get a description. Every time someone appears on the screen, I work out who it is, and note down what they are doing. By the time I've finished, I should have accounted for every guest and worked out if there is anyone in the hotel who isn't a paying guest.'

'And once you've done that?'

'I check out each one, and look for someone giving false details.' Lowther smiled. 'That's the fun part, because I can bet that we'll drag at least a couple of people in who gave false addresses to keep their stay secret. You can't beat the twitch of a cheating spouse to brighten your afternoon.' When Sheldon scowled a rebuke, Lowther added, 'We've been getting plenty of calls from the press.'

'Speak to the Press Officer and make it official then,' Sheldon said. 'Have we had any fresh information about Billy since the news broke?'

'Just a few calls about his lifestyle, but nothing we

didn't know. We've had a few putting Ted Kenyon's name forward.'

'That's where I'm going next,' Sheldon said.

'You've got to go somewhere else first,' Lowther said. When Sheldon raised his eyebrows, he added, 'The Chief has been looking for you.'

'What, Dixon? How long ago?'

'A few minutes. She said to go down when you were free.'

Sheldon let out a breath and stepped out of the Incident Room. He looked along the corridor, towards the Chief Inspector's office. It was darker down there, furthest from the entrance. He took a deep breath and set off walking. He guessed what this was about, but that just made the walk seem longer. As he got to the door, a nameplate facing him, he knocked lightly. He waited until he heard 'yes', and then he walked in.

The atmosphere changed immediately, from the hubbub of the station to the refined calm of a gentlemen's club, except that the room's occupant was a woman. He had last seen her in the corridor before, when he had brought Christina in. Her head was down, looking at some papers, her hair cut short and streaked by grey. There were paintings of hills on the walls and a wine-coloured leather chair dominated one corner, high-backed, as if it was just short of a cigar and whisky glass. Framed family pictures were on a cabinet, although Sheldon kept his focus on her as he stood in front of the desk, his hands clasped in front of him, and waited for Dixon to notice he was there.

When she did look up, Sheldon said, 'You wanted to see me, ma'am.'

Chief Inspector Dixon pointed to the chair in front of the desk. 'Sit down, Sheldon, please.' Her voice sounded tired, and as he got a better look at her, he saw dark rings under her eyes and broken veins just starting to flush across her cheeks.

Sheldon did as he was asked, his legs tightly together, his hands on his knees.

Dixon leaned forward, her arms folded on the desk, and stared at Sheldon. 'We know now that the body found last night is Billy Privett.'

Sheldon didn't respond, except for a small stretch of his neck, his collar too tight.

'How do you feel about that?' Dixon said.

Sheldon gave a small cough before he spoke. 'I don't know, ma'am, if I'm honest. I feel for Alice's family, because the secret of her murder may go to the grave with Billy Privett, but at the same time I feel like there is something fateful about it – that if it had to be anyone, I'm glad it was him.'

The Chief nodded and then twirled a pen slowly in her hand. 'I want you to handle the investigation, Sheldon. I know that FMIT want it, but I'm fighting for you to keep it. The answers will come from local people, and you were very close to Alice's case. You know all about Billy Privett.'

Sheldon licked his lips. He tasted sweat. 'That's why I should have it. I know about Billy, and the victim is where murder cases should start.'

'But you need to be careful, Sheldon.'

A pause, and then, 'What do you mean?' His fingers gripped his knees tighter.

Dixon stared at Sheldon. 'I'm taking a risk for you, and giving you the opportunity to redeem yourself, and to prove that this station is worth keeping open. You're a good officer, I know that, but I don't want a repeat of what happened when Billy Privett was a suspect.'

'I don't understand.'

Dixon put her pen down and put her hands together. 'You

do understand, and don't make me force you from the team. Alice's case made you ill, you know that. It was taken from you because you didn't get anywhere. And I know what has been going on, with you and Billy Privett.'

Sheldon looked down. He rubbed his left hand with the fingers of his right.

'Billy complained, Sheldon.'

Sheldon looked up. 'About what?'

'About you. You were harassing him, watching him all the time, parking on his street, following him when he went out.'

'I didn't do anything wrong, ma'am.'

'Don't take me for a fool. I know that you were doing this on your days off, just sitting in your car, watching Billy's house. The case had stopped being yours by then.'

Sheldon brushed some lint from his knee. The room had got warmer. 'I was just trying to find answers,' he said eventually.

'And did you?'

He shook his head. 'No, I didn't.'

The Chief smiled, although it looked forced. 'So show everyone that I'm right. I'm fighting for you, but I'll be watching. If I see that you are going the same way, I'll stop everything. Keep me up to date.'

'I thought FMIT were coming over today, ma'am.'

'I've stalled them,' she said. 'So can you do it?'

Sheldon took a deep breath. 'I can.'

Dixon nodded her approval. 'Don't forget to keep me updated,' she said, and then pointed towards the door. The meeting was over.

Sheldon didn't say anything as he left, and once he got outside, he leant back against the wall and closed his eyes.

He stayed like that for a few seconds, listening to the

chatter filtering down from the Incident Room, and then pushed away from the wall. He ran his fingers around his collar. It felt damp from perspiration.

It was time to take control.

Chapter Fifteen

Charlie looked out of his window. The kids in black had gone, as had Ted and the press. He had watched as Amelia gave her quote, and since then, the street had returned to normal.

Donia was in the corner of the room, reading files, just to get a taste of what being a criminal lawyer was all about. It's the files that earn the money, not what happens in court. That's just a sideshow. Playing out, Charlie called it, when he got to have some fun. The real work was done in the office, clocking up billable hours reading police statements.

Charlie turned round quickly and caught Donia looking at him. Her eyes darted back to her file, and he saw a flush jump into her cheeks. He was going to say something, but she was only going to be with him for a week. There was no point in making friends.

He left his office and went towards Amelia's, leaning against the doorframe once he got there. Amelia was looking at her desk, a dictation machine in her hand, but she wasn't saying anything into it.

It was a few seconds before she noticed him.

When she looked up, he said, 'What's going on?'

She shook her head. 'Nothing,' she said, but it came out too quickly.

'Come on, Amelia. You're staring into space. Our office was burgled, and it was your room they went through, not mine. And your two goons in suits were hanging around outside.'

'Goons?'

'Those clients of yours. They were coming out as I came in, except they didn't seem keen on moving on.'

Amelia leaned back in her chair and sighed. She looked tired. Charlie detected some vulnerability he didn't normally see. 'I've told you, it's nothing.'

He stared at her, and she held his stare. He was aware of Linda, the receptionist and secretary, becoming suddenly interested in her computer screen, and so he stepped into the room and closed the door.

'It's my business too,' Charlie said. 'We're partners, remember, and I don't normally see you like this.'

'I didn't know you did caring.'

'And I didn't know you did vulnerable, so come on, Amelia, what's going on? Are there bills we haven't paid or something?'

That made Amelia smile. She considered Charlie for a few seconds, and then shook her head. 'It's nothing to worry about, like I've said.'

Charlie wasn't convinced, but if Amelia didn't want to tell, he knew that was the end of the discussion.

'If we have a problem, I need to know,' he said. 'Promise me you'll tell me.'

She nodded, and then said, 'What are you doing for the rest of the day?'

'I've got a couple of trials to prepare for, and I need to brief counsel on something, but then I'm going for a drink.'

'On a Monday?'

'Monday in a pub is better than a Monday sitting at home.'

Amelia smiled with more warmth this time, and he returned it. 'I mean it,' he said. 'I can't help you with any personal stuff, but if it's about work, share it.'

Charlie went back into the reception area, and saw Donia duck back into his room, as if she had been eavesdropping in the doorway. He looked at Linda, who just shrugged.

Something about Donia wasn't right.

Sheldon drove quickly to Ted Kenyon's house, accompanied by Tracey. Christina had given a statement and made her own way home.

'How are we going to play this?' Tracey said.

Sheldon thought about that for a moment. He had a history with Ted, because Ted blamed his team, including Sheldon himself, for his daughter's killer still being free. Ted had been angry with Billy Privett at first, but as Billy kept his secrets, Ted had turned on the police. Had it gone full circle and Ted taken the ultimate revenge?

'We have to treat him as a suspect,' he said.

'Are we bringing him in?'

'No, not yet, unless we find something.'

Sheldon's mood darkened during the trip along the edges of Oulton until he turned into a street lined by hedgerows, with large detached stone houses set high from the road, sitting at the top of terraced lawns, the borders awash with colour. It was pretty, a bit of old Lancashire charm, and it was those qualities that had propelled Alice's story into the public consciousness. Ted had grafted for what he had, to give his daughter the best chances in life – until her life had been taken away by someone who most people thought didn't deserve his wealth.

Sheldon thought back to the drive he had made a year

earlier, to tell the Kenyon family that Alice had drowned in Billy's pool.

Ted Kenyon's house was in the middle of the row, with a dark wooden bay window and a hanging basket filled with bright purple flowers next to double wooden doors. Clematis clung to a wall trellis like large tissues that fluttered in the light breeze. There was a small knot of photographers outside.

'Should we carry on?' Tracey said. 'It might look bad with the cameras there.'

Sheldon shook his head. 'Just be casual and make it look like a courtesy visit.'

He parked further along the street, just so that the reporters wouldn't crowd round. As he climbed out of the car, he checked his pocket for the rattle of the blue pills, before marching up the sloped drive, towards the front door. Sheldon rapped on the door and waited, Tracey catching up with him.

'They're just killing time before the press conference,' Sheldon said, staring at the door, ignoring the clicks from the camera lenses.

When the door opened, it was Emily, Alice's mother. She had been less vocal than Ted, had dealt with her grief more privately, but from the shock of grey hair that had appeared since her daughter's death, Sheldon knew that the sorrow was just as deep.

Emily's polite smile faded. 'I thought it was another reporter,' she said, and folded her arms.

'Mrs Kenyon,' he said. 'Can we have a word?'

'We know about Billy Privett,' she said, her voice quiet.

'And that's what we need to talk about.'

Emily frowned and stepped aside. 'All right, come in.'

Sheldon went past her, wiping his feet as he went, Tracey

behind him. Alice's brother walked towards them along the hall. A young man, twenty years old, his hair dyed black, but the paleness of his skin told Sheldon that he had the same colouring as Alice. Bright red hair. He looked briefly at Sheldon before going upstairs.

Sheldon followed Emily into the front room. He knew he had interrupted something. There were two cups on a table, both half full, with wisps of steam coming from them. No television, no radio, no newspapers or books left open. Ted and Emily must have been talking.

He hadn't seen Ted for a few months and Sheldon was surprised to see how he looked. Ted had gone quiet once the press caught him with that young woman, and it looked like the bad publicity had taken its toll. His skin looked more drawn, some of the colour gone, as if he didn't get as much fresh air. He didn't acknowledge Sheldon at first, just stared straight ahead, but when he looked up, he gestured towards the chair. 'Sit down,' he said, his voice terse.

Sheldon did as he was told, the leather on the large green sofa creaking as he sat down. Tracey sat further along.

Ted considered them for a moment and then said, 'You're going to want to know where I was last night.'

Sheldon was about to say no, that they had come just to give him the news about Billy, but he could tell from the rise of Ted's eyebrow that he didn't expect to be taken for a fool. He was a suspect and he knew it.

Sheldon nodded. 'Yes, I would like to know.'

'I was here,' Ted said, and then pointed to the doorway. 'Emily will confirm it, and so will Jake.'

'You don't know what time I'm talking about.'

'It doesn't matter what time,' he said. 'I was here. If it was early, I was watching television. If it was after midnight, I was in bed.'

'What did you watch?'

'Just the usual rubbish. There was a police thriller on. You know the type, where plenty of people die before the killer is caught.'

Sheldon swallowed at the dig. 'Can anyone else verify that you were here last night?'

Ted smiled, but there was no warmth to it. 'What, other than my family? Isn't their word good enough?' When Sheldon didn't respond, Ted waved his hand towards the rest of the house. 'Have a look round. See if you can find anything suspicious.'

Sheldon looked at Tracey, who nodded that they should, because they might not get the invite again.

They went to the kitchen first. Tracey went to the washing machine to look for bloodied clothes, but it was empty. Emily was right behind her. 'Have you got a dryer?' Tracey said.

Emily pointed to a door. 'In the garage.'

'What were you watching?' Sheldon said.

Emily looked confused.

'On the television,' he said. 'I can check the listings, to see if there were any police shows on last night. Can you remember the name?'

Emily folded her arms. 'Like Ted said, a police drama. I forget what it was called.'

Sheldon nodded an acknowledgement that he wasn't going to get any more information, and then he went into the garden as Tracey went to the garage.

The lawn was long and neat, with plenty of colour, as if it was tended regularly. He was looking for evidence of recent bonfires or digging, but couldn't see anything. He walked over to the dustbins and lifted the lids, but there was nothing suspicious.

As he walked back to the house, Tracey joined Sheldon

as she came in from the garage. She shook her head. Nothing.

They went back into the house, Emily leaning against the kitchen worktop, glowering as they came in. Sheldon ignored her and went towards the stairs. They were lined by pictures of Alice, so that going to bed must be like walking through a memorial; Alice as a young girl, pigtails and thick glasses, and then as a teenager coming to bloom, her school skirt too short, her jumper too long. There were no pictures of Jake, Alice's brother.

There were three bedrooms upstairs. The door to one of the bedrooms was open and so they went there first. The double bed confirmed that it was Ted and Emily's bedroom. There were more pictures of Alice in there, on the wall and in small frames on the shelves. Sheldon opened a wardrobe and had a look around, but there wasn't anything suspicious. He was looking for wet shoes, or anything with blood on them. Perhaps some clothes or shoes in a bag, waiting for disposal. Nothing.

They backed out and went to the door next to the bedroom. There was a low voice coming from the other side, and so Sheldon knocked and then opened it slowly. It was Jake, in front of a computer screen, with a microphone and headset wrapped around his head, playing some kind of online game. He looked round but then went back to his game.

'Do you mind if we look?' Sheldon said.

Jake shrugged.

His bedroom was small, with just enough space for his single bed and a desk, with a small wardrobe next to it. Tracey got down to the floor to check under the bed and Sheldon looked in the wardrobe.

When Sheldon thanked Jake, he got no response, although he heard Jake's voice start up again as soon as the door closed. He nodded towards the remaining bedroom door. 'That will be Alice's room.'

Tracey looked at the door and then back to Sheldon. 'You seem reluctant, sir.'

Sheldon looked back to Jake's room. 'Did you notice how he is still crammed into the smallest bedroom, and how the house is all about Alice?' he said. 'Their lives are all about Alice. Her room will be like a shrine.'

'It might hold a vital clue.'

Sheldon shook his head. 'I don't think they would soil it like that, and I don't want to intrude any more than we have to for the time being.'

Tracey thought for a moment and then said, 'We won't find anything anyway, and that's why they're letting us search, because they know that.'

'Perhaps because they're innocent.'

'Do you think they are?'

Sheldon thought about that, and then said, 'I'm not sure. Removing Billy's face was vicious, and I think Ted would just kill him and dump him. That hotel scene was meant to attract attention, and Ted wouldn't want that.'

'Double bluff?' Tracey said.

Sheldon allowed himself a smile. 'We could go on counting bluffs all day, but we've found nothing, and I don't think we should bring him in. Not yet, anyway.'

They went downstairs and back into the living room. Sheldon was about to say thank you and goodbye when he noticed that Ted was gripping the chair arms, his knuckles white, his eyes glazed with rage.

'What's wrong?'

Ted looked up and pointed at the television. 'Even in death it never ends.' When Sheldon looked confused, Ted pressed the rewind button on the remote and watched as the footage moved backwards. When he pressed the play button, a face that Sheldon recognised came onto the screen. Amelia Diaz, Billy's lawyer. It looked like she had spoken to the press outside her office.

'A lot of people held a lot of opinions about Billy Privett,' Amelia said, 'and they were mostly to do with Alice Kenyon, a poor young woman who died in tragic circumstances. Before the press decide that they can print what they like, I just want everybody to remember one thing about Billy Privett; that nothing was ever proven against him. He was an innocent man in life, and he is still an innocent man in death. Thank you.'

And then she gave a brief smile and turned to walk into her office.

Ted clicked off the television. 'Now do you see why it couldn't be me?' he said, a tear now running down his cheek. 'I wanted to change things about Billy Privett. Now it will always stay the same.'

Sheldon wanted to say how he prayed that it wouldn't be Ted who had done it, that he had suffered enough. But he didn't. Instead, he nodded that he understood and thanked him for his patience. He placed a business card next to Ted's hand and then turned to leave. As he closed the front door behind him, he saw Emily in the kitchen at the end of the hall. She was staring at him, her arms folded. She was still staring as the door clicked shut.

Chapter Sixteen

John was outside the farmhouse, at the old man's window, nailing a wire grille to the frame, as Arni ordered. The breeze ruffled the leaves on the trees opposite and brought a glow to his cheeks. Dawn appeared in the doorway next to him, her arms folded across her chest.

She stayed silent for a few moments, before saying, 'That won't stop them.'

'What, the grilles?'

'They should be on the inside of the window, because if someone does come, they'll just rip them off.'

'Who are *they*?'

Dawn shrugged. 'Whoever Arni is trying to protect us from.'

'But who do you think they are? And why now?'

'Things have changed,' Dawn said, and then she shook her head. 'We weren't about all this at first.'

John was wary. This could be a test. Henry had once said that he should trust no one.

'Isn't it more important to be about where we are now, rather than where we once were?' he said.

'Don't give me that,' she said, her eyes narrowing. 'You don't believe in what's going on here. Not truly, deep down, in here,' and she banged her chest with her hand.

'What do you mean?'

'You watch them too much, as if you are working out the right thing to say, not what you truly believe. What is it, just some fun?'

He shook his head. 'You're wrong. I believe in Henry's message. And what do you mean by *them*? Don't you mean *us*?'

Dawn looked at John, her lips pursed, wariness in her eyes. 'I don't mean anything.' She pointed towards the window that now had a metal grille hammered into its frame. 'The old man. Is he awake?'

John put his face against the grille and saw the old man turn his head towards him. His breaths looked shallow, and there was pleading in his eyes. He had no hair, apart from the wisps around his ears. His scalp seemed almost translucent, the veins visible through the tired pallor of his skin, his cheekbones just sharp edges.

John nodded. 'How long has he been like this?'

'He was always frail, that's why he let us stay here, so that we could help him with the farm, and shop for him. He told us he had no family. We're not helping him anymore though.'

'How many were there of you, when you first came here?'

'About ten of us, plus Henry.' Tears popped into her eyes. 'Some have left, some more have come. When we came here, it was an escape, that's all.'

'From what?'

'From what we were doing. We were travelling round, going to all the demos. It was fun, but sometimes you've got to get away and have some downtime.'

'What got you into all of the political stuff?'

She shrugged. 'It was the togetherness, I suppose, the people you meet. A lot of us didn't have that when we grew up.'

'What about you?'

'I grew up in care. The first lot of us did.'

'How was that?' He banged another nail into the window frame and then bent it around the grille.

'Just typical, I suppose. You get warned about stuff, or hear about them, and you think it will be different for you, but it isn't. It's just the same. We'd hang around, and the men would come cruising. They were always too old for us, but it didn't matter, because they could get us drink and fags, and we could ride around in cars with loud music and spoilers and stuff. It seemed like fun, but then you realise it's a trap, that no one cares for you.'

'Where were your parents?

'Not with me,' Dawn said, her sadness showing in her voice. 'I went into care and they never tried to get me back. The care workers did their best, but they couldn't give us the love we needed, the affection. But when you're young, you confuse affection with sex, and so if you're getting fucked, you're getting love, except that you're not. You're being used. So one day, six of us left and never went back. We went to the festivals, and then the camps, you know, the protest ones, climate change and ones like that. The people were nice. No one used us, because they wanted to teach us stuff, and we listened.'

'When was this?'

'Three years ago.'

'Are you all from care, the ones who came here?'

'The newer ones are different. Posh kids, just looking for an adventure. Take your Gemma. She's from a good home, but she wanted to break away. We all have different reasons. I was living in a hostel when I first met Henry. A lot of the girls were talking about him. He was older but different to the others, because he seemed more determined. He had things to tell us, his take on the world. Then he started to talk about getting away from the city, starting on our own, like a commune, where we made our own rules.'

'And so you ended up here?'

'Only by a fluke. We were between squats and we came to a party in the field next door. It was just a bonfire and people sleeping out, but in the morning the old man let us use his toilet and bath, and so we cleaned up for him, and then we ended up staying. And then Henry attracted more people, because, well, people follow Henry.' Dawn smiled, although John detected regret in it. 'It was great at first. We had a base. We could go to the camps but we had somewhere to come back to. The student demos were the best, because the nice kids would join in too. That's when we hit on the masks.'

'The masks in the pictures?' John said. 'I saw them in the house, but I didn't know you'd started that. I used to see them on the news. They're creepy. All white and expressionless.'

'Shop dummies,' she said. 'It was symbolic, you know, because that's what we had become, faceless. And it made it harder for the police to identify us, which was the real reason. When other people see you like that, they see you as a group who are getting their stuff together, and so they want to join, and people followed us on the marches, rather than us following them.'

'I saw the masks on the news during the riots last year.'

'The riots were just the best times, but then they became sort of the worst times.'

'Why the worst?'

Dawn's jaw clenched. 'Because that's when Henry changed. And *we* changed, as a group.' She looked at the Seven Sisters and took a deep breath.

John followed her gaze. 'I like them,' he said.

'What?'

'The stones. They're atmospheric, sort of mystical.'

Dawn closed her eyes for a moment. When she opened them, she said, 'They are not what they seem.'

'What do you mean?' John said, as he turned to hammer another nail into the frame.

'You don't really know what they stand for,' she said. 'If you did, you wouldn't think that.'

'Tell me then.'

Dawn looked towards the Seven Sisters again and tears came into her eyes. She looked like she was about to say something, but then there was some quick movement, and Dawn yelped as Arni's cane was thrust through the open doorway, the metal handle under her chin. She turned round slowly, John following her gaze.

Arni was standing in the hallway, his arm outstretched. John hadn't heard him. Arni was glowering, his anger giving him a flush to his cheeks and a quiver to his arm.

Dawn's breaths started to get ragged, eyes flicking between John and Arni.

The cane stayed there for a few more seconds before Arni lowered it, still staring at Dawn.

'We were just talking,' she said.

Arni ground his teeth and then said, 'Be careful what you say. You are either with the group or you are not.'

'I am with the group,' Dawn said quickly, nodding apologetically.

Arni stared at her, making Dawn more agitated, until they were distracted by soft footsteps on the stairs as Gemma came into view. John felt a small burst of pleasure. He smiled, he couldn't stop himself, but before he could say anything, Gemma looked past him, her eyes widened.

'Someone's here,' she said. 'It's Henry.'

John followed her gaze towards the woods on the other side of the field. There was movement in the trees from a band of people dressed in black, Henry at the rear of the group.

Gemma waved at them, and someone waved back. She turned to Dawn. 'Henry's back.'

Dawn didn't respond at first, as if she was weighing up the right thing to say, but then she flickered a smile. 'That's good.'

Gemma held her gaze for a moment, and then went towards the door.

John watched as the group walked across the field, Henry encircled, and then as he looked, he saw someone new, a woman he hadn't seen before. She was tall and attractive, her clothing more provocative than the others, in tight blue shorts and a cropped vest top, making her breasts bulge out.

'It's Lucy,' Gemma cried, and she darted past John, running barefoot across the grass. When she got to the group she threw her arms around the newcomer, and the laughs of the crowd drifted across the field. Arni scowled and went back inside.

John watched as Henry got nearer, and when Gemma got back to the house, she skipped excitedly, clapping her hands.

'What's the excitement?' John said.

'Lucy's home,' Gemma said, and giggled.

John was surprised. He'd never heard of Lucy, but from the way the others spoke to her, it seemed like everyone knew her.

Before John could ask anything else, Henry came towards him, looking wound up and edgy.

'What's on your mind, John?' he said.

'Sorry, I was just wondering who she was.'

'Interested in her?' he said, and looked round at Lucy. 'She's very pretty.'

'No, not like that,' John said quickly, catching Gemma's glare. 'I'm just curious, that's all.'

Henry cocked his head, his dark twists of hair flopping with him. 'It's not just about what we do on the demos, or even from here. There are people out there, doing vital work. Lucy is one of them.'

'And she's back now?'

'Yes, she's back, because the time is getting nearer for positive action.'

'How do you know?'

Henry's eyes showed his excitement. 'I just sense it. Don't you?' He banged his chest with his hand and grinned, his teeth bright white, matching the gleam of his eyes. 'If you have belief, you know it. Do you have belief, John?'

'I believe in you, Henry.'

'That's all you need,' Henry said, and grinned again.

'So what do we do?'

Henry looked back across the fields, towards Oulton. 'You stay here, John, because I trust you to keep watch. When they come for us, fight them. We have a message, and they will try to stop it being heard. We have to be ready.'

John smiled. 'Whatever is coming, Henry, I'm with you.'

Chapter Seventeen

Charlie tried to focus but the movement behind the bar seemed blurred, patches of light shimmering in front of him. He lifted his nearly empty glass, drained it and went to put the glass on the table, but misjudged it, so that the glass made a bang. The landlord looked over.

He was in The Old Star, a low-ceilinged pub of small side rooms that had avoided the open plan craze of the eighties. The lighting was subdued and the place kept warm by log fires. It was too easy to fall asleep there after a long day at the office.

He put his head back, closed his eyes and the sounds of the bar went distant. The smell of stale beer filtered into his nose, what used to be hidden by cigarette smoke before the smoking ban. He almost laughed. He knew this was too much for a Monday night, but it didn't feel like the evening would get better if he went home. Then he realised that he was laughing, just a chuckle, but he was on his own, his eyes closed.

Charlie stopped himself as he thought of the message he'd had from Julie that morning, complaining about his Saturday night call. He felt for the phone in his pocket. Perhaps he ought to give her a ring, just to say sorry. But something stopped him; a last shred of common sense still making itself heard above the jangle of drunken musings.

He picked up his glass again. There was solace in there.

There was a noise in front of him. He knew who it would be: the landlord telling him that he'd had enough. He wasn't interested in hearing that, and so he kept his eyes closed. Then he heard someone say, 'Mr Barker?'

That ruled out the landlord or any of his clients. He was Charlie to everyone.

Charlie opened his eyes slowly and then waited for them to adjust, as the bar seemed to focus in and out and swirl in front of him. Then he saw that the person who was in front of him was Ted Kenyon.

Charlie closed his eyes again. He didn't want an argument. He had left his job behind when he locked the door to the office.

'Mr Barker, please wake up.'

He sighed. There was no escaping it. He sat up and moved around the side of the table. 'I wasn't asleep, I was resting my eyes,' he said, his head bobbing as he spoke. When Ted didn't respond, he added, 'I'll need a drink for this. Can I get you one?'

Ted looked uncertain at first, and then he nodded. 'I'll join you.'

Charlie went to the bar. The barman gave him a look as if he was about to refuse service, but then he glanced over at Ted and poured Charlie the same again, along with a pint for Ted.

When Charlie sat down, slumping back into his seat, Ted said, 'Don't you think you ought to slow down?'

Charlie lifted the pint to his lips, let some of the beer swim into his mouth, and then put his glass down. 'Yes, I do, but I'm not making plans for it yet,' he said, his voice coming out with more of a slur than he expected. He smiled. 'I'm guessing this is no coincidence. Twice in one day. How has it been for you?'

'Mixed.' When Charlie frowned, Ted added, 'The man I blamed for Alice's killer still being free is dead, and so I should be happy, even though that is a bad thing to say, but I'm not.'

'Perhaps because you're a good man.'

'That's not what people think anymore.'

'What, the girl in the car?'

Ted closed his eyes for a moment. 'That was a set-up. I wasn't doing anything.'

Charlie shrugged. He had stopped being a judge of human behaviour a long time ago. He helped to clean up the mess, not wonder how it happened.

Ted didn't say anything for a few seconds, and Charlie thought he was going to leave, but he didn't. Charlie gave it a few more seconds before he said, 'You haven't come here to watch me drink. So what can I do for you?'

'I want you to tell me about Billy Privett.'

'I can't do that. It's confidential.'

'But Billy is dead now.'

Charlie sighed. 'I'm sorry, but the Law Society won't see it like that.'

Ted looked down at that, and suddenly Charlie felt shitty. He leant forward.

'Look, I'm sorry. I didn't mean to be so blunt, but what did you expect me to say?'

'You know things about how my daughter died,' Ted said quietly, still looking at the floor. 'When Billy was alive, I didn't have to think about you, but now he is, well, you are all I have left.' He looked up. 'I know things that I've been told, but not the full story, and that's what I need to know.

I won't tell anyone.' Then he shook his head, answering his own query. 'This was a stupid idea. I'll go,' and he stood as if to leave.

Charlie shook his head. 'Sit down. Finish your drink.'

Ted looked at him unsure, and so Charlie said, 'I don't know anything about Alice's death. Amelia looked after Billy Privett in relation to Alice's case. She knew it would get media attention and we decided that she would be better for the interviews.'

Ted looked dejected, and for a moment, despite the boozy fog, Charlie saw his turmoil, that he just wanted answers.

'I can tell you one thing, if it makes you feel any better,' Charlie said.

Ted looked at him, expectant.

'I have never heard anything from Amelia that suggested that Billy killed your daughter. I don't know what part he did play, but if he murdered your daughter, he didn't blurt it out to Amelia.'

Ted considered that for a moment, and then said, 'Do people ever lie to their lawyers?'

Charlie smiled ruefully and took a drink. When he put his glass down, he replied, 'All the time, Mr Kenyon. All the fucking time.'

Ted sighed and got to his feet. Charlie could tell that he wasn't going to hang around anymore.

'Thank you for your time, Mr Barker.'

'It's Charlie,' he said.

Ted nodded at that but didn't answer, and then turned to go.

Once Charlie was alone again, he looked at the full glass Ted had left behind and then wondered about what thoughts he was taking home with him. He could only guess at the injustice he must feel every time he woke up. Then Charlie thought of how he must have looked to Ted, drunk on a Monday night. Charlie felt the creep of self-pity, knowing that he was just avoiding an empty house.

He pulled his phone out of his pocket. He thought again about calling Julie, but stopped himself. He put his phone away and tried not to think about her. Instead, he picked up his glass.

He would have just one more and then go home.

Chapter Eighteen

The night crept into early morning as John did what Henry had asked him: be a lookout. He had spent the evening sitting in a plastic chair with one of the old man's shotguns in his lap. He had watched the night turn dark, the spread of stars take over the valley sky and the hill opposite turn into silhouette, just the occasional bleat of a sheep or the sweeping beam of a car interrupting the solitude.

Henry had left the house again, along with Arni, Gemma and the new woman, Lucy, all out for some fun. The ones who were left behind had been drinking home brew, some mixture Arni made from potato peelings that burned John's throat, along with whatever the group had managed to steal on outings. People were sprawled on the floor, on cushions, glasses next to them, smoke drifting from ashtrays.

There was the sound of an engine. John got to his feet, his hand gripped around the shotgun. Was this what Henry had talked about, people coming for them? Then he relaxed as the engine noise got closer and he recognised the rattle of the Transit van. As he watched it approach, the headlights were off, and there was laughter coming from an open window.

Dawn appeared behind him and handed John a spliff. He took a long pull, grinned as that leaden feeling crept through his body. As the van rumbled to a halt, everyone jumped out, Henry from the passenger seat, Gemma and Lucy from the back. Lucy was carrying the face masks. Five of them, one for each of them and a spare.

Henry walked quickly, and he looked restless, excitable, wide eyed.

'How was it?' John said.

Henry didn't speak at first. He just walked quickly to the living room, accompanied by the crackle of logs and the smoke that drifted in the light from candles flickering in each corner. John followed, and everyone sat upright when they saw Henry, who paced up and down and rubbed his hands, his gaze filled with concentration.

'Henry?' John said, smiling now at Henry's excitement.

'It was exhilarating,' Henry said, grinning. 'But we need to be careful. We have just brought everything closer. There's not much left of tonight, and so we need to party.'

Whispers went round the room.

'So where did you go?' John asked. 'Why have you brought everything closer?'

Henry shook his head. 'When the truth needs to be told, it will be told. Have faith in me, that's all you need right now.' He hopped onto a stool at one end of the room and snapped his fingers. John went over to pass him the spliff. As he got close, Henry moved quickly. His hands clasped the back of John's neck and pulled him in, so John could smell the staleness of his breath. 'No more questions, John. There are too many.'

John nodded, wincing at the grip. 'I just want to know things, that's all. For me, it's all new. I'm not questioning you, Henry. I feel something here, like a bond, a brotherhood, but I don't know everything about us. I want to know everything.'

Henry sucked hard on the spliff in his hand, so that John's eyes stung from the smoke and the tip glowed hot close to his skin. Gemma appeared alongside him, and so Henry passed the spliff to her.

'What do you think we are about?' Henry said. Smoke seeped through his grin and his hand relaxed on John's neck.

John stepped back. Henry's words seemed slow to him, as if he couldn't process them quickly enough, and the people in front of him seemed to sway. He looked down for a moment. His head felt heavy. 'We are what you said – that we are a freedom movement, where there will be new rules, and the rule will be that there are no rules. And I believe that Henry, I really do, but I need more answers.'

John thought he saw Gemma tense, but when Henry grinned, she relaxed.

'You know why we came for you,' Henry said. 'Because you shared our ideals. I remember what you sprayed on the walls. That was a cry for help, and we heard you.'

'What made you first think like you do?' John said.

'Just a developing truth. It is something you feel, but then things happen that makes it clearer, that the little mutters you hear rise above the doubts and you begin to understand the message you've always heard. The world was changing, and when I wondered why, I realised that I had the answers all along, had always known them. I first knew it back on the eleventh September.'

'The Twin Towers?'

Henry nodded. 'What do you think happened?'

'Two planes flew into them. I saw it.'

'You saw what they wanted you to see,' Henry said, shaking his head. 'You saw the planes, but that's just deflection, because you saw just the obvious. Who was flying the planes?'

'Terrorists. Islamists.'

'Why? Because *they* told you? Corporation USA? And you accepted that?' Henry laughed. 'It's bullshit, man. Half the hijackers are still alive, working in other countries. One is a pilot in Saudi Arabia. And what evidence have they produced? A charred passport below the towers? What about the flames it went through, the crash? What did it do, just fall out of his pocket?' Henry gripped John's shoulder. 'It's crap, all of it. People made money on the stock exchange on those airlines just before the crash, betting that the stocks would go down. People knew, John.'

Henry let go and whirled around, animated now. 'Look at the Pentagon, just over the river from the centre of the Western world, but there are no cameras anywhere showing a fucking jet flying at ground level. And we're supposed to believe that someone could hit the Pentagon, which isn't a high building, after a few lessons in a tiny plane and playing computer games? Come on, John, that's precision flying. The hole in the Pentagon wasn't big enough for a plane. They were on long-distance flights and had just set off, but the rooms around the site don't show fire damage. They were filled with fuel, kerosene, which goes up like a fucking bomb, and what do you get, apart from a hole? Nothing, that's what. It was a missile, John, and it was the beginning of the end, and I saw that. Everything came together that day for me.'

'But I saw the planes, on television.'

'You saw planes, but you didn't see the passengers. If they can send a probe to a dot on Mars, they can fly planes into high buildings, by remote control. It was like the veil slipping away and I saw everything with such clarity.' He stroked his beard. 'Look at everything since. What did we do? We used it to invade other countries, to take over oilfields, and faith turns on faith, West against East. They told lies to spread their power, but people fought back. They thought it would be easy, but it wasn't, and now it is our turn to fight back, because all they fought for has crumbled. The banks, the money men. All busted.'

'So what can we do to fight it?'

Henry grinned. 'We move the battle on. Direct action.'

John smiled in return. 'I'm ready.'

'We must get this place ready. You started the work today in making it secure. Tomorrow, we need to make it so that we can defend it.' Henry shuffled in his seat, grabbing the spliff back from Gemma. 'Are you prepared to do more, to become fully involved, to be one of our soldiers?'

John nodded.

'That is good to hear. If you promise that, you'll get the answers. Just be patient. This is a process, and you have to prove yourself before you get all of them.'

'But how can I truly commit if I don't fully understand?'

Henry stared for a few seconds, and John was aware that the others around him had gone quiet. He licked his lips, but then Henry smiled.

'What do you think about our country now?' Henry said, his voice low, so that everyone leaned in to hear. 'I'll tell you; it's gone sour and forgotten how to look after its young people. You remember the riots last year. There's your answer. They have tried to pass it off as just kids pinching trainers, but it wasn't that. They are called feral and sent to prison just for getting the things that they need. They were so desperate that they scrambled through broken glass, just to get shoes for their feet. Look around the room.'

John did so.

'We were all there, John, in the middle in Manchester, and we felt the mood. People are angry, because all they see is greed. That's why we have rejected society. But the people in power are scared, because all movements start small, but some are unstoppable. People are joining together, and the authorities know that, and so they are watching, because they are scared of a repeat. It won't be the same this time though, because you can't repeat spontaneity, it doesn't work, and so they know this time it will be planned. They are looking at us now, I know that, but we are smarter than before.'

'So what do we do?'

'We bring everything forward and move now. They will try and crush us if we give them the chance, but they can't, because we have made promises to ourselves, and so all of this will be soon worthwhile. The sacrifices, the pledges.'

'I don't understand.'

'You are still tied to your old life. You can't just live here and pretend that is enough. You need to do more.'

'So what do I have to do?'

'Cast everything off that you once had,' Henry said.

John looked at the other women sat with Henry, and he saw that they were listening intently, their lips pressed together in tight smiles. Two of the women were holding hands.

Henry leaned forward, and his voice turned into a whisper.

'Just trust me, and follow me,' he said. 'Feel it, in here, like I do,' and he banged his chest with his hand.

'I do, Henry, I do. Tell me what to do.'

'First, you sever your ties, because if you leave the link to your old life, you are accepting their will. If you have family, you don't see them anymore. If you have money or property, you hand it over to us, for the good of this group, so that we can use it to do more.'

'I understand, Henry,' John said, nodding.

'Don't be afraid, John. Stare down your fear, look into its face, and you will no longer fear it. That is freedom.'

'What else?'

'Just do as I ask, because whatever I ask, it is for the good of the group and the cause.' Henry pointed around the room, towards Gemma and Lucy, who were huddled in a corner, talking earnestly. At the Elams, Jennifer rocking herself, her arms clasped around her knees, her eyes vacant, and Peter next to her, staring into his cup of home brew. 'I worry that someone in here will betray us, because some are not strong – but I trust you, John, I don't know why.' Then he waved it away. 'But tonight is for a party.'

John nodded, his head heavy again, and sat down on a cushion on the floor. He heard Henry click his fingers, and then Gemma appeared in front of him. She was holding the spliff, and she straddled John and took a long pull, tiny sparks flying in the air in front of her. Then she leaned forward so that her face was in front of his. He knew what to do. She started to blow smoke out slowly, and so he sucked it in hard, felt it burn the back of his throat. His world started to spin, and as he flopped back onto the cushions, he started to laugh, uninhibited, gleeful. He felt Gemma fall onto him, her lips on his cheeks, her hair over him, her fingers entangled in his. And the room started to fade as she drew him in, and he knew that he was home, his entire body consumed by happiness. She kissed him, and he responded, and it didn't matter that other people were there, because it felt right.

As his hands started to lift Gemma's dress, Henry let out a slow growl.

Chapter Nineteen

Charlie thought he heard a noise.

Like always, he thought it was in a dream. Movement around him, whispers, just shadows creeping around. He saw a man with a pale face and long dark hair. He was laughing.

Charlie's eyes flew open. Something wasn't right. His bed felt hard, and as he looked around he could see shadows. The black plastic wheel of a chair, the strong wooden leg of a desk. The curtains weren't closed. Then reality started to filter through. He had slept at the office. The curtains weren't closed because there weren't any. Just blinds.

He checked his watch, eight thirty, and groaned. He put his hand to his forehead. It wasn't the first time he had done this.

He moved to try and get up, but he had to pause as the room seemed to spin and lurch. His mouth was dry and his hair felt wild. He got to his feet gingerly and then tottered for a few seconds before pulling on the cord for the Venetian blinds. Charlie shielded his eyes as the sun streamed in. The sun rose behind the office, but it was bounced off the windows opposite, so that looking out was like staring at brickwork decorated by squares of sheet metal.

The noise he had heard was just the sound of the day

starting up. A takeaway wrapper tumbled down the road and there was the warning beep of a street cleaner, the brushes scraping on the pavement and leaving behind a damp trail.

He shut the blinds again. Daytime could wait. He looked down at the floor. His jacket was there, crumpled from where he had been sleeping on it. He knew he had a tough day ahead now.

Then he saw it.

There was a knife next to the jacket. It was steel-handled, like it was from a kitchen set. It was distinctive though, with a twist at the end of the handle. He bent down, curious, knowing that he had never seen it before. Then he noticed something else. A stain on the knife. He thought perhaps it was a trick of the light, and so he got closer, just to make sure. The blade was wide, like a carving knife, and it looked new and sharp, except that there were reddish-brown streaks all along it.

Charlie reached down to pick it up, curious. There were more of the stains on the handle, and it was sticky to the touch. Then he saw something on his hand, some red stains on his palm. As he looked at it, the room seemed to sway.

It was blood, he knew it straight away. He had seen enough crime scene exhibits to know what he was looking at.

He closed his eyes. Was he imagining it, some drunken remains of the night before? He expected to open his eyes and find an empty floor. Except when he did that, the knife was still there, and the blood was still on his hands.

Panic surged through him. He looked at his clothes. There were smudges on his shirt, probably from his hands, but whose blood was it? What had he done? He checked his own body for cuts, his best hope being that he had hit some drunken low and tried to harm himself, knowing he wouldn't do that, because even in his lowest moments, he knew there was always a better day ahead. His hand was grazed, the skin red and exposed.

He looked towards the window again, just to focus on something different, to clear his mind. How did he get here? He couldn't remember leaving The Old Star. He had a drink with Ted Kenyon, and then another one after that. Were there more? As he looked towards the window, he saw that the cord for the blinds was now stained with the blood from his hand.

Charlie was fully awake now, adrenaline chasing away the hangover. He rushed out of his room and into reception, where Linda spent her days. Had someone been into the office? He looked down the stairs, towards the door that came from the street, a wooden panel door with a glass porthole. It was locked. He could see the latch. No one had broken in and placed the knife there.

He went back into his room, unsure what to do. He had to think rationally. What could it mean? Had he found it and brought it with him, out of some kind of drunken curiosity? But why would he do that? He'd never done anything like that before. Was it a discarded butcher's knife? Could it be animal blood, something left out by the kebab shop downstairs?

Then he thought about Julie and her message the day before. Had he called her? Worse still, had he gone round? Oh fuck, what had happened?

He checked his watch again. He couldn't hang around, Amelia liked early starts, but what should he do with the knife? Discard it? Except being caught throwing it away would almost be as bad as being caught with it. No, he had to conceal it somewhere until he could work out what was behind it all.

Cleaning it was the first job though.

He rushed into the kitchen, nothing more than a small space with a couple of cupboards, a small fridge and a kettle. There was a sink, and so he ran it under a tap, the water turning pink as it swirled into the sink. Once the water ran clear, he dried it on a towel and then looked around for a bag to carry it in. He would wash the towel too, just to get rid of any traces, but before he bagged it up, he wet it to rub against the blood on his shirt. It made the stain a little paler but didn't remove it.

He bundled the knife and towel into a plastic bag he found under the sink and then fastened his jacket to conceal the stain. He checked his reflection in the chrome of the kettle. His eyes looked wild and scared, and that's how he felt, his heart drumming fast against his ribcage. His jacket was dishevelled. He ran his hands down it to straighten it out, and he even tried out a smile, but it looked forced.

Then he noticed a red mark on his face, over his cheekbone. He touched it and then he winced. It was another graze. When he brought his fingers down, there was more blood on them. This wasn't good, he knew that.

There was a noise coming from the bottom of the stairs. It was the sound of a key in the lock. Amelia or Linda coming into work.

Charlie froze, unsure how to react. He listened as the door pushed against the post on the mat and then watched as the sliver of light that came in through the doorway expanded, before Linda's familiar silhouette came into view.

When she got to the top of the stairs, she jolted and put her hand to her chest.

'Oh, you surprised me,' she said, laughing to herself 'You're here early, Charlie.'

He put the bag containing the knife into his jacket and

then shrugged, unsure how to respond at first. 'I came to get the court files. I'll go home first. You're early too.'

'I know, but I've got some post to get out today. It was supposed to go out yesterday, but you know how it was, with the burglary.'

As Linda walked to her desk, she wrinkled her nose and frowned. She looked at Charlie suspiciously, and he realised why she was doing that. Charlie could taste the booze on his breath, and he guessed that the office smelled like a wino had been dossing down in there. Which, of course, was true.

She went to her desk and handed him three thin files. He took them from her and was about to go down the stairs, when he stopped.

'I was looking for a sharp knife before, but I couldn't find one,' he said. 'I thought we had a carving knife in the kitchen.'

Linda shook her head. 'I don't think so. Why did you need a knife like that?'

'I just did. I'm sorry. I thought we had one.'

'What's happened to your face? Your cheek. It's grazed.'

'I tripped,' he said, and then turned away, walking quickly down the stairs, not wanting the same discussion with Amelia, who was due into the office at any time.

Charlie grimaced and shielded his eyes as he went onto the street. Someone shouted his name. He looked over. It was one of his clients waving at him.

He turned away. He wasn't in the mood to be pleasant. The plastic bag with the towel and the knife was clasped tightly against his chest, and so he put his head down and walked as quickly as he could.

He needed to work out what had happened.

Chapter Twenty

Sheldon stared out of his windscreen at the brick wall of the police station. The skin underneath his eyes felt sore. He looked into the mirror and saw dark rings. It was late, almost nine o'clock, and he was angry with himself. He had wanted to be the first one in, but images of Alice Kenyon had taunted him as he tried to sleep, of the swirl of her hair in the water, and the post mortem photographs he had copied, kept securely in a metal box that he hid under the bed, fastened shut with a combination lock. He had looked through them again, once more hoping to find that elusive answer. He had turned in his bed for hours and then drifted off as the first licks of daylight painted his room soft blue.

He remembered reaching out to the empty side of the bed when he finally stirred, as he did most mornings. His wife had left him six months earlier, because she hadn't understood about Alice. Neither had Hannah, his daughter. Like Alice had been, she was at university, but they didn't speak anymore. His family didn't understand that it wasn't just Alice. It was all of them. The victims. The forgotten ones.

He climbed out of his car, feet crunching on loose stones on the tarmac. There was a police officer standing by a patrol car. He seemed to be looking over but pretending not to be. Sheldon tugged on his cuffs and headed for the entrance.

The corridor was quiet as he got inside, although he heard low rumbles of conversation as he got closer to the Incident Room. The talking stopped when he walked in and everyone looked round. It was the detective sergeant, Tracey Peters, surrounded by a small group of detectives.

Sheldon smiled, but it felt strained. 'Good morning. Nice to see you keen.'

There were some mumbled greetings but nothing more than that.

There was a newspaper on one of the desks. It was open at the Billy Privett story, a picture of Alice Kenyon prominent, Jim Kelly's by-line at the top. Sheldon turned away. He didn't want to know what the press were saying.

'Anything come in overnight?' he said.

It was Tracey who spoke. 'We did the calls to the neighbours last night, like you said, and guess what; someone went out in Ted Kenyon's car the night Billy was killed. He remembered because it was late, past eleven o'clock.'

'So Ted lied about staying in?'

Tracey nodded. 'Is it enough to bring him in on?'

Sheldon thought about that for a moment, and then shook his head. 'We need more than that, and if news gets out that we've arrested him, people will think the case is closed and stop calling with information. But I want to know why he didn't tell us the truth.'

He turned towards the board at the front and looked at Billy's body, the face missing, so that he looked anonymous, and the very essence of him taken away at the point he died. It wasn't how Sheldon remembered him. The Billy Privett he knew was bullish, had a swagger, the knowledge that

Sheldon couldn't touch him. The Billy in the pictures was different to that. He was a victim. Helpless.

Sheldon started to feel some pity, but he shook that away when he thought of Alice Kenyon. He remembered how limp her body had been as he'd pulled her out of the water, so that she flopped onto the wet tiles like a caught fish. Sheldon had seen the bruises straight away. Blue marks around her neck where strong hands had held her under the water, and there were bruises around her wrist, as if she had been held down before she was drowned. And there were marks on her thighs, and between her thighs. There were some cuts on her stomach, small slashes.

It was the face that he remembered though. Alice had been a beautiful young woman. Young, with high cheekbones and smooth bright skin, and red hair that seemed to swirl over her face in the pictures he saw. When she was dragged out of the water, it was lank and wet, draped across her cheeks.

Then there had been Billy's behaviour after she had been found. He'd refused to answer questions, and so was brought in to get his side of the story, but he had stayed silent. He'd seemed frightened at first, but once he was in the station, familiar territory, he acquired an arrogant smirk as he sat across from Sheldon, his arms folded. He looked to his lawyer, Amelia Diaz, every time a question was asked. She gave the same response each time; a small shake of the head, and then he would repeat, 'No comment.'

Sheldon had tried to speak to Amelia after the second interview, when he knew that he would have to watch Billy walk out, but she hadn't been interested. 'Just doing my job,' was all she'd said.

So he'd kept watch, waiting for Billy to slip up, to meet up with the others who'd been there. But what had he found out? Only that there had been a party. Just another raucous night, except that by the time Sheldon and the young cadet arrived, the house was deserted. Even Billy was gone.

The blood had been a mystery. A pool of it had been congealing in one of the party rooms, with spray on the walls. They never did find out whose blood it was. It wasn't Alice's. It wasn't Billy's. It wasn't on the DNA database. But it had been spilled that night and so was part of the story. Had someone else died?

He heard someone behind him. It was Duncan Lowther.

'Sir, about Christina.'

Sheldon nodded. He remembered her. Billy's housekeeper. 'What about her?'

'She's gone.'

Sheldon turned from Billy's death pictures, confused. 'What do you mean, gone?'

'Just that. I went up to the house last night, after you'd gone, just for a welfare check, and to see whether she remembered anything else. She was gone, no trace of her. Her clothes. Toiletries. No sign she had ever been there.'

'She might have gone home, wherever that is. She'd just been made jobless. There was no point in hanging around.'

'I checked that,' Duncan said. 'The address she gave us doesn't exist. There's a street, but not that number. We checked with the DVLA. No one of that name holds a driving licence around here.'

Sheldon closed his eyes. He felt the tension build again.

'So we need to find her,' Sheldon said quietly.

'We're trying,' Lowther said. 'We could release her picture. She'll be on the CCTV in the station.'

Sheldon thought about that, and then he shook his head. 'Keep it internal for now. Don't let the press know. It might be a misunderstanding. Get a picture from the cameras in here and circulate it across the county, see if any other cop knows her. If we get nothing, then we go to the press.'

When Lowther nodded, Sheldon said, 'Do it now though, no delays,' and then jumped out of his chair. He was too warm, needed some air. He went quickly towards the door.

He turned back to Lowther to see him exchange raised eyebrows with Tracey.

Sheldon banged through the door and made for the exit at the end of the corridor. When he got onto the street, he settled back against the wall and closed his eyes. He felt the morning breeze just cool the sweat on his brow and his shirt collar felt tight. He opened his eyes and looked down at his fingers. They were trembling.

Don't let this one go wrong, he said to himself. Please, not this one.

Charlie tore off his clothes when he got into his apartment and put them in the washing machine – he bought washable suits because he had spilled beer down them too many times. The towel from the office went in too. He didn't know where the blood had come from, but he didn't want any trace of it left. The knife went in the dishwasher, and once that was turned on he relaxed slightly, although the uncertainty about what had happened made his stomach perform loops every time he tried to work it out.

He went for a shower, unsure of what other traces he might be carrying, and once he was under the hot water he examined his body for more injuries. There were none. No scratches or cuts or bruises, apart from the grazes along his hand and his cheek. His knuckles looked normal. If he had been in a fight, he'd come off best by a long way.

He put his hands against the cold tiles and let the shower pummel him for a while. He winced as the grazes got used to the water and tried to recall more of the night before, but he couldn't. It would come back in flashes, he knew that, it was always the same after a late night, but he wanted the answer to the bloody knife sooner than that.

Then he thought of Julie and straightened up, his hands rubbing his face awake. Since she'd left, he had called her sometimes when he got drunk. Had he gone further this time, perhaps argued more violently if she had threatened to arrest him, like she had hinted at?

Charlie put his back against the tiles and slid slowly downwards, until he was sitting in the shower tray and his head was against the wall. That couldn't be right. He wouldn't hurt Julie, he knew that. It wasn't in him to hurt anyone.

Or was it?

He knew he had to call her, to confront it, but it was a call he didn't want to make, just in case his worst fears came true. The water drummed against his legs as he sat there, until the urge to call became too strong.

He dried himself quickly and threw on a dressing gown. He picked up his phone and paused with his finger over the keypad. Yes, it was a call he didn't want to make, but he knew he was just stalling.

He dialled quickly and paced up and down, waiting for her to answer. Then he heard the click.

'Hello?' It was Julie's voice, although her drawl told him that he had woken her up. Then he remembered that she had missed her rest day because of Billy Privett's murder. She must have got it back. There was a man's voice in the background.

'Julie, it's me,' Charlie said.

'Charlie? For Christ's sake,' she said, her annoyance snapping in.

'No, I'm not ringing for that. I just wanted to know if you are okay.'

There was a pause, and then, 'You're not making any sense.'

He put the phone against his chest as he thought what he could say, and then, 'I heard a police officer was hurt last night. I was worried it might have been you.'

'I'm fine, and so is Andrew.' Then her voice softened. 'Thanks for the concern, Charlie. Now if you don't mind, I want to get back to sleep.'

Charlie was relieved, although he heard the male voice whisper something and Julie giggled. He closed his eyes.

'I'll leave you to it,' he said, and clicked off the phone.

So what now? He wasn't hurt. Julie was fine. So how could he explain the knife, and how could he explain the blood?

Chapter Twenty-One

Sheldon drove quickly through the gates to Billy's house, his wheels throwing up gravel against the gateposts and making Tracey grip the door handle.

He was first out of the car, running towards the front doors, Tracey following. They weren't locked. He pushed at them and watched as the hallway came into view.

Billy's house felt different straight away. Empty, quiet; cold even, despite the warmth outside. He shouted out Christina's name. There was no response.

Sheldon ran for the stairs, ignoring Tracey's footsteps behind him. He went straight to Christina's room. He had been in there the day before. He had seen her clothes, her things. Photographs on the wall. Cosmetics on the dresser. Christina had lived there, he knew it.

As Sheldon flung open a wardrobe door, he saw it was empty, just the jangle of the coat hangers to greet him. He checked the drawers. There were no clothes or jewellery or personal things. It was the same in the bathroom. Lowther was right. She was gone.

Sheldon went from room to room, checking for Christina's clothes, but there was no trace of her.

He walked slowly down the stairs and saw Tracey looking up at him, concerned. He slumped onto the bottom step.

His hands hung from his knees and he stared at the floor. Why did it feel like he had lost control over whatever went on in this house?

'Sir, are you all right?'

When Sheldon looked up, he took a deep breath and nodded assertively, but the clench to his jaw gave him away. 'Yes, I'm fine. I just stayed up too late.'

Sheldon got to his feet and walked out of the front door, striding past his car and towards the gates at the front of the house, his ears filled with the sound of his footsteps on gravel. The house next door wasn't too far away. He knew the road from his late night surveillance. Maybe they had seen Christina go, or knew more about her.

He went through the gate and along the fence at the front of the house, his feet swishing through the long grass. As he turned onto the driveway of the house next door, he saw the door begin to open. They had seen him.

'Mrs Taylor,' Sheldon shouted. He knew their names, of course. She had made the most complaints about Billy before Alice died, and had been the one who called in the complaint that led to Alice being found.

She looked nervous as the door opened fully, a woman in her sixties, with a pinafore dress and tight curls that had been dyed into a deep brown. Her husband was just behind her, in slippers but dressed smartly, a shirt and tie and pressed blue trousers.

'We knew you'd come round eventually,' Mrs Taylor said, as Sheldon got closer, her voice coming out with a tremble. 'It was awful what happened to Mr Privett. We saw it on the news and, well, we just want you to know that although we didn't get on with him, we would have no part in anything like that.'

Sheldon was confused. 'What do you mean?'

'Mr Privett's murder. I know how you find out who had a grudge against the dead person, to work out who killed him, and I suppose we're some of those people. So we are suspects.'

Sheldon smiled, a moment of relief. 'You're not suspects, I promise you.'

She visibly relaxed, and so opened the door to let him in. 'Can I get you anything? Tea? Coffee?'

He was about to refuse, he just wanted to find out if they knew where Christina had gone, but he felt the sudden urge to relax, to sit down and enjoy the warmth of their hospitality. 'Coffee, please. That would be nice.'

He sank into a high-backed chair that looked towards the view at the front. He closed his eyes, just for a second, and felt the comfort of the chair send him drifting off somewhere, where he couldn't feel his doubts anymore, where Billy Privett didn't matter.

He woke up with a start. Mrs Taylor was in front of him, holding out a cup of coffee.

'Have you been working too hard?' she said, as she handed it to him.

Sheldon nodded. 'It seems that way sometimes.' He took a sip of coffee, felt it perk him up. 'Did you know the girl next door, Christina, Billy's housekeeper?'

'Blonde girl? Yes, we used to see her around. We thought it was Mr Privett's girlfriend, because since, well, you know, Alice, he had been quieter. Not as many parties.'

'She's not there anymore. Did you ever speak to her?'

'No, not ever. Not even a smile. But why would anyone from there say hello to us? They knew what we thought of them.'

'She left yesterday. Did you see her go?'

They shook their heads.

Sheldon put the cup on the floor and put his head back against the chair, as the sound of the blood rushing through his head overwhelmed him. He thought he could hear someone talking, getting closer, but he ignored it. Someone's hand was on his but he didn't look up. He saw Billy's smirk, and Alice's body. He remembered when his wife left him, her clothes packed into bin liners, her screams that she couldn't compete with Alice Kenyon anymore. So it had come to this, his life defined by what he couldn't solve, not what he could.

The hand around his became tighter. He could hear voices shouting at him. 'Inspector. *Inspector.*'

He opened his eyes slowly and the room blurred into view. Then he saw that it was Tracey Peters, her hand shaking his.

'Sir, are you all right?'

He looked at her, and then at Mr and Mrs Taylor, their eyes filled with concern, and he nodded.

As he stood to go, following Tracey, he glanced over to Billy's house, visible over the hedges and rhododendron bushes. He thought it looked dark, a cloud in front of the sun casting the house in shadow, while everywhere else was bathed in sunshine.

Sheldon turned away.

Charlie faltered as he got near to the court building, the three files Linda had given him earlier tucked under his arm. First hearings. A guilty plea and two not guilty. One long, two quick. He could do this.

But he wasn't sure that he could, because the blood-covered knife dominated his thoughts. He had to try though, because he had to appear normal. If he had hurt someone with the knife, appearing different could count against him if the police started asking questions. Same old Charlie, that's what he had to be.

Donia was waiting for him, standing just to the side of the main doors, looking smart in a navy skirt and jacket. She waved as she saw him.

Charlie took a deep breath and smiled as he got closer.

'I hope you don't mind, but I knew you were coming here,' she said.

'I tripped,' he said, knowing that she was looking at the graze on his cheek but not wanting to discuss it. He looked around for police officers, and felt a jolt when he saw a dark uniform on the other side of the courthouse door. He went closer, needing to reassure himself, and as he got closer he breathed more easily. It was an officer in uniform, but he was in his parade dress, best tunic and shiny buttons, so he must be giving evidence.

Charlie hustled his way through the crowd huddled around the door. It was the daily gathering, and the usual smells assaulted his nostrils, of cigarettes and sweat, unwashed clothes smelling like sour milk. There were grunted greetings, and one or two scowls from those people whose days in court hadn't gone so well in the past.

Charlie nodded at the people he recognised, but he wasn't in the mood for conversation. He was at court because it was what he did. He could have asked Amelia to do it, feigned illness, but it was all about appearing normal, just another day. Except that he needed his anxiety to keep him alert, because whenever he was able to convince himself that he'd done nothing wrong, the fear was replaced by fatigue. The fog of a hangover felt heavy and waves of nausea swept over him from time to time. He hadn't eaten anything, apart from the steady supply of mints intended to keep the boozy smell away.

Donia fell in behind him as he went inside, elbowing his way through the crowded waiting room and towards the door to one of the courtrooms. He could see the respectful calm of the court on the other side, visible through a glass porthole. He practised his smile, so that it looked natural, not forced, but when his eyes focused on what was in the courtroom, he backed away.

It was the usual scene. Two rows of wooden benches, like church pews, facing towards the high bench occupied by the Magistrates, the backdrop a high velvet curtain, the royal coat of arms hanging in front of it, the lion and the unicorn. The prosecutor was ready in his seat, the white file covers piled up on the desk in front of him, but it was the person he was talking to that made Charlie back away.

It was one of the local detectives. He was standing over the prosecutor, talking. It wasn't unusual for the police to attend the court hearings. Sometimes they had updates to pass on, and sometimes they just wanted to see the prosecutor put up a fight. This might be different though. They might be waiting for him.

'Are you Charlie Barker?'

He started. When he looked round, there was a man in his early twenties, scowling, holding some papers in his hand.

'I'm sorry,' Charlie mumbled, backing away. 'I just need some fresh air.'

Charlie bolted outside, banging through the entrance door, and made it to the street before he threw up. It was booze and nerves and tiredness, but that didn't make him feel any better as he heaved to the cheers of the crowd behind him.

Once he had finished, he propped his head on his arm and leant against the wall. His forehead was clammy, and for as long as he didn't look up, he could pretend that no one had seen him. There was a hand on his shoulder. He looked round, bleary-eyed. It was Donia.

'Are you all right?' she said.

Charlie nodded. 'Just a bug, I'm sorry.'

His phone buzzed in his pocket. He fumbled for it and checked the screen. It was the office.

'Linda?' he said.

'Have you seen Amelia?' Linda said. 'She hasn't come in and she's got an appointment.' Her voice turned into a whisper as she said, 'He's sitting opposite me and he's stinking the place out.'

Charlie took some deep breaths. He didn't need this. Linda kept a can of air freshener under her desk for clients like that. 'Have you called her?'

'Yes, landline and mobile. And one of her friends called. She didn't make their dinner date last night.'

He wiped his mouth with a handkerchief. 'Okay, I'll go round when I've finished here.'

'And what do I tell her client?'

'Just tell him to come back another time,' he said, and then hung up.

Charlie leant back against the wall and enjoyed the feel of the cold brick against his head. Cold sweat prickled his forehead again, before he felt another surge in his guts, and there were more cheers as he retched once more against the brick wall of the courthouse.

Chapter Twenty-Two

John squinted as the bright morning sunshine streamed in.

The night had become raucous, with too much home brew, too much cannabis. Laughter, drinking, some people naked, as if it was the best party they had ever been to, Henry moving from person to person, asking for promises of loyalty. They had all given it, even Dawn.

He collapsed back onto the bed, sucking in air to calm the nauseous roll of his stomach. Gemma's body was warm next to him. She mumbled and moved, her arm going over his chest as she shuffled closer, her head against his body. He smiled and ran one hand over her hair and then along her back, her skin soft, just the sharp ridges of her spine disrupting the smooth feel of her body. His mind went back to the night before, but it came back to him in flashes. Gemma on him, passionate, her shouts of pleasure, uninhibited and joyful. And there were other people with them, their hands on him, on Gemma.

He closed his eyes. It had got too wild. Gemma didn't move as he climbed out of bed. He got to his feet, groaning, and then stumbled his way to the bathroom. He sat on the toilet for a while, wondering what lay ahead for the rest of the day. Henry had said that things were happening now, that the day ahead would be important.

There were footsteps on the landing. John coughed to let whoever who it was know that he was in there. There was no door on the bathroom. Henry didn't like doors. Whoever was on the landing was walking softly, sounding like they were barefoot.

He froze when he heard a voice say, 'John?' It was Henry.

John flushed the toilet and scrambled to his feet, before stumbling onto the landing.

'Morning Henry,' he said, trying hard for normality. 'The home brew came back and bit me.'

Henry grinned. 'It can rot you from the inside if you don't keep an eye on it.'

'Were you looking for me?'

'I was. Come with me, for a walk. You look like you need some fresh air,' and he headed down the stairs and out of the main door, the one that opened onto the field, the Seven Sisters in view.

John ran to get some clothes. He paused to gaze down at Gemma, and he felt a moment of longing, a need to be with her again, but he looked away. Henry was waiting for him.

When John joined him outside, Henry was sitting on the stone slab of the Seven Sisters.

'What do you think when you look at the stones?' Henry said.

John placed his hand on one. It was cold, just stone, but he remembered Dawn's description. 'It's a legacy, something for people to remember us by.'

Henry nodded and smiled. 'We'll need a legacy, because we are nearly ready,' he said. 'We just need people to help us with our mission, and only those people will know about it.'

'What mission is that?'

'The fulfilment of our plans,' Henry said. 'We've had them in place for a while, but it is about picking the right moment, and the right people. You are one of those people. We need you.'

'But I can't agree to something I don't know about.'

'You trust me?'

John nodded. 'Of course I do, Henry.'

'So trust me on this.'

'And if I change my mind when I know the details?'

Henry glanced towards the rest of the stones. 'We find someone else.'

John rubbed his eyes, still tired, as he thought about what Henry was saying. 'Why me?' he said eventually.

'Because no one will know you. That's important. How long have you been with us? Three weeks?'

John nodded.

'That's why we kept you up here,' Henry said. 'You got to know the group, and I got to know you, but also so no one would know you were with us, because the police watch us, I know that. They won't know you though. You are our secret weapon.'

John nodded slowly, taking in what Henry was saying. 'So what are your plans?'

Henry grinned. 'We are going to strike at the heart of it all.'

'I don't understand.'

'Soldiers, John, that's what we are. You too. But you have to agree, because that is how we are, that we live our lives by consent. If you want me to tell you, there is no backing out. Do you understand that?'

John nodded. 'Tell me.'

Henry smiled paternally and stepped closer to John. 'We have explosives,' Henry said in a whisper. 'Bad stuff.

Ammonium nitrate. But we are at a farm. No one would suspect. It's fertiliser.' Henry began to laugh. 'Genius, isn't it? The detonators are with a different group. Just phones and wires, nothing sinister on their own.'

John's mind flashed back to the white crystals in the metal drum. 'Is it legal?'

'It's lawful rebellion, John, they can't punish us for that.'

'I don't understand.'

'The Magna Carta. You've heard of it? It's our country's constitution and Parliament cannot take it away. If we are being ruled unjustly, we can fight back, and that starts with us not obeying their laws, because the Magna Carta says that we can.'

'But they can just lock us up, can't they?'

'They can't unless we are doing something contrary to the law of the land, and if the Magna Carta allows us to conduct lawful rebellion, how can it be unlawful?'

'So what do we do?'

'We do what others won't. There are a lot of people who think like us, but they don't have the heart that we do, because they take the fight to the courts, by not paying taxes and bank debts. Except that doesn't hurt the slugs who rule us. No, we are launching the real rebellion. So we are going to London, to the heart of the beast.'

'London? What's the target?'

'Trafalgar Square,' Henry said, his eyes wide with excitement. 'We are taking down the column.'

John let out a slow whistle. 'Why Nelson's Column?'

'Because it is symbolic of our wonderful fucking empire, when we ruled and robbed and pillaged our way round the world. Think about it. Where does everyone go when we celebrate our greatness? Trafalgar Square, like it is some kind of magnet, a totem for our great nation. But what if we could take it down? It would show what we can do, how it is just a start.'

'Won't people get hurt?'

'This is our war,' Henry said. 'There is always collateral damage.'

John nodded slowly. 'I can see how it would send a message, but how will it work?'

'There'll be three of you, just playing at being tourists. No rucksacks, too obvious. We'll line your coats instead and go when the weather is bad, so that your coats don't look conspicuous. You'll be the excited visitor, clambering on the lions, posing for pictures. Just take off your coat for a better picture, as will the other two, and you'll leave them at the base of the Column. You need to be in the Square when it goes off though, because you will use the confusion to get away.'

'And where will you be?'

'I'll be one of the decoys. We will go to the financial district, and so if they think we are planning something, they will follow us and not you.' Henry smiled. 'I've been watching you, and you can do this.'

John frowned. 'I'm not sure. I mean, what if people get hurt? How near is this thing from happening?'

Henry stepped forward and grabbed John by his T-shirt. He pulled him close, Henry's breath rancid from stale home brew and lack of sleep. 'You can't back away now. I said direct action and you stayed interested. That was your consent. If you back away, you are saying that you don't want to be with us anymore. You don't want to be the one who betrays me.'

'I don't want to betray you.'

'So agree, once and for all.'

John grimaced as he tried to pull away. Henry pulled him

closer. 'You made your decision a moment ago. There is no going back, I told you that.' He pushed John away, making him stumble over the standing stones, so that he ended up on the grass.

John closed his eyes, his breaths short from fear. Eventually he said, 'All right, yes, I'll do it.'

Henry nodded, smiling. 'I have to go somewhere today, to make preparations. You will have to look after everyone. You will be the man here. Don't let anyone leave in panic. We must stay together.'

John nodded. 'I understand.'

Henry stood over him. 'I knew it,' he said, and stepped closer to John, his head tilting, first one way, then the other, staring down into John's eyes. 'You are my newest disciple, but also my closest. I think we can be special together, John, work some magic. Do you feel like that?'

John flushed. 'I do, Henry, and it's an honour.'

Chapter Twenty-Three

Sheldon banged on the door to Ted Kenyon's house.

'What are you going to do, sir?' Tracey Peters whispered.

'Get some answers.'

There was no answer, and so he banged again. When Ted opened the door, surprised, Sheldon barked, 'Why did you lie?'

Ted took a step back and said, 'About what?'

'You said you'd stayed in. You hadn't. You went into Oulton on the night Billy died, and then you lied to me.'

Emily appeared from the kitchen. 'What's all the shouting about?'

Tracey went to her, her hands out, placating. 'It's all right, Mrs Kenyon. My inspector is just talking to your husband.'

'He's shouting.'

'It's nothing to worry about.'

Emily pushed past Tracey. 'Ted, are you all right? What's going on?'

Sheldon tried to ignore her as he stared at Ted. He wanted to see the flicker of recognition, that moment when he knew that he had gone too far in going after Billy Privett, and that he had been found out. But there was only anger.

'Are you going to arrest me?' Ted said, and then held his hands out. 'Go on then, here they are. You couldn't get it right last time. Why not repeat it?'

Sheldon paused, remembering what he had said in the Incident Room, that there wasn't enough to arrest him yet. As he thought of that, some of his anger subsided. He looked at Tracey, and then at Emily, who appeared distressed, her hand over her mouth.

'So why did you lie?' Sheldon said, his voice softer now.

'Because the last time I followed up a lead like this, I was set up and photographed with a young woman. You remember, the thing that made the front page and ruined my reputation, but I'm not rich enough to fight a libel case. And what did they say anyway? That I was with a young woman who wasn't wearing a top, that's all. All they had to do was print the picture.'

'You explain it how you want, Mr Kenyon,' Sheldon said.

Ted stepped closer. 'That's how it was,' he said, his voice more threatening now. 'The calls and the letters about Alice dried up afterwards, but I bet you can guess that. So why set me up? Do you know what I think? Someone didn't want me to get any closer. The girl promised me some answers, and so I turned up. Somewhere quiet, she said, because she was scared. We were talking, but she wasn't saying much, just putting on the tears, and so when I leaned across to her, there was a flash. Before I knew what was happening, her top was off and she was trying to straddle me, and the flashes were still going on. It was a fix, designed to make me go away, and it worked.'

'I've been in the police more than twenty years, Mr Kenyon, and so I've heard plenty of people try to explain away tricky situations. That was one of the worst efforts I've ever heard.'

'I don't care whether you believe it or not, but you asked me why I lied, and so I've told you.'

'I don't understand,' Sheldon said.

'I got a similar message,' Ted said. 'It wasn't the same person. It was a man this time, someone who said he was a friend of Billy Privett, and Billy had told him what had happened when Alice died. The full story, he promised. He told me to meet him in Oulton, outside the Crown and Feathers, just down the road from the hotel where he was found. I went, but he didn't turn up, and so I came home. When I heard that Billy had died, I wondered whether it was a set-up again, and so I lied. So go on, lock me up, if you think it will help. But that's all I did, tell a lie.'

Sheldon closed his eyes and rubbed his temple. Glimpses of Billy Privett came into his head. Grinning, taunting, brash and arrogant. Then he thought of the corpse on the hotel bed, his face ripped off. It was nasty, vengeful, so it hinted at Ted, but he knew it was too obvious.

Sheldon spoke the words before he thought to stop them. 'I think of Alice all the time,' he said. He opened his eyes. 'I found her, but you know that. It's more than that though. I see her body when I'm asleep, and when I'm on my own. I feel like I can't rest until I know, because all we found was Alice, with no one else there. Even Billy had gone, and no one knew who else was there.'

Sheldon felt a hand on his arm. It was Tracey Peters, raising her eyebrows, a hint that they should leave. He pulled his arm away.

'If you are lying to me again,' Sheldon said to Ted, 'I will make sure that everyone knows that you lied, so that even if we can't prove it, people will think you as much a murderer as an adulterer.'

'You don't need to threaten me,' Ted said. 'Take my car. If the reports in the paper are true, there will be traces of Billy everywhere. Just to eliminate me, take it and check it out. Then you can leave me alone.'

Sheldon looked at Tracey. She had moved further down the hall and was speaking into her phone, her voice just whispers.

Sheldon turned to Tracey. 'What is it?'

She looked at Ted, and then back to Sheldon, before saying, 'I need to talk to you, in private.'

Sheldon moved down the hall, away from Ted and Emily. 'What is it?'

She leaned in and whispered, 'Jim Kelly has called in. There's been another package delivered to the paper.'

Sheldon clenched his jaw. 'Another one?'

Tracey nodded. 'He didn't open it this time, but on the box this time are the words *The Face of Lies*.'

Sheldon had to reach out for the wall, just to stay on his feet.

Charlie was outside Amelia's house, sitting in his car and staring through his windscreen. He had persuaded Donia to return to the office, because Amelia wouldn't welcome visitors if she was ill. If Donia wanted work experience, she could read some files.

Amelia's house was as he remembered it, although he had only been there a couple of times before. It was a grey stone cottage, with black timbers set into the ceiling and roses that curled around a slate-covered porch. At the back, it looked out onto a reservoir by an abandoned paper mill, so that it was dark at night, except for when a bright moon turned the water silver.

The setting had surprised him when he first saw it. Amelia was business-like and unemotional, but the street was a chocolate box image of country living, the sort of place where tea came in china cups and people rode bikes with baskets under the handlebars. Her house was detached, although only just, with space for a small path around each side.

He climbed out of his car, a five-year-old black Seat Leon, and strode confidently towards Amelia's front door, his determined gait bearing little resemblance to how he felt. He had to confront the nagging doubts about Amelia's absence. He knocked on the door. It came back as a dull thud, but there was no answer.

Charlie stepped away from her door and looked at her window. The curtains were closed. Amelia didn't strike him as the type for a duvet day.

He stroked his stubble as he looked to the other side of her house, towards the gate and the path round the side. As he went towards it, Charlie fought the urge to look around and check who could see him, because it would arouse suspicion. The gate opened with a clink, and as he went through and walked to the back of the house, he expected someone to shout out. No one did or tried to stop him.

He walked slowly, so that he could retreat quietly if Amelia *was* there. The path opened onto a long stretch of lawn, with a small patio next to the house. Her view was towards the paper mill, the tall stone chimney and corrugated roof spoiling the outlook.

The kitchen window was next to him and so he peered in, gazing over the black granite and oak cupboards, looking for some sign that she had been up that morning, like an opened cereal packet or aspirin packet, maybe wisps of steam from the kettle. It all looked clean.

Then he saw something that made his knees go weak and the colours in front of him fade, so that the world seemed to bleach out for a few seconds.

Charlie closed his eyes and put his forehead against the sill. This could not be happening. He was sure that he was going to wake up and discover that it was all a dream, or that he was still drunk and not seeing things correctly.

Except that he knew it was neither of those things.

Charlie straightened and took some deep breaths before he looked through the window again. He cupped his hands around his face to block out the light from behind him, leaving his finger marks on the glass. He needed to satisfy himself that he had seen it right, although he knew that the image had burned itself into his memory.

In the corner of the granite worktop, next to a microwave and a steel utensil stand, was a knife block. Six knives. Or at least that was how it was supposed to be, because one of the slots was empty. The other five slots were full though, and they each held knives of the same design. Shiny steel, with a twist at the end, a small metal ring hanging down. Just like the one he had woken up to.

He clenched his jaw as he tried hard to think of how the night before had ended, his eyes squeezed shut. He couldn't have come to Amelia's house, he was sure of that. It was near enough to walk, but there was no way he could pass it accidentally, more than a mile from his house and even further from The Old Star. And why would he have done?

What if he had though? It would have been by taxi, and so someone would remember taking him, the drunken lawyer who tipped too much, because he liked to be everyone's friend when he was drunk.

He looked along the wall, towards the back door. It was a sliding patio door, sheltered by a wooden pergola covered in Russian ivy that was starting to swallow up the back of the house. The handle was broken, the white plastic hanging down and held on by just one screw.

He reached out for it, shocked, but then he stopped himself. He didn't want to touch anything, and so he put his hand into his jacket sleeve and pulled at the door. It opened smoothly and then he stepped into the kitchen.

It was a small house, with the kitchen at the back having just enough room to squeeze a table in, the living room occupying the front part of the house. As he looked through the kitchen door he could see the stairs going out of the front room. The house was warm, as if the heating was on, despite the sunny day outside. He swatted at a fly that buzzed him.

He listened out for the noise of someone else in the house. A radio or television. The trickle of the shower. It was silent. 'Amelia?' he shouted, but there was no answer.

As he turned towards the living room, he gave another shout of 'Amelia' before stepping through the doorway.

That was when his whole world turned into a nightmare.

Chapter Twenty-Four

Sheldon followed Tracey into the police station. He'd been silent all the way back to the police station.

As they walked along the corridor, they saw Jim Kelly, the local reporter, being led into a side room.

'Inspector Brown,' he said, when he saw Sheldon. 'Anything to say before I give my statement? Do you feel you have a grip on things?'

Sheldon went towards him, but Tracey pulled at his sleeve and said, 'We have to go to Dixon's office.'

Sheldon nodded and walked in front of her, tugging at his cuffs, easing out a crick in his neck. His hand went to his cheeks, remembering that he hadn't shaved. As he pushed at the door, he caught his reflection in the glass. There were dark shadows under his eyes, and for a moment he thought he looked haunted. The image made him pause. It was a snapshot of how other people saw him. He went to tug at his cuffs again, but as he looked, they were grubby and frayed. Was it the same shirt he had worn yesterday? Perhaps the day before? He couldn't remember ironing a shirt recently.

Tracey breezed past him, and he caught the scent of her perfume. 'Sir?'

Sheldon nodded and started to follow.

Tracey opened the door into Dixon's office, and as Sheldon

followed her, he saw that there was only one chair in front of Dixon's desk. He gestured for Tracey to take the seat, but she went to stand alongside Dixon instead.

Sheldon was surprised.

'Thank you for coming, Sheldon,' the Chief Inspector said. 'Sit down.' Her voice sounded tired.

Sheldon sat in the chair, his knees together, his hands on his legs. There was a man sitting in a chair along one of the walls. Sheldon recognised him from earlier in his career, when they had both been younger and more ambitious. Sheldon had acquired a separation from his wife and a house he couldn't afford, and the man opposite had got himself dyed hair and a moustache, along with a growing reputation in FMIT. Sheldon tried to think of his name, but it wouldn't come back to him.

The chief inspector leaned forward on her desk, her hands clasped together. She glanced at the man sitting against the wall. Sheldon noticed that her hands were trembling.

'Sergeant Peters has been reporting back to DI Williams,' she said.

Williams. That's right. He remembered now.

Williams coughed. 'At my request,' he said. His voice was soft, almost velvety, and Sheldon recognised it from the numerous press conferences and Crimewatch appeals. It was the voice of reassurance.

'I wanted DS Peters on your team to keep her eye on you, Sheldon,' Williams continued. 'Oulton likes to go its own way, we know that, and we were tied up with other cases, but that doesn't mean we were happy for you to take over.'

'So you sent someone to spy on me?' Sheldon looked at Dixon, aghast. 'Ma'am, you trusted me with the investigation. You said so.'

Dixon shifted in her chair. 'In the end, it wasn't up to me.'

'I wasn't sure if you were ready to lead the investigation,' Williams said. 'It's gone a little higher profile now and so we're taking over.'

'I am managing,' Sheldon said, his voice terse. 'We just haven't had the breaks.'

Williams shook his head. 'That's not what I'm hearing. You're not in control. You look awful. I'm sorry, but it ends now. Take some time off, for your own good. FMIT are taking over.'

'It's not right though. You took the Alice Kenyon case from me and got no nearer than I did.'

Williams sighed. 'It's not about being right or fair. It's about catching a killer, and Sheldon, you're not up to it.'

'Ma'am?' Sheldon said, appealing to Dixon.

She exhaled wearily and then shook her head. 'It's time to hand it over. We don't have the resources. Take some leave, Sheldon, until I decide otherwise. Full pay.'

'What, I'm suspended?'

'No, just sick leave. Here's the number of the welfare officer,' and she passed over a leaflet that Sheldon had seen pinned to noticeboards around the station. 'Speak to him, take some advice. Go on holiday. Just get the old Sheldon back.'

Sheldon didn't know what to say. He looked at the leaflet, turned it over in his hand. 'So this is it?' he said.

'Only for now,' Dixon said.

Sheldon rose slowly out of his chair. The silence seemed heavy in the room. He looked at Williams, who simply crossed his legs in response, his lips firm under his moustache. Tracey looked embarrassed, but her position in the room, just behind Dixon, told Sheldon where her allegiance lay. He turned away and went towards the door. As he stepped through and clicked it shut, the corridor felt empty and quiet. The light reflected from the blue and white tiles that ran along its length seemed to guide him towards the exit at the other end.

His footsteps were hesitant as he passed the doorway to the Incident Room. There were a few detectives in there, and they stopped whatever they had been doing as he went past. The ones that caught his eyes turned away when he returned their stares.

Sheldon kept on walking until his hand thumped on the final door, and then it was bright outside, making him squint, the hum of traffic breaking the echoes of the corridor. He went towards his own car but didn't climb in. Where would he go? He couldn't go home. There was nothing for him there. Instead, he kept on walking, going past his car and towards the road that ran in front of the station, where the traffic noise got louder.

Sheldon stared ahead, not sure what he was going to do, or where, and finally set off walking, the buzz of the investigation replaced by the sound of his feet on the tarmac. The further he got from the station, the more certain he was that he was never going to return.

Charlie sank to his knees and closed his eyes. He got the acid burn in his mouth and knew that he would struggle to keep down whatever was left in his stomach, but he gritted his teeth and tried to get through it.

Oh Amelia, he thought to himself. Oh Christ, what had he done?

He braced himself before he opened his eyes, knowing what he was about to see.

Amelia was on her back on the floor. She was virtually

naked, her clothes ripped off, her blouse in shreds around her wrists, as if it had been pulled off her shoulders from behind. Her skirt was pushed up her legs, her knickers in the corner of the room. The long tanned legs that he had admired during slow afternoons looked stiff and lifeless, although crooked, so that in death she retained some modesty. Trails of blood had run down her thighs and onto the floor, where it pooled in a dark stain and merged with the streams that had run from her chest and torso.

Her chest was exposed, but it was hard to make out the smoothness of her skin for the dried blood. It was smeared, like finger painting, with long streaks running to her neck, where an electrical flex from a lamp had been tied tightly around it. But it was what was above the flex that he knew would haunt him for the rest of his life.

Where there had once been Amelia's face, there was now just bloody flesh and the protrusion of bone. Her eyes stared at the ceiling like two glass balls, her teeth set in a permanent grimace. Her face had been cut away.

He closed his eyes again. He couldn't look. He hadn't done this, he just knew it. He would have been covered in blood, and he hadn't been, except for the stains he had made as he brushed against the knife as he slept. But the missing carving knife was in his dishwasher. How would he explain that? And his clothes? How could he say that his clothes were not covered in blood when he had put them in the washing machine?

Then something else occurred to him. Billy Privett, then Amelia. Would he be next?

Charlie sat back against the doorframe, his hands on his head. There were photographs behind Amelia, lined up along the mantel over the fire. Her parents mainly, Amelia looking much different to the person she had been around the office.

She was laughing, her arms wrapped round her father, his face brown and deep-lined, love and pride etched into every wrinkle to his smile.

He shook his head. What had Amelia gone through in her final moments? The flex was around her neck like a dog lead – not to mention her face. Charlie hoped fervently she had been dead when that happened.

Charlie put his hand over his mouth and looked back towards the kitchen. But if it wasn't him, how did he end up with the knife? Then he noticed that he had been stepping on patches of blood, and so there would be blood on his soles. Just tiny traces, but enough for a forensic scientist to find. And then there was the sweat on the wall where he had put his head back.

He had to think like a lawyer. There is always an alternative theory.

He should call the police and brazen it out, he knew that. But they would spot the missing knife, and so they would guess that it had been used. And he would have to stay with them, to tell them what he saw. They might even ask where he had been? He couldn't just tell them that he couldn't remember. If he tried to make something up, someone else somewhere might contradict it, and then he would be a liar. They would ask about the business, because that is what tied him to Amelia, but what could he say? That they were losing money and surviving on an overdraft, and that Amelia blamed him for the partnership failings, that their relationship was not always harmonious? And then the rest would come out. How he looked at her when she was in the office, and the more drunk he got, the more it was a leer. How he had acted strangely earlier in the morning. Vomiting in public. Sleeping on the office floor. Bloodstains on the cord on the Venetian blind, which would be Amelia's blood, because it came from the knife. It will start to add up against him, and so they'd lock him up just so that they can have a poke around. And what would they find? The clothes he wore the day before in the washer, matched against the CCTV from the court waiting room, and the knife missing from Amelia's knife block in his dishwasher. It would be like writing his own prison sentence.

Charlie was being selfish, he knew it, but he couldn't bring Amelia back. He had to look out for himself, because they wouldn't get any nearer to finding out who killed her if the police focus was all on him.

Except that what he was about to do could look even worse, because if he just left and someone remembered him through the twitch of a curtain, they would want to know why he hadn't called it in. Charlie felt like the last piece on the chessboard, the white king being pursued around the board, with no winning move possible but not willing to give it up.

He looked at Amelia and told her that he was sorry, that he hoped she would forgive him if it turned out that his religious views had always been wrong, and that she was looking down on him. Then he backed out of the room.

Charlie was about to go to the back door when he heard a car pull up outside.

He went to the window, stepping round Amelia. As he looked through, he saw the two men in suits who had been at the office the day before, the private payers, emerging from a silver Audi. What were they doing here? They were clients, Amelia had said that.

They were talking to each other, looking around, and then they set off towards the front door.

Charlie panicked. He looked down at Amelia, and then

back at the two men getting closer along the path. Did they have something to do with it?

He bolted for the back garden, the patio door opening with a swish. There was a knock on the door as he ran along the lawn, the pounding of his feet loud in his ears. He scrambled over the fence at the back, and then lay on the floor as he tried to get his breath back. He waited for a shout from one of the neighbours, but it was quiet.

The grass tickled his cheeks, his breaths hot as he panted into the ground. There was the sound of cars in the distance and the loud thump of his heart, and then he heard the clink of the gate. He remembered it from his own walk around the side of the house. They were going in the same way, so would find the same thing that he had. Amelia, dead. Or perhaps they already knew that?

Charlie was trapped. His car was further along Amelia's street, but he couldn't go back to it. They would see him. They might even know that it was his car, so would come looking for him. He had to get away from there.

Noises came from the back of the house. Hisses, angry voices.

Charlie started to crawl along the ground, trying to keep his head down. He looked along towards the reservoir and the paper mill, wondering if anyone was watching. There was a path that ran alongside the water and then disappeared into trees before coming out by a grid of terraced streets. If he could get that far, he knew a short cut back to his apartment building.

He crawled quickly so that he could get to a point where he could look natural, as if he was coming from a different direction. He tried not to grunt or shout out whenever his knees hit a stone, and soon he knew that he was out of sight of the house. He straightened and tried to make like he was out for a walk, although he was in a suit and there was a sheen of sweat on his face, putting a gloss to his grey pallor and making the graze on his cheek brighter. None of this was natural, and he knew that people would remember him, because as soon as Amelia's body was discovered there would be shockwaves in the town. People knew her. That was the way with defence lawyers, because the court stories are what people read in the local paper, and so the defending lawyer gets a name. So they will remember the tall man in a crumpled suit, his hair wild, his face covered in greying stubble, creeping round the house and crawling through the field. He would have to explain why he did nothing, but until then he had to work out what had happened to Amelia. He owed her that much.

Chapter Twenty-Five

Sheldon walked slowly through the streets of Oulton. It seemed quiet to him, even though the streets were busy. People were still curious about the murder, and so the activity around the police station attracted onlookers, those who were grateful to have something to fill their day, just hanging around, sharing cigarettes. But it was as if they knew to stay away from him as he shuffled along, each step taking him further away from the police station, one step nearer to an uncertain future.

The parish church was ahead, dark grey stone with a high Norman-style tower at its centre, square with castellated ridges and a white-faced clock on each side. It had dominated the skyline of the town for five hundred years, from when Oulton was just a small wool trading village and the church served as the religious centre for the surrounding farms. It had drawn Sheldon today, as if he was seeking somewhere quiet to reflect.

The low drone of the traffic was lost immediately as he went inside. Sheldon's movements echoed and seemed to bounce between the majestic stained-glass windows. He looked up and felt small, insignificant. The ceiling was high and arched, traversed by oak beams, the lines broken by carved rosettes where they intersected, overlooking the black and white checks of the aisle. He let his hand trail over the pews as he went towards the altar, and when he got there, he sat down. He closed his eyes and tried to find some solace in all the years that the church had been there, that his problems meant nothing.

But as he sat on the pew they all came back to him, the deaths, right back to his first, a bony old man found dead in his flat, killed for his pension money, the bravery that had made him carry a gun in wartime spilled over a blood-soaked rug, his life taken away in front of framed pictures of his grandchildren. And so the movie flew forward again, past car crash victims and fights that went too far, once more juddering to a halt at Alice Kenyon, floating lifelessly in Billy's pool, her hair trailing around her like rags caught on a branch.

Sheldon got to his feet. The church brought him no comfort. For all the years of prayer, he wasn't sure any had been answered. Good people died, bad people lived. That seemed to be always the way, and Billy's murder didn't change that balance. It was a blip. He stepped up to the altar, unsure of what he was doing, but then saw a stone doorway that opened onto steps that would take him upwards in the tower. Sheldon thought of the view, the fields and hills surrounding Oulton, and he had an urge to go up there.

He looked around to make sure no one was watching and then stepped into the tower. As he started to climb, the steps felt suffocating, winding in a tight spiral so that all Sheldon saw as he got higher was more stone, more steps, turning, getting narrower, so that he wondered whether he would reach nothing but a dead-end. But he was wrong. He burst gasping onto the roof, a small square hemmed in by the castellated ramparts of the tower. As Sheldon headed for the wall, he was breathing hard, the effort of the climb making his chest pump hard. Sweat flashed across his forehead, and as he pitched forward, the ground below swayed and blurred.

Sheldon looked forward instead and sucked in clean air as he let the horizon settle down. It was as he imagined. The roll of the hills on the other side of the valley, and the chimneys and terraced streets in the nearby towns. As he looked further, he could see how the green around him turned grey and ugly as the sprawl of Manchester took over.

He was cold. He was wearing just his suit, and although the sun was shining, the exposed tower chilled the wind, so that he folded his arms to try and keep warm. He felt his ribs under his fingers and wondered how they had got there. He knew he hadn't been eating that well, surviving on sandwiches and microwave meals, but he was surprised. But then as he thought about it, he couldn't remember his last meal.

Sheldon looked down at his shoes. They were worn and scuffed. He could feel the ground through his soles, cold against his feet.

How had he got to this? Pushed out of the station on forced leave. He had only tried to do what was right, to track down a killer. Why wasn't that enough?

The view held his attention for a few minutes, the rumbles of a diesel engine reaching him as a bus struggled up a hill. Cars threaded through the town. A train ran along the valley floor, Manchester-bound. The trains will keep running, the people will keep praying, and then his life would get lost in the fade of time, so that nothing about Alice Kenyon would matter anymore. Nothing about him would matter anymore.

Sheldon put his head back and looked up, let the blue sky swirl above him, the view broken only by the occasional wisps of cloud. There was nothing of his life up there, just infinite emptiness. None of the failures, or the obsessions. For a moment, he felt a tight grip around his throat as he realised how his life was turning out. There was no real way forward.

He stepped forward to the wall. He looked ahead and not down, just towards the roofs of distant buildings, and all he had to do was keep on walking. The stones scraped his hands as he lifted his foot and let it settle on the wall, and then the other one, so that he was crouching and the view below opened up in front of him.

The ground was just stone a hundred feet below. As he looked down, he thought he could hear voices telling him to jump, that the ground would end it and bring him peace. But the voices got louder. He looked round again. There was a woman behind him. She was young, with long red hair, her face kind but worried. She looked like Alice.

'Are you all right?' she said. She looked scared, a tremble to her voice. 'I saw you come up. I was at the back of the church.'

He didn't have the answer to that. He hadn't seen her. His eyes welled up with tears, or maybe it was just the sharp cut to the breeze.

'You shouldn't do what you're thinking of,' she said, her voice softer now. She brushed her hair away from her face, the wind sending it into a tangle. 'Things get better. They always do.'

He swallowed.

'Why should you care?' His words came out thick with emotion.

Her hand went to her mouth. She closed her eyes and took a deep breath, just to calm herself. When she opened them again, she said, 'I just don't want you to do it, not here, not in front of me. Just step down. Please. For me.'

Sheldon looked at her and the young woman reminded him not just of Alice, but also of Hannah, his daughter. He couldn't let her remember him like this. He wiped his eyes and took a step back so that he was off the wall, level with her again. He looked at the floor for a few seconds and clenched his fists, trying to hold back the tears. But he couldn't. They rolled down his face, his mouth quivering. He looked at her and said, 'Thank you.'

His pace was quick as he walked away. She was right. There was so much still to do. He looked back just once, and he saw her watching him leave, her arms folded around her chest.

Sheldon headed swiftly down the stone steps, and when he burst out of the stairway and into the open spaces of the church, it felt like he'd been given another chance.

He ran out of the church and looked towards the town. All he could see were the stone buildings and slate roofs, dark and moody, but they were just facades, because behind those buildings was the rest of the town, and somewhere in there was the killer of Billy Privett. And as Sheldon thought of Billy, he remembered Alice Kenyon – as if he could ever forget her. The thought of the empty days ahead scared him, but of course they didn't have to be empty. He could fill them. He could keep looking for Alice's killer. And Billy's.

As he crossed over the road, he walked with more purpose. He knew where he was going next.

Chapter Twenty-Six

Charlie went straight to his apartment, a long run from Amelia's house. He was sweating and feeling sick, but speed was more important than appearances. He needed to get in and out quickly without being noticed, knowing that he needed to do something with the knife. Perhaps return it to the knife block and then call the police – provided that the two clients in suits had gone. He knew that was the riskiest option.

He sank to his knees when he got into his apartment, panting hard from the run. All Charlie could hear was the peace and quiet of his home. The hum of his fridge. The sound of the television from the apartment below. He closed his eyes, just to take stock, but his head was filled with the image of Amelia once more. That told him that he had to keep moving.

He went towards the bathroom, but the sight of his living room made him pause when he went past. It was just as he had left it the previous morning, with beer bottles and an empty pizza box. There was just one boozy night between then and now but suddenly it seemed like a different life so that just worrying about some untidiness seemed like bliss.

He went to the bathroom and rinsed his hands and face, not sure what forensic traces he had picked up at Amelia's, like traces of her blood. He scrambled in the cabinet above the sink for a grooming kit that Julie had bought him a few months earlier, a hint that he had ignored. It had ended up at the back, pushed behind mouthwashes and razor packets. He pulled out the nailbrush and scrubbed his fingers under the hot tap, not sure what he needed to scrape away but feeling that it would be a good idea to do it.

When they were clean, he paused with his hands on the sink, his hair hanging down, sweat dripping onto the porcelain. Once more he thought of Amelia, but he willed himself through it. He didn't have time for that.

As he looked in the mirror and stroked at his beard, he knew he had to look more respectable, not like a drinker bogged down with worry. Those that look guilty are guilty, experience had taught him that. But guilty of what? That was the problem. He had no idea. He just knew that it would all look bad to an outsider. A shave was a gamble though, because for every second he spent in the bathroom, it was another second with Amelia's knife in the apartment.

As he held the razor, he thought of the people who might have seen him at Amelia's house. He needed to look different. It was worth the gamble.

His hand shook, and so he took a few deep breaths to steady the tremble, not wanting to give himself away with nicks and cuts. He watched in the mirror as haggard was slowly replaced by smooth, some remnants of his younger days creeping back as the grey-tinged whiskers ended up in the sink. He couldn't do anything about the graze though, and it just added to the redness in his cheeks. When he'd finished, he pulled on his other suit, still creased from the weekend, and went to the dishwasher, taking a step back as the steam assaulted him when he opened the door. The knife was there, hot and clean.

He picked it up using a paper towel and dropped it into a plastic bag. It was time to take it back. He paused for a moment, aware of the risk he was about to take, and had a last look around the apartment, wondering when he would return.

As he turned towards the door, Charlie glanced out of the window and down towards the street. He jumped back. The two men were there, getting out of a car, the same ones he had seen outside Amelia's house and at his office.

Why were they there? Who were they? Had someone spoken to them, one of Amelia's neighbours? Perhaps they had recognised his car. He had left it just a short distance along her street.

Charlie went behind the curtains and peered around the side. The two men were looking up towards the apartment. He hid behind the curtain again. It was no coincidence. It was time to go.

But where could he go? To the police? Of course not. It would be his last moment of freedom if he did, and he would never come out, protesting his innocence to the grave. He knew exactly how it looked. He could feel the weight of the knife in his hand. He felt a jolt as the words *murder weapon* came into his head for the first time, but he knew that he couldn't dwell on that. He would have time to mourn Amelia later, but if he didn't get moving he would have more mourning time than he needed, with just the four walls of a cell to distract him. His avenues of escape were narrowing.

Charlie's apartment was on the top floor of a four-storey block. He didn't want to take the lift, because there would be no escape if the door opened to them in the lobby; really just a corridor lined by mailboxes, accessed using a secure key.

He tucked the knife under his left armpit, the blade

pointing downwards, and fastened his suit jacket. He switched on the burglar alarm and then left the apartment. If they broke in, he would hear it go off, and then he would know how serious they were.

Charlie thought about his way out of the building. There was CCTV on the landings, fed through to the building manager, so he had to look normal. Charlie jammed his hands into his pockets so that his arm held the knife against his ribs. It looked like he wasn't carrying anything. He made a play of looking at the lift and then shaking his head, as if he didn't want to wait around. Every cell in his body screamed at him to run, to get out of there as quickly as possible, but he had to think of the longer view, of how the footage would look in front of a jury. All it would show so far was a man deciding that the stairs, rather than the lift, were the best route. He did his best to make his walk look natural, almost a saunter, and he just hoped that the camera didn't pick up the sweat on his forehead, or the nervous way he licked at his lips.

He got to the stairs and pushed open the door. He pushed himself against the wall and waited, so that he could make sure they were on his floor before he set off down.

It seemed like an age. The knife was sticking into his side, and he was worried that it would prick the skin too much and just add more of his DNA to its tip. But still he waited, trying to keep his breathing silent. He felt the sting of sweat as it trickled into his eyes. Then he heard the noise of the lift as it went upwards, and voices in the hallway.

Charlie set off down the stairs, trying to keep his footsteps light but moving quickly. There was a knock on his door, and then a pause, before he heard loud bangs and shouts, closely followed by the shriek of his burglar alarm.

It was no courtesy visit.

He bolted down the stairs, not worrying about the noise. It was just about getting out. He was holding the knife in one hand now, still wrapped in the bag, the stair rail sliding through his other hand, his footsteps in time with the fast pant of his breaths all the way to the ground floor.

There was no pretence anymore. The door to the street was made out of glass and Charlie could see the way ahead was clear. He ran at it, feeling it thump against the flat of his hand, and then he was outside, running.

He got some looks as he ran for the pavement, but that wasn't his concern. He had to get away. He slowed to a fast walk, his chest tight, his heart hammering, ignoring those who gave him strange looks, sweat pouring down his face.

Just as Charlie got to the end of the street, he looked back towards his apartment. There was someone on his balcony, looking out. It was the first man in the suit, and before he turned away, Charlie was sure that the person looked right at him, their eyes connecting even over that distance.

He had to keep moving.

Chapter Twenty-Seven

Henry clapped his hands and everyone turned to look. He had been talking to Arni in angry whispers, whilst the rest of the group were discussing how things were changing. The wire mesh. The visitors to the house. They seemed almost palpably nervous. Fingers were chewed, eyes wary.

Henry held out his hands. 'I need to go out, to see if the authorities are watching us,' he said, his voice low. 'I'm going to make myself visible, just to see if I'm followed. The rest of you, prepare up here, be ready, in case I don't come back.'

'I'm scared, Henry,' a woman said. It was Jennifer Elam, the older woman.

'Just hold your nerve,' Henry said. He closed his eyes for a moment and his fingers pinched the bridge of his nose. 'Just believe in what we are doing.' His voice was almost a whisper now. His hand gripped his shirt and he opened his eyes. 'Feel it. We have something special in this group, and you have made me realise who I am. What I am. Rely on that to get you through, because, all I am doing is thinking of us, of what I can do for the group. People will talk about us in years to come, of how we fought back.'

Henry looked slowly around the group, taking in each one of them. 'We need more help though, because we have to fight them in their world. Their shallow, pitiful, material world.' He pointed to John. 'Do you feel the freedom now?'

'I do.'

'How does it feel?'

John smiled. 'Like whoever doesn't have what we have is somehow empty.'

Henry's grin spread slowly. 'That's right. They are just magpies. They get excited by shiny things, or they worship false faiths like some fad. We are the future, our movement, and so give up everything you own, John. Whatever property you have, or savings, they just tie you to your past life. Donate it to me, for the group.'

John nodded, encouraged. 'That will feel good,' he said, but then he took a deep breath. 'But there are some things I still find difficult.'

'What do you mean?'

'Well, Gemma,' and he looked towards her. 'You say we shouldn't feel bonds, that we should be free to share, but I feel like we have a connection, and I know she feels it too.' Gemma blushed. 'I don't want to share her, but you say that I should, and I don't know how I feel about that.'

Henry glowered for a few seconds, and no one seemed to be breathing, waiting for his response. When he did speak, his voice was quiet, measured. 'We do not have possessions in this group. Everything belongs to the group. Even Gemma.'

'But you make her sound like a thing, not a person.'

Henry's jaw clenched. 'What do you want? Marriage? The union of one man and one woman? One more contract with the State?' He shook his head. 'You think Gemma is special, but you want to deprive the rest of us of that special thing. You want to keep it all for yourself. That isn't thinking of the group. I chose her for you, John, because I knew you would like her. You cannot just throw it back in my face and say that you want her all for yourself?'

'No, it isn't like that.'

'So what is it like?'

John looked at Gemma, who was staring at her lap. Her cheeks were red, and John couldn't work out if she was embarrassed or angry. 'I just like her, that's all,' he said.

Henry paused for a moment, and then he smiled. 'You are allowed to like her. We all like her.'

John nodded. 'All right, I'm sorry.'

Henry stepped off his stool and approached John. 'Are you sure you believe in me? In us, as free men?'

'I believe, Henry, but how will we know when we've won the fight?'

'Because there will be no rules, no possessions, no restrictions. We will take back what has been stolen. People lost their homes because the banks got greedy. There are empty houses but people live on the streets. None of this is right, and so anyone who isn't with us is our enemy, you understand that?'

John nodded.

Henry grinned. He pointed at Lucy, and Arni, and David, the youngest male, skinny and twitchy. As they got to their feet, Henry ran out of the room, pausing only to collect some boots.

'How long do we wait?' John shouted, as he followed them outside.

Henry paused, and then turned back towards the house. 'Until we come back. Don't leave. If anyone else tries to come, don't let them in.' He pointed to the grilles. 'The house is more secure, but stock it so we can defend it. Food. Oil. Wood. We might have to barricade ourselves in. Remember Waco, how the police underestimated them?'

'Everyone died in the end.'

'There is always a price to pay,' Henry said.

'But what about what we talked about earlier?'

Henry looked angry for a moment, but then he raised his fingers to his lips. 'Remember what I said. There are things I've got to attend to first, because events might derail us.' Then he ran to his van along with the others, laughing excitedly. There were knives in their pockets; John could see the glint of shiny metal where they jutted out.

He watched as the engine started and then they set off towards Oulton, bumping along the farm track, throwing up dirt in a cloud.

John closed his eyes for a moment as the van's engine faded into the valley, and he was left with just the breeze in the trees and birdsong. Images from his past life came at him. Work. Family. Money. But it had been empty, he felt that now, as if his own life had been working towards this, and it felt like a rush, a surge of adrenaline, that feeling of belonging, of purpose.

He heard soft footsteps behind him, just light crunches in the dirt, and then arms encircled him gently, a head resting on his back.

It was Gemma, and so he turned around and took her face in his hands. She looked up at him, and for a moment he saw some doubt, fear flashing across her eyes.

'Things are changing,' she said.

John thought about what Henry had asked him to do. He kissed her on the forehead. 'Yes, changing, but moving forward,' he said.

'But I'm scared.'

He closed his eyes so that she wouldn't see the lie in them. 'We've nothing to fear,' he said. 'Nothing to fear at all.'

Chapter Twenty-Eight

Sheldon came to a stop outside Ted Kenyon's house. He'd collected his car from the station car park, and had driven straight to Ted's house again. Except this time he was off-duty, officially.

There wasn't much movement inside. He stepped out of his car, the clunk of the car door loud in the street, and then walked slowly to the door. He let the gate clink shut behind him and as he paused, he went to straighten his cuffs. Then he stopped himself. The cuff edges on his shirt were threadbare, with threads of loose cotton trailing over his wrists, and the sleeves on his suit jacket were shiny with wear.

It was too late to turn back though, because Ted was in the window, watching as Sheldon walked up the path. Ted was at the door by the time Sheldon reached it.

'Here again?' Ted said, but still he stepped aside to let Sheldon in.

'Mr Kenyon.'

Sheldon went through to the living room, where he had been before so many times, the scene of terse exchanges, although this was the first time that he could call his visit unofficial. He sat down without waiting to be asked.

'What can I do for you, Inspector? Another search? An arrest this time?'

'It's not inspector,' Sheldon said. When Ted looked confused, he added, 'I'm on leave, just so that I can sort some things out. I'm here in my personal capacity.'

'Personal?'

Sheldon nodded. 'As someone who cares about what happened to Alice.'

Ted sat down. He looked at the floor for a few seconds, his lips pursed, before he spoke. When he did, his voice was quiet. 'I never doubted that you cared,' he said. 'It was whether you had done enough.'

Sheldon's hands trembled, and so he gripped one set of fingers with the other. 'I did everything I thought I could, and more. If it wasn't enough, and it was down to me, then all I can say is that I'm sorry for not catching Alice's killer.'

'And now Billy is dead.'

'Yes. Now Billy.'

'So, you're done,' Ted said. 'You've said your piece, and so you can go back to whatever you want to go back to with a clean conscience.'

Sheldon shook his head. 'It's not that.'

Ted considered him for a few moments before he said, 'Go on.'

'I want to help you find out what happened to Alice.'

'You've been trying for long enough. What makes you think you can do anything now?'

'I might know things that you don't, and I can guess that you know things I don't. If we work together, perhaps we can get somewhere.'

Ted tapped his fingers on the chair arm and stared silently at Sheldon for a few seconds, until he said, 'Do you think Alice's killer is lying in that mortuary?'

Sheldon thought about that. There were only three outcomes; that Billy had known who had killed Alice, that he hadn't known, or that he had been Alice's murderer. Sheldon still didn't know which one was the truth. 'It's possible.'

Ted shook his head. 'I don't think so.'

'I don't understand.'

'Billy Privett did not kill my daughter.'

'How do you know?'

'Because I could do one thing you couldn't do, and that was speak to him as another human being. You represented something that could lock him away, the police, and you were prepared to try. I was just a grieving father. He could be more honest with me.'

Sheldon was surprised. 'When did you speak to him?'

'Just before the anniversary of Alice's death. I went to his house. He let me in, which surprised me. He didn't say anything at first. He took me to the pool room and mumbled something about leaving me for a few moments.'

'And did he?'

Ted nodded. 'He was respectful, until I came out of there and asked him to tell me what he knew. No, not asked. I begged him. I cried, pulled on his clothes, lost every shred of dignity I had left.'

'And what did Billy do?'

'Nothing, except that he looked like he wanted to tell me, but something was stopping him.'

'How do you know it wasn't just guilt at something he'd done?'

'Oh, there was guilt, but there was something else too; fear. He knew damn well who killed my daughter. He was just too scared to tell anyone.'

Sheldon was about to say something, but Ted held up his hand. 'You don't need to tell me that he was just scared of getting caught. I've gone through every possibility in my head, but each time I come back to what I thought when he looked at me, and it was a certainty that he was scared of telling me.'

'But yesterday you were angry at what his lawyer said to the camera, that he died an innocent man,' Sheldon said.

'Just because he didn't kill Alice doesn't mean that he's innocent. He was a coward, and I can't forgive him for that.' Ted rose up out of his chair. 'Follow me,' he said, and went towards the stairs. Sheldon went after him, not sure what to expect.

Ted was quiet as he climbed the stairs. Sheldon kept a respectable distance as Ted headed straight for the room that he and Tracey had avoided: Alice's old room. Ted undid the bolt at the top of the door and pushed it open gently, stepping aside to allow Sheldon to enter.

It was a square room, with fitted cupboards at one end and a single bed below them. There was a corkboard of photographs; teenagers having fun, family pets, some people holding beer bottles. The room was clean, and Sheldon could tell that it was cleaned often. There was a picture on the side, in front of a switched-off clock radio. He didn't need to get too close to know that it was Alice, and that it was the one item that had been added after she'd died. Her head was cocked, smiling, the sunlight shining through her hair like a halo. Sheldon imagined Ted and Emily sitting on the bed, clutching her photograph in the room that Alice had grown up in, from a toddler full of promise to a party-loving student, all of it snatched away by one night at Billy Privett's house.

Sheldon thought that he had been brought to the room to be reminded of Alice, but he didn't need to be reminded, because he thought of her every day. Then Ted opened one of the cupboards and Sheldon saw folders lined up, each with a title marked out in bold red on the spine. *Friends. Parties. Neighbours.*

'These are all the notes I've made from the people I've spoken to,' Ted said, and then he gave a bitter laugh. 'At least, those who would speak to me.'

Sheldon went towards them and ran his fingers down one of the spines. His fingernails looked long and dirty.

'Can I look?' he said.

'I'll bring them downstairs,' Ted said. 'But first you eat.'

Sheldon was confused. 'I don't understand.'

'Inspector . . .'

'Sheldon.'

'Sorry, Sheldon. You don't look well. You look tired and hungry.' He pointed out of the room. 'Have a bath, relax for a few minutes. I'll find you some clothes. I think I've got some that will fit. I'll make you some food. Then we'll talk.'

Sheldon felt tears jump into his eyes, and his mind went back to the moment on the church tower, to how that young woman had saved him. He knew Ted was right.

'I don't think I've been dealing with it very well,' Sheldon said.

'No need to explain.'

Sheldon smiled his gratitude, but the choke of his emotions caught in his throat stopped him from speaking.

Chapter Twenty-Nine

Charlie knew he had to get rid of the knife first, and so he turned towards Amelia's house, wanting to put the knife back in the block. Then he would call the police, tell them what he had found, and all about the two men in suits.

He followed the same route back, ducking down back alleys, dodging round the discarded boxes and junk and dogshit, the knife inside his jacket. He was able to circle the town centre without venturing onto the street, his eyes always looking out for an unlocked gate so that he could hide out of view if a police car passed the end of the alley. He emerged onto the main road further down the hill from the town centre, with Amelia's house on the other side. He wanted to walk there casually, so that he wouldn't seem suspicious, but just as he was about to cross the road, there were police cars bunched up ahead, blocking off the road near Amelia's.

Charlie jumped back into the alley, the knife digging into his side. Someone had found her; the news was out.

He turned to retrace his steps, not taking as much care, just wanting to get away from where the police were. He jogged along the alleys that ran behind the terraced streets, short parallel strips that stacked up the hills. His apartment was somewhere to avoid as the two men would still be there, but he knew he had to get rid of the knife before anything.

Then Charlie remembered a quarry, now filled with water, a favourite for the local kids whenever the sun came out. If he followed the line of the houses, he would get to it. So he moved quickly, one arm clenching his side to keep the knife lodged there.

A shale path went towards a bramble-covered waste ground and then curved downwards to the lip of the quarry. He checked around, even though he knew it made him look more suspicious, but he couldn't stop himself. Charlie wanted to know who might have seen him, so he would know who might one day give evidence against him. He had never been in this position before, so he didn't know the rules.

The quarry appeared as a cliff behind some wooden fencing twenty feet above the water. Charlie peered over. The surface was deep blue and still.

He took the knife out of the bag and looked at it one last time. The sun caught the blade and sent flashes of light to his eyes. He thought of Amelia again, of what harm the knife had done to her, and then took another look around, to make sure that no one was watching. It was quiet, just a brief moment of calm in a day that had so quickly turned his life the wrong way. Then he shook his head, suddenly angry with himself. What about poor Amelia? What had she suffered before she died?

As Charlie held his hand out over the wooden fence, towards the quarry edge, he paused. What he was doing was wrong. He was disposing of a murder weapon. Then he remembered how the evidence looked stacked against him, and so he had to act.

It didn't take much more than a flick of his wrist and then the knife was tumbling in the air, bright silver flashes as it arced downwards. And then it was out of sight. Charlie didn't even hear a splash.

Now he just had to work out what had happened.

Images of Amelia kept on coming back to him, and not just her body in her house. Her smile, or the elegant sweep as she came into the office most mornings, tossing her black hair and putting her sunglasses onto her head. They hadn't been close, but there had been a bond, he realised that now, and suddenly he felt lost.

But he shouldn't think like that. Sadness over Amelia was no good now. Or was it just self-pity? Whichever it was, it was draining, self-destructive. Everything had changed so quickly, the length of time it took for him to take in what had happened to Amelia. And now there were men in suits looking for him, ones he had seen coming out of the office the day before. The murder weapon had been next to him as he woke.

Charlie thought briefly about the possible explanations, like a jealous boyfriend or disgruntled client, but he came back to one obvious answer: Billy Privett, because Billy was Amelia's client. But where did Charlie fit into it all? He had nothing to do with Amelia's death, he knew that. He wasn't a murderer, it wasn't in him. If something had happened, he would have remembered it, he was sure of it.

Then the other reality hit home, that if someone else had killed Amelia, they had tried to frame him, and had planted the knife on him. What was the reason for that?

Charlie tried to think that one through, wanting it clear in his head before he went back into Oulton, so that he would have a plan. He didn't dare go to the police, because if someone could plant a knife, what else could they do?

Whoever had put the knife there hadn't expected him to be in the office, because he hadn't planned to sleep there. So they must have gone to the office for a different reason. And the answer was so obvious; the Billy Privett file. He remembered the burglary. Amelia's room had been the target, not his, and nothing was taken. That was the night Billy was killed, and the file was the one thing that Amelia had that connected her to his murder. It told Billy's story. So Amelia must have given up the secrets, Charlie thought, or else why was he still alive?

Charlie got the shivers as snippets of memory came back, snapshots from the night before. He was with Ted, in the pub, The Old Star, but when he left for home, he went for a walk. He had stumbled and fallen into a wall, which must have been how he got the graze on his cheek and on his hand. He remembered people laughing at him, and someone used his name. Then he was in the office, rummaging around Amelia's room.

He put his hands to his face. There was a hazy recollection now of finding Billy's file and looking through it, trying to find some snippet to help Ted Kenyon, because in his drunken haze, it had seemed like such a good idea. When he was drunk, he was everyone's friend. But like all drunken thoughts, such as late night calls made to his ex-girlfriend, it was only ever going to be a bad idea. What had he wanted to do; turn up at Ted's house, staggering, holding out the file, hoping to be invited in as his saviour, giving him the details of how his daughter died? Not very heroic, when viewed in the harsh glare of sobriety.

So he had been reading the file, but because he was away from the pub and the alcohol had stopped flowing, he'd fallen asleep. So he ended up on the floor, and someone came looking for the file, and then the knife had been planted.

Why hadn't he been killed too? Was he nothing more than a deflection?

Charlie pulled out his phone and called the office. If the police were there, he wondered whether it would be answered.

It rang out a few times, and then a voice came on, meek and nervous. It was Donia.

'Don't react,' Charlie said, talking low so that no one passing by could hear him. 'If the police are there, just say that Charlie isn't in the office at the moment.'

There was a pause, and then she repeated what he had told her, that Charlie wasn't in the office.

So the police were there already. They had moved fast, had obviously found the body, although he realised that the link with Billy Privett sent the investigation straight there.

'I was reading Billy Privett's file last night,' he said. 'I need to know if it was taken.'

'I don't know if I can help you,' she said, her voice quiet.

'I need to know about the file, Donia. Is Linda talking to the police?'

'Yes,' she said, her voice a whisper.

'Can you go into my room for me? It will be on the desk, or perhaps on the floor.'

Another pause, and then, 'What do I do?'

He tried to picture the scene, the police everywhere, but he knew they wouldn't be able to take all the files. They would want Billy's though.

'Just find it,' he said, some desperation creeping into his voice. He knew what he was going to ask her to do, and it was wrong. Donia was just a kid, a wannabe lawyer looking for some work experience, but he couldn't think about that. 'Try on the floor in my room, near to my desk. If it's there, just put other files on top of it, and my dictation machine. They won't expect it to be there. Bluff it, say that it's my typing pile.'

There was a pause, and then the phone went quiet. She had hung up.

Fuck!

Charlie paced up and down and gripped his phone, almost threw it into the quarry. He would have to go to the office for the file, if he was going to get it at all. But what alternatives were there? He could just come out of hiding, blame it all on a bad hangover and invite them to prove something against him. But that was too risky, and he wasn't ready for a prison cell. No, he had to see what was in the file, if it was still there.

Then his phone buzzed in his hand. He looked at the screen. A text.

Got file. Im in weekly rental flat. Marshall Ave. 66. Fl 6. Go there. Donia.

Charlie looked at the screen, unsure what to make of it. It could be a trap. He didn't know Donia's number, so how did she know his? The police might be behind it.

He knew one thing though; he had few options.

He texted her back. *OK.* Then he turned away from the quarry edge and started jogging towards the town.

Chapter Thirty

Sheldon came down the stairs, rubbing his hair dry with a towel, dressed in Ted's old clothes; jeans that hung low on his hips and a shirt that revealed the bones in his shoulders. They showed how much weight he had lost, but at least they were clean. As he walked along the hall, Ted was standing in front of a microwave oven, and as he got closer, the smell of curry drifted towards him.

'Emily has gone away to her sister's,' Ted said. 'This is the best I could do at short notice. Jake hasn't got beyond the microwave with his cooking skills, but I found this in the fridge. Chicken Madras.'

Sheldon smiled. 'That's perfect,' he said. 'Did I have anything to do with Emily going?'

'Yes, you did,' he said, a scowl appearing for a moment. 'She was expecting more visits from you and couldn't stand the thought of me being locked up.' He sighed. 'It was more than that though.'

'What do you mean?'

'You remember the girl in the car? Well, she believed me about that, or at least she said she did, but there is that small part of her that doubts me, because it sounds implausible, doesn't it? It sounds like bullshit, but I can't change what happened, and Emily knows that since Alice died, well, we've been pretty quiet in the bedroom.'

'I don't need to know this,' Sheldon said.

'I know that, but who do I have to talk to?' Ted said. There was some desperation in his voice, as if he needed to explain himself, his words coming out quickly. 'Alice being killed affected both of us badly. I dealt with it by becoming more vocal about it, but Emily just retreated. She spends hours in Alice's room, just lying on her bed, hoping that one day Alice will walk back in. I can't blame her for not being interested in sex anymore. Hell, I don't think I'm too bothered. It just wouldn't seem right to be so carefree, as if we had forgotten about her already. But Emily thinks I'm lying, just to be kind, because I'm a man, and we have urges, right? So there is a small part of Emily that wonders if I was with that girl, because I just needed something, like some closeness, or even just a release. And so I could see it in her eyes, that if I lied about that, perhaps I lied about Billy Privett, and that I did kill him.'

'So Emily thinks you killed Billy?'

Ted shook his head. 'No, she doesn't, because she knows me, but there is a small part of her that is not prepared to rule it out, like with the girl.'

'I'm sorry if I made it worse,' Sheldon said. 'I just haven't been myself lately.'

'No need,' Ted said, and pointed Sheldon through to the dining room, next to the kitchen and separated from the living room by wooden double doors. There was a conservatory behind, filled with cane furniture and potted plants. In the dining room, there was a large mahogany cabinet with glass shelving units. On top there was a framed photograph of the Kenyon family, showing Ted and Emily sitting at the table, beaming proudly with their children behind them, Alice's arms wrapped around Ted's neck, and Jake's around his mother's.

Ted brought the curry through, and saw Sheldon looking at the photograph.

'That's the last picture of us together,' Ted said. 'I didn't donate it to the police for a press release because it would taint it. It would be the picture they splashed on the news when they talked about her. I wanted to remember the afternoon as it was, everyone happy. Alice died the weekend after.'

Sheldon felt a wave of sadness as he thought of his own family. It was still intact then, or at least he thought it was. As he thought more about it though, perhaps it wasn't. He couldn't remember a family photograph as happy as that, not since Hannah was a small girl, when all he had to do was be there.

Sheldon turned away from the photograph and thanked Ted for the food. As he sat down to eat it, he became ravenous and realised how much he had neglected himself. Ted watched him eat for a while and then said, 'If we are sharing information, you tell me: what suspects did you have?'

Sheldon paused as he thought of it. 'None, other than Billy. We knew who some of his friends were, because we had been up there enough times over party noise before Alice died, but everyone had an alibi that they could prove. And anyway, we believed them, because they all said the same thing, that Billy hadn't invited them up for a few weeks. It was as if he had got himself new friends.'

'And you couldn't find out who they were?'

Sheldon shook his head. 'There was blood at the scene, but we don't know whose. Did you find anything out?'

Ted shook his head. 'I thought people were embarrassed at first, about what had gone on up at Billy's house, because his money loosened clothes and no one would tell me too much. Except that Billy had new friends, but no one knew who they were. Some people had gone up and Billy wouldn't let them in, and on the drive were old vans, and there were Goth-type kids, all in black, different to Billy's usual crowd. Billy's old friends were from the estate, people with no money helping Billy to spend his.'

Sheldon stopped eating for a moment and said, 'Do you have any suspicions?'

'Drugs,' Ted said. 'People told me that there were always a lot of drugs at the house, but they thought Billy was running out of money. He used to buy cars just so they could race them on the field behind his house, but for the few months before Alice's death all he had done was repair the old ones. And he was starting to buy dodgy vodka, and was selling the drugs, cocaine and cannabis mainly, not giving it away. That's why people weren't as bothered about missing out on the parties. Too many people had watched their boyfriends or girlfriends sleep with other people, just because the mood was right, but if they were going to have to pay for it, what's the point, right? Billy thought he was Mister Popular, but he wasn't. He was just the mug willing to spend his money.'

'So why drugs?'

'Because he must have been in debt to dealers if he was stocking up so much but running out of money. It would explain why he was so scared to say anything. I think he got a visit from someone big, and things got out of hand. Alice was a good girl, but she would speak her mind, and so I wonder whether she had said the wrong thing, tried to show that she couldn't be bullied. But she wouldn't know what those people were like, and so things just got nasty.'

Sheldon nodded as he ate his curry. 'That makes a lot of sense. He was still taking drugs before he died, because we found a dealer list in his house, but his silence might have extended his credit line. We looked at the drugs angle, but there was no intelligence about where he was getting his drugs. Because of the quantities, we thought that he had gone higher up the chain, to the wholesaler, not the street dealer, and they are harder to track. We always know the street dealers, because your bottom-rung junkies will tell you anything to keep on your good side, just to make sure they always get bail, or so we won't bust their door down. The higher up you go, the more it becomes about money, and so people stay quiet. No one knew where Billy was getting his drugs from.'

Ted sighed. 'So we both came up with nothing except theories.'

Sheldon nodded. 'It seems that way.'

Ted stayed silent as Sheldon finished his food, until the chirp of Sheldon's phone disturbed the peace.

Sheldon reached into his pocket and saw that it was a number he didn't recognise. He clicked the answer button.

'Hello?'

'DI Brown?' It was a man's voice.

'Yes.' There was no need to correct him.

'I'm PC Ellis. I work in Southern Division. I saw the email that was sent round earlier, with the young woman's photograph. Your number was on it.'

Sheldon looked at Ted, who was sitting up straight, watching him. 'Go on.'

'I know her,' Ellis continued. 'There is a care home here, New Pastures. It keeps most of us busy. I recognised the girl in the photograph, although it threw me, because she isn't called Christina. It's Lucy, Lucy Crane.'

'Any form?'

'Not much, but she was a constant misper, always turning

up in the houses of the local pervs, her pockets filled with fags and stinking of booze. I don't what happened to her because I got posted elsewhere, but it looks like her.'

'How sure are you?'

'Pretty sure.'

'Thank you, PC Ellis,' Sheldon said. Keep this conversation to yourself for the moment.'

'No problem, sir. Glad to help.'

When Sheldon clicked off, he got to his feet. Ted looked at him curiously, and then scrambled to follow him when Sheldon said, 'I think we've got something.

Chapter Thirty-One

Charlie walked quickly away from the quarry, heading straight to Donia's flat in the town centre where she had the Billy Privett file.

Marshall Avenue was one of the main roads out of Oulton, down a hill and lined by trees, an attempt to create some suburbia amongst the industrial units and workers' cottages. Charlie didn't look up as he went past dusty shop fronts and neglected pubs. He straightened his clothes so that people wouldn't recall the dishevelled man in the suit, because the best chance he had was to blend into the background.

He kept on looking round as he walked, always ready for the shout of the police, wary in case it was a trap. He turned quickly onto Marshall Avenue and saw how it stretched downwards, grass verges bordering the road, the trees forming a canopy so that it was all in shadow. Number sixty-six was a double-fronted building in pale glazed bricks, with yellowing net curtains in every window. He had another quick look around, to check for dark uniforms hidden behind lampposts, but then realised that he must have watched too many films. He had no weapons, and was just some scruffy lawyer heading too quickly for his fortieth birthday. They could approach him at a saunter and he would have little chance of getting away.

He pushed at the door and it opened into a communal hallway. It was all shades of brown, with plywood-finish doors and a number 1 in fake marble pinned to the first one. The stairs were narrow and dark, but it was the only way forward.

There was a television playing in one of the flats, and as he climbed, the landings just got darker. The switch for the lights was a push-button timer that slowly released itself, but it didn't give him enough time to get upstairs. By the time he got to the top floor, flat number six, he had to feel his way along, the number visible only in silhouette against the faint light that came through a glass door. There were small steps on the other side, and so he guessed that it was the loft flat.

Charlie knocked at the door, but there was no answer. All he could do was wait.

His phone rang. He checked the screen. It was Julie, his ex. When he pressed the answer, he let Julie speak first.

'Charlie, it's me. I've heard about Amelia. We need to talk to you about what happened.'

Charlie thought about whether to answer, but the urge to know what was being said was too strong. 'What's the word? Why do you want to speak to me?'

'I can't tell you that. You know how it is.' There was a pause, and then, 'You need to come in, Charlie.'

'What, to the station?'

'Yes. They need to talk to you.'

Charlie closed his eyes for a moment. It felt like everyone was closing in on him.

'No, I can't,' he said, and then he clicked off his phone.

More than an hour passed before he heard footsteps. He had spent that time with his head in his hands, expecting the sound of the police rushing the stairs, but it had stayed quiet. So he had gone over Amelia's death in his head, trying to make some sense of it all. But he couldn't, however much he tried, because he didn't know what was behind it, other than it somehow involved Billy Privett.

He heard footsteps, and tensed up, waiting for the glimpse of a uniform, but he knew it was Donia before he saw her. The footsteps weren't heavy enough to be the police. When she rounded the corner, she smiled and held out her shoulder bag. It looked heavy.

'I got it,' she said.

'Let's get inside,' Charlie said, nodding gratefully but not up to returning the smile.

Donia's apartment was dark and smelled fusty and damp, or perhaps it was just old cigarettes. There were two bedrooms, but there was a bunk bed in the hallway as well, and so he guessed that in the summer it was all about cramming them in, living off the hill walkers. The carpet was rough carpet tiles, cigarette burns in some, and as he turned into the living room, he saw that it was just a collection of chairs with wooden arms facing a small television, heat provided by a three-bar electric fire topped by plastic coals.

'Is this low rent, or some kind of retro trendy thing I don't quite get?' Charlie said, in an effort to appear normal.

Donia laughed and put her bag down on one of the chairs. 'It was cheap and not far from your office. I'm thinking of spending the summer here, if things work out.' Then she blushed and became apologetic. 'I'm sorry. I wanted to spend the summer working for you, but things have changed, I know, with what happened to Amelia.' She paused, and then asked, 'What happened to her?'

Charlie sat down opposite her and closed his eyes. He put

his head back against the wall. 'Make me a drink and we'll talk about it,' he said. 'It's been one hell of a day.'

He listened as Donia bustled around in the kitchen, and not long after he opened his eyes to see her holding out a mug of coffee and what looked like a cheese sandwich.

'You look hungry,' she said.

He was, although he'd hoped the drink was going to be colder and stronger. He thanked her anyway. She watched him eat, her head in her hand as she sat at a table by the window, a white placemat and a vase of plastic flowers adding some fake grandeur to the scuffed surface.

When he put the plate down and drank some of the coffee, she said, 'The police wouldn't tell us what happened to Amelia.'

'How was Linda?'

'Upset, and she didn't know what to do, because you weren't there. She let the police look round the office. Was that all right?'

'Yes, fine,' Charlie said. 'Did they take anything away?'

Donia shook her head. 'Linda printed Amelia's appointment list and client list for them, but that was it. They said she had been killed, and that they needed to speak to you, but didn't say why.'

'How long were they there for?'

'Not long.' Donia took a drink of her own coffee and then said, 'Those people were hanging round outside the office again.'

'Which people?'

'Those people all in black. You spoke to them yesterday.'

Charlie felt uneasy. 'What were they doing?'

'Just waiting around.'

'Did they follow you?'

'I don't think so.' Donia looked worried. 'What, do you think they might have done?'

'Check out of the window. If they have, it will be me they are interested in, not you.'

Donia went past him and pulled the curtain to one side. She peered out of the window and then shook her head. 'I can't see them.' When she turned back to Charlie, she said, 'Why are you running?'

Charlie sighed. He knew that if there was enough planted evidence to put him in a dock, the fact that he ran would be the first thing in the minds of the jury.

'Because I want to try and find out what happened,' he said. 'I'm worried that if the police think I did it, they'll stop me.'

'Why would they think you did it?'

Charlie didn't want to answer that, because it would mean disclosing the knife. 'Do you think I might have done it?' he said instead.

'I don't really know you,' she said, her teeth chewing at her lip.

'So if you're not ruling it out, why have you let me in?'

She shrugged but didn't answer.

He put his cup down. 'I need a proper drink. Have you got anything?'

Donia shook her head. 'I don't drink much.'

'Sensible.'

'You drink too much.'

'Depends on the reason. If I'm drinking so that I don't have to face up to my life, I'm not drinking enough.'

'Is your life that bad? It looks good to me.'

'Go on, make it better for me. Why is it good?'

'You live in a nice place. It's got countryside, views, fresh air, and you can walk everywhere. You've got an interesting job, and you're healthy. My mum once wanted a career like yours. You should be grateful for what you've got.'

Charlie gave a small laugh, but it was bitter. 'Thank you for the life-coaching. I'll tell you about this town; it is stagnant. No, it's more than that. It's dying. Everyone is waiting for it to be rescued as a Manchester commuter town, but there isn't enough charm to make it work, and it is too bleak in winter. Pound shops, they're the only things that work, and don't start me on my job.'

'I want your job,' she said.

'Good. You can buy me out when you qualify, because I'm sick of it.'

'You don't mean that.'

'Don't I? What is there to like? At the beck and call of people who think I'm their friend because I speak up for them in court, but I have to say things I don't believe, about how prison won't work and bullshit like that. Because prison isn't good, I know that, but at least it gives everyone a break from them. So my whole life is a fake, because people who don't deserve my help spend their lives making other people miserable, and it's all about them when they get caught, bleating self-pity. So you want to be a lawyer? Well, don't, because you'll never get to do what you want to do, just what other people want you to do.'

Donia raised her eyebrows and then started to laugh.

'What's funny?'

'I've never seen anyone so wound up,' she said.

She had an infectious smile, her teeth bright against her skin, but Charlie couldn't muster a smile.

'Okay, maybe I've just having a bad day,' he said. 'No, more than that. I'm having a stinker of a day, the worst fucking day I have had for a long time. I've got a hangover, and now my business partner is dead, perhaps because of a file I've now got,' and he nodded towards Donia's bag. 'So let me have a look.'

'Can I help you?'

'You're here for work experience.'

She pulled the file out of the bag, resting it on the table with a thump. 'Just let me get changed out of these clothes,' she said, and then she went out of the room.

Charlie watched her go and shook his head. She was young and pretty and she wanted to spend some time with him. Then as he went towards the table, he caught his reflection in a mirror. His cheeks were flushed and his hair was grey and messy, his graze darkening. His eyes looked tired, as did his skin, and he knew then why Donia was relaxed around him. To her, he was middle-aged. He was safe, not a sexual threat. Good old Uncle Charlie.

His smile faded, and instead he sat at the table and opened the file.

It wasn't the usual sort of file for criminal clients. They have separate inserts for the different things that make up a file. The legal aid forms. The prosecution statements. Defence witness statements and the typed-up version of the defendant's bullshit, something for him to rehearse for his trial. All the correspondence on a clip. But Billy's case never got as far as the court, and so it didn't have all that clutter. Instead, there were just the sheets from the police station, with Billy's details and a summary of what he had told Amelia, along with a deep pile of correspondence and attendance notes. There was a separate insert for press cuttings.

Charlie's fingers trembled as he put the police station forms on the table, along with the correspondence. Was he going to find something out that should stay secret, or might even suggest that Amelia had been less than frank with the police and courts? It wouldn't bother her now, but he didn't want her name dragged through the press. At least let her name retain the dignity that her death had taken away.

Donia came back into the room, pulling on a baggy grey jumper over loose jeans.

'You've started without me,' she said.

'You haven't missed anything,' Charlie replied flatly.

As he pulled the contents of the file out onto the table, he knew that the next hour could change his life.

Chapter Thirty-Two

John scoured the barn with Gemma, looking for ways to make the house more secure.

Gemma kicked a roll of barbed wire. 'Can we use this?'

He nodded. 'We can wrap it round the grilles, or nail it to the window frames on the inside.'

'What are we defending against?'

John licked his lips nervously, not knowing how much Gemma knew. 'The authorities don't like what we do,' he said. 'Henry is worried that they'll do a raid. We've got cannabis here, remember, growing in one of the barns.'

'But we can't stop that with wire and mesh on the windows.'

'I know, but it will slow them down and give us more time.'

'For what?'

'Just to defend ourselves. Or even get away, if we can hold off until nightfall.'

Gemma didn't look satisfied by that. 'Do you think Henry wants us to be martyrs or something?'

'I don't know,' John said, not meeting her gaze, 'but if we are going to change anything, we have to be prepared for that. It might just be prison, and that will be easy. We'll be out in less than half, and we'll be heroes, because we'll have made a stand. We're fighting back, but we must be ready for it.'

'It won't be prison,' Gemma said.

'How do you mean?'

She rolled her eyes. 'Because we don't recognise their courts, silly. Don't you remember what Henry said, that their laws only bind us if we agree to it? That's why we are free.'

He nodded. 'Yes, I'm sorry. Henry told me about the Magna Carta thing, that we can carry out lawful rebellion.'

'I don't understand all the details, because every time Henry explains it, I get lost, but I trust him, because it isn't just us who feel this way. You've just got to remember to give up everything.'

'What, you mean my property?'

'More than that, because you have to give up your legal name. If you are dealing with anyone official, don't go by the name you used to have, because your birth certificate is just your membership card to their society, and so if you use that name, you accept membership. But this is the clever thing; if you don't use your given name, you have opted out. If you have no contract with society, they can't enforce the penalties under the contract.' She grinned. 'Clever, don't you think?'

'It can't be that simple.'

'It is, I've seen it work.' Gemma started to pull at the coil of wire, an old rag wrapped around her hand to protect it. 'And like you say, if they try to use force, we will just defend ourselves. It's exciting, sort of.'

'Gemma?'

She stopped. 'Yes?'

'All I want is for us to stay together, that's all,' John said. She started to say something in response, but he held up his hand. 'I know what Henry said, and I know that you won't be with me exclusively, but whatever time you've got spare, if Henry is all right about it, I would like you to share it with me.'

Gemma grinned and then bit her lip seductively.

He laughed, she knew how to play him, and went back to rummaging, pulling old pieces of machinery to one side, a bit more skip in his step. At the back, covered in dust, he found some animal traps, with metal hinges and strong serrated jaws. They were dusty, with rust on the edges, and so he wasn't sure if they worked anymore.

He set one of the traps, his arms straining as he pulled on the jaws, until he felt it click into place. He found an old bamboo cane against the wall and placed it in the trap. He didn't have to push hard before the jaws snapped together, sending one end to the floor, leaving him with a piece of bamboo with a jagged end. He liked it. There were six of the traps, and he carried them outside. Three for the field, two on the path that ran in front of the house, leaving one by the back door. It got dark there, with no lights shining at the back, and so whoever was coming wouldn't find out until the jaws snapped around their ankle. He just had to make sure that everyone knew about them.

John took a deep breath and looked around to see what else he could use to secure the compound. Then he saw it. The red fuel tank, filled with the petrol they used to run the quad bikes and the old cars that were parked behind the end barn. They bought cheap cars from auction and ran them until they broke down. He could make petrol bombs, because there was a store full of bottles, ready for use with the home brew.

He went outside to set the traps and then he filled a barrow with empty booze bottles and wheeled them towards the house. When he got inside, he saw that the Elams were already nailing the barbed wire to the windows, following Gemma's lead, creating a spider's web across each one, nailing the wire half in and then bending the nail over. Peter wasn't doing much good. He wasn't the sort who was used to physical work, and so he bent more nails than he pushed in, but it was the effort he was putting in that John admired.

Jennifer looked back and grinned. 'This will keep them out.'

'I hope so, I really do,' John said, 'but leave a space in the middle of each one. We're going to make petrol bombs. If they get the grilles off, we can fight back with those.'

Jennifer's eyes widened at that. She liked the thought.

John pointed to the wheelbarrow by the door and addressed the other young women that were left. 'Fill those from the fuel tank. Dip a rag in the petrol, get it soaked, and then jam the cloth hard into the neck. I want ten under each window. We'll work out how to make a catapult, so we can use them when they are further away.'

As the women scurried off, John went to the cabinet where the old man kept his shotguns. There were three of them, and a box of cartridges. The last firearms licence was a few years old now, due for renewal. John guessed that he wouldn't be applying for another.

The cabinet was in the hallway next to the old man's room. As he pulled out one of the shotguns, there was a moan from the room.

John pushed open the door, one of the few rooms that had one, the shotgun still in his hand. Henry wanted to keep the old man locked away. As the door creaked open, the old man looked at him. His eyes were yellow, his skin pale grey. He tried to make sounds, but all that came out were strangled moans. His head lifted as if he was making an effort to get up, but he just flopped back onto the bed, his head turned to one side.

Dawn brushed past him, pushing John into the doorframe. 'I'm going to feed him, and change him,' she said, her eyes fierce. 'Don't think about stopping me. Henry hasn't said that we shouldn't.'

John didn't say anything. Instead he just watched as Dawn went to him and lifted a cup to his lips. He drank gratefully, even though he couldn't lift his arm to grip the cup. As the sheet fell away, John saw the ribs jutting through the skin, through the soiled vest, his shoulders sharp and bony.

'Get some bread,' Dawn said. 'And heat some soup. He's starving to death.'

The old man shook his head, not much more than a tremor, and then looked towards the gun. He nodded, almost invisibly, his mouth hanging open, his eyes yearning, but John saw it all the same. He was straining towards the gun before he flopped back onto the bed, his chest rising up quickly, his lungs working like pistons, his breaths coming out as loud rasps.

'He wants me to kill him,' John said quietly, looking down at the shotgun in his hand.

Dawn shook her head. 'No, that is not what we are about, you know that, John. Come on, get some soup. He's dying.'

There was a click next to him, the snap of metal, and Gemma appeared in the doorway alongside him. She was holding one of the other shotguns.

'Henry hasn't told us to feed him.' Gemma raised the shotgun. 'So are you going to go against him? Are you going to be the one who betrays us?'

Dawn's eyes flashed between the shotgun and the old man, then to John, looking around the room, pleading, scared. 'We can't do this,' she said, her voice cracking. 'It's inhumane.'

'Come out,' Gemma said, her voice lacking in tone, flat and emotionless, and she twitched the shotgun.

Dawn put the cup down and walked towards the doorway, her shoulders slumped. When she went past John, she looked up at him, stared into his eyes, and he read what she was thinking, that it was all wrong.

John looked towards the old man, and doubts surfaced, because he looked close to death, emaciated and bedridden, and John knew it was cruel.

Gemma spoke up. 'John, help me.'

When he glanced back towards her, he felt his doubts slip away.

John turned round to push Dawn on her shoulder, so that she stumbled towards the bottles now piled in one corner.

'Sit there, don't move,' he said, and then he walked towards the door that opened onto the field.

Someone had to keep watch.

Chapter Thirty-Three

As Charlie looked at the contents of the Billy Privett file spread across the table, Donia asked, 'So what is the story? The real story?'

'You've heard of Billy Privett?'

She nodded. 'Everyone's heard of Billy Privett. That's why I came to Oulton.'

Charlie was surprised. 'What, because of Billy?'

'Not exactly,' she said, smiling, knowing how it sounded. 'I knew which firm represented him, and so I guessed that you were important.'

'And now, you're disappointed?'

'I didn't expect you to be how you are,' she said.

'What, some small practice above a takeaway?'

'Something like that,' she said, embarrassed.

'You don't need fancy offices if you do criminal work,' Charlie said. 'Just somewhere convenient for the clients and not too far from the court.'

'So about Billy?'

Charlie sighed. 'He was just a loser who got lucky once in his life,' he said, waving his hand dismissively. 'Six numbers, that's what changed him. He was a pain in the arse before he won it. Afterwards, he was a pain in the arse who suddenly thought he was a big deal.'

'But was he a murderer?' Donia said. 'Did he kill Alice Kenyon?'

Charlie shrugged. 'He said not. Perhaps there'll be something in here,' and he patted the papers on the desk. 'I know that Amelia fought hard to keep him away from the inquest.'

'Could he do that? Stay away, I mean.'

'Inquests are just to find out how someone died. They're not there to find the murderer. It's the *how* and the *why*, not the *who*. Billy provided a written statement that said he didn't remember anything, even who else was there. The coroner decided that there was no point in making him give evidence at the inquest if that was all he was going to say. Ted made a real stink in the papers about that, but he just wanted the inquest to be something different to what it was.'

'I feel sorry for him,' Donia said. 'I've seen him on the news. He seems like a nice man.'

'He is, much nicer than me, but he'll go to the grave waiting to find out what happened, now that Billy is dead.'

Charlie reached for the correspondence clip and went to the back, to the first time Amelia had spoken to Billy, when the police had dragged him in after Alice had been found. Most of the information was just personal, just what they would need to conduct the case. There was a sheet at the back where she had written out Billy's version of events. When he looked, Charlie was surprised. He had expected to read Billy's story, all set out in Amelia's neat script, but there was just one sentence. *I do not wish to disclose to anyone what happened at my house on 14th May 2011*, with his signature underneath.

He tapped his lip. That was unusual. Billy Privett didn't even want Amelia to know what had happened. That isn't how clients work. They try to get their lawyer to believe the lies, as if it somehow makes it true when it becomes the official version. They never realise that the lawyer never truly believes, or even cares. It is only ever about two things; what can be proven, and how will they get paid.

'What did Billy say?' Donia asked, leaning forward.

'Not much,' Charlie said, and showed her the piece of paper.

She frowned and sat back. 'So the file isn't important.'

He started to flick through the other sheets of paper, with letters sent to Billy demanding that her bills be paid. Once the police station work had finished, Amelia billed Billy privately for her work. As he got to the end, to the letter sent most recently, he opened his mouth to speak, but couldn't think of what to say.

'What is it?' Donia said, trying to get closer.

Charlie looked up. 'Amelia sent out letters yesterday, when she found out Billy had died, enclosing a DVD.'

'Show me,' Donia said.

Charlie tilted the folder towards her. The letters were short, just *I enclose a video shot by Billy Privett recently, and which I have been authorised to disclose in the event of his death.* It was the recipients that interested Charlie. There were ten letters, all identical. There was one sent to the police, one to Ted Kenyon, three to television companies and five to newspapers.

'Does it say what was on the discs?'

Charlie shook his head. 'I don't know, but it is certainly unusual. It makes it sound like a final statement, a message beyond the grave or something.'

'The story of what really happened to Alice?' Donia said.

'What else can it be?' Charlie said, nodding. 'Which means that someone wanted to silence him, scared of what he would say.' He frowned. 'But why now?'

'What do you mean?'

'The timing must be important, because he kept quiet for over a year and then decided to commit something to video. He was killed a few days later. The timing seems crucial. So he must have been scared of something. And there is something else too.'

'Go on.'

'How did whoever killed Billy know about the DVD?' When Donia looked confused, Charlie continued, 'Think about it. The killer must have known that he was talking, or else why silence him?'

'Yeah, but if that was the case, why kill him? It was his death that prompted Amelia to send the videos.'

'That was their mistake. Billy was talking, they knew that, but they didn't know that it was only to be released after his death. Only Amelia and Billy knew that.'

'And now they are both dead.'

Charlie nodded. 'Billy must have spoken up about the video when he was being tortured, and so Amelia was the next target because she would know where they were.'

'But isn't there another problem?' Donia said. 'If they were sent yesterday, why hasn't it been in the paper or on the television?'

'I don't know,' Charlie said. 'Perhaps the police suppressed them, and asked the press to hold it back.' Then something occurred to him. His stomach started to roll knowing that the reason for all of this was becoming clearer. 'No, it's not that,' he said quietly. 'Linda came in early this morning. She said she wasn't up to date with her post, because of the burglary.'

'What do you mean?'

'The videos were never posted. They were left overnight in the office, because things got messed up, and whatever was on them must have been important, because it was for distribution only after his death.'

'They might still be at the office,' Donia said. 'Everything closed down once the police had gone.'

Charlie shook his head. 'No, because I'll bet they were stolen.'

Donia looked confused. 'I don't know what you mean.'

'Did you know I spent the night in the office?' Charlie said.

'Yes, Linda mentioned that she thought you had. She said you'd done it before, and I think she told the police that.'

'I didn't see the letters when I woke up, and I think someone had been into the office,' he said, although he realised that he couldn't tell her the rest of the story, about the blood-stained knife.

'So if the discs were taken, we'll never know what Billy said.'

Charlie thought about that, and then said, 'There will be a master copy somewhere.' When Donia looked up, he added, 'It's probably in the safe.'

'That might have been taken too.'

'Yes, it might, but it is worth checking out.'

'When shall we go?'

Charlie shook his head. 'No, you've taken enough risks getting me this. I need to get it on my own.'

As he thought of that, he felt sweat flash across his forehead. What could be on that video that someone would be prepared to kill for it, and would he be the next target?

Chapter Thirty-Four

Sheldon drove towards Penwortham, a suburb on the edge of Preston, once the county's largest cotton town, but its history now obliterated by retail parks and an identikit city centre, with just a university to provide a buzz. Penwortham was not far from the police headquarters, where it fashioned itself as a sleepy area on the other side of the River Ribble, the vibe being delicatessens and cyclists and tree-lined avenues. Sheldon and Ted were following the lead from the telephone call that Christina was really Lucy Crane, and had lived in a care home there.

Ted had been quiet most of the way, but as they got to the final part of the journey, he said, 'What are you hoping to find when you get there?'

Sheldon thought about that as he looked down the hill ahead, and replied, 'Just confirmation about the woman who pretended to be Billy's housekeeper.'

'And you think it will help, knowing that?'

'It will be more than what we have now.'

They crossed the wide river that separated Preston from Penwortham and then headed past shops and more takeaways before they turned off at the police station, a low-rise red brick building on a corner waiting to be sold, a victim of the cutbacks. After fifty yards or so further on, they came to a double-fronted detached house in dirty white pebble-dash. As they came to a stop, there were three teenagers sitting on the front step, smoking cigarettes. They started to laugh as Sheldon led the way.

'Your clothes don't fit, man,' one of them said to Sheldon, making the other two laugh more loudly than the jibe deserved.

Sheldon smiled at them. 'Who's in charge in there?' he said, and pointed towards the house.

'We are.' More laughter. 'No, I'm serious.'

Sheldon rolled his eyes and stepped past them, going through the front door, Ted behind him. As they crossed the threshold, the same teenager shouted, 'Marian?'

A large woman appeared from a room at the end of the hall. The kitchen, Sheldon guessed. She had hair cropped short, dyed purple, and a stud in her nose, although it didn't match the lines round her mouth that put her somewhere near to fifty.

'Can I help you?' she said, stepping towards them.

Sheldon pulled his identification from his pocket. 'From Oulton police.'

'You don't look like the police,' she said, looking at his clothes. And then she pointed at Ted Kenyon. 'I know you.'

'It's a long story,' Sheldon said, interrupting. 'I want to ask you about Lucy Crane.'

She looked confused for a moment, and then her eyes widened. 'I haven't heard that name for a long time. You need to update your records if you think she's here though. She left, oh, three years or more.'

'Tell me about her.'

She looked suspicious. 'Why do you want to know?'

'It could be important,' Sheldon said. 'I don't want to see her records. I just want to know about her.'

Marian thought about that, and then she nodded them through to the kitchen. It was wide and spacious, with plates piled high on the side, waiting for their turn in the dishwasher.

'So I'll ask again; why do you want to know?' Marian said, as she hauled herself onto a high stool next to a breakfast bar.

'I can't tell you that.'

'So I can't tell you about Lucy,' she said, and shrugged, her hands held out.

Sheldon had expected that, but he thought it was worth trying for information without giving anything away.

'It's about the Billy Privett murder,' Sheldon said. 'She might have some useful information.'

Marian pointed at Ted. 'Now I know you. You're Alice Kenyon's father.'

Ted smiled, trying to win her over. 'This could be important. Please help us.'

Marian looked at Sheldon, and then back at Ted. Then she softened. 'She was trouble.'

'Aren't they all?' Sheldon said.

'Most are *troubled*, yes, but trouble? Not always. The kids that come here are like any group of people. They form hierarchies, where some follow, others lead. Whether the kids get in trouble depends on who is doing the leading. Sometimes you get kids who just like some fun, and will even work at school. The home is a good place to be then, and all the kids have a chance.'

'But?'

Marian smiled. She knew the *but* was there. 'But sometimes you get leaders who are just too much trouble, and they drink too much, get into drugs, and they take at least a couple with them.'

'And Lucy?'

'Lucy, well,' and Marian laughed. 'She was all about sex. I tried not to judge her, because I knew the background she brought into the home, from her family background, and I am sure as hell not going to tell you, but she was good looking, and she knew it gave her a weapon. She developed early, and she used what she had to get what she wanted. I think she realised that her looks would take her further than her academic skills, and so she would flaunt it. There was even a care worker who lost his job over her, who forgot where the line was when she came at him fresh from the shower. She just wanted him to let her go out drinking, but she had to persuade him. Someone walked in on him groping her, but she was on her back, letting him touch her.' Marian shook her head. 'He said she came on to him, and I believe that, but he was supposed to say no, he was the adult, except that Lucy didn't know the word *no* when she heard it.'

'What happened to her?' Sheldon said.

'She was always going missing, although she was never really going missing, if you know what I mean. She was just hanging out with adults. They would get what they wanted, and they would keep her in booze and fags. It was just the local men at first, the deadbeats who hang around the parks with beer cans, but then other people started calling round for her. They thought of themselves as artists, anarchists, squatters, people like that, but they were just people who had opted out. She would go missing for days at a time, and we called the police, but then one day she never returned.'

'Don't you worry about them, the ones who end up like that?'

Marian thought about that, and then said, 'Some I do. It's the ones who are weak that I worry about, because they will give in to whatever pressure is put on them. Drugs, crime, prostitution, and so just about any bad thing that can happen to a person will happen to them. They are the ones who end up hanging themselves in jail when they get to thirty and realise that their sorry little life was going to stay sorry. The strong ones I don't worry about. They'll manage somehow. Lucy was one of the strong ones, in her own way.'

Marian was lost in her memories for a while, before she said, 'So what did she have to do with Billy Privett? I saw on the news that he had been killed.'

'There was a young woman who was at his house the morning after his body was discovered, and we think it might have been Lucy, which if it was, I'm suspicious, because it means that she lied about who she was. Do you have any photographs of her?'

'We don't keep mug shots,' Marian said, scorn in her voice, and then she paused, looking unsure, as if something had occurred to her. 'Wait there.'

She bustled out of the room. Ted raised his eyebrows. 'What do you think?'

'It sounds like the same kind of person, but it's all based upon one officer's memory jolted from a police station CCTV still.'

'She has probably been in trouble,' Ted said. 'Won't you have mug shots?'

'I'm on sick leave, remember.'

'That isn't the same as suspended though, is it?' Ted said. 'You could still go in and look at the computers.'

Before Sheldon could answer, Marian brought in a photograph album.

'This is from four years ago,' she said. 'We went on a weekend in the Lakes. Rafting, adventures in the woods, that kind of thing.'

Marian put the album on the breakfast bar and started

to flick through the pages. Cellophane-covered photographs went past in a blur, children in red lifejackets by water and boats. Marian stopped occasionally, and then she stepped back. 'There,' she said, and tapped a photograph at the top of a page.

Sheldon got closer to have a look, and then he started to nod to himself.

The picture was of a teenage girl, laughing, her blonde hair in a ponytail, but it was wet, with strands across her face, the top of a bright red lifejacket visible. It was Christina. The cheeks were less defined, but the smile was the same, and that confidence he remembered in her eyes.

'That's her,' Sheldon said. He moved to one side to let Ted Kenyon have a look, but when Ted got close, he put his hand over his mouth.

'What is it?' Sheldon said.

'I know her,' Ted said, and he headed for the door.

Chapter Thirty-Five

Charlie was in Donia's bathroom when he heard something. It was a knock on the door to her flat, loud and urgent.

He had been washing his face, just watching the clock move on until it was dark so that he could go back to his office, the cold water waking him up. The police would have searched some of the office, but they were limited in how far they could go, because most of the things worth looking at were in confidential files. They would get a warrant eventually, but Charlie wanted to find out first whether the original video was in the safe. If he knew what was on it, he could go to the police confident that he wasn't a suspect.

The water dripped from his face as he stayed quiet, praying that Donia wouldn't answer it. Then he heard her footsteps, skipping along the hall.

There were muffled voices, and then heavy footsteps.

The bathroom went into Donia's bedroom, and so his hand went to the door handle, ready to rush through. If it was the police, it was time to surrender. He knew he hadn't done anything. He just needed to convince them.

He paused when he heard the shouting. That wasn't the police. Too many expletives, the words hissed out.

He opened the door slowly, taking a deep breath, wanting to see who was there. The light from the bedroom illuminated his face, and as he stepped out, he was wary of creaks from the floorboards, the carpets too thin to muffle anything.

The voices got louder. He got to the bedroom door and saw that the hallway was dark. He tried to stop his breathing and listen above the tick of the clock on the wall. His shadow grew in the fan of light from the bedroom door. He stepped back and listened out. There was a male voice, and he was talking. Had Donia let the police in? Or perhaps the two men he had seen at Amelia's house.

He peered around the doorway and towards the living room. He could see black clothes and movement. There was no sign of Donia though.

Charlie flattened himself against the wall. He was trying to keep himself free, but he didn't know where Donia was, and he felt responsible for her. He closed his eyes and took a deep breath before he stepped out again, further this time. There was the rustle of paper, excited chatter. They'd found Billy Privett's file on the table. It confirmed what he knew, that it was information about Billy Privett that was behind everything.

His foot made a creak on the floor as he felt his way across the carpet. He looked down. His silhouette spread across the hallway and against the wall on the other side. His skin shot up in goose pimples.

Charlie took one more step out, and this time he could see who was there. It was the kids who had been hanging around outside the office, dressed all in black. They had followed Donia.

His eyes looked back into the bedroom for another escape route or somewhere to hide, but there was nothing. The bed was a box frame that went all the way to the floor and any hanging space for clothes was just an open rail. There was a window held by a clasp, not much by way of security, but he was three floors up. It didn't need to be locked tight. The next thing on the way down was the concrete yard.

Where was Donia?

Charlie moved further out, keeping watch on the main door, knowing that if he had to run for it, he had an exit. His heart was beating hard, and he was trying to calm his breathing, certain that they would hear. Then he remembered Amelia's body. He knew he couldn't leave Donia, but he wouldn't be able to handle them on his own. He would have to get help for her. It was no good if they both died.

He started to back away down the hallway, leaving them to read the file, hoping they would be distracted, but as his footsteps moved backwards, his spine went cold when he bumped into something. Or rather, someone.

Chapter Thirty-Six

Ted was silent until they were back in the car, ignoring the shouts of the kids on the steps, Marian watching them go.

As Ted looked at his lap, his jaw set, Sheldon asked, 'Who is she?' his key poised in the ignition, not willing to go until he had an answer.

Ted turned to him, and there was still confusion in his eyes. 'She was the girl in the car, the one who leaped on me when the camera was there. That was her, Lucy Crane.'

Sheldon was surprised. 'Are you sure?'

'Of course I am,' Ted said, exasperated. 'I was talking with her in the car for five minutes, before she jumped on me. And now I found out that she is connected to Billy Privett, and so maybe she did know something.'

'She was always connected to Billy Privett, because she told you she had information,' Sheldon said. 'Perhaps she did at first, but then decided that she could just sell you out instead. Or maybe she got scared. She must have had the photographer waiting, and was hoping she could trap you in a blackmail plot, or just sell you out to the papers. But you weren't interested, and so she had to jump on you and hope the pictures told a different story.'

'I wouldn't have been interested,' Ted said. 'I just wanted to know about Alice, and I still love my wife. We are more distant now, I know that, but I wouldn't do that to her. She has suffered enough.'

'Lucy is still a link to the case though, but how? She was Billy's housekeeper. Why didn't you see her when you went up there?'

'She would keep out of my way, wouldn't she, if she knew I was on the way,' Ted said. 'Do you think she was really his housekeeper? She might have been Billy's girlfriend, trying to protect him?'

Sheldon shook his head. 'No, she was more than that. She'd have no reason to lie to us if she was his girlfriend, and she wouldn't have disappeared.'

'You've still got your identification,' Ted said. 'There is a police station just up the road. Can't you find out something about her?'

Sheldon thought about that, and then remembered his moment on the church tower earlier that day, and the promise he had made to himself that he would find out the truth.

He started the engine and drove the short distance to the police station, a one-storey L-shaped block on the verge of being closed down as it waited for a buyer. There was no public reception and so no frosty civilian officer to get past.

'Wait in the car,' Sheldon said, and then swiped his pass card along the reader. It worked for all the Lancashire stations, and so he found himself at the meeting point of two corridors, the floors tiled, the walls painted in cold light blue. Fire doors intersected the corridors at intervals. It was Sheldon's first time in the Penwortham station, and so all he could was walk and look for a computer terminal.

He turned left and when he got to the room at the end, there were three rows of desks filled with computer screens. There were no cells at Penwortham, and so Sheldon realised that it was a hideaway, somewhere for the officers to get their files together without getting landed with an urgent custody investigation, the only risk being a call-out to chase some kids on the Kingsfold estate, the main source of aggravation for the Penwortham force.

There was only one other person in the room, a young female officer in uniform. She looked up once, curious at first, but didn't investigate further, satisfied by the identification swinging from Sheldon's neck.

Sheldon jiggled the mouse to clear the screensaver and sat down. Once he had logged in, he brought up the intelligence system and typed in Lucy's name. The pale screen of grids and boxes threw up three people, but the dates of birth narrowed it down pretty quickly. When he clicked on her details, he leaned forward to get a better view.

Christina was really Lucy Crane, he saw that straight away, except that some of her flirt was missing. It was a picture taken after she was arrested, with rings under her eyes and her hair dishevelled. There was no smile, just a tired and sullen glare at the camera, another kid caught doing something bad.

When Sheldon clicked on her personal details, her address was still listed as the children's home they had just visited. It looked like she had kept out of trouble since she left.

He scrolled down to the intelligence file, and saw that it ended a couple of years earlier, when she turned seventeen. The entries before then were just as Marian described. Calls to the police from the home to report her missing, and then an entry to report that she had been found. A few men had been issued with Child Abduction Notices, where it was noted officially that the care home did not approve of her being with them, and one more time would mean a court appearance and a reputation as a paedophile. Apart from that, it was quiet.

Sheldon frowned and clicked on her antecedents, the list of her convictions and cautions. Lucy was only nineteen, and it was as Sheldon expected, filled with her route to a court appearance. A youth reprimand for theft, and then a final warning for criminal damage, followed by her climb up the ladder of youth sentences. A referral order for an assault, then an action plan order, followed by a supervision order. It was the usual trail of one more last chance, another failed attempt to reform a troubled youth. Sometimes they worked, sometimes they didn't, and often it was the child who decided that there were better things to do.

It seemed like Lucy had got into scrapes when she was at the home, and then she stopped. The Youth Offending Team would call her a success. Or perhaps she had just learned that it was more fun to get other people into trouble. Leering men maybe, an outlet for her new-found power, tinged by anger from her earlier life experiences.

Sheldon was about to click off and admit defeat when he scrolled through to the *non-conviction disposals*, the list that was made up of acquittals or fixed penalty notices, sometimes cases that were investigated but never got as far as a charge. For Lucy, there was just one entry.

Six months earlier, Lucy had been arrested for shoplifting some booze from a late night grocery shop in Oulton. At least that put her in the right area. Penwortham was more than twenty miles away. The case was dropped before she got to court though.

Sheldon clicked on the related case file, which would consist of an incident log and a crime report, along with a record of the outcome. The witness statements would be held over in Oulton.

It was nothing remarkable. Lucy had been caught trying to leave the shop with a bottle of whisky hidden in her coat. Sheldon scrolled through the crime report, and as he got to the bottom, he saw an entry that said RNC, no public interest.

Released No Charge? Why was that?

He made a note of the custody number and searched the database for it. It wasn't a long record. She was brought in and booked in, but she didn't even get as far as an interview. There was an entry forty minutes after her arrival. A visit from CI Dixon, who spoke to Lucy in her cell.

Why was a chief inspector talking to a shoplifter in her cell?

The custody sergeant had done his job well. He had noted when Dixon went in and when she came out. He was looking after himself, making sure that if anything went wrong, it wasn't going to come back to him. Dixon was in there for thirty minutes. Five minutes after that, Lucy was released, no charge.

Sheldon sat back and stared at the screen. Sometimes senior officers did interfere with suspects, particularly for minor things. It might be a deal, an exchange for information, or because the suspect was being looked at for something bigger. A sergeant would be used to that, but why Dixon? She didn't work on a team dealing with informants or undercover work. Her job was to run the Oulton station, to argue her case for a bigger budget at headquarters and to allocate resources.

But it was the timing that bothered Sheldon, and he remembered how Dixon had been earlier. The way she had almost dropped her cigarettes when she saw Christina in the corridor. Or Lucy Crane, as Sheldon now knew her. There was something else going on. Something more personal.

He clicked off the computer and headed for the door.

When he got to the car, he asked Ted, 'How long ago was it that you were caught in the car with Lucy?'

Ted did some quick calculations in his head. 'Just over five months ago.'

Not long after Lucy was released by Dixon, Sheldon thought.

He climbed into the driver seat. 'We need to get back to Oulton.'

Chapter Thirty-Seven

Charlie turned around in the hallway. There were sounds behind him, people in the living room, everyone suddenly aware that he was there. The way out was blocked by the shadow of a man, large and threatening. It wasn't just his size that told Charlie that he was in trouble. It was his readiness. Charlie hadn't had a fight since he was at school, and the spread of the man's arms and the gleam of his teeth as he grinned told Charlie that he would enjoy whatever came next.

There was movement from the living room. Charlie looked round and saw the man he had spoken to the day before, with the wild black hair surrounded by teenagers.

'Charlie Barker,' he said, laughter in his voice.

'Who are you?' Charlie said, trying to watch the man in the hallway at the same time.

The man with the wild hair stepped closer. 'I thought you'd lost interest in us?'

Charlie looked past the man and into the living room. Donia was there, kneeling down, a young woman holding on to her hair, making Donia grimace. 'What are you doing to her?'

'Don't worry about her. She looks like she could give us some fun. She's safe, for the moment.'

Charlie got the smell of cannabis and unwashed clothes as the man stood in front of him.

'Fun? What do you mean?' Charlie said, and then looked down. There was a knife in the man's hand, the blade protruding from his clenched fist. The shock was like a kick to his stomach. 'You killed Amelia and Billy.'

The man tilted his head, amused. 'They wrote their own destinies, don't you think?' he said. 'Now you can write yours.'

Charlie closed his eyes. He swallowed when he felt the prick of the blade in his neck. When he opened them slowly, the large man had his arm stretched out, and Charlie could feel moisture on his skin. He didn't know if it was blood or sweat.

'You know what we want,' the man said.

'I don't know what you mean.'

'Don't be foolish, Mr Barker. Amelia tried to keep her secret, but everyone has a pain threshold.' He nodded slowly. 'She was good, better than Billy, but it ended just the same. So we want the footage. Where is it?'

'What footage?'

The blade pressed in more, making Charlie wince.

'The video of Billy,' the man said coldly, the laughter gone from his voice.

'You took them,' Charlie said, his mouth dry, swallowing hard.

'Not the original, but you know that,' he said. 'We've just got copies put onto discs. I want the original footage, and any copies that are left.'

Charlie took no comfort from the fact that he had guessed right. He tried to think of what to say, but his mind was confused by adrenaline, so that all of his thoughts rushed him at once. He knew the original footage would most likely be in the office safe, but he remembered the sight of Amelia, and how she had ended up.

'We use an off-site facility for things like that,' Charlie said, hoping that they couldn't detect the lie. 'We keep the child witness videos there, and only Amelia or I can get access. We are the only signatories.'

Charlie closed his eyes again and felt the rise and fall of his chest, his heart beating hard. If they believed him, they would have to keep him alive.

'And if you or Amelia couldn't go to the facility anymore?'

'The child witness videos belong to the prosecution, not us. We have them just for the trial. Everything we have stored there would be sent to the prosecution.'

Charlie opened his eyes and saw the two men exchange glances and shrugs. The blade moved from his skin, just a fraction, but it was enough of an opening.

He stamped hard on the big man's foot and pushed at him, the surprise move giving Charlie an advantage. He bolted towards the door. Someone shouted. There was the rumble of heavy boots. Charlie's hands were slick on the latch as he panicked, but he was able to turn it and pull the door open as someone came up behind him. He ran through and slammed the door shut, so that the chasing figure banged into the glass, knocking Charlie onto the landing, the door slamming shut. It gave him more time.

He thumped the light button and ran for the stairs. He had little idea of what he was doing. There were shouts from the flat, and all he knew was that he had to get away, driven by panic and instinct.

The door to Donia's flat flew open as Charlie reached the stairs. There were people coming after him. He couldn't stop.

His hand slid along the painted rail as he ran, his feet banging on each step. He stole a glance upwards. The large man was running along the landing and got to the top of the stairs as Charlie reached the bottom. Charlie didn't stop to get a good look.

As Charlie ran along the landing below, just two flights to go, something metallic flew at him. He didn't have a chance to avoid it, and he cried out as it stuck into his shoulder, only the shoulder pads in his suit stopping it from sticking too far in. He yanked on it and winced with pain as it came out.

He got to the next stairs, and thought he was losing the race. There were more people running after him, loud shouts in the confined space of the stairway that turned quickly into screeches of rage.

Charlie looked back. The large man looked strong, his teeth set in a grimace behind a goatee beard, his biceps bulging from the black T-shirt that was tight to his chest.

Someone opened a flat door, probably curious about the noise, but closed it quickly again. Charlie's feet skipped down the next set of stairs, barely touching each step, his skin hot against the stair rail as his hand ran along it. The chasing feet were quicker, hitting the top step before Charlie had got to the bottom. All Charlie could do was try to go faster as he dashed along the landing and then turned to go down the stairs. He was breathless from fright and exertion. As he rushed for the final set of stairs, he saw the front door ahead and tried to speed up, but when he was halfway down, one of his feet missed a step. He skidded forward, his arms flailing for balance.

Charlie stumbled into the hallway, his hands and knees hitting the floor, but he couldn't stop. The footsteps were getting closer, and so he ran at the front door, the street visible as the orange glow of streetlamps through the glass panel.

The night air outside turned the sweat on his forehead cold but Charlie kept on running, his shoes making loud slaps on the tarmac, his arms pumping hard, his throat hoarse with effort. The door banged behind him, but as Charlie ran down the street, he couldn't hear his pursuers anymore.

He looked back. The small group in black were emerging onto the street, watching Charlie as he got further down the street. One of them went towards a white van. Were they going to chase him in that?

Charlie ran across the road and into an alleyway, too narrow for the van. He didn't want to stop yet, just in case they appeared round the corner on foot, but as the evening echoed with the sound of shoes pounding hard on the bricks under his feet, he began to realise that he was alone.

As he rounded a corner where the alley emerged onto another terraced street, Charlie stopped to put his head against the wall. His chest ached with effort as he gulped down air, and sweat streaked down his temples. The pain in his shoulder began to make itself known as sharp jolts, and once he was able to straighten himself, he looked at his jacket. There was a tear and a dark stain. It looked like blood.

He put his back against the wall and looked upwards and blinked at the stars. He let his breathing get back to normal and then started walking across the road, heading for the shelter of another alley, where it was long and dark, no streetlights, just chinks of light that came from the houses that backed onto it, and the occasional glow of a side street.

He had to keep moving though, and so Charlie hobbled along, wincing, his shoulder sending sharp jolts of pain. He thought about Donia. She was in danger now. He had to help her, but then he realised how little he knew about her. Why would anyone believe him? Julie's phone call earlier told him that he was someone, and he knew how blinkered investigations could get when the police fixated on a suspect.

Charlie had worked out where he was going next. He just needed to get there without being seen.

Chapter Thirty-Eight

John was walking round the house, checking each window, when he saw her.

He shouted, banged on the window, but it was no use. It was Dawn, running across the field, her hair streaming behind her, pausing only by the Seven Sisters, just for a moment, touching one of the stones. Then she looked back and set off again, before heading for the wall.

'Shit! No, you don't,' he shouted, and then he bolted towards the stairs, taking them two at a time. People called his name in the house, curious, but he kept going. Dawn must have heard him as he ran out of the house, because she looked round, but it just made her run faster, sprinting for the tumbledown section of the wall.

His footsteps were loud in his ears as he ran, and he remembered to avoid the traps. As he went past the Seven Sisters, Dawn was scrambling over the wall, crying, sounding desperate, heading into the woods and making for the path.

John hit the wall at a sprint, vaulting over, ignoring the scrape of his knees on the top or the judder in his ankle as he landed. His lungs ached, but he had to keep going. Panic was driving her. All he had to fall back on was his own strength. He almost stumbled on tree roots, and his knees gave way as his feet hit hollows in the path, but still he kept on going. She was still within sight, a dark shadow moving quickly, not heading for the long path towards Oulton but for the road, hoping to stop a passing car.

Dawn looked back as she ran though. A mistake. It slowed her down, so that he gained on her and could hear her fear coming out in yelps and cries, audible over the thumps of his feet and the urgency of his breaths. She wasn't going to make it to the gate.

He got within ten yards of her, and Dawn went to her knees, gasping for breath, her arms over her head. 'I'm sorry, I'm sorry,' she cried, between gulps of air. 'Please don't hurt me. I won't do it again. I was weak. I'm scared. I'm sorry. Forgive me.'

John stood over her, his heart beating hard in his chest, his lungs dry from exhaustion. 'Why did you run?'

Dawn scrambled to her feet, and so John grabbed her, to stop her running again. She looked down and her shoulders started to heave with sobs.

'It's not going to end how you think, believe me,' she said. 'There is no rebellion, no uprising. So help me, please, just let me go.'

John pushed her to her knees. His fists clenched and Dawn shrank back, frightened, her eyes frantic. 'Don't hurt me.'

He closed his eyes, one hand gripping her shoulder. He breathed through his nose, deep and angry. A flush crept up his cheeks.

'Why are you trying to escape?' he said in a growl. 'We have to stay together. It's important.'

'You sound like Henry.'

'Of course I sound like him. We are part of the same group. We have the same ideals, don't we?

Dawn shook her head and started to laugh, but it was hysterical, tears streaming down her face.

'You say *we*, but you don't know who Henry is.'

'I know what he has taught me.'

'Bullshit! It is all fucking bullshit. You know nothing.'

John shook her by the arm, his own eyes blazing now. 'I know that if you get away, you'll talk about Henry, and so whatever great plans he has, they won't happen, and so it will all have been for nothing.'

She yanked back. 'Fuck Henry. Fuck Arni. Fuck you. All of you. Think about Henry. What do you know about him? I mean, really know?'

John paused at that, and his mind went back to what he knew about Henry before he arrived, and what he had been told. He shook his head. 'I know him differently now.'

'From what? The petty thief? The burglar? The fraudster? What about the sex offender, that kid at the party? Did you know about that? He doesn't mention that too much, does he, how he went to prison for buggering some teenage boy.'

John swallowed. He glanced back and could see people gathering outside the house, just visible through the trees, cast against the light shining through the doorway.

'Why do you think he ended up hanging around with the likes of us?' Dawn continued. 'Because he was shunned everywhere else. For his violence, his attitude, the way he thinks the world owes him for his own failures.'

'You need to keep your voice down,' John said. 'We've all trodden difficult paths to get here.'

She screeched with laughter and then wiped her mouth with her hand. 'Do you believe all that? It was fun, John, that's all. But Henry had to take control, because he does that, likes being the focus, except that this time people listened to him. And if they want to believe it enough, they start to believe it, because it gives them answers. But it was never meant to be like this.'

'Like what?'

'Murder.'

John's eyes widened.

'We were peaceful, loving,' she continued. 'Not killers.'

'Who has he killed?' John's grip loosened on her arm.

'Look around you,' she said. 'The stones you're so fond of, the Seven Sisters.'

John was confused. 'What do you mean?'

'You don't know, do you?' When he didn't answer, she continued, 'It's not a memorial, or a legacy John. It's a graveyard.'

'I don't understand.'

'People have tried to run away in the past, or have stood up to him, or not done as he said.' She flicked her hand towards the field. 'They are all there, under the ground, a stone for each of them.'

John looked over, the blood rushing through his head making sounds disappear, the shadows amongst the trees getting darker.

'Seven?' he said, eventually.

'Get a spade, John,' she said. 'Dig around the stones and you'll find them, the ones who tried to leave. That was the message – that if you threaten Henry, you die. *Fear* keeps us together, not love, or fellowship, or revolutions.'

John tried to take in what Dawn had just said. He looked back towards the field again, and the stones seemed different now. Darker. Colder. He looked at the woman in front of him, and he thought back to the nights he had spent with Henry, the truths that Henry had asked him to believe.

'I'm scared, John,' Dawn continued, her voice broken by sobs. 'That's why I'm still here, because I'm a coward. Henry made us take part, like it was some kind of thrill taken too far, our joint secret.'

'You're not making any sense.'

'You've heard of Billy Privett, and that poor girl, Alice, who was found in his pool?'

'Billy Privett? What has he got to do with this?'

'Because he's got money, and Henry wanted it, like he wants yours. That's all you are, an asset to be stripped. You've got a house, and you've got money. Henry saw it in the paper.'

'But what about the girl at the party, Alice?'

Before Dawn could explain, Gemma appeared further along the path, striding towards them. Her mouth was set, her fists clenched.

Dawn looked up at John, her eyes pleading, tears making a slow trail down her cheeks.

Gemma marched past him and grabbed Dawn by the arm.

'Back to the house,' Gemma barked at her, and then looked at John. 'Henry said someone would betray us. Don't listen to her.'

And with that, Gemma pulled on Dawn, making her get to her feet. Once she was standing, Gemma gripped her hair and started to drag her, stumbling, back along the path.

'I didn't mean to do it,' Dawn shouted, her voice desperate. 'You don't have to do this.'

John walked behind them. He looked at the standing stones as he got closer and started to think that he should have let Dawn escape, because what if she was telling the truth, that there were people under the ground? Then Gemma turned to smile at him, and he felt the same flutter in his chest whenever she did that. A glow, a warm feeling inside, despite what had happened. He knew then that he couldn't leave just yet, because he couldn't abandon Gemma. He loved her, he had known that from the start, and so he would do whatever it took to keep her safe.

Chapter Thirty-Nine

Charlie moved quickly along the alley, despite the pain in his shoulder, always keeping an eye on the exit, waiting for someone to appear. The walls were high, and so for as long as he kept in the shadows he was safe. Then he passed an open gate, a thin stream of light just reaching across the bricks. He glanced in and saw someone he recognised. A client, sitting on his back step, smoking.

'Patrick?' he said, sighing in relief.

The smoker stopped and peered into the gloom, his cigarette disappearing into his hand. 'Who is it?'

Charlie stepped into the light that was coming from the kitchen door.

'Fucking hell, Charlie Barker,' Patrick said, laughing. 'What the fuck are you doing, creeping around behind my house?'

Charlie shrugged, and then winced as his shoulder sent a sharp stab of pain. As he looked down, he saw that his suit was ripped where his knees had hit the floor. 'Trying not to get killed.'

Patrick must have noticed Charlie's blood-stained and torn clothes, because his gaze went to his body and then back up to his face. His look grew serious. 'Oh yeah, man, I heard about Miss Diaz. It was on the news. What the fuck's going on?'

'That's what I'm trying to find out,' Charlie said, breathing heavily, the relief chasing the adrenaline away. 'Except that some people don't like the idea.' He looked at his hand. It was shaking. 'Look, can we go inside, Patrick? I need some help.'

Patrick nodded and got to his feet. 'You've always been there for me, man. Come in.'

Charlie mumbled his thanks and followed Patrick inside.

The house was a typical terraced house, except without the kitchen extension. There was a room at the back and one at the front, and then straight onto the street. Once the door closed, Patrick opened out his palm to reveal what he had been smoking outside, and Charlie got the hot, sweet smell of relaxation.

Charlie reached out for it, and as he passed it over, Patrick looked surprised. Charlie inhaled deeply, the roach wet from Patrick's lips, but it was what he needed. 'I wasn't always a lawyer,' he said, and the pain began to recede from the wound in his shoulder.

'What the fuck happened to you, man?' Patrick said, his voice low.

'I fell down some steps,' Charlie said, and then passed the reefer back. 'Have you got a car?'

'Depends who's asking,' Patrick said, and grinned.

Charlie smiled, despite himself. 'Call it legal privilege.'

'I use an old Corsa,' he said. 'It's out the front, but if anyone asks, it's nothing to do with me.' He reached over and grabbed some keys from a worktop. 'Bring it back when you can.'

As Charlie thanked him, he noticed something in Patrick's eyes, and realised what it was: gratitude for Charlie never looking down on him. Charlie had put forward Patrick's excuses over the years as if he believed in the whole truth of them, and so Patrick saw him as an equal, despite the letters after his name and the lawyer label. Charlie had turned to Patrick because he knew Patrick would help him, and he was right. This was Charlie's circle of support, and he needed them. And what Charlie knew about his clients was that although their morality seemed to point in different ways to most people, they would always help out someone in trouble, because they recognised some of that need in themselves.

Charlie shook Patrick's hand and then cut through the house. In the living room was a young woman he had seen trailing Patrick at court, a lank-haired brunette with home-made tattoos on her wrist and blackened teeth. She didn't look up when Charlie went in, and then he spotted the bottle of bargain sherry. There was a young child, maybe eighteen months old, lying alongside, playing with a cuddly toy, but his mother was fast asleep, in a stupor.

Charlie looked away. He didn't feel like judging. Not today.

'Thanks, Patrick,' he whispered, nodding down at her.

'Don't worry about speed cameras,' Patrick said. 'The plate goes back to a scrapped Ford Mondeo. Nothing will come back here.'

'There are some things I don't need to know,' Charlie said, and then clicked the door closed, before bolting into an old sky blue Corsa.

It started on the third turn, and as he drove along the terraced street, Charlie started to feel some of his dread lift. He needed to get to the office. He knew where the video would be, and if it was important enough to murder for, he knew he had to get it before Amelia's killers found it.

His mind went back to Donia. He should call the police, he knew that, but something made him uncomfortable about her. It was all too neat. She arrived to do work experience, and then people started dying. The people in black knew where to go. Was it all a set-up, Donia in on the whole thing? They had threatened to hurt her, but what had it been? Hair-pulling? It could have been an act.

The journey to his office was brief. He drove to the end of the road and then some way up the hill.

He didn't go in the front way, where the takeaway owner might tell someone that he'd seen him. Instead, he drove to the street behind and then went into the alley that came out behind his office. There were black wrought iron streetlights lining the route, so it made it harder for people to hide there. Charlie blocked the alley with the car. He had a quick look round as he got out and then dashed into the yard, before running up the fire escape that went to the rear door of the office.

Charlie didn't turn on any of the main lights once he was inside, because he didn't want anyone to know he was there. Instead, he closed all the blinds and relied on desk lamps.

He went to the desk in reception and found the key for the safe. That was where they kept all the videos, in a small storage cabinet in the reception area. As he fumbled with the key and unlocked it, he saw rows of discs. They were logged by file reference, a sticker on each case. Charlie couldn't remember Billy's reference, but he knew it would begin with PRI. His fingers clicked through the discs, but there was no disc with Billy's reference on.

Charlie slammed the door closed. If the master disc had been in there, they had taken it, which was why they had left the knife behind and not killed him. They thought they had everything. The letters that Linda hadn't got round to posting. The disc from the cabinet, if ever there was one. But if they had those, why were they still hunting for something?

He went into Amelia's office. It was obvious that the police had been through it. Not looking through the files, but checking drawers and at the back of cupboards. As he looked, Charlie felt the sadness for Amelia rush at him, the shock of seeing her dead, and how she died. He picked up a photo frame she kept on her desk. It was her family again, close and smiling.

Tears jumped into his eyes, took him by surprise. She was a young woman, beautiful, her life unfulfilled. He thought he could still smell traces of her perfume, and he expected to hear the click of her heels or the angry snap to her voice. He wiped his eyes, angry with himself. He had no time for grieving now.

Amelia's client files were not in cabinets, but on shelves, in alphabetical order, alongside large folders that contained materials from whenever she went on a training course, the compulsory hours they both had to do to keep their practising certificates. Charlie's just piled up on the floor until they made their way to the bin.

Amelia did a lot of personal injury work, and the cases always moved slowly. So she did what most lawyers did; she worked her way through her cabinet methodically, going through each file in turn, writing an update letter, each one billable, or doing any chasing that needed doing. It took around three weeks to get to the end, and then she would just start over again. Updates, chasing, generating paperwork that generated money.

So he went to her files and started to flick through them, looking for a file that was out of place.

Charlie wiped his eyes as he started to pull out files. His exhaustion came at him quickly, and the names started to sway in front of him, not really taking them in. It took him thirty minutes to get to the end. Nothing.

He sat at Amelia's desk and looked for something that

gave it all away. Whatever the intruders had wanted, they hadn't got. They must have tortured Amelia, but because they were still looking, it must still be in the office somewhere. But he couldn't see anything on her desk, and if it had been visible, then they would have found it.

He clicked the button on her computer monitor. The screen slowly came to life, pale blue, and then the password dialogue box. Except that there was a red cross next to it. The password had been entered incorrectly. He tapped his lip with his finger. The police might have turned it on, but they wouldn't need to, because Linda could access everything from her own computer, but she wouldn't have done that, not without his permission, because she'd be worried about confidentiality. So if it hadn't been the police, it must have been whoever planted the knife on him, because they had been in the office. They had been looking for something on the computer and been locked out.

Charlie typed in his own username and logged on.

He went to the client search box and typed in Privett. Twelve client numbers came up, all Billy's case files, although ten of those were from before Alice Kenyon's death in his pool. There were two from the last year, which surprised him, as other than Alice's death, Billy had kept out of trouble. One of the files was at Donia's flat, and so what was the other one?

Charlie clicked on Billy's most recent client number. He expected to see a list of consultations and letters, so that he could trawl through the history of the file without having it in front of him. Amelia didn't always put everything on the paper file.

There was just one entry from a week earlier, an attendance note, along with a few telephone calls and letters.

Charlie clicked on the attendance note and started to read.

It said that Amelia had visited Billy's house, and that they had recorded a video. That's all it said. Two hours.

He sat back. That note was too brief for Amelia. Attendance notes contained detail, so that they had a record of exactly what the client told them. That note was just so that she didn't forget to bill him for the time, which confirmed his suspicions from the other file, that if there was nothing on the note that disclosed what was on the video, it told Charlie one thing; Amelia didn't want a record of it on the file. That must be the disc that had been sent to the press and to the police and to Ted Kenyon. The video was the important thing, and there was no sign of a master copy.

Charlie sat back and ran through the events of the evening in his mind. He was missing something, he was sure of it. Where was Donia? Who was Donia? Just a work experience student all the way from Leeds. A long way to come to work for nothing. And staying in a flat too. It was costing her more than her time.

They had gone through the file together, and when it didn't contain anything obvious, those people in black arrived. Had she let them in? Was Donia working for the group, and so had applied for work experience just to find whatever it was they wanted, which he knew now was the video?

But that didn't sit with how she had been in the flat. Or was he failing to see past the pretty face?

He ran out of Amelia's office, wincing, and went to the desk in reception. The job applications were kept in a folder underneath the desk, the applications for training contracts in one side, the requests for work experience in the other. He flicked through until he saw a neatly typed piece of paper with Donia's name at the top.

He sat down and read it quickly. Donia Graham. An

address in Leeds. Her education. A paragraph about why she wanted the experience in Charlie's firm. Nothing unusual. Just another request for a foothold in a law firm, hoping that it might come useful later. They hadn't checked whether any of it was true.

He put the paper down and realised that he didn't know what was going on anymore.

Chapter Forty

John stood by the front door on guard duty, holding the shotgun, his eyes scanning the dark hills, trying to see into the shadows. He was still shaking after Dawn's attempted escape, because he didn't know what Henry would have done if she had got away.

It was still quiet. There were no headlights on the road, no people coming across the field. If Henry was right, people were coming to get them, but all he could hear was the crack of the branches in the woods opposite, and the occasional rustle of leaves as a bird took flight. The light from the house spilled over onto the edge of the field, the stone circle taking on an amber hue. He remembered what Dawn had said, that it was a graveyard, Henry's legacy just a field filled with dead bodies.

John looked back and along the hall to where Dawn was trussed up, her hands bound in front of her. He wanted to go to her and find out more about Henry, but the rest of the group were sitting and watching her, making sure that she didn't make another attempt at running.

Gemma walked along the hallway towards him. She looked distracted, her teeth teasing at her lip. As she leant against the doorjamb and looked over the field, John said, 'Where did Henry come from?'

She looked at him. 'I don't understand.'

'How did he become the leader? What's his background?'

Gemma shrugged. 'Just like us. I know what he told us, that he grew up the hard way and so understands.'

'But those are just words. They don't mean anything.'

'You want specifics?' Gemma said, and then she sighed. 'He's from Manchester. His father was a drinker, and he used to beat Henry, so Henry left home. He learned the guitar and survived by busking. That's how he fell in with the festival crowd. He roamed around until eventually he ended up here. Just about being lost and found.'

'What about prison?' John said, and when Gemma scowled, he added, 'Dawn said that he'd done some bad stuff, and had gone to prison for abusing a young boy.'

'That was a set-up – Henry told us about that. It was just some daft kid who liked to make things up.'

'He was convicted though, and went to prison.'

'Prison is full of innocents,' Gemma said. 'He told us that his beliefs were founded there, because it gave him space to think.'

'If you are in prison, you will think about being free,' John said. 'It's natural.' He turned to Gemma. 'Dawn talked about Billy Privett.'

Gemma looked back into the house towards Dawn. 'We're not about the past anymore.'

'She was going to tell me something about Billy Privett.'

'So it's good that she didn't.'

'What do you mean?'

Gemma shook her head. 'You don't need to know. We're about the future now, about fighting back.'

'Was it anything to do with Alice Kenyon?'

'Why do you say that?' Gemma said, her eyes suddenly flashing angry.

John took a step back. 'Hey, I didn't mean anything by that,' he said. 'But why else would Dawn mention Billy, because she was talking about other things Henry had done?'

'Why is that your concern?'

John thought about what to say, but as Gemma scowled at him, all he could think of was not upsetting her, and so he smiled an apology and said, 'I just don't want anything to stop us.'

'Why would that stop us?'

'I don't know,' John said, shrugging. 'If the police come for Henry because of what happened to Alice, they won't care about his vision.'

Gemma thought about that, and then, 'Do you trust him?'

John considered that for a moment and then nodded. 'Henry? Of course I trust him.'

'So stop worrying,' Gemma said. 'Henry has it all under control.' Then she frowned. 'If the police go after Henry, we all go down. Henry, Arni. Even me. Is that what you want, to see me go down?'

'Were you there?'

Gemma stepped forward and stroked John's cheek with her fingers. She leaned into him and kissed him softly. 'We don't need to talk about that night,' she whispered.

John's misgivings about Billy Privett seemed to dissolve as he tasted her lips on his. He wanted to feel her body under his, the soft feel of her skin under his fingers. He closed his eyes. 'I just don't want to lose you.'

'If you stick with us and trust Henry, you won't lose me.'

He opened his eyes and smiled at her.

'You do still trust him? And me?'

John looked at Gemma, and her eyes were wide, appealing to him, and he felt that pull, a need to hold her, almost as if it didn't matter what she might have done. What any of them had done.

'I'm falling in love with you,' he said.

Gemma started to laugh.

'Stop it,' he said, feeling embarrassed.

'I'm not laughing at you,' she said, and kissed him on his cheek. 'I'm loving you. Stay with us, babe. We'll get through this.'

John flushed. He wanted to hold her, for them both to run away and leave Henry behind, but he knew one thing; he wasn't going to leave Gemma there.

'Stay strong,' she said, and hugged him. He pulled her in close, inhaled the scent of her hair, felt her ribs under his fingers.

They stood there together, Gemma in the crook of his arm. Watching. Waiting.

Chapter Forty-One

Charlie went back to the computer. There was more information on there, and so he wanted to read as much as he could before he left the office. He glanced out of the window, towards the alley at the back, where Patrick's car was parked, expecting to see shadows moving, or perhaps blue flashing lights, but it looked quiet.

Amelia's note had been typed on the computer and so Charlie looked again at what she had written. He knew there had to be something that he was supposed to see. It was a niggle pricking at his subconscious. As he read it again, he saw it. The exact words were *Videotaped interview with Billy Privett.* It had been recorded on tape, not on disc or a memory stick. Had the intruders realised that?

Charlie started pulling out drawers in Amelia's desk. They were tidy, pens and staples stacked neatly together, but when he pulled out the bottom drawer, he saw a small video camera, still with the leads attached that connect it to the computer. Amelia had downloaded the footage and made the discs.

He lifted out the camera. There was no tape in it. He banged the desk in frustration. Where was it?

He went to log off from Billy's file and click off the computer when he saw another entry. It was the time that stood out. Amelia had made three calls just after she had written the attendance note about the video. He leaned into the screen, curious, and clicked on one. The entry contained little detail. It stated that Amelia had made a phone call and cross-referenced it with a different file with the reference ABB003/1. Everything Amelia had done in the office, she had billed for it. The reference meant that he was the third client with those three letters at the start of his surname, but that it was the first file for him. A new client. There was no more activity that day, and now Billy was dead, along with Amelia.

Charlie went back to Amelia's shelves. It was the first file he got to, right at the start of the alphabet. He pulled the lamp a bit closer so that he could see it properly.

The file was a criminal file, from one court appearance. Charlie looked at the instruction sheet. John Abbott. An arrest for criminal damage, some graffiti on the side of a building in the town centre. *I am a free man* and *My rule: no rules.* Another one was *Smash the world.*

It stirred a memory in him.

Charlie read on.

John was a loner. He lived on his own after his mother died. He'd been left money and property, but his life seemed empty. He was angry at the world, because it had left him with no one to care for. He had wanted to find answers and started to read on the internet how governments were colluding together to create one world power, with the so-called free world's power concentrated in a small number of families. It made John angry, he didn't want any part of society anymore, but he didn't know what to do. He had told Amelia that he scrawled on the building through frustration. He wasn't sorry though, and he was going to carry on finding the answers and fighting.

Charlie closed the file and threw it onto the desk. Something clattered onto the desk but Charlie ignored it. Abbott was just some local crackpot who was unhappy with the direction of his life, and so he was making it someone else's fault. He had caused some damage and had wanted Amelia to turn the court speech into a protest. But why was Amelia making calls about Billy Privett using that file reference? The case was four months old. It should have been closed and billed.

Charlie reached for the file again, knowing that the answer was in there somewhere.

He went to the call logs on John Abbott's file. All they said was that Amelia had spoken to M at NPOIU. Nothing more. Three times. Charlie didn't know what they meant and so he pulled out the bill, hoping it would explain more. When he read it, he was shocked.

He leaned back in his chair, just quietly nodding to himself. He picked up the bill again, confused, to make sure that he had read it right. He had.

The bill was made out to the police. But why would the police pay the legal costs for a defendant in a criminal case?

He realised that there was only one thing to do, despite what he had said to Julie. He did need to speak to the police. But on his terms.

He called Julie. She answered on the third ring.

'What's going on, Charlie?' she said, her voice in a whisper. 'Andy doesn't like me being worried about you, but I am.'

'It's been an eventful day, and I don't think it's going to lay off just yet,' he said. 'I need you to get Sheldon Brown to call me.'

'I can't just go calling inspectors.'

'I thought you wanted me to come in.'

'I do, but only to make it easier for yourself. And anyway,

the rumours are that Sheldon Brown has been taken off the case. DI Williams from FMIT is running the show now. He's walking round the station like it's beneath him.'

'No, it has to be Sheldon Brown,' Charlie said. 'We haven't always got on, but he's straight and I trust him. I don't know Williams.'

She sighed and then said, 'I'll see what I can do.'

Charlie was about to hang up when she said, 'Look after yourself, Charlie. I don't know what's gone wrong today, but I still care about you.'

He would have laughed on a different day. Instead, he thanked her and put the phone down.

As he went to grab his car keys, he saw something on the desk. He was sure it hadn't been there before. A small videotape. He remembered something clattering on the desk when he had put the Abbott file down.

There was a connection between Billy Privett's video and the Abbott file, because Amelia had made calls straight after making it, and now a videotape had fallen out.

Charlie scrambled in the drawer again, looking for the video camera. He fumbled with the tape and then found the button that would make it play. He rewound it to the beginning and pulled out the screen at the side. As the tape scrolled forward, Billy Privett appeared on the small screen. He was sitting in a chair and looking nervous, messing with the jewellery on his wrist.

Charlie punched the air. This was it.

He turned off the camera and put it into the pocket in his jacket. He took the file too, along with Donia's application, grabbed the car keys and headed for the door.

Chapter Forty-Two

Ted's eyes were fixed on the road as Sheldon drove them towards Oulton. Sheldon hadn't said much since he had been into the police station in Penwortham, but he was in a rush, screeching his car around the tights bends lined by stone walls, the long slope towards Oulton visible ahead as a long line of orange lights.

'Do you know what is the hardest thing about losing Alice?' Ted said.

Sheldon looked at him briefly, and then turned back to the road. 'The thought that her killer is still out there?'

Ted shook his head. 'No. It's the way it hits when you are not expecting it, and so you feel like you can never live your life. I've tried to channel my anger, because it felt like I could control it that way, even start to rationalise it, because I know that being angry won't bring Alice back. So it's not that.' He let out a long sigh and swallowed. 'You think you are dealing with it, and then you see something, and you forget for a moment that she is dead, and so when it comes back at you, it feels like the hurt has never gone away.'

'What like?'

'Stupid things. A trailer for a film, some fluffy chick-flick, and the first thought you have is that Alice would like that, but then you remember that she can't, and it seems so unfair, because everyone else's kids will queue up for it, and Alice never will. Or a dress that would make her look pretty, or a book she might like. We tried to go on holiday, and we went to a lovely place in the south of France. The sunflowers were out and everywhere had charm and sunshine, but all we could think about was that Alice would have loved it.'

Sheldon didn't respond, there was no point, and so they drove in silence for a few miles until Sheldon said, 'I need to go to the station in Oulton.'

'I'm coming with you.'

Sheldon shook his head. 'You're too well known. They'll spot you and throw you out.'

'They might do that to you.'

'No, they won't,' Sheldon said, and he clenched his jaw.

Ted stayed silent for a few minutes and watched the flash of the houses past the windscreen. As Sheldon started on the long climb to Oulton, he said, 'So what do I do?'

'You go home until I get there.'

'What will you do if you find out something crucial?' When Sheldon glanced at him, Ted added, 'Do you tell the police, or me?'

Sheldon thought about that, and then said, 'I don't know.'

Ted frowned. 'So it's all one-way. I tell you what I know and then you shut me out.'

'It's not like that.'

'It seems like it is.'

'I'm still a police officer, Ted. I'm sorry about that, but I do still have to do the right thing. I can promise you one thing though.'

'Go on.'

'Whatever I tell the police, I'll tell you too, and so we can both look at it. You never know, we might beat them to it.'

Ted nodded and then he smiled. He seemed happy with that.

Charlie checked around as he got onto the fire escape outside his office. He couldn't see anyone watching, but the onset of night had turned the alley behind into shadows. He was looking out for blue lights as well, not just threats in the dark, and he needed to move quickly but quietly.

Despite his efforts, his footsteps clanged on the metal and echoed between the buildings. He had the John Abbott file hidden in his suit, and as he got to the yard, he paused, waiting for the rush of an attacker, his breath held. There was no one, just the light cast by the kitchen of the takeaway and chatter in Turkish he couldn't understand drifting through an open window.

The rear gate clicked open. Patrick's Corsa was still there. There was nothing unusual in the alley, but there were gateways all along, small dark spaces that would hide someone, and they could block him in.

He climbed into the car quickly. He hadn't locked it, and so he sat there for a moment and checked his mirror, waiting for the shadow of someone to appear from the back seat, a growing threat blocking out the rear window. He turned around slowly, just to look in the back seat, and then let out a sigh of relief when he saw it was empty.

There was a bang on the bonnet, and so he whirled around quickly, his eyes wide, teeth bared. It was a cat, making its way to the floor from an alley wall. Charlie closed his eyes to let his heart rate calm down, and then turned the ignition key, the engine loud as he pulled away. He relaxed when he got onto the street, where he was in control of where he went next.

He drove away from the town centre, turning down side streets and through estates to make sure he wasn't being followed. His phone vibrated in his pocket and so he stopped in a parking bay outside an off-licence. He didn't want to get pulled into a cell just because he had used a phone when driving.

It was a text from Julie. *I did some ringing around*, and then there were some numbers highlighted in blue. He called the number, and Sheldon's familiar measured tones came through.

'Brown.'

No introductions. This man was used to being in charge.

'This is Charlie Barker,' he said.

Sheldon didn't respond at first, until eventually he said, 'What can I do for you, Mr Barker?'

It sounded like Sheldon was in a car. Charlie could hear the whoosh of passing traffic.

'I've got some information for you, about the Billy Privett case,' Charlie said.

'I'm listening.'

'No, I need to show you.'

'How do I know it's important?'

'Dare you take the risk?'

A pause, and then, 'I'm going to the station. Meet me there.'

'No, I can't go there.'

Sheldon was silent for a while, and then he said, 'Okay, go to Ted Kenyon's house. We won't be long.' He gave Charlie the address before his phone went silent.

Charlie drove quickly towards Oulton town centre, and then dropped away on one of the country roads towards Ted Kenyon's house. The street was quiet when Charlie pulled up. The sodium orange of the streetlights curved away ahead and he couldn't see anyone on the pavement. There had been no cars behind him.

As he closed the car door, he thought that Ted's house looked like there was no one in. Some of the lights were on, but the curtains were open, and all Charlie could see were walls and furniture. But then there was the rumble of an engine. Charlie tensed and wondered if it was the people who had been in Donia's flat, guessing his next move, but as it got closer, he recognised Ted Kenyon in the passenger seat.

As Ted and Sheldon climbed out, Ted said, 'Mr Barker, I was sorry to hear about Miss Diaz.'

Charlie nodded his thanks. 'It doesn't compare to your loss.'

Ted started the walk up his drive, Sheldon with him. Charlie took it as an invitation to follow, and when Ted opened the door and stepped aside to let Charlie walk in, he was surprised at how quiet it seemed.

'Is this some kind of trap?' Charlie said.

'What do you mean?'

Charlie nodded towards Sheldon, who was walking into the living room. 'Inspector Brown told me to come here. I'm wondering if it was the right thing to do.'

'It's no trap,' Ted said. 'Can I get you a drink?'

Charlie sighed and nodded. 'Just make it strong,' he said, and then followed Sheldon into the living room. They stared at each other, neither saying anything, until Ted came back into the room and passed him a glass. The amber fluid and the oak smells were warm and comforting. A single malt. He took a sip. It was good.

Once the whisky had filtered down to where it would do most good, Charlie got a good look at Sheldon, and was surprised by his appearance. His clothes hung from him and there was a film of sweat on his forehead.

'Can we talk openly?' Charlie said to Sheldon, glancing towards Ted Kenyon, unsure about what he could discuss in front of him. When Ted didn't leave the room, and Sheldon let him stay, Charlie guessed that there was no problem.

'You sounded scared on the phone,' Sheldon said.

'My business partner is dead.'

'Not your friend?' Sheldon said.

Charlie's eyes narrowed. 'What do you mean?'

'You worked together. Even if you didn't socialise, she must have been your friend too.'

'Why the hell does that matter?' Charlie said, getting impatient.

Sheldon shrugged. 'I just thought it might matter to her, to be missed.'

'Whatever I call her, she is dead, and we both know that whoever killed her also murdered Billy Privett.' Charlie looked up at Ted. 'I'm sorry for being drunk last night, but I meant what I said, that I've never heard anything from Amelia that Billy admitted killing Alice.'

'So what information have you got?' Ted said, not giving away his emotions.

Charlie pulled out the John Abbott file from under his jacket.

'Two days before Billy died, he made a video. I think whoever killed Billy did so because of the video, because the person who made the video with him, Amelia, has been killed too. They came into my office and took all the copies of the disc.'

'How do you know this?' Sheldon said.

'Because Amelia sent copies of the footage to the police, to the press, and also to Mr Kenyon here.' Charlie turned to him. 'Did you get a copy?'

Ted shook his head.

'No, I didn't think so. There had been a burglary the night before, and so my secretary was late sorting out all the post. I think they stole the lot of them. They got lucky.'

'So what was on it?' Sheldon said.

'My guess is it's Billy telling his story. The instructions to Amelia were to post it out if he died.'

'So what's that?' Sheldon said, and pointed at the file in Charlie's hand.

'Part of the puzzle, but you can provide this part.' Charlie held up the file. 'Amelia made three calls to the same number after that video was made, and she billed this file for the calls. There were another three calls made on this file after Billy had been found.'

'So that makes a connection, does it?' Sheldon said.

'It does in my mind, because this file finished four months ago. Why would Amelia start calling someone in connection with this file after Billy has made a video?'

Sheldon held out his hand for the file.

'I've not finished,' Charlie said. He reached in and pulled out the bill. 'This file is a criminal file. So why has she sent the bill to the police?' He passed over the piece of paper and let him take in its contents. 'Why were the police settling bills for petty criminals? I've never heard of that before.'

Sheldon eased out a crick in his neck as he took in the bill, and Charlie could tell that he didn't know the answer.

'What is the file about?' Ted said.

'Some wannabe anarchist,' Charlie said. 'His mother died and left him money and a house, and so he got a conscience about all the poor people in the world and painted slogans on buildings in the town centre. Political rants. So why were the police so interested in him that they would settle his legal bills for him?'

Sheldon looked at Charlie, and then at the piece of paper again. 'I don't know,' he said.

'Why don't you go find out?'

'What do you mean?'

'There's the file,' Charlie said. 'Take it. And find out who are the two men in suits who visited Amelia at the office and who broke into my apartment.'

Sheldon reached out for the file and then turned it over in his hand, as if he could find out the answers without opening it.

'What about you?' Sheldon said eventually.

'I'll wait for you to come back,' Charlie said. When Sheldon glanced at Ted, as if to seek his approval, Charlie added, 'I've had a rough day. I just need to have a rest.'

Ted nodded at Sheldon, who returned a thank you and headed for the door.

As the sound of Sheldon's engine grew faint along the street, Ted said, 'What's really going on?'

Charlie reached into his pocket and pulled out the video camera, the connection leads hanging from it.

'I don't know how much time I've got, because I'm a target now, and I'm worried about a young woman who came to the firm this week. I don't know if she is on the killer's side, but I know that I wanted to help you last night, and I still do.' He held up the camera. 'This is the tape.'

Ted looked at the camera, and then at Charlie, his eyes wide. 'What about confidentiality?' Ted said. 'It was a big thing for you last night, when you were in the pub.'

'I don't care anymore,' Charlie said. 'Amelia is dead. All it would cost me is my career, and right now, that doesn't bother me.'

Ted didn't hesitate. He pulled out the television and plugged in the wires from the camera, taking a few moments to work out how to get the camera onto the right setting. As the screen flickered into life, Ted sat next to Charlie, sitting forward, his fists clenched.

Charlie had only watched a few seconds of the footage when he had found the camera. It seemed more real now that it was on the big screen. Billy Privett was sitting on a high-backed chair, fidgeting, looking nervous. He glanced towards someone off-camera, Charlie presumed it was Amelia, and then Billy cleared his throat.

'My name is Billy Privett, and I'm going to tell you what happened on the night Alice Kenyon died.'

As those words came out of the television Ted's hand went to his eye. Charlie caught the shimmer of a tear, glistening in the light from the screen.

Chapter Forty-Three

John heard the van before he saw it. He was still standing in the doorway, looking down the field and towards the road, the shotgun cradled in his arm. The night had slipped into darkness and so all he could see were the outlines of the hill opposite against the light from the moon.

He looked back into the living room, where Dawn was tied up below the window, a strip of cloth binding her hands, Gemma in front of her, glaring at her. There was blood from a cut on her lip. Gemma had lost patience with Dawn once already.

Gemma caught him looking and so she gave him an impish wave. It was all a game to her. He waved back without thinking. It felt like events were spinning out of his control, and he didn't know how to deal with things anymore. What they were doing was wrong, he knew that, but every time he got a smile from Gemma, he felt that skip of new love.

He stepped outside to wait for Henry's arrival, to warn them about the traps. As John stood in the glare of the headlights, the van rolled and bounced along the farm track, the engine straining, until it came to a stop in a cloud of dust.

Arni jumped out of the driver's seat, Henry following.

John pointed towards the window. 'I've done my best,' he

said. 'Barbed wire on the inside. We've got petrol bombs, and those,' and he gestured with the shotgun towards the dark shadow of an animal trap. 'Watch your step.'

Henry grinned as he got closer, the whites of his eyes catching whatever shreds of light there were 'You've done well,' he said, and then laughed. 'We've gone one better though.'

'What do you mean?'

Then John heard the shouts. Shrieks and then cries of fear, mixed in with anger. Lucy appeared from the back of the van, pulling on someone. It was a woman, young and skinny and dark.

'Look what we caught,' Lucy said, laughing. 'Our new pet.'

'I don't understand.'

'This little bitch is our exit strategy,' Henry said. 'When they get closer, she will keep them away.' He strode towards Lucy and grabbed the young woman by the hair. She yelped. As Henry pulled her towards the house, Lucy jumped up and down in excitement, clapping her hands.

'Who is she?' John asked.

'Donia, she's called,' Lucy said, animatedly. 'And she's going to have some fun.'

As they got into the house, Donia trying to pull away, Henry stopped and looked at Dawn. He turned to John. 'What's going on?'

'She tried to leave. I caught her. She was heading for the road.'

'And you brought her back?'

John nodded.

Henry started to laugh. 'You are complete, John. Welcome to the flock.' He whirled the young woman around by her hair, so that she screwed up her face and cried out in pain, and pushed her towards Lucy. 'Tie her up in there,' and he gestured towards the old man's room. 'We'll deal with her later.'

Henry walked towards Dawn and stared down at her for a few seconds. She shrank back, frightened. He smiled, knelt down in front of her, then reached out and ran some of her hair through his fingers. 'You've let me down,' he said, in a whisper.

She started to sob again. 'I didn't mean to. I'm so sorry.'

'I knew someone would betray me,' Henry said, his voice a low hiss. 'What were your plans? Turn me over to the police? Or just bring them here, so that they could arrest me, perhaps bring a film crew, and so they can have their little show trial? And then what? Lock me away for the rest of my life? Is that what you wanted for me?'

Dawn hung her head. 'Please, Henry, I'm sorry. Don't do it.'

Henry snarled and stood up quickly. He lashed out with his foot, kicking her hard in her ribs. She gasped and cried out, but she couldn't hold herself where she was in pain, because her hands were still tied together.

'I didn't mean to do it,' she shouted, her voice desperate. 'You don't have to do this.'

Lucy appeared behind Henry, and she put her arms round him, her chin resting on his shoulder. 'I made sacrifices,' Lucy said, her voice cold and even. 'Why couldn't you?'

Henry lashed out, backhanding Dawn. Lucy's grip slackened and the slap made a loud crack. He turned to the rest of the group. 'You know what to do.'

No one objected; it seemed that there was no regret for what was about to happen. Four people went outside, three of the young women and Jennifer, who seemed excitable, bustling the others along. They disappeared around the side of the house, and John was just about to shout a warning about the traps when he heard the clatter of tools and they ran onto the field holding spades and pick-axes. They went to some grass by the largest standing stone and started to dig. Henry grabbed Dawn by her hair and pulled her close to him.

'You were special once,' he said. 'Why you?'

'I want to tell the truth,' she said, her voice hoarse. 'No more lies.'

Henry slapped her again, and this time a thin drool of blood ran onto her clothes from her lip. He stood there for a few seconds, his chest heaving, his fists clenching and unclenching. Lucy stepped forward and whispered into Henry's ear, 'She needs you one last time.'

Dawn heard it and started pleading. 'No, no, no, no.'

Henry cricked his neck, teasing out some tension, and then pulled on the cloth that bound her wrists. As she was pulled to her feet, John saw that Henry's eyes were unfocused, wide and wild.

He pulled her towards the stairs. Lucy was laughing, singing, 'Henry's gonna party.' Dawn tried to pull back, wailing, but Henry just pulled harder.

John knew what Henry's intentions were. He turned away to try and block out Dawn's cries, because he could have just let her go. But he couldn't block them out. All he could do was listen as their footsteps went upwards, and as the door closed, he heard Dawn's wails turn to cries of terror.

He looked towards the field. Everyone was grim-faced, mouths set into scowls, digging hard.

He jumped when he felt a soft hand on his forearm. It was Gemma. 'It was always this way,' she said, her head resting against him. He reached up to stroke her hair, and then kissed her gently on the top of her head.

'I know,' he said, although when he tried a smile, it was unconvincing.

Ted was quiet as Billy Privett started to speak on the videotape.

'Things were getting too wild,' Billy said. He was fidgeting, rubbing his hands together and sitting forwards and then back again.

'What do you mean, wild?' a voice said off-camera. Amelia.

Billy shrugged. 'Just that. What do you think I mean?'

'It's your story, not mine.'

'Okay, I get it,' he said, some impatience in his voice. Then he sat back, one leg crossed over the other. 'It was fun at first. All that money and so people wanted to know me.'

'Was that fair on you, that you were only about the money?'

'I was having a good time, what was wrong with that, better than I could have had without it. I knew it was about my money, but so what? There were women coming to my house who would have never looked at me before the win. But there they were, in my house, getting naked and getting off. I didn't care why they were there.'

'So what went wrong?'

Billy sighed heavily. 'People come to expect it, because when they are only coming for a good time, I have to give it to them. But the money doesn't last forever. What could I do when it started to run out? I couldn't tell anyone that, because then I would be at the house on my own.'

Ted shook his head. 'This is where I'm supposed to feel sorry for him.'

Charlie didn't answer. He felt for Ted, but he wasn't interested in attacking Billy. He just wanted answers.

Ted fell silent again as Billy talked about the parties, and the drugs and the group sex. He was enjoying the recollections too much, and so Amelia brought him back to why he was making the video.

'Tell me about the night Alice died?' she said.

Billy took a deep breath and sat upright.

'I hadn't met her before that night,' Billy said. 'I didn't really meet her that night, if I'm honest, until, well, until it was too late, because she was just one of the girls at the party.' Billy paused to wipe his eyes. 'She came with that group.'

'Remember, Billy, this is the first time you've told me your story,' Amelia said. 'Don't make me drag it out. We can stop and start again, if we have to. So which group?'

'Henry's group.'

'Henry?' Amelia said. Her voice came quick, almost like an interruption.

'Yeah. Do you know him? They used to come up to the parties not long before Alice died, and I don't even remember how it started. Perhaps he tagged on to someone else, I don't know. Things were getting out of hand back then, almost an open house. Henry was intimidating, even though he wasn't that big. He was sort of intense, and he frightened people away.'

'Do you know his full name?' Amelia said. Her voice sounded keener than before.

'Henry Mason.'

There was a pause, and then Amelia said, 'Henry Mason? Are you sure?' Her voice was quiet, almost distant.

'Of course I'm sure. You do know him, I can tell.'

'It's not about me, Billy,' she said. 'Why didn't you just stop Henry from coming up, if you didn't want him there?'

Billy rubbed his hands together, nervous about replying.

'You don't have to be scared,' Amelia said.

'But what if this video gets out?'

'It won't,' Amelia said. 'It's only here in case something happens to you, so your story gets out there. Are you in danger?'

Billy nodded.

'Why do you think that?'

'Because Henry told me he would kill me if I said anything, and I know they suspect something.'

'What, that you're going to go to the police?'

Billy nodded again.

'I keep on sitting in the pool room,' Billy said, a tear visible on the footage. 'I know it's self-pity, and Alice's father won't care about me, but I keep on seeing Alice in the pool. So I sit there and look at the water, I can't help myself because that was where it all went wrong. My life, Alice's life. Everything changed, and it wasn't my fault, and sometimes I just want to jump in and sink to where she was, where I can't hear any noises above, because it will all be muted, and so for a few peaceful moments, I'll be free.'

Amelia paused for a moment as Billy wiped his eyes, and then she said, 'Why does your remorse make Henry think that you're going to the police?'

Ted turned to Charlie. 'He didn't use the word *remorse*, she did,' Ted said. 'That's what you lawyers do, isn't it, repackage their words to make them fit?'

'Remember the girl you were with in the car?' Charlie said. 'Perhaps you might have needed a lawyer then.'

Before Ted could respond, Billy coughed. 'That bitch in my house, that's why,' he said.

'Bitch?'

'Christina, although I know that's not her real name. She calls herself my housekeeper, but she isn't. She is Henry's spy. I don't pay her, but Henry moved her in, just because he was worried I would talk.'

'How long has she lived at your house?'

'Three months. Henry kept out of the way at first, but I knew he was watching me. He would turn up behind me when I was walking down the street or driving somewhere, even if it was somewhere I hadn't planned to be. It was his way of letting me know that he was there, so I wouldn't do anything stupid.'

'So what made him move in Christina?'

Ted turned to Charlie. 'She's not called Christina. She's called Lucy, and was the girl they caught me with in the car.' When Charlie raised his eyebrows, he added, 'I told you it was a set-up.'

Billy was speaking again.

'My old friends drifted back and so the parties carried on. Then Henry turned up again, and I told him to stay away, that I didn't want him round anymore.'

'Why not?'

'Because it just wasn't right. What happened to Alice, and because some of the girls he brought with him were, well . . .'

'Too young?'

'Maybe. I'm not a good person, I know that, but I'm no child molester. And Henry was cruel.'

'How do you mean?' Amelia said.

'If someone didn't want to take part, he would make them.'

'You need to explain, Billy,' Amelia said, some tension creeping into her voice. 'This is your story, not mine. You have to tell it.'

Billy nodded and took a deep breath. 'Before Henry started coming to the parties, things happened because everyone wanted it to. Random sex, sometimes threesomes, even more occasionally. And women together. It was just everyone getting off in every room, like every man's fantasy. It was fun and everyone had a good time. If you just wanted to drink, or take some coke, that was okay, but not in Henry's world. He made people do things. To him, to each other.'

'And he made you do things?'

'Sometimes,' Billy said, looking down, his cheeks flushed red. 'Some of the girls Henry brought would start to cry, say that they didn't want to, but Henry would make them. Or the other guy, the one who killed Alice.'

Ted gasped at that but stayed silent. Charlie knew he had been waiting a long time to hear this story.

'Tell me about him,' Amelia said.

There was another long sigh from Billy. 'He's a big Scandinavian guy. Arni, they called him. Muscles and long hair. But it wasn't just his build. He was nasty and vicious. He didn't smile much, and if people didn't do what he wanted, he would hit them. Usually just slaps, but if someone that big hits you, it hurts, and so you do as he says.'

'What happened to Alice?' Amelia said.

Billy looked up at the ceiling and another tear ran down his cheek. 'It was the same old crowd, Henry's lot, all in black, but there was someone new with them.'

'Alice?'

Billy nodded. 'She was different. Her clothes were brighter, and she was talking politics at first, because she seemed interested in what they had to say, how they lived their lives.'

'So how did it go wrong?'

'It went the usual way, with the women naked, and Henry telling them who to have sex with, as if he was dishing out treats. Alice looked embarrassed, as if she didn't want to be there, but was too polite to leave. Then one of the girls didn't want to take part, and so Arni tried to make her. He held her down and told one of the men to, well, you know. Alice tried to stop him, said that it was wrong, that it was rape, which made Arni angrier.'

'What happened?'

'Arni did to the girl what Alice accused him of. He held her, face down, and had sex with her, and everyone else just watched and let him carry on as the girl screamed.'

'Everyone?'

Billy swallowed.

'Yes, me too,' he said, and then shook his head. 'Everyone except Alice. She tried to stop it, but people held her back.'

'Did you hold her back?'

'No, I didn't,' he said, 'but I did something just as bad.'

'Which was what?'

'I did nothing. I let it happen because I was scared, except that Alice wasn't, and the more the girl struggled and cried, the more Alice tried to stop it.'

'What happened next?'

'Henry told Arni to *shut the bitch up*, and so Arni took the knife from his waistband. It was long, with a serrated edge, and he slashed the girl's throat. He held her hair back and ran the blade across her neck like he was in a slaughterhouse or something. Blood went onto the floor. Big pools of it.' Billy wiped his eyes. 'She died pretty quickly. And then it was Alice's turn.'

Charlie leaned forward and put his hand on Ted's shoulder. 'Are you sure you want to do this?'

Ted shrugged it off. 'I've got to do it,' he said, his voice breaking. 'I've got to know.'

'Arni went towards Alice,' Billy said, 'and Henry encouraged him, shouted at Arni to really hurt her, because it will be her last time with a man. Some of the other women held Alice's arms, Christina too, but Arni couldn't do it so soon after the other girl, and so Henry took over. Everyone just laughed as Henry raped her, and brutalised her. I couldn't believe it. They were women, and so what hold must Henry have over them to make them do that? It was almost like he was commanding them, and so if they could do that to Alice, what could they do to me?'

'How did Alice end up in the pool?' Amelia asked.

'Arni dragged her when Henry had finished. Just pulled her through the house by her hair, naked, and put her in the water. She tried to fight, but Arni was too strong. He held her head under until she stopped struggling. Henry put on the dishwasher first, so that their traces were gone, and then we all left, like we were running away.'

'What about the other girl Arni killed?'

Billy shrugged. 'They took her away. I didn't go with them. I just drove around. I didn't know what to do.'

Ted turned to Charlie. 'You can turn it off now,' he said. Charlie could tell he was crying.

When the screen went blank, the only sounds were Ted's sobs. Charlie didn't say anything, but then there was a noise in the corner of the room. When he looked, it was Jake, Ted's son.

'I know who they are,' Jake said.

Ted looked surprised. He wiped his eyes. 'You do? How?'

Jake looked down, nervous. 'I guessed some of that story, from things I've heard.'

Ted looked at Charlie, and then back at Jake, before pointing at the sofa.

'You need to talk,' Ted said.

Chapter Forty-Four

Sheldon was wary as he approached the police station. He was on leave, which really meant an unofficial suspension, but he needed to find the connection between Billy Privett and John Abbott, about why Amelia Diaz had made calls relating to John Abbott after videoing Billy.

He was interested first in why the young woman who had ended up as Billy's housekeeper had seen a theft case against her dropped. He remembered how Chief Inspector Dixon looked shocked when she saw her in the court corridor, and it had been Dixon who had visited the young woman not long before she was released. It wasn't too long before she was being photographed in a car with Ted Kenyon, and then the press lost interest in Alice Kenyon and the story became all about Ted.

The station was mostly in darkness, just the small lamp over the public entrance and a few windows casting any brightness over the darkened millstone. The press had gone home for the night, nothing to report until someone was arrested, and so it was quiet around him as he walked up the cobbled street that led to the station, holding the John Abbott file in his hand.

He went through the car park to get to the entrance in the corner, which used to be the prisoner walk-out door.

The public entrance was closed, but his swipe card still worked, and so he was soon in the nearly empty station.

Most of the doors were closed along the corridor, the uniformed officers out in their cars. There was a light on in the Incident Room, but the filing room was in the other direction. Sheldon turned away and put a set of fire doors between him and whatever progress they were making in there.

The filing room was for those cases that had finished but not yet reached a destruction date. The details of minor cases sometimes became important later on, when a series of them establish a pattern of behaviour.

He had a reference number and so he found Lucy's file quickly. It was just an envelope containing two statements, along with a copy of the custody record stapled to the front.

Sheldon pulled open the envelope and leant against the wall to read the statements. They were routine, as he expected, with just enough information to prove the theft. The shopkeeper had been working the till in his shop when a young woman loitered near the alcohol section. When it looked like his back was turned, she put some whisky into her coat and tried to leave the shop, except that the shopkeeper had been watching her in the convex mirror on the wall above the till. He blocked the door before she got away.

Lucy Crane hadn't put up a fight. She had said she was sorry and asked to be let go, promised that she wouldn't do it again.

The shopkeeper hadn't agreed to that. He worked hard for his money and so why shouldn't she? He called the police.

The second statement was from the arresting officer. He hadn't expected any problems from Lucy, and so he let her stew in her cell for a while as he wrote up his statement. Sheldon knew how it worked, particularly on the night shift, that if he had processed Lucy quickly, he could have ended up with another troublesome incident as his shift drew to a close. No one would pull him out of an interview though, and so all he had to do was hide away as he shuffled papers and then interview her an hour before his shift was due to end. He had expected a guilty plea, and so it would be a fifteen-minute interview, a quarter of an hour with the sergeant as she was charged, and then a quick thirty minutes putting the final pieces of paperwork together.

The statement was nothing more than a summary of the arrest, and her comment after arrest had been, 'Fair enough.'

It was an ordinary shoplifting case against a woman with only youth convictions to her name. It was an easy one. Either a charge, or perhaps a fixed penalty notice, or even a caution. Sheldon could see no reason why Dixon would interfere.

Which made him suspicious.

He put the file back and left the filing room. He was going to go to Dixon's room to confront her, if she was still there, but he wanted to look into the John Abbott file first.

There was an empty room across the corridor, with five desks, each with a monitor on, all connected to small servers on the desk. It was the room used by the burglary team, with trays teeming with paperwork and photographs of Oulton's most prolific thieves plastered on the walls. There was a list of names on a whiteboard, with descriptions of their trainers underneath, so they knew whose door to smash down when a footprint mark turned up at a scene. It was the team Tracey Peters worked on, and he scowled as he thought of how she had spied on him.

He put his anger to one side; he didn't have time to be distracted, and logged in. Once he was in the system, he keyed in Abbott's details, and there were five people with that name on the computer, although only one had an arrest from that year. When Sheldon clicked on the link, he was able to access the custody record and incident log.

Abbott had been caught spraying the graffiti after an anonymous call, and he didn't answer any questions when interviewed.

Sheldon paused, his fingers drumming a beat on his lips. Why didn't John Abbott answer the police questions? He clicked on the case result, and he saw that Abbott had pleaded guilty at the first court hearing. He had admitted the damage at court, but if he had confessed to the police, he wouldn't have had to go to court. He had never been in trouble before, and so would have received a caution, and possibly an add-on of paying the cost of the clean-up, although the graffiti was on a building scheduled for demolition a week later. All of this on the advice of his solicitor, Amelia Diaz. It was almost as if he wanted to go to court. Sheldon pulled on his lip. That troubled him.

The custody photograph of John Abbott showed a man in his mid-twenties, with his hair around his collar and unkempt, like someone who hadn't realised that once Glastonbury comes to an end you are supposed to go back to the real world.

Sheldon scribbled down the address John Abbott had given on his arrest and headed along the corridor once more.

He was heading for Dixon's office, wanting to speak to her about Lucy's case. As he got closer though, he saw the light from the Incident Room spilling into the corridor. He slowed down, and as he passed the doorway, he couldn't stop himself from looking in.

Only Lowther and Tracey Peters were in there, along with DI Williams. Lowther was perched on a desk, looking down at Tracey. From the smile on her face, it seemed that she was enjoying the attention.

Sheldon paused to listen. DI Williams was telling some anecdote about something he once said. The scrawls on the whiteboard and the papers already accumulating on desks gave Sheldon a tinge of envy that he was no longer part of it, but then Williams spotted him in the doorway.

'What brings you back, Sheldon?' Williams said, his grin gleaming beneath the unnatural darkness of his moustache.

'I'm just checking in, wondering how you were getting on,' Sheldon said. He felt some of his tension return as he was reminded of being taken away from the investigation.

'I thought you were on leave, sir,' Lowther said.

'I'm just looking in on one of my other cases. A shoplifting. You wouldn't be interested.'

Williams snorted. 'You're right, I wouldn't. Things find their own level, I suppose.'

Sheldon ignored the jibe. He didn't want to be ejected just yet.

Except Williams didn't seem to want to stop taunting him.

'What I can't understand,' Williams continued, 'is why Dixon was so keen for you to stay in charge. We had to force her into letting us in. Why would that be?'

Sheldon turned away, grinding his teeth. He didn't want to get into a shouting match with him. He walked along the corridor and tried to ignore what he thought were sniggers from the Incident Room.

When he stopped outside Dixon's room, he smoothed down his clothes and looked at the ceiling. He took a deep breath. If his suspicions were wrong, this could end his career.

The knock on Dixon's door was followed by a quiet, 'Come in.'

It seemed Dixon hadn't been doing anything before

Sheldon's knock, as he'd heard no scurrying of papers and there was nothing open on her desk.

He didn't bother with the formalities. 'Why didn't you tell me about Christina, Billy's housekeeper, when I brought her in?' he said, sitting down.

She seemed to sink lower in her chair. Her mouth opened for a second before she spoke. 'Christina?'

'We thought she was a young woman called Christina, but you knew differently.'

'I don't keep track of your cases, Sheldon.'

'But you did with Billy's murder. You spoke to me about it, wanted to know how things were going, and when I brought in Christina, you knew her. I saw it in your face, when you met her in the corridor. You looked shocked.'

'You must be mistaken.'

Sheldon felt the anger build in him, more than a year of frustration of not knowing the answers about Alice Kenyon. His late night vigils outside Billy's house. His wife walking out on him. Hannah, his daughter, growing distant.

He slammed his hand on the desk. Dixon jumped back, startled.

'Liar!' he shouted. He held up Lucy's file and waved it angrily. 'You took quite an interest in her six months ago. Except that Christina was called Lucy Crane back then. You made sure her shoplifting case went away. Why did you do that?'

Dixon's eyes widened and she swallowed. 'I am your senior officer,' she said, although Sheldon heard the tremble in her voice.

'Report me then, and I can tell everyone about this,' and he threw the file across the desk. It slid towards her.

'Sometimes I decide which cases we are proceeding with,' Dixon said. 'Cases cost money and manpower.'

'So you remember her now?'

Dixon looked as if she was about to say something, but then she stopped and looked at her desk.

'But why this case?' Sheldon said, leaning across to jab the file with his finger. 'It was an easy hit, an admitted shop-lifting. Why would you want a tick in the wrong column for a case like that?'

'I don't know what you mean?' Her fingers trembled.

'Okay, try this,' he said, his words coming out quickly. 'Lucy's shoplifting case was just a few weeks before Ted Kenyon was caught in a car with a young woman. You might remember that, it was all over the papers, and guess what; that was Lucy Crane as well. She made a bit of money is my guess, but I can't help wondering whether there was something more to this, because Ted Kenyon being caught with Lucy took the public sympathy away from him. Once the stories became about him, they stopped being about how we couldn't find his daughter's killer.'

Dixon's tongue kept flicking onto her lips. 'Come on, Sheldon, spit it out.'

'That's the thing, ma'am. You're not throwing me out. You are sitting there, listening, wanting to find out what I know, which means that the reason behind this is something you would rather I didn't find out. And now I'm really curious.'

'Don't think you can mess with me, Sheldon.'

Sheldon laughed, but it was filled with bitterness. 'I'm sorry, ma'am, it must be a sign of my sickness. If you remember, you put me on sick leave that I hadn't requested, for the sake of my mental health. So what I will do is leave you alone, but trust me when I say that I will keep on looking for the reason. You noted yourself that I have a tendency towards, shall we say, obsessive behaviour.'

He stood up as if to leave. Just before he turned away, he

noticed that some photographs had been taken from the wall, as all there was left was a picture hook.

Sheldon took one last look at her. She was staring at her desk, and she looked frightened.

Once the door had closed, Sheldon paused for a moment. He looked at his hands. They were shaking. He had done the right thing though, he was sure of that. He marched off down the corridor, and when he got outside the station, he ran to his car. It was time to find out more about John Abbott.

Chapter Forty-Five

Jake sat down on the chair opposite Ted, facing each other over the dining room table. From the pictures Charlie had seen of Alice, he could see the family resemblance, although there was a sadness to him that he had never seen in photographs of Alice.

Jake sat hunched up with his knees turned inwards, his shoulders bony through his black T-shirt.

'So what do you know?' Charlie said.

Jake shrugged, and then said, 'They used to talk to us when we were hanging out in town. They were into being free, so they said. I don't know why they spoke to us. Maybe it was because of how we were dressed, as if they thought we wanted to join some kind of Goth gang. They were friendly at first, but the second time they found us, they started to talk about leaving society and having no rules, and how we had to be there on the big day.'

'Big day?' Charlie said.

'The uprising, that's what they called it.' Jake shook his head. 'It was rubbish, all of it.'

Charlie knew it was the same group he had seen outside his office. He thought of Christina, how she had been placed into Billy's home and felt angry about Donia, about how she had set him up. It was obvious now that she was a plant, put into his firm just so they could find out what Billy had told Amelia. Was that why they had been outside the office, waiting for Donia to take whatever they needed to them?

'Did they go round all the young people in the town?' Charlie said.

'I don't know, because I don't hang out with other kids. Anyway, it wasn't really *us* they were speaking to.'

'I don't understand.'

'It was the girls, not the rest of us. They were just trying it on. They realised soon enough that we weren't interested and so left us alone. We get enough shit from the local kids, all the hoodies picking on us, without the political freaks joining in.'

As Charlie thought back on how the group had watched him, Jake said, 'A couple of them were pretty scary. Like Billy said on the video, one was a huge guy. Solid, over six feet, with a beard that was kind of twisted, with beads in it. And the smaller guy, Henry, he had long hair, and with a really intense look to him. All the girls were in awe of him, I could tell.'

'When was this?' Charlie said.

'Not long before Alice died.'

Ted's mouth opened in shock. 'So you've always suspected them?' Jake responded with another shrug. 'How did you know?'

Jake ground his teeth and looked down.

Charlie moved closer to him. 'Jake?'

He looked away.

Charlie banged his hand on the table. Jake jumped and stared, scared now.

'Jake, if you know something, say it.' Charlie was breathing heavily, his temper rising. 'The time for silence is gone.'

'Jake?' Ted said, confused.

When Jake looked up again, there were tears in his eyes. 'I'm sorry.'

'For what?' Ted said.

'For not saying anything.'

'Tell me now.'

Jake took a deep breath and wiped at his eyes. 'One of Alice's friends had become involved with them. Alice had gone away to university, but do you remember Marie, her friend from school? She failed her exams and she drifted, but Alice would hook up with her when she came home, except that Marie was hanging around with this group. Marie was with them when they were speaking to my mates and me. She was talking about going wild at Billy's house, and that we should go up too, that we'd enjoy it.'

'And so you thought that this group might have had something to do with Alice's death?' Ted said, his voice rising.

Jake looked at his hands for a few seconds, and then said, 'Maybe.'

'And you didn't say anything?'

Jake shook his head.

'Why not?'

Jake swallowed. He looked at his father, and then at Charlie, before he sighed and said, 'We don't know everything about Alice. She was all grown up, not a little girl anymore. She will have had secrets from us. It's natural. When I was talking to Marie, she told me they were having a great time. She was smoking a spliff, and the nods and the winks hinted that it was like a group thing, you know, orgies. What does everyone think about Alice? That she was sweet and lovely and respectable – and she was, but if she had got involved with them, got out of her depth or something, well, it would all change, and I didn't want that, because then she would be the girl who died in some drug-fuelled party. No, I preferred it how it was reported, that she was innocent, that she wasn't part of their crowd. So I kept quiet.'

Ted took some deep breaths, and Charlie could see some anger in his eyes, that his own son knew some of the answers but had kept them from him. But Ted's furrowed brow showed he was wrestling with his feelings, because he understood why Jake had kept quiet, because he had tried to protect Alice's memory.

'Who's the girl?' Ted said. 'Marie?'

'Marie Cuffy,' Jake said. 'She was a friend of Alice's from the sixth form, but Marie had changed. I suppose Alice had, but all of Alice's other friends had gone away too, and so Marie was someone to hang round with when she was home.'

'Find me a picture.'

Jake left the room, and Charlie listened as he rummaged in what he guessed was Alice's room. When Jake came downstairs again, he was holding a photograph. 'That's her,' he said, pointing to a picture.

As Charlie looked, he saw an attractive young woman, her eyes flirty, smiling with Alice, each holding beer bottles in their hand.

'When was the last time you saw her?' Charlie said.

'I haven't seen her since Alice died.'

'We need to find her,' Ted said, tapping the photograph. 'She knows something about Alice. Jake, do you know where she lives?'

Jake nodded and gave an address. 'That's where her parents live.'

Charlie's thoughts were interrupted by the buzz of his phone in his pocket. He checked the number. It was Donia's.

'Hello?' Charlie said, expecting to hear her voice, ready for the next stage of deceit.

'Mr Barker,' said a deep voice. Charlie recognised it from the hallway of Donia's flat.

Charlie swallowed. His mouth had gone dry. 'What do you want?'

'You know what we want.'

'Tell me.'

'The videotape of Billy Privett. We've got the discs, but we want the original tape.'

He felt the hot flush of anger creep up his cheek, mixed in with helplessness about how it was all out of control. 'You killed Amelia. Why should I do anything for you?'

'Because we've got something you want.'

'You've got nothing I want.'

'Haven't we?' the voice said, and then he laughed, loud and mocking. 'What about poor little Donia here?'

'The work experience girl you put into my firm. Very clever, but I'm not falling for that.'

'If you knew the truth about Donia, you would help. The tape. Bring it, and it must be you. Call me when you've got it. I'll give you an hour. Then we start to kill her, slowly.'

His phone went dead, and he looked at it in disbelief. And what did he mean about Donia? The truth?

Charlie remembered that he had grabbed Donia's CV before he left the office. He reached into his pocket and pulled out the crumpled piece of paper. It looked routine, headed with her name, Donia Graham. He doubted its truth, but there was a phone number.

He dialled the number and waited as it rang out. When the phone was answered, a timid voice said, 'Hello?'

Charlie put the phone against his chest for a moment, just to think about what to say, and then, 'Mrs Graham?'

'Miss,' she said. 'Miss Graham.' Her flat Yorkshire vowels were given some lift by the lilt of the Caribbean.

He took a deep breath. 'Is it Donia's mother?'

'Yes.'

'It's Charlie Barker,' he said. He expected Donia's plan to unravel now, because he doubted she was the real Donia.

Instead, he heard just a gasp. He waited for her to say something, anything that would kick-start the conversation, but she said nothing.

'Miss Graham?'

'It's Wilma, you know that,' she said, her voice stronger now. Then she sighed. 'I'm sorry to hear about your business partner.'

'She told you?'

'Yes, she was quite shaken by it.' There was a pause, and then, 'Has she told you?'

Charlie was confused. 'I'm sorry, told me what?'

'About her. And me.'

'I don't understand.'

Another pause. 'You don't remember me?'

Charlie was getting exasperated now. 'I'm not calling about you. It's about Donia.' And then he realised what she had said. 'What do you mean, why don't I remember *you*?'

'Hasn't Donia said anything to you?'

Charlie closed his eyes. She sounded genuine, and so the possibilities started to race through his head. The scene at the flat, the members of the group there, and now the phone call, the demand for the videotape and the threat to kill Donia. He had it wrong, and she wasn't a plant. She was just a young law student getting some experience, which meant that the threat was real. He felt nauseous.

'Do you know anything about an anarchist group near Oulton?' Charlie said.

'No. Why should I?' Her voice started to crack. 'Why, what's happened?'

Charlie wanted to put off the moment, knowing what he was about to say would wreck her, but he knew that he couldn't.

'The same people who killed my business partner have got Donia,' he said quietly.

Wilma let out a whimper. '*Got?* What do you mean?'

'Just that,' he said. 'They called me and told me they have her.'

'And they're going to hurt her?'

He paused again, wished that he could end the call and not say it, but he knew that he couldn't. 'Yes, that's what they told me.'

Wilma's voice turned into a scream. He moved the phone away from his ear and put his head in his hand. He let her shout, and she was shouting at him, saying that he was supposed to look after her.

'Call the police, Wilma, please.'

'I told her to stay away from you, Charlie Barker! I tried to tell her not to, that it wouldn't end well, but she wouldn't listen, and now she's in danger.'

Charlie thought about telling her that it wasn't his fault, but it wasn't the right time to talk about blame.

He tried to speak calmly. 'The person who spoke to me said that there was something about Donia that would make me help them. What did they mean?'

Wilma went quiet for a few seconds, and then she said something that sent everything into background noise, blurred, out of focus, the words burning into him like a slap.

'Charlie,' she said. 'Donia is your daughter.'

Chapter Forty-Six

John was outside the old man's room. There were screams and sobs from upstairs, the sounds of Henry with Dawn, and people digging outside. Arni was on the telephone, and he heard what he said about the girl they had brought back with them, that her name was Donia.

He pushed at the door so that it swung open gently. The old man didn't look up, but the girl did.

Donia was fastened to a metal strut on the bedstead, a chain wrapped around her wrist and made tight with a padlock. As John went over to her, she shrank back, her feet pushing against the floor, as if that would somehow help.

'What are you going to do to me?' she said, the words coming out as a wail.

'I don't think anyone knows yet,' he said.

Her breaths came in gulps. She tried to speak in a whisper. 'Why don't you let me go? I won't tell anyone, I promise. I just want to go home.'

'Henry has brought you here for a reason. I can't stop that.'

The old man moaned, but John ignored it. He had learned to do that.

John knelt down to her level. 'Just be patient, Donia. It will be all right.'

'I haven't done anything wrong to you,' she said. 'You can't let them keep me. I'm scared. Let me go.'

John shook his head. 'I can't do that. I have to wait for Henry.'

There were footsteps behind him, and when he looked round, it was Gemma and Lucy.

'Have you taken a fancy to her, John?' Lucy said, laughing.

'No, no,' he said, looking at Gemma, flustered, suddenly embarrassed, standing up straight. 'It's not like that.'

Lucy went towards Donia and stroked her hair. 'Why not? She's a pretty girl.'

Donia pulled her head away, but Lucy grabbed her hair more tightly, making Donia cry out in pain.

'He's saving himself for you,' Lucy said to Gemma, mocking him. 'Isn't that right, John?'

He didn't answer. Instead, he just blushed and looked down.

Lucy gripped the collar of Donia's jumper and pulled it back, making Donia's chest jut out, Donia gasping.

'She is very pretty though, John, don't you think?' Lucy said, and reached down with her other hand and pulled up the bottom of Donia's jumper, exposing her stomach and her bra.

'Do you like her now, John?' Lucy said, her voice softer now, but it was pretence, because she was enjoying herself too much, a malevolent gleam in her eyes.

John didn't respond. Lucy had a close bond with Henry, and so he didn't want to say the wrong thing.

'Why don't you party with her, like Henry is with Dawn?' Lucy continued, pouting. 'Gemma won't mind.'

'No, it's not that,' John said quietly, and then stopped himself from going any further. Don't form bonds, that was the rule – because couples become apart from the group and start to look after themselves.

Lucy yanked Donia's jumper again, exposing her chest, small beads of sweat running down to the lace of her bra. 'Final decision?' she said, laughing. 'If you don't, I might.'

There was a loud bang and they all jumped. As John looked round, he saw Arni there. He had hit the doorframe with his cane.

'Leave her for now,' he said.

Lucy let go of Donia's jumper, and she slumped back towards the floor, her head hanging down.

'If that's how you want it?' she said.

Arni nodded. 'That's how I want it.'

John followed Gemma and Lucy out of the room, not acknowledging Arni as they went past, who was staring at the captive girl.

As they went back into the hall, Arni didn't shift his gaze away from Donia, and when he finally turned away, there was a smile on his face.

He was keeping Donia for himself.

Chapter Forty-Seven

Charlie had the phone to his chest. Donia couldn't be his daughter. It didn't make any sense. Then he thought of her age. Eighteen. He did the sums quickly. Nineteen years since she was conceived. She was from Leeds, where he went to university, nineteen years ago.

'Charlie, what is it?' It was Ted, but his voice seemed faint, as if he wasn't really in the room with him.

Charlie's mouth went dry. His fingers tingled with nerves. His daughter? But she is mixed race. Charlie was white.

Then a memory came back to him. A party. The last night of his second year. His farewell to exams for the summer, reckless living, sleeping in until lunchtime. He had to get a summer job, and so he was going the next day, heading for Bridlington, where a friend had fixed him up with some work. There was drink. Too much drink. And a local girl, but on the same course. Pretty, dark, her hair cut in a short afro. A room upstairs. She was naked. Charlie had thought about her sometimes, but he had forgotten her name. He remembered her body under him, her gasps, but had he ever known her name? They had taken a risk, but he'd heard nothing from her afterwards. He had forgotten about her, except when he was horny and alone, and he trawled through his memories for stimulation.

Then he remembered that Wilma hadn't returned for her final year. People had talked about it, but it was soon forgotten in the whirl of exams and having a good time. And it turned out that all the time he was trying to be the hotshot lawyer, he had a daughter growing up in Leeds.

He put the phone back to his ear. 'I didn't know,' he said, his voice quiet.

'It doesn't matter what you know,' Wilma snapped. 'This is about Donia. She is all I have, but Donia wanted to know about you, Charlie, naturally, and so I told her. That's why she's there, with you, to get to know you, and I didn't want her to go, because I didn't know how you'd react when you found out. I didn't want Donia to be hurt emotionally, and now this?'

'We'll find her,' Charlie said. 'Just call the police. I'll do the same,' and then hung up.

He called Julie, his ex-girlfriend.

'Charlie, are you going to come into the station?' she said.

'No, not yet,' he said. 'I need your help though.'

'What is it?'

'Amelia Diaz was killed last night, as you know. There was a work experience student. Donia Graham. I've had a call. The people who killed Amelia say that they have Donia, and they'll kill her if I don't hand over what they want.'

'How do you know it's not a prank?'

'Because it's not funny,' he said. 'She was with me. We were at her flat,' and he gave her the address. 'Then she had intruders. It's genuine.'

'So why are you calling me?'

'I don't think I can come in to the police just yet.'

'Why not?'

He thought about that, and realised that it was for one reason; he was scared. 'I just can't, but you can pass this on.'

'Who are these people?'

'Just a bunch of kids really, but there are a couple of older ones. Black hair, black clothes. They've been hanging around the town centre the last few days. I think they killed Billy Privett and Amelia.'

Julie gasped. 'Are you sure?' When Charlie didn't answer, she said, 'Okay, I'll do it, don't worry.'

'Thank you,' Charlie said, and he gave her Donia's home address. 'Her mother will be calling,' and then he hung up.

He put hands to his face. This couldn't be happening. His mind raced through the last nineteen years. The career, his firm, nineteen years of girlfriends and drink. Just years of being an arsehole, and all the time he'd had a daughter. He thought of Donia. Beautiful, intelligent. His life had drifted along for nineteen years, and there was something there all along, a person who would have given it meaning.

'Charlie?'

He opened his eyes. Ted was looking at him.

'We need to find this group,' Charlie said, and he headed for the door.

Chapter Forty-Eight

Sheldon peered out of his windscreen as he tried to make out the house numbers, looking for John Abbott's house. He was on a street of seventies semis, with wood panelling under large windows and bright glass porches. He came to a stop at the right number, marine blue on a white tile, like something bought on holiday, but he was confused. There was a large *To Let* sign outside and the house looked vacant. Sheldon remembered the story. His mother had died and he had been left the house. Except that John Abbott was no longer living there.

Sheldon stepped out of his car and looked at the house, and then up and down the road. It was quiet but unremarkable, just low garden walls and saloon cars on the drives. The street was forty years old. People who bought the houses from new would have seen their children grow up and leave, and so now the street looked like pensioners filled it, with heavy floral curtains in the windows and china ornaments visible on the sills.

The wooden gate creaked open and then he went towards the living room window, stepping across the small square of lawn that was unkempt and long, seeded ends blowing in the light breeze. There was a gap in the curtains where they didn't quite meet, and so he pressed his face against the glass, his hands cupped around his face to keep out the glow from the streetlights. The house was completely empty. There was no furniture, nothing. Just bare floorboards and the red glow of the burglar alarm sensor in the corner of the room, disturbed by his face pressed against the window.

Sheldon stepped back and pursed his lips. He had disturbed the alarm sensor but there was no noise coming from the metal box on the side. Why was that?

He looked around and saw that most houses were in darkness, and he didn't want to raise suspicions by getting people out of their beds. Then he saw a light shining along a driveway three houses further down the street.

The light came from a pebble-dashed garage at the end of a concrete drive, a man visible through the gap where the battered green wooden doors wouldn't close properly. As Sheldon got closer, he saw the man was wearing safety goggles and sending up sparks as he messed with something on a workbench.

Sheldon got his identification ready and coughed lightly so as not to alarm him. He stepped around an old bike leaning against the house and tapped on the garage door.

The man lifted up the goggles, surprised. He was in his sixties, with grease etched as black lines along his cheeks.

'DI Brown from Oulton police,' Sheldon said. 'I'm sorry if I've disturbed you.'

The man put down a soldering iron and nodded. 'It's late,' he said, confused. 'Am I making too much noise?'

'No, it's not that, and I apologise for the hour, but I want to ask you some questions about the occupant of number nineteen.'

The man frowned. 'What about him?'

'How well did you know him?'

'Hardly knew him at all. No reason why I should, he wasn't here long enough, despite what it said in the paper.'

'What do you mean?'

The man put his goggles on an old red biscuit tin filled with tiny light bulbs and screws. The whole garage was like that, filled with drawers and boxes piled haphazardly on each other, filled with rusted old nuts and bolts and different coloured electrical wiring.

'He was in court, I read about it, and it said that he had inherited number nineteen from his mother, but he hadn't. He was lying.'

'Why do you say that?' Sheldon said.

'There *was* no old woman in that house. He had only been there a few weeks himself. Whatever he told the police and the court was a lie, because there was no inheritance. A young family lived there, but they had it repossessed when the husband lost his job. A nice man, a real shame. But that is why it is empty, because the bank took it back and sold it in auction to a property company. We've had all sorts living there since.'

'Back to John Abbott,' Sheldon said. 'So everything that was in the paper was a lie?'

'Yes, apart from the fact that it was his address, but not for long.'

Sheldon thought about what had been in the paper, and how it matched what was in the file. The paper hadn't got it wrong. He remembered his thought from earlier, how Abbott seemed determined to get himself before the court, almost as if he wanted to draw attention to himself.

'Did you see much of him?' Sheldon asked.

'No. He didn't come out much, but he used to get visitors. All in black, they were, and used to arrive in a dirty old van.'

Sheldon nodded. It all fitted. 'When was the last time you saw him?'

'A few weeks ago now.'

Sheldon thanked the man and turned away. Just as he walked along the pavement, a pair of headlights swung into view around the corner ahead and then drove quickly towards him. Sheldon's eyes narrowed and then he tensed.

The car was a silver Audi, and it pulled up sharply behind his car, the tyres grinding along the kerb. The doors opened quickly and two men got out, in their forties, both in dark suits and bright white shirts, thin ties above the three jacket buttons that were fastened tightly.

Sheldon pulled out his identification again and thrust it forward, as they advanced quickly towards him.

'DI Brown, Oulton police,' he said quickly.

The two men exchanged glances, and then the taller one nodded. 'We know, and we need to talk.'

Chapter Forty-Nine

Charlie drove quickly onto a large estate filled with wide new-build housing.

'What was in the phone call?' Ted asked, his hands gripping the door handle as tyres screeched, the noise echoing around the curves of white-fronted garages and open plan lawns.

Charlie shook his head. He wasn't ready to talk about it. 'We need to make progress,' he said. 'Let Sheldon find out about John Abbott. We'll follow this lead.'

'Marie Cuffy?' Ted said.

Charlie screeched to a stop. 'This looks like the right number,' he said, looking at a house shrouded in darkness. He was out of the car and heading along the drive before Ted had his seat belt undone.

A light went on as he approached the house. Charlie checked his watch. Nearly eleven o'clock. What response would they get when they rang the doorbell?

As the chimes rang through the house, Charlie knew he was about to find out. Ted appeared behind him but didn't say anything.

There was the sound of feet on the stairs and then the door flew open. It was a man in shorts and T-shirt, fresh out of bed, in his fifties, his hair grey and short, his skin too tanned.

'Oh, I thought it might be the police,' he said.

Charlie stepped forward. 'Why do you say that, Mr Cuffy?'

His jaw clenched and his eyes narrowed, but then he saw Ted Kenyon and he faltered. 'Mr Kenyon. What can I do for you?'

'Can we come in, Mr Cuffy?' Ted said. 'It's about Marie.'

His eyes flickered and Charlie thought he paled under his tan. 'Do you know something?'

'Please, can we come in?'

'Yes, of course, I'm sorry, and it's Ray. No need to be formal.'

As they walked in, they were shown into a spacious and comfortable living room, too big for its purpose, the television large in the corner, the chairs around the edges. It was a picture of suburban serenity, the impression dented slightly by the remains of an evening in. Two empty wine glasses and the smell of Chinese food in the air.

A woman in a silk dressing gown came into the room. 'I'm Janet Cuffy,' she said. 'It's very late.'

Ray Cuffy stood in front of the fireplace, one arm resting on the mantelpiece. Janet glanced at him and gave a small shrug as she sat down.

Ray spoke first.

'Mr Kenyon, I know that we've never met before, but I just wanted you to know that I'm sorry about, well,' and he fell silent, dropping his arms.

'Alice?' Ted said, and then shook away the sympathy. 'Everyone starts with saying how sorry they are, and it's never necessary.'

'We're here about Marie, not Alice,' Charlie said, still standing, trying to convey his urgency.

Ray and Janet exchanged worried glances again, and Janet looked down first, a flush of red to her cheeks.

'We don't hear from her,' Ray said, his arms folded again. 'It's been more than a year now. When you came to the door, I thought perhaps you knew something, with Alice and Marie being friends.'

'Where was she when you last heard from her?'

'She was in lots of places, just doing her own thing,' he said, looking confused. 'Why do you want to know about Marie?'

'She's discovered politics, I understand,' Charlie said. 'Part of some revolutionary movement.'

A flush started to creep up Ray's neck. 'If you know about her already, why are you asking?'

'Tell me all about it.'

'Why should I?' he said, his voice becoming hostile. 'You come to my house at nearly midnight and start demanding answers about my family. Give me one good reason.'

Charlie pointed towards Ted. 'Because he lost a daughter,' he said, his voice raised. 'If that isn't a good enough reason to inconvenience you, I'm sorry, but it's the best I can do.'

Ray looked at Ted for a few moments, before saying, 'All right, I'm sorry. But Marie had nothing to do with Alice's murder.'

'Is that why you think we're here, to accuse her of it?'

Ray licked his lips and paused before he spoke. 'No, I mean, of course not, but it must be something to do with Alice, because Ted is here, and the only thing that links us is Alice's death.'

'Why is that?'

'What do you mean? I don't know Ted Kenyon, except for when I've seen him in the press, but Marie and Alice were friends.'

'But you said that it was Alice's death that links you, not Alice's life.'

Tension crept into Ray's voice. 'You're playing with words.'

'With *your* words, Mr Cuffy, not mine.'

Ray looked over to his wife again, but she was still looking down, her knees together, sitting forward, her arms folded across her legs. Ted was keener now, leaning into the discussion, but Charlie held up his hand to stall him.

'Tell me about Marie,' Charlie said, his voice lower now, softer, more cajoling.

'We don't believe in her politics,' Ray said. 'She is her own person.'

'And who is that person?'

'A kid, someone who believes in a simpler world. I thought similar things, back in the seventies, but then as you get older, you start to see things differently, less black and white.'

'Easily influenced?'

'Like most young people, she'll follow the good times. She'll grow out of it.'

'Perhaps she is just kicking back against this,' Charlie said, and he waved his hand around at the house.

'What do you mean?'

'It's always the same with little revolutionaries,' Charlie said. 'Most are just suburban kids looking for a bit of shock value. They flock to groups with names that get your attention and start wearing Che Guevara T-shirts. It's as much a cliché now as it always has been.'

Ray started to get angry. 'What do you want me to do? Change her politics? Because I can't. She found a bunch of oddballs and squatters and left.'

Charlie leaned in. 'Who was in the group?'

Ray sighed and then rubbed his eyes. 'It was the biggest *fuck you* she could give,' he said quietly. 'I tried to be tolerant at first, thinking that she might grow out of it, but she started asking for money, saying that the group needed it.'

'And you said no?'

'It was the money they were interested in, that was my guess, and so I wouldn't give her anything.'

'How did she react?'

'She left and stopped coming back.'

'Is she still with them?'

Janet Cuffy started to sob softly, her face in her hands.

'We don't know,' Ray said, and Charlie saw a tremble to his chin.

'I don't understand,' Charlie said.

'We haven't heard from Marie in over a year,' Ray said, his voice cracking. 'The last time she was here, she was asking for money for insurance and the release fees, because the police had seized their vehicles for being uninsured. I wouldn't give it to her. She stormed out and we haven't seen her since.'

No one spoke for a few seconds, until Charlie said, 'You were nervous when you saw Ted.'

'What do you mean?' Ray said, looking at his wife.

'You think Marie might have had something to do with Alice's death, don't you?' Charlie said.

Ray swallowed. 'What makes you say that?'

'I've been a lawyer for quite a while now, and people who answer questions with a question are usually trying to work out what to say.'

'What's your point?'

'I think you know what Marie was getting up to, and where they used to go for their parties,' Charlie said. 'Billy Privett's house. You knew that, right?'

Ray shook his head and looked at Janet, but she was looking at the floor, rubbing her hands together.

'I think you ought to be going now,' Ray said.

'Where is she?' Charlie demanded. 'They need to be caught. More people will die.'

Janet looked up. Her cheeks were streaked with tears. 'We don't know where she is,' she said. 'We went looking for her, and we can't find her.'

'What did you tell the police?'

'We didn't tell the police,' she said.

'What? Why not?' Charlie said, surprised.

'She's just a young woman. That group she was with? They go travelling. We went to where they stay, and someone told us that she had moved on, had found a different group to mix with.'

Ted stepped closer. 'Where are they, this group?'

'Some farmhouse on Jackson Heights,' Janet said. 'She's not there now though.'

'Is that the real reason you didn't tell the police?' Charlie said. 'Or was it because you are worried she was involved in Alice's death, and you want to keep the police away from her?'

Ray pointed at the door. 'Go.' There were tears in his eyes now.

Charlie got to his feet but walked up to Ray. 'Nice house, ugly conscience. You've got the balance wrong,' and then walked towards the door.

Chapter Fifty

Sheldon followed the two men towards the empty house where John Abbott had lived. They were police officers, but were being cagey about where they worked. Horne and Murch were the names they gave. Sheldon knew he hadn't seen them before. When they opened the door and clicked on the light switch, Sheldon saw a house as empty as it seemed from the outside. He went to the living room and perched on the windowsill. It was low and gave a view over the front garden, the curtains open now.

'So you want to talk?' Sheldon said. 'You first. How did you know I was here?'

The taller one, Horne, pointed at the alarm sensor. 'We had that installed a few weeks ago and you tripped it.'

'So why are you monitoring it?'

The two officers exchanged nervous glances, and then Horne said to Sheldon, 'Tell us what you know.'

'Why do I go first?'

'Because you do. That's just the way it has to be, sir.'

Sheldon noted the *sir*. As he considered them, he saw nervousness, not disrespect. Sheldon reached into his pocket and pulled out the bill that had been in John Abbott's file.

'Why were the police paying the legal bills for a petty

criminal?' he said, and he passed Horne the bill. 'Abbott lived here, except that he didn't really, not for long.'

Horne looked at the bill, but Sheldon could tell he knew what was on it, that he didn't need it shoving under his nose. Horne handed it back. 'Can't you guess?' he said.

'I'm starting to get an idea,' Sheldon said.

'Well, you tell us what you think, and I'll tell you if you get close.'

Sheldon stood up and started to pace, tugging at his lip. He looked at the men in suits. 'Okay, this is how I see it,' he said. 'John Abbott wanted to get noticed. He adopted a strategy that would put him in a courtroom. He sprayed some graffiti and was caught by an anonymous call. He kept his mouth shut, to make sure he was taken to court, and then told a story that was untrue, but interesting enough to get in the local paper. Then we, the police, paid for his legal bills.' Sheldon smiled. 'There is only one answer.'

Horne held out his hands. 'Tell me then.'

'John Abbott is undercover.'

The two officers exchanged glances. Murch exhaled heavily and shook his head. Horne nodded and said, 'Carry on.'

'There is a group near here who are into the protest thing. You put John Abbott in there. You spun some yarn that he had ideas of rejecting society but had an inheritance to spend that he didn't know what to do with. Quite clever. So they went to him, because they wanted his money, and so they didn't suspect him. And he fed you information on their protests, and perhaps links with other groups.'

Horne held out his hands. 'Nearly right, sir.'

'How near?'

'Near enough so that I might as well tell you,' Horne said, and then he sighed. 'We're from the National Public Order

Intelligence Unit. We monitor environmental and protest groups, anarchists, people like that.'

'And you use undercover officers.'

Horne nodded. 'We've got operatives in a few of the groups. They feed information back, just so that we can cut down on the disruption.'

'So what's the thing with this group near here?'

'The leader of this group is Henry Mason,' Horne said. 'When he first started to pop up in intelligence briefings, we thought he was just some petty crook and occasional pervert with an ego problem.'

'Pervert?'

'Always had a thing for children, boys and girls, and became a bit of a Pied Piper figure, with a lot of young teenagers following him around. It was the usual story; he would get them drunk and things would get seedy. He didn't always take part, but sometimes he did, until someone broke ranks and reported him. He went to prison for three years, and when he came out, he started drifting around. He's an attention seeker, thinks that he is some kind of undiscovered genius and that people need to hear what he's got to say. That was the attraction with the young teenagers I think, because they would listen to him. Most people older would just see him for what he is, some small town crook with delusions of grandeur.'

'So what changed?'

'Because an undiscovered genius who stays undiscovered becomes bitter, and sometimes can become dangerous.' Horne glanced at Murch, as if to query whether he should continue, who just nodded.

'We got diverted for a while by the Islamic groups,' Horne continued, 'and so a lot of other groups grew without us knowing what they were doing. Before we knew it, there was a whole protest scene, and so the student marches and the riots took us by surprise. We didn't know who any of them were. So we've turned our attention back to them, and as we started looking, Henry Mason's name started to come up.'

'In what way?'

'Just whispers, but it was enough to make us listen. The thing with a lot of these protest groups is that they are well-meaning, decent people whose emotions sometimes get the better of them. On the whole, they want to make their point and have some fun, and that's it. They like the excitement, the kicking against things, but don't want to hurt anyone. Direct action is one thing, like cutting down fences or breaking into power stations, but the operatives were all reporting the same thing: that Mason was planning something bigger.'

'What like?'

'We don't know, and that was the problem. We can follow mobile phones, get into voicemails, spy on social networking sites. The point for most of them is that protest has to be seen and heard, or else what's the point? And most of the protest groups can't keep off internet forums, and so we used to just tune in. It was harder with Henry, because although people were talking *about* him, we never heard from Mason himself, or any of his followers. His group went off the grid. No computers, no phones, and you have to be more worried about what you don't know.'

'So what's his thing?'

'It's hard to pin down,' Horne said. 'As far as we can work out, he pinches the interesting bits from other groups. There's some who have wild ideas that if they refuse to obey the laws, they somehow don't apply, and it's all to do with the Magna Carta or something. They might even be right, what the hell do I know, but even they were getting worried that Mason was going to wreck everything by doing things in their name.'

'And that's why you put John Abbott in there?'

Horne nodded. 'We had to move quickly. Normally, an operative may take months to integrate and build up trust. They have to take part, be seen at the right places. Most importantly, the operative has to be trusted. We didn't have that time with Henry, because the hints we were getting were that he was planning something soon.'

'So you had to make Henry come to you,' Sheldon said, nodding.

'That's right,' Horne said. 'We had tried it once before. The operative had an old bus, a coach with the seats ripped out, but he was too obvious. He was older than Henry's usual crowd and he just imposed himself on the group. Henry spotted him straight away and so they burnt out his bus and told him to leave. We tried to get cuter this time. We set up the story, made Abbott sound like someone gullible and with money, and receptive to all that conspiracy rubbish that Henry liked. It worked great at first. We paid Amelia to represent him and make it look legitimate. The group started to follow Abbott around, and eventually took him in.'

'So what went wrong?'

Horne sighed. 'We chose the wrong officer.'

'Don't these people have thorough training?'

'Oh, it's thorough all right, except that the life of an operative can be attractive for all the wrong reasons.'

'How do you mean?' Sheldon was pacing now.

'You know how it is for undercover cops. They have to live the life. They can't have nights off, clock off at five on Friday and go back at nine on Monday. They have to leave everything behind. Wife, children, family. They have to make do with occasional visits, and the more they do the work, the more they become the person they are pretending to be – but that doesn't mean that they leave their home life behind completely. The undercover life becomes all about getting home, because he doesn't know what is going on there. Who's keeping his wife company, or tucking his kids in.'

'So why was John Abbott the wrong officer?'

Horne let out a long breath. 'We needed the right sort of person, someone who could project that vulnerability that would make Henry see him as a victim, as a follower, not a threat. We found the officer, and he projected vulnerability perfectly, except for the wrong reason; he *was* vulnerable.'

'What do you mean?'

'We didn't know it, but during his previous undercover posting his wife changed the locks, said that she'd had enough. John was doing test purchases, living the life of some junkie on an estate, wired up with button cameras. He went home one day and there was another man in there. So he had no home anymore, and the only life he had was his undercover post. That's why we think he volunteered for this one, because it gave him a different life again, where he didn't have to think about the man fucking his wife every night, or making breakfast for his kids. It was a refuge, not an assignment.'

'So what happened when he got invited into Henry's gang?' Sheldon said.

'He went native, we think, pretty much straight away. He was supposed to seek us out three times a week to fill us in. It seemed a pretty loose set-up at Henry's farm, and so we didn't think it would be a problem for him to get away, but he didn't even turn up for the first meet. One minute he was here, in this house, waiting to be invited into Henry's circle, and then he was gone.'

Sheldon thought about that. He knew it made some sense. Undercover officers lived lives of deprivation, but it was exciting too, being at the heart of it all, like some kind of adventure story, except that it took a toll on those you were close to. And it was too easy to be sucked into the scene you infiltrate, because you end up making friends, build up new loyalties, create some kind of fake world that you start to like. What happens if you fall in love with someone when undercover? It has happened, and not everyone realises the risks and pulls out.

'So why are you here now?' Sheldon said.

Horne grimaced. 'This is the part where it gets difficult.'

Sheldon tilted his head. 'I'm listening.'

Chapter Fifty-One

Charlie and Ted headed towards Jackson Heights, an area of fields and valleys a few miles from Oulton. The route took them on a steep drive, towards the dark shadows of the hills, brooding shoulders that blotted out the stars, just the occasional dim light from hillside farmhouses and barn conversions. They lost the streetlights as they climbed out of Oulton, and then turned onto a road that narrowed and rose and curved, the way ahead never visible for more than fifty yards, the car echoing between drystone walls.

Charlie was quiet, just trying to get his thoughts in the right order, but they only ever went back to Donia. He remembered how she had looked at him, part-disappointment, part-wonder. He was the father she'd never known, and all he had been was drunk, complaining, throwing up outside the court.

He had to find her, had to make it right. Perhaps it was for selfish reasons; if he could rescue Donia, then maybe he could make his own life better. The reason didn't matter, provided that he found her.

Ted spoke up.

'I thought you were a bit harsh in there,' he said. When Charlie glanced over, he added, 'That thing you said about dirty conscience.'

'They knew about Alice but didn't say anything.'

'And perhaps they have lost their daughter too.'

Charlie gripped the wheel a bit tighter but didn't respond. There were too many thoughts swirling around in his head to give a proper answer.

They drove in silence for a bit longer, until Ted said, 'What do we do when we get there?'

'We see what's going on.'

'Shouldn't we call the police when we find them?'

'Yes, we should, but I'm not going to wait around for them. At least we can relay what's happening.'

'Pull over,' Ted said.

Charlie looked at him. 'Why?'

'You are breaking all the rules and taking gambles. It doesn't seem right. You're a lawyer. You fight with paper and words, not this.'

Charlie took a deep breath and put his head back. He thought of all he'd found out that day, and of how things would never be the same again. Because of Billy Privett. Because of Donia.

He saw a space ahead, next to an old wooden gate, and pulled in. He sat there for a few seconds, just staring out of the windscreen, and then turned to look at Ted.

'The work experience girl, Donia,' Charlie said. He closed his eyes for a moment as he thought about how his life had somersaulted during the last hour. 'She's my daughter.'

Ted's eyes widened, and then he frowned. 'Why didn't you say something?'

'Because I've only known since I called her mother.'

'What, the phone call at my house?'

Charlie nodded. 'I thought she was involved with them, because she got me to where she was staying, and then the group turned up. I wouldn't have run if I'd known the truth.'

He realised that his voice sounded desperate, but he didn't know how to deal with what he had just found out. 'Donia had sought me out to get to know me, but she hadn't told me yet.'

Ted nodded to himself. 'I didn't have the chance to save Alice,' he said, determination in his voice. 'We'll save Donia.' He peered through the windscreen. 'We need to work out where they are. We can't just keep driving around.' He reached for the door handle and stepped out of the car.

The night air came into the car, cold and sharp, and it reminded Charlie that he was only in a suit. He joined Ted outside. Charlie fastened his jacket and pulled the lapels to his neck. He looked up at the stars, and they were bright spots of light.

They were high on the side of the valley. The land fell away in front of them, sheep clinging to the slope further down, their wool reflecting the moonlight. The orange clusters of towns and villages broke up the darkness, the lights more concentrated further away, as the fringes of the Pennines turned into the larger towns nearer the coast.

As he looked around, there was no sound. No cars or pub shouts. Just the rustle of their clothes as they got used to the chill.

Charlie scoured the hillsides, looking for anything, a chink of light from a barn or a fire burning, anything that hinted of something out of the ordinary.

Ted blew into his hands. 'Let's just keep going,' he said. 'We are looking for something unusual. We'll go with our instincts.'

It sounded like a plan.

As they jumped back into the car, Charlie shivered. Except that this time it wasn't from the cold. This time it was fear of what lay ahead, and whether he would ever get to see the sunrise.

Chapter Fifty-Two

John turned round when he heard footsteps on the stairs.

It was Henry, pulling on his shirt, his trouser belt still undone. He was dishevelled, his hair sticking up, two scratch marks down his cheek.

'How's Dawn?' John said.

Henry took a breath and then scowled. 'Against us.'

'So what now?'

As Henry passed John, he glanced outside to where the hole had been dug. 'Our mission is the important thing. We can't be distracted. Dawn was going to betray us. If we let her go, we're finished, all of us.'

John turned to follow Henry into the living room. When he got there, Lucy looked up.

'We need to deal with the problem,' Henry said. 'She needs to join her sisters.'

The mood in the room improved. Jennifer smiled. Gemma jumped to her feet, and Lucy grinned. She held out her hand, and Henry grabbed it and helped her to her feet.

Arni banged his stick on the floor. When everyone turned to him, he said, 'Let's do it. John, go get her.'

John ran upstairs. As he got higher, he heard soft cries coming from Henry's room. When he opened the door, Dawn was curled up in a corner. She had put her clothes back on, but her top was ripped, so that she had to hold it over her chest. Her trousers weren't fastened properly. As John got closer, he saw swelling around her eye and a trickle of blood from her nose.

'You need to come downstairs,' he said.

She looked up at him, and her eyes were pure hatred, her brow heavy, lips clenched tightly. 'You could have stopped this.'

He closed his eyes. He had no control anymore. 'Downstairs,' he said.

Tears started to run down her face. 'I won't say anything. Just let me go.'

John shook his head. 'No, downstairs.' He went over to her and gripped her arm. She pulled against it at first, thumped him a few times in his chest, but he ignored it, so her shoulders slumped and she went with him.

As John got to the top of the stairs, he looked down and saw everyone waiting for him. Dawn pulled against him again but he held firm. When they got to the bottom, Arni grabbed her and took her outside, everyone else following.

She shrank back at the cold. The warmth from the day was gone. Arni kept pulling and so she stumbled as she went, her cries lost in the clamour from the group. Footsteps on grass, gleeful shouts. When Arni got to the stones, he pulled her towards the flat stone, the large one that was horizontal like a table. Arni held her by the hair, so that her legs and body thrashed, but she couldn't escape. She started to scream, but no one tried to stop her. There wasn't anyone near enough to hear.

Henry appeared by her feet, and she looked along her body towards him, her eyes wide. Her screams turned to a whimper and her head went back in despair.

'We need a knife,' Henry said.

Gemma ran back into the house. No one said anything, so that the only sounds were those of Dawn's cries as she struggled against her captors. When Gemma emerged from the house, she was holding a carving knife. The blade glinted in the moonlight.

John could feel the tension, everyone watching as the knife was passed along the line to Henry. He held it and turned it in his hand before he nodded at the two women stood closest to Dawn.

They smiled and then each grabbed a leg of her trousers and pulled, and although her hands reached down to stop it, it was no use. They kept on pulling until her trousers were off, her legs skinny and pale. Then they pulled at her shirt, ripping it, until it was just shreds of cloth on the ground. Dawn was naked apart from her knickers. She crossed her legs in a vain attempt to keep some dignity, but it was futile. Her underwear was torn off, so she lay there, naked and sobbing.

John was transfixed. Her body was skinny, so that he could see the sharp bones of her hips and ribs, her legs bony and mottled and pale. He knew that Dawn hadn't participated as much as the others. Some of the people enjoyed the sexual aspect of the group, the lack of inhibition, but Dawn had never really taken part.

People rushed forward to grab her ankles and wrists, spread-eagling her. Her head was back and she was panting hard. She tried to pull against them, but she couldn't, they were too strong for her. John could hear her skin scraping on the stone, could see the blood on her heels. She was looking at the sky, until her gaze blurred over from her tears.

He didn't know what to do. What they were doing was wrong, he knew that, but he felt powerless against the group.

Henry stepped up to the stone, so that he was at her

side. He looked around the group, tried to look each one in the eye.

'If we are to take our movement forward, we cannot afford traitors,' Henry said. 'That's just the way it has to be.'

People mumbled that they understood.

He smiled. 'Apology is of the other world,' he said to the group. 'The one where life is about accumulation and greed. That's how man deludes himself, because he does what his heart desires, not caring about others, but then he is racked with guilt, and so he apologises and tries to make amends. But why? It's just a candle in a dark place, an illusion of light, because he knows it is wrong and so he tries to pass the burden by apologising.' He looked down at Dawn. 'No one here apologises for anything, but yet you still do.'

Dawn shook her head frantically, moaning, scared. More tears squeezed out of her eyes.

Henry held up the knife. 'We know how it is,' he said. 'Who goes first?'

Dawn knew what was coming next, because her struggles became more frantic.

Gemma stepped forward. 'Me first,' she said, and held her hand out for the knife.

Chapter Fifty-Three

Charlie and Ted followed the road as it ran alongside the hillside, looking out for wherever the group might have taken Donia. It had been a fruitless search, just tracks and hedgerows and stone walls that hugged the valley sides. They were about to curve back towards the valley floor when Ted shouted, 'Stop!'

The car skidded as Charlie stamped on the brake. 'What is it?'

'Back up.'

Charlie moved the car slowly backwards, looking up the long slopes, trying to see whatever had caught Ted's attention.

Ted shouted for him to stop again. 'There,' he said, and pointed.

Charlie looked past him, followed his finger, and then he scowled. He looked round for somewhere to park and headed towards a small leafy track that ended in front of a metal gate. He turned off his engine and the night turned silent again.

Charlie tried to see along the track, but it disappeared into woods that climbed up the hill. It hadn't been the track that had caught Ted's attention though.

There was a small cottage a couple of hundred yards away,

high up on the hill. The moonlight shone from an old slate roof and weak yellow light shone as tiny yellow squares. It had been more than the cottage though, because there were jagged stones set against the bright silver of the moon, and there was movement between them, cast into silhouette. Charlie could tell that it was a group though, and that something was happening.

'This way,' Charlie said, and started to climb the gate. It clanged against the post as he jumped over, Charlie wincing as the noise echoed around them. Ted followed him, and once they were both on the other side Charlie pointed at the trees that ran up the hill. 'We need to go through there, to stay hidden.'

The hill was steep, and as they disappeared into the shadows of the trees the loss of the moonlight made it harder to see. Stray branches and roots snagged at their feet, and unseen dips and hollows almost sent them tumbling. Charlie's ears were keen, listening out for the sound of someone approaching, sure that the rattles of Patrick's car must have attracted their attention, but all he got was the soft rustle of leaves and the creak of branches straining under their own weight. Ted's breathing seemed laboured, and he shouted out as he stumbled to the floor.

'We need to go quieter,' Charlie whispered.

Ted didn't respond, just scrambled himself upright and walked on ahead, his footsteps faster now, so that all Charlie could hear were the rustles of his feet as he rushed to keep up. The view ahead was just gloom and darkness, the brightness of the moon just slipping through in places, lighting up their faces as ghostly apparitions moving through the trees. Charlie's white shirt caught the light, so he buttoned his jacket and pulled up the lapels.

Charlie was breathing hard too, his legs aching from the

climb, his lungs fighting back against too many long nights bar-hopping and the escape from Donia's flat. Neither of them was in suitable gear; Charlie's suit was torn and ragged, his feet clad in leather-soled brogues.

Charlie stopped. He put his arm out. There was something ahead. Mumbles and murmurs, but the voices were fast and sharp, as if they were angry. They couldn't be far away. Charlie tilted his head to the edge of the woods. They needed to get a better view.

They moved slowly to the edge of the treeline. Charlie sheltered behind a dead tree, the top gone, as if it had once been caught in a storm, so that all that was left was the trunk and two large branches sticking out to the side. He peered out over the field towards the cottage. They were more level with it now, near the top of the slope, and the cottage was framed against the glow coming from the moon. As he focused on it, Charlie saw again what had attracted his attention. There was a small cluster of standing stones, spread out into some kind of haphazard semicircle. There were people gathered in the middle of the stones, around a large rock that was flat against the ground, fifty yards from the house and in the middle of the field.

'We need to get closer,' Charlie whispered, and pointed towards the hedgerow at the top of the field. 'We'll go along there. It will get us nearer to the cottage.'

The hedgerow was twenty yards away, but it provided some shelter from the moonlight, so that Charlie thought they could get closer without being seen.

He ducked back into the shelter of the trees and crunched his way to where the hedgerow joined the wood. Ted was behind him, making his way more slowly, carefully.

Charlie stopped to let him catch up.

'They won't harm Donia,' Ted said, looking towards the stone circle. 'Not yet anyway.'

'What do you mean by that?'

'Think about it. They've got her because you've got something they want. If they kill her, they won't get it.'

'And just in case you've forgotten, they don't seem too humane,' Charlie hissed. 'So let's not pretend there's going to be any kind of amicable handover.'

'So what are we going to do?'

'We're going to find out what's going on, and then call it in.'

'The police will think it's some kind of prank,' Ted said. 'Anarchist nut-jobs in the woods, and my name won't help it too much.'

'The police already know about Donia. They just don't have a location.' Charlie stepped out of the shadows of the trees and into the darkness of the hedgerow. He looked along and tried to work out the landscape.

There was a ditch that ran in front of the hedgerow, and as he jumped into it, he knew that it wasn't waterlogged. They would be able to go along its length until they were just a short dash from the house. It would at least give them a chance to see what was going on so they could report it.

They moved slowly, hunched down, trying not to make a noise. It was hard to work out what was going on. There were around six young women standing around the central stone, and three or four men. They were struggling with something, but Charlie couldn't make out what it was.

They got to the far side of the ditch, where it met the wall that ran up from the house. There was some shouting, an increase in activity. They tried to keep low in the ditch, just to watch. He could see an outline of someone through a window at the side of the cottage. He thought he recognised the frizz of her hair. Donia.

Charlie gripped Ted's arm when he saw, and was about to say something, when he heard something that made his stomach pitch and cold shivers ripple up and down his skin.

A long, shrill scream came from the group and echoed around the valley.

Chapter Fifty-Four

Horne looked to Murch.

'So go on, I'm listening,' Sheldon repeated. 'Why now?'

Murch and Horne exchanged glances, until Murch held out his hands in a gesture to continue.

Horne sighed. 'Amelia called us,' he said. 'It was last week. She said she was worried about Abbott, but she wouldn't tell us why. She just said we had to get him out. She seemed agitated. No, more than that. She seemed scared.'

Sheldon remembered what Charlie had said, that the calls had been made after she had spoken to Billy Privett.

'You had no idea at all about why she was worried?'

'No. There was something wrong, we knew that, but if Abbott had contacted her, she would have told us, because he would have contacted her in order that she could pass it on. Or he could have called us directly. We could have gone up there and pulled him out, and we were talking about doing that.'

'How?'

'Just go up there and arrest him. Produce a fake warrant, for non-payment of fines or something.'

'So why didn't you?'

Horne looked at Murch, who was silent, with his arms folded.

'Because we weren't sure,' Horne said. 'We thought that perhaps Abbott was biding his time, so as not to attract attention.'

'But Amelia's call came last week. What has changed? Why this week?'

Horne started to look more nervous. He rubbed his thumb on the palm of his other hand, as if he was trying to rub some dirt away.

Sheldon stepped closer. 'No more bullshit,' he said, his voice quieter. 'I want the full story. This is cop-to-cop, so it stays confidential, but I want to know.'

The two men exchanged shrugs and raised eyebrows, and then Horne relented.

'Amelia called us again, the morning it was discovered that it was Billy Privett who had died. She told us that Billy had called her the day before, said that he was going to keep out of the way for a while, that he was going to that hotel. On the way into work, she saw the police cars there. When she tried to call him, she got no reply. So she called us. She was angry now, and more scared. Someone had tried to break into her office. So we went to see her.'

Sheldon thought back to what he had been told, that the two men in suits had been seen coming out of Amelia's office, and they had gone looking for Charlie in his home.

'You found Amelia's body, didn't you?' Sheldon said.

They both nodded.

'And then you broke into Charlie Barker's home.'

They nodded again.

'We were worried for him as well,' Horne said. 'We tried his phone, but it was switched off, and so we kicked in his door to find him. Except that when we got in there, we saw him running away.'

'He thought you were after him,' Sheldon said. 'He

didn't know who you were.' When neither Horne nor Murch said anything, he continued, 'What did Amelia tell you at her office?'

'Not enough,' Horne said. 'She said she had specific instructions from Billy. She was to disclose what Billy had told her, but everyone had to find out at the same time.'

'Why?'

'Maximum effect, I suppose. She said there wasn't too much of a rush, because Billy was dead.'

'Except she hadn't planned on herself being in danger,' Sheldon said. 'Amelia had prepared copies for the local police, and the BBC, the local paper, and to Ted Kenyon. Billy knew he was in danger. He feared for his life. Billy's instructions were to send this out if he was killed, so that the truth wouldn't stay silenced. Billy was scared, that's all. That's why he stayed quiet.'

'So why hasn't anyone received them? They must have been sent yesterday?'

Sheldon gave a rueful smile. 'Her secretary didn't realise the importance, because Amelia hadn't told her what they were, and so she just didn't get round to sending them. Mason's group pinched the discs.' Then something occurred to him. 'You don't seem surprised.'

'What do you mean?'

'Your involvement with Amelia was to get John Abbott into the group. That had no connection with Billy Privett.'

'We didn't know at first, but then when Amelia called us after Billy was killed, we started to wonder about it. When Amelia was killed, well, it became more than a guess.'

'So why didn't you tell me?' Sheldon snapped. 'I was in charge of the Billy Privett investigation then. You should have come to me.'

Horne started to say something, and then he stopped and looked at the floor.

Sheldon stepped closer. 'It was time to cover your arse, wasn't it?' he said, glowering. 'You'd lost your undercover man, and so you thought that if Henry's group had killed Billy Privett, then perhaps Abbott had taken part. How close am I?'

Horne nodded but didn't look up. 'Too close.'

'So you let them stay free because you were protecting your department?' Sheldon said, incredulous. 'They killed Amelia the next day. If you had passed this on, we could have locked them up straight away. Amelia would have been alive.'

'I know,' Horne said, all the resolve gone in his voice.

Sheldon sat back down on the windowsill, shaking his head.

'Chief Inspector Dixon,' Sheldon said. 'She has looked worried the last couple of days. Is that why? She let you onto her patch and you've caused mayhem?'

Horne shook his head. 'Dixon doesn't know about Abbott.' He exhaled noisily. 'You might as well know. Dixon *couldn't* know about Abbott.'

'Why not?'

'Because Dixon's daughter is with the group.'

Sheldon paled. He remembered how Dixon acted when he brought Lucy into the station, when everyone thought she was Billy's housekeeper.

'It was Dixon who arranged for Lucy to be seen with Ted Kenyon,' Sheldon said, trying to work it out through his head. Now, it seemed clearer. 'It was done to stop him campaigning and getting too close to the truth. She was protecting her daughter.'

'That's how we read it now,' Horne said, 'but we hadn't known there was any connection with Billy Privett.'

Sheldon went to the door. Before he got there, he turned round and said, 'What's the name of Dixon's daughter?'

'Gemma,' Horne said. 'Gemma Dixon.'

Chapter Fifty-Five

Henry handed the knife to Gemma, his eyes wide with excitement.

Dawn was screaming, long lung-bursting shouts of fear, but Henry showed no reaction. They were a long way from anyone who might hear them.

John's heart felt like fast finger taps. Dawn was thrashing in front of him, and he knew he should intervene, but he was excited by it. He tried to shake it away, but it was there, seeing Gemma enjoying it so much. Gemma looked at him and gestured with a cock of her head that he should join her. He looked around the group. Everyone was looking at him, expectant, and so he stepped forward, stood alongside Gemma.

She smiled as he got next to her. He glanced over at Henry, who smiled almost paternally. Arni glowered, the intensity in his eyes telling John that he was turned on by this.

He looked down at Gemma's hand, at her slim fingers around the handle of the knife. The blade seemed to blink with reflected light. He could feel the presence of everyone else. The breaths they were holding, the anticipation. He looked up once more at Henry, who nodded. It was time.

All John heard were the sounds of Dawn's struggles. Her

heels and elbows on the stone, the bang of her head, skin catching on the rock. Panicked cries.

Gemma's hand moved forward until the tip of the knife rested against Dawn's skin, just pressing inwards, making a dimple, just under the ribs. Dawn winced.

Henry held up his hands, and everyone turned to him.

'No battles are won without spilling blood,' he said, his voice low. 'It's been the same throughout history; progress has cost lives. And so without the shedding of blood, we cannot move ourselves forward. We are free men and free women.'

Gemma grinned and whispered, 'As it is.' Then she pushed with her hand.

Dawn bucked as the blade disappeared into her side, blood rushing onto the knife. It went in so easily, John thought. Dawn screamed again, except this time it was the sharp scream of pain. John shuddered and he felt himself go light-headed. The field swam in front of him. He had to hold on, he knew that. He was the only one reacting. This had happened before. There was nothing new. And they were watching him. This was his first real test.

He looked down and watched as Gemma withdrew the knife. Blood ran quickly from the wound down to the stone, gushing out in spurts as Dawn's chest rose and fell rapidly. Her eyelids flickered. She was in shock.

Gemma turned to John and held the dagger to him. 'Now you,' she whispered.

John looked around the group. Everyone was smiling.

'Don't be uncertain,' Gemma whispered to him. 'This is the way. We all take a turn, so that we have all banished her.'

John swallowed and felt his mouth go dry. He looked at the hole in the ground, waiting for her, a large stone lying flat alongside.

Gemma followed his gaze and smiled. 'We bury her, in the stone circle. A stone for her, just like the rest.'

A headstone, John thought.

Gemma's hand went around his. Her fingers felt warm, and he remembered how they had been on his body. He could feel her breath on his cheeks, the soft brush of her hair against his neck.

The knife was placed into his hand and the blade pushed against Dawn's skin. She was saying something, and he paused as he listened to hear her words.

'The Lord is my shepherd; I shall not want,' Dawn said, pausing to lick her lips. 'He makes me lie down in green pastures.'

Gemma whispered to him that he should push, smiling, her teeth on her lip, biting, coy. Her hand went to his neck, her fingers caressing softly, and she was nodding at him.

He didn't know how it started, but he felt his hand move forward, and when he looked down, the blade was disappearing into Dawn, just as it had done when Gemma had done it. Dawn was shaking now, her eyes rolling, and he just kept on pushing until he felt the handle of the knife rest against her skin.

He looked at Gemma. She was smiling, her eyes showing her arousal.

Dawn groaned when he pulled out the knife, her voice already getting weaker.

The person next to him, Jennifer, took the knife from him and moved to take her position next to Dawn. The blade went in quicker this time, as if they had all become impatient, and John watched as the knife moved down the line.

Dawn stopped moving after the fifth person, when the blade had found its way between two ribs and into her chest. Her body suddenly became flaccid, as if they had watched her life leave her, but still the knife went down the line, so that everyone had their turn, the ceremonial stab.

Gemma turned to John and kissed him, her lips urgent, and John realised that his body was already responding, knowing that Gemma was aroused by the display. She pulled away.

'You're truly one of us now,' she said. He just smiled and nodded. There was no turning back.

Chapter Fifty-Six

'We've got to do something,' Ted hissed at Charlie, who pulled out his phone. He had a message. He shielded it with his back to hide the glow from the screen.

'It's from Sheldon,' Charlie said. He read it and nodded to himself.

'What is it?' Ted said.

'I don't know why I didn't think of it before,' he said, almost to himself. When Ted frowned, Charlie said, 'It's about John Abbott. The police paid our bill to represent him, because Abbott works for the police.'

'What do you mean?'

Charlie showed Ted the message. It just said, *Abbott is undercover. Infiltrated group.*

'Undercover?' Ted whispered, surprised.

'It looks like Amelia represented a fake defendant to attract the attention of Henry Mason.'

Ted's eyes widened, visible in the moonlight. 'Which is why Amelia called the police after Billy made the video. She was worried about Abbott, because she knew that Henry Mason wasn't just some political activist.'

'He was a murderer,' Charlie said, nodding.

Charlie sent a message back to Sheldon to let him know

that people were in danger, and that they were at an old cottage on Jackson Heights. Once he clicked *send*, he looked at Ted and said, 'We have to wait for the police. There's too many of them. They'll turn on Donia if they catch us.'

'We can't just sit here and watch someone die,' Ted said, and started to climb out of the ditch.

Charlie grabbed his arm and pulled him back. 'It's too late to save whoever that is,' he said, desperation creeping into his voice. 'Think of Donia.'

Ted shrugged him off but didn't say anything.

Charlie looked towards the figures by the stones, and in the moonlight, he saw the blood on the woman on the stone, dark against her pale skin. She was still now. He looked across to the window where he could see Donia's outline, and he realised she would be next, whatever they did.

Ted was right.

'I'll go,' Charlie said, and started to clamber out of the ditch.

'What do I do?'

'Sit tight,' he said, and then jumped out of the ditch and ran the short five yards to the wall. He was in the open, and knew that movement might attract their attention, but it was the only way. His hands went onto the wall. The stones were loose, but his choices were limited. He threw his leg towards it and scrambled over, heard the clack of stones as he fell to the ground on the other side. He sat there, panting, waiting for some sign that he had been seen or heard. He couldn't hear anything.

Charlie took a deep breath and tried to work out the layout. There was movement nearby. He jumped, and then clasped his hand to his chest as he saw the outline of a sheep. The deep thump of his heart made him realise that he couldn't afford to get this wrong.

He went onto all fours and shuffled along, his fingers moving through the coarse grass. The cottage got nearer all the time, and he could see light through the windows. Donia wasn't visible, and he started doubting that it had been her, but he had to keep going, just in case.

He got to a gate, a metal five-bar that kept the sheep penned in. He peered through. He was level with the standing stones, visible along a stone path than ran alongside the cottage. His eyes shot to the window again. He saw Donia's outline again, the curl of her hair. And he noticed something else this time; the metal grille on the window, and the sharp knots of barbed wire.

There was excited chatter coming from the group at the stones. The woman on there was naked and still, and Charlie could see blood on her, some of it seeping onto the stone. He smacked his hand against the wall in frustration. He should be helping her. He sat back, felt the cold stone against his body, and hung his head for a moment. But he couldn't focus on that. He had to find a way inside without being spotted.

He went to the gate again and peered through. The woman on the stone had not moved, but it seemed like the group was distracted by her.

The gate was held closed by a small loop of rope. Charlie lifted it away from the stone gatepost, watching the group all the time, waiting for someone to spot the movement, and then pulled at the gate. It didn't creak. He let out a long breath, and then put himself into the gap. He kept on watching the group and made a silent prayer that there was still enough darkness around him to hide the pale glare of his face.

There was a small stone courtyard behind the cottage, sheltered by an outbuilding that spurred off the main house. It would give him shelter, but he couldn't see a way in. As he looked along the cottage though, he saw a shaft of light going onto the grass. It was the main doorway. He would have to go in that way.

Charlie ran across the path, kept low and headed for a dark shadow in the grey stone that was created by the overhang of the roof. There were no shouts, no one looking towards him.

He tried to absorb himself into the wall so that he was enveloped by darkness, but everyone seemed too engrossed in whatever was going on at the stone circle to hear him.

His footsteps were slow as he crept forward, careful of where he was standing. The darkness at the side of the house made him feel more secure. His foot kicked something metal, and so he paused, to make sure that no one had heard him. As the metal object caught the light from the window, he saw the jagged teeth of an animal trap.

Charlie knew then that it wouldn't be easy.

As he edged forward, he saw that he had to cross the window where he had seen Donia. He moved quickly, knowing that he would cast a shadow across the path. As he got back to the relative darkness, he took another look around. There was nothing there except the light from the window reflected back against the eyes of a watching sheep, like yellow glints in the black.

He was close to the corner of the house and could see more clearly what was happening on the stones. The woman on the stone wasn't moving, but the blood still ran from the wounds along the side of her body, gravity doing the work, her heart no longer pumping it out.

Charlie closed his eyes. What the hell was going on up here?

Then when he opened his eyes again, he saw that everyone was looking up the field, distracted now. He followed their gaze, and then he put his head back against the wall.

It was Ted, walking towards the group.

Chapter Fifty-Seven

Sheldon arrived at Dixon's home and jabbed at the doorbell, which sounded loud in the night. When Dixon answered the door, it looked like she had expected visitors. There was no surprise. She turned away from him without a word and walked into the house. She slumped onto a large leather recliner, and as she settled, Sheldon thought her eyes took too long to refocus on him. There was a large wine glass half-filled with a deep red liquid, and the bottle on the floor next to her was empty.

She saw him looking. 'So, I'm getting pissed. So what? I'm entitled to celebrate.' Her voice sounded bitter.

'Celebrate what?'

'What do you think? The end of my police career,' she said, and she raised her glass. 'A-fucking-men to that.'

Sheldon sat down on the sofa opposite, the soft leather squeaking as he made himself comfortable. He thought about offering some words of comfort, but she was right. It was all over, and she knew it.

'Where is Mr Dixon?' Sheldon asked.

Her lip curled. 'Mr Dixon isn't here anymore. He doesn't like the way I do things. And do you know what, Sheldon; neither do I.'

'So tell me,' Sheldon said. 'How do you do things?'

She didn't answer, just stared into her glass instead.

'Answer me something else then,' Sheldon said.

She looked up.

'Why did you want me to lead the investigation?' he said. 'You tried to keep me. Why?'

Dixon considered him for a few moments, and then she shook her head. 'You don't want to go there.'

'But I do.'

'You know the answer.'

'I want to hear you say it.'

She took a gulp of wine, and then went to the room next door, coming back with another bottle, picking at the foil seal with the end of a corkscrew. Once she had opened the bottle, she refilled her glass and held the bottle out for Sheldon. 'Do you want some?'

Sheldon shook his head.

She scowled. 'Didn't think you would,' she said. 'Too fucking pure and controlled. That's always been your problem. Not enough fun away from the job.'

'You don't look like you are having fun to me.'

She leaned forward, wine spilling out of her glass onto the carpet. 'Don't be smart, Sheldon, it doesn't suit you.'

'So tell me,' he said, his tone firmer. 'Why did you appoint me as head of the investigation?'

'Why do you think? Because I admired you? Is that what you think?' she said, the words snapping out, becoming strident. 'No, Sheldon, you have it all wrong.' She laughed, but it was exaggerated, filled with drunken scorn. 'I knew you would mess it up, and so I fought for you.'

'So you wouldn't get found out?' he said. He had guessed that as a reason, but it didn't lessen the feeling of betrayal, of humiliation, that he was the force joke. 'Or was I just getting too close, by bringing in Lucy? You put me on leave to keep me away, hoping that the files would eventually become cold cases, and so that you could hold on until retirement, hoping that Gemma grows out of her little gang of misfits.'

Dixon looked like she had been slapped when he said Gemma's name.

She took a drink. 'I protected my daughter, that's all. Is that a crime?'

Sheldon nodded slowly. 'You know that it is, the way you did it.'

Dixon paused at that, and then her lip trembled, her eyes glassy, tears brimming onto her eyelids. She swallowed and gritted her teeth as she tried to maintain some control.

He felt like he ought to go over to her, to offer some support, but he couldn't get over the fact that people had died, due to her actions.

'When did it start?' he said.

'Huh?'

'How long have you known about Gemma and Billy Privett and Alice Kenyon?'

She took a deep breath. 'I didn't know. That was the problem. I still don't. I just know that Gemma is with people she shouldn't be with. But what can I do? She's twenty now, although she doesn't look it. I followed her a few times, and I found out they were hanging around with Billy Privett. They were having parties there, just a couple of weeks before Alice died. As soon as I heard about Alice, I feared the worst, I suppose.'

'Did you interfere with any of the evidence?'

She smiled a watery smile. 'Are you going to caution me? Take me to the station?'

Sheldon didn't respond.

'The answer is no,' she said eventually.

'But Ted was getting closer, wasn't he? He wouldn't let the media forget about Alice. So you found your own way to silence him. You set him up with Lucy Crane.'

She nodded slowly. 'She was locked up for shoplifting. I knew who she was, one of Henry Mason's little gang. I saw her when she was brought into the nick. I told her I could make the case go away if she helped me keep Ted quiet. She was happy to go along with it, because she was part of the group. The set-up was her idea. She tipped off a local press photographer, but I put it in motion.'

'It almost worked.'

She put her head back. 'That was the beginning of the end. I hadn't planned it. I just saw it, and I had the idea, and so I went with it. But they thought they had me then.'

'What do you mean?'

'Come on, Sheldon, what do you think? Henry's gang. I had to tip them off about any drug searches, and the same with Billy Privett. Anything that might cause them problems, I had to pass it on. It was blackmail, but I was caught in it. Everything I had worked for was slipping away from me, and I couldn't even hold on to my conscience. But what could I do?'

'Why are you telling me all this? You know I'll do something about it.'

'Because I've been waiting for this day,' she said. 'I knew it would come. It's almost like a release.' She exhaled loudly. 'I just wanted to protect my daughter, that's all.'

'People have died this week,' Sheldon said. 'Things might have been different if you had told me what you knew.'

'I know that.'

'How does that make you feel?'

Dixon looked at the glass, and then at the floor. 'Like hell,' she said.

Chapter Fifty-Eight

John whirled round as someone approached them across the field. 'Who's that?'

There were gasps as everyone followed his gaze. It was a man, striding purposefully, marching straight towards them.

Arni stepped away from the group, holding his hand out to keep them back, and picked up his cane which was propped against one of the stones. As the man got closer, he raised it, brandishing it like a baseball bat. 'Big mistake, mister.'

The man stopped. 'You know who I am,' he said.

Arni tensed, the cane took a twitch.

'Mr Kenyon,' Henry said, and grinned, his eyes glaring. 'Nice of you to call in. You know some of us, I believe. Lucy, say hello.'

Lucy curtsied, mocking him.

Ted flushed and scowled.

Arni looked back at Henry, and then back at Ted Kenyon. Then he started to smile. 'You're brave.'

'Killing young women may be your thing, but I'm not going to let it happen,' Ted said.

Arni looked at Dawn. 'You're too late,' he said, his smile getting broader. 'And you are on your own.'

'Am I?'

John felt a jolt of panic as Ted looked towards him.

Arni looked around, trying to see into the trees. 'Are you?'

'John Abbott?'

Everyone looked towards John.

Ted followed their gaze and pointed at John. 'I know who you are, John Abbott. Do your duty, for Christ's sake.'

Arni looked at John. 'What do you mean, "do your duty"?'

John was thinking of some way to bluff it out, but Ted spoke again. 'I don't know your real name, John Abbott, but remember your promise to serve the public. I'm relying on you now.' Ted looked at Dawn. 'Whatever you have done.'

'What are you talking about?' Gemma said, stepping forward.

'He's an undercover cop,' Ted said, and nodded towards John.

There were murmurs amongst the group. People were looking at him, pulling away.

'You've no choice now,' Ted said. 'So what's it going to be? Do your duty, or be at the mercy of these people? You know what they can do. Don't let another daughter die.'

John felt a churn in his gut, his hands slick with sweat. He looked at Gemma, who was backing away from him, her eyes angry, a tremble in his lip. He saw Dawn, naked and stretched out, the stone stained by her blood.

Then he heard Henry begin to laugh.

Everyone looked round.

Henry just laughed louder.

'Henry, what is it?' Gemma said.

'Do you think I didn't know?' he said.

'You knew?' Gemma said.

'Of course I did, I've known all along. Lucy, take a bow.'

Lucy bowed extravagantly.

Henry's face straightened, and now there was a glimmer

of anger in his eyes. 'They think we are stupid, just misguided nobodies, but we are the people with the vision for a better life. We've talked about how the world is, how we want to change it. They know what we stand for, and then suddenly someone is in the paper for writing graffiti about wanting to be a free man, and when he says sorry in court, the lawyer does a long speech about how he is rich but lost, looking for a meaning.' He shook his head and scowled at Ted. 'John was just cheese in the mousetrap, waiting for me to spring forward. Except that it doesn't work, if I can see the trap as well as the cheese. Am I wrong yet, John?'

John didn't answer. He swallowed and licked his lips.

'Lucy did well,' Henry continued. 'They put your address in the paper, but you knew that, John, because that's how we were supposed to find you. Except that Lucy checked you out first, followed you around. She saw your little meets with your minders.'

'Why didn't you say anything, Henry?' Gemma said, her voice filled with anger. 'I slept with him. You told me to.'

'Because it was a test of my message,' Henry said. 'What if my message was so strong that it could turn the mind of someone who came to us to betray us? And it worked. John is with us now, not against us. He proved that tonight.'

All eyes turned to John, who nodded, panting and scared. 'I'm with you,' he said.

'So prove yourself,' Henry barked, and pointed towards Ted. 'You know what to do.'

Ted took a step back. 'So Billy Privett was about your message, and my daughter, Alice?'

John stopped.

'One of these people killed my daughter,' Ted said, tears jumping into his eyes. 'If he is your inspiration,' and he pointed at Henry, 'then I pity you, because he is just a murderer. And just as greedy as everyone else, because he hooked up with Billy Privett because of his money, nothing more.'

'John, kill him,' Henry said, his voice rising in pitch.

'And then when Billy wanted to tell all, they silenced him. You know nothing of humanity. Who did you use as bait? Lucy?'

'John!'

'I know what happened to my daughter,' Ted said. 'And so will everyone else, because you didn't get every copy of the video.'

Henry clenched his jaw and took a deep breath through his nostrils.

'What happened, Henry?' John said.

Henry pointed at Arni, and then grinned. 'Tell him, Arni.'

Arni put his cane under Ted's chin. When he spoke to John, his eyes never left Ted. 'If the girl doesn't want to join the party,' he whispered, 'sometimes it takes a little persuasion.'

Ted swallowed but didn't move. A tear ran down his cheek. 'You raped her, Mason,' he said. 'A sweet, intelligent, beautiful young woman.' Then he snarled at Arni, 'And you killed her, you cowardly bastard.'

Ted went to lunge at Arni, rage in his eyes, but Arni jabbed the tip of his cane into Ted's neck and he stopped. His hands were balled into fists.

'We drowned the evidence,' Henry said. 'We had to protect the group. No man is perfect, and Arni did wrong, but my humanity, my kindness, forgave him. You are just vengeance, nothing more. A little bundle of hate.'

'I look at you and I see cowardice,' Ted said.

'John, kill him,' Henry said.

John's breaths were coming fast now. He looked at Henry and then at the knife that was next to Dawn's sprawled body.

Ted was looking at him, shaking his head, eyes wide and imploring.

John looked towards Gemma, but she shook her head, her mouth set in anger. He cast his eyes to the sky and the stars seemed to swirl around him, some faded out by the moon, small wisps of cloud moving across it. Emotions welled up inside him as he was assailed by past memories. The thrill of his passing out parade, the early days in uniform. Arrests. Escapes. Deaths. The laughter of those who walked away. The tears of those who didn't get justice. His first year undercover, living amongst the junkies and thieves, and how he came to like them, knowing that he could have ended up like that himself, just a few decisions in his life that went the right way. He had sat in judgement too much, and forgotten that everyone is the same, just people trying to make their way through life. He had ended up lost, not knowing why he was doing what he did. Going undercover had cost him a lot, he knew that. His marriage. His life. All the police had done was strip his life away. Henry hadn't given him the answers, it was the group. The togetherness. The bond. It felt like he belonged somewhere.

John thought of Gemma. Her touch, her hair soft in his fingers. Her skin under his fingertips.

He looked round at the group again. Gemma had a tear in her eye. He had let her down, had kept secrets, but that was Henry's way. They left their old life behind when they entered the group.

The knife was still sticky from Dawn's blood as John picked it up. He pushed his way through the group and stood in front of Arni, who pressed on Ted's shoulder with his cane, so that he went to his knees.

John took some deep breaths. He glanced back at Gemma, who was nodding slowly. Henry was grinning now.

John nodded to himself and moved towards Ted Kenyon.

Chapter Fifty-Nine

Charlie watched, transfixed, as Ted confronted the group. He fought the urge to go across and help him, but Ted was outnumbered and Charlie wouldn't change that. He needed to stay alive to get Donia. But it was such a waste, because the woman on the stone slab was obviously dead, and so nothing Ted could have done would have saved her.

He realised then why Ted had done it. Ted was acting as a distraction, because he couldn't let another daughter die. It was a message to Charlie to get Donia out of there.

He looked at his phone again. There was one bar, just, but it kept flickering, the signal wavering. He scrolled through the numbers he'd dialled before and called Sheldon. He cupped his hand around the phone, and when it was answered, he whispered into it, 'It's Charlie. They've just killed someone, and now Ted is in danger. A farmhouse on Jackson Heights, with standing stones. Hurry.'

He couldn't hear anything. He looked at his phone again to see that he'd lost the signal. He didn't know how much of that had gone through.

Charlie looked back towards the group. They were looking at Ted. This was his chance to slip into the front door. He would be in view, but it seemed to be the only way.

He gripped the corner of the wall and edged forward

slowly. Nobody looked over. As he moved towards the doorway, the light from the hall started to shine on him. The best thing to do was not to go too quickly, to make sure that nothing attracted their peripheral vision. He just kept on moving steadily, and then he was facing down the hallway, and those people at the stones were fifty yards behind him. He couldn't see them, because he was facing away from them, and so he wouldn't know if they could see him until he heard the shouts from behind.

When he stepped inside the house, he put his back to the wall, so that he didn't make shadows across the grass. He edged along, his hand making light brushing noises as it ran along the wallpaper. The cottage smelled of stale food, boiled vegetables, and of piss and shit. He covered his mouth and nose with his arm as the stench made him recoil.

He looked along the hallway and saw that he was heading towards some kind of living room. There were ashtrays on the floor and cushions around the edges of the room. There was a clock on a mantel, but the hands were still. The way ahead was dark.

He didn't have an exit plan, he knew that. What would he do when he got in there? What if the door into where Donia was held was locked? He hadn't thought any of this through, and the more he moved inside the cottage, the more his escape routes narrowed. He had already seen from the outside that the room had a metal grille on the window. He thought again on what Ted had said, that Donia was just bait, for whatever it was that they wanted.

The thought of what they would do to her when she wasn't required as bait anymore emptied his mouth of moisture.

It was too late to go back.

His nose itched from the dust. The further he went, the

more the room came into view. There was no one there, just the signs of communal living. A large dirty pot in the middle of the floor, the remains of some kind of stew around the sides. There were dishes scattered around the room, the remnants of spliffs in an ashtray made out of a large shell. There was a window, and he saw the metal grille on the other side of that glass. There were bottles underneath containing liquid, rags sticking out. Petrol bombs. It looked like Henry's group were getting ready for a siege.

As his hand felt along the wall, he came across a door-frame, and then a doorknob, round and wooden. He turned it slowly. As he pushed, he expected to feel the rattle of a locked door, but instead it started to open.

He looked quickly towards the group outside. Still no change. Then he heard a whimper from the room. A young woman.

He made a silent prayer that he was making the right choice, and then pushed the door open fully and stepped inside.

When he closed the door behind him, he put his sleeve across his nose and gagged.

Ted was pushed to his knees, gasping as he felt the crack of Arni's cane on his shoulder. The grass was damp underneath him.

He looked up at John Abbott, whose arm was stretched towards him, gripping the knife tightly. He could feel the tip against his throat, just pushing, not piercing. A sharp pinprick. It felt wet from blood. Was it his own? The blade trembled lightly, but he knew he couldn't move.

'You don't have to do this,' Ted whispered, swallowing, pushing his skin harder against the tip. 'We could stop this. You could blame it on drugs or a breakdown. I could even forget what I saw, because she would have died anyway. But John, let's end this.'

'What's he saying?' Henry said. 'Don't listen to him. It is temptation, that's all. Remember who he is, what he represents. Think of our mission, what we have planned.'

John faltered.

'Come with me, John,' Ted whispered. 'Just put the blade down. Use it against them.'

'John, kill him!' Henry shouted. 'Don't give him an opportunity. The time is now.'

John looked back to Henry. The tip of the blade moved away, just a fraction. The grip on his shoulder slackened. Ted moved quickly, his hand snapping upwards to grab John's forearm.

John yelped, pulled away, making the blade sweep sideways, an instinctive reaction.

Ted gasped as he felt the slash as heat across his skin. John stepped back, shock on his face. He looked at the dagger in his hand, and then at Ted. He turned to the group. Henry was laughing.

Ted coughed. Liquid splashed down the front of his chest. He looked down. There was blood down his shirt. His hand went to his throat. It felt wet. He pulled it away. More blood.

He coughed again, and when he tried to breathe in, the air didn't make its way to his lungs.

John looked down at him, the dagger limp in his hand now.

Ted could hear laughter. He tried to take another breath, and the night air made him grimace as it rushed into the wound across his throat. But he couldn't fill his lungs. He coughed again, and he felt the warm, oily taste in his mouth.

He tried to stand up so that he could escape, but the ground didn't feel even. It was moving so that he swayed with it, his arms out. He felt clammy, his vision speckled, small dots of colour dancing in front of him. He looked at Henry and shivered. Sounds faded, the grass lost its colour, his view like television interference.

He put his hand to his throat again. It was slick now. He tried to look around the group, but nothing was clear. The colours swirled into one and faded out, the sounds gone.

But Henry's laugh made it through, one last time.

Ted started to fall, the grass rushing to meet him. He knew he wouldn't feel it hit him.

Chapter Sixty

Sheldon looked at his phone. His hand trembled. Someone else had died. And now Ted Kenyon was in danger.

Dixon put down her glass. 'What is it?' she said.

He looked around the room. There were family pictures everywhere. In most of them, there was a young woman, a teenager, skinny, pale and blonde, almost fragile. He guessed it was Gemma, and Sheldon didn't know who had died at the farmhouse.

'The farm where Gemma is living,' he said. 'Where is it?'

'Jackson Heights.'

'I know that, but where?'

'I don't know the exact address. I don't send them bloody Christmas cards,' she said, bitterly. 'Some farmhouse, that's all I know. On a hill somewhere. Why?'

He wondered whether he ought to say something, because only half a story doesn't tell you whether it has a happy ending.

'Something's happened,' Dixon said, her voice getting shriller. 'Tell me.'

Sheldon cleared his throat. Whatever Gemma might have done, she was still her daughter. 'Someone has died up there.'

Dixon's hand went to her mouth, shaking, tears jumping onto her cheeks. 'Gemma?'

'I don't know.'

As her face went into her hands, Sheldon said, 'I'm going up there.'

'Let me come with you.'

'No, you're drunk,' Sheldon said, and then he went towards the door.

'Sheldon, don't go!'

He didn't stay to listen. As he slammed the door behind him, he heard her start to wail. It might not be Gemma, but waiting to find that out wouldn't help anyone.

When he got outside, he felt the cold night air through his clothes. He didn't know what to do at first. He wanted to see this through, to be there when Alice's murderer was caught, but he knew from Charlie's voice that he had to get people up to the farmhouse.

He jumped in his car and set off towards the police station.

The streets were quiet as he drove. He passed a couple of taxis but that was all. He drove through speed cameras at a rate that would get him a driving ban but there were no flashes to worry him.

His tyres rumbled loudly as he raced up the cobbled ramp. He parked it as close to the door as he could and then he ran into the station, banging against doors. As he got to the Incident Room, he saw that there was only Tracey and Lowther there. No Williams. They looked surprised to see him.

He didn't wait for any greeting.

'You need to get some cars. Blue lights, sirens, everything. You need to announce your arrival.'

'I don't understand,' Tracey said.

'Billy Privett's murderers are at a farmhouse on Jackson Heights. They've killed someone already. Ted Kenyon is next.'

Tracey and Lowther exchanged glances, and then grabbed their coats.

'I'm coming with you,' Sheldon said.

'You're suspended,' Tracey said.

'No, I'm on sick leave, but I feel better again.'

Tracey smiled, and then she ran past Sheldon, heading for the car park.

Donia gasped when she saw it was Charlie.

He felt a surge of relief. She looked uninjured, just scared, with tear stains dried out on her cheeks. He had to keep his arm across his nose though, as the smell in the room was overpowering.

There was a man in a bed, old and frail, with sharp cheekbones that jutted through his grey skin, his mouth like an open wound, red lips around a dark hollow. He smelled like he lived in his bed, left to wallow in his own piss and shit.

Donia was next to him, standing up, but her hand was tethered to the bedstead by a metal chain, padlocked around one of the metal struts. She was trying to put some distance between her and the old man, and Charlie could tell it was because of the stench coming from the bed.

Charlie went towards her. Fresh tears ran down her face, and when he got next to her, she wrapped her free arm around him, sobbing.

He pulled her close. The enormity of it was too much to take in, but in that moment, something passed between them, the sudden knowledge that they both knew what they were to each other. It didn't have to be said.

'We need to get you out,' Charlie whispered. 'I promised your mother.'

Donia bit her lip at that, but then nodded vigorously. 'I think they're going to hurt me,' she said, and her voice cracked.

Charlie looked at the chain. It was a solid metal chain looped around her wrist, with a padlock fastening the other end to a metal strut on the bedstead.

'I won't allow that to happen,' Charlie said, and when he said it, he meant it. Except that as he looked at the clasp, he didn't know how he was going to live up to it. He tried to prise it open, but it was solid, as he knew it would be. 'I don't how to do this,' he said, despair in his voice.

Donia looked at him, scared, hope wilting, more tears running down her face. Then there was a noise from the bed. Charlie looked down. It was the old man, his head turned towards him. His eyes were yellow, and as Charlie stared into them, he saw fear.

'Who are you?' Charlie said.

The old man tried to shake his head, but it came as a tremor, nothing more. His eyes went towards a cup on the other side of the bed and he nodded, his eyes widening. A plea.

There was a cup with water in it.

'They taunt him,' Donia said. 'They put the water where he can't reach, and put food in front of him and then take it away. That's what they're like. And there's other stuff too. I heard it.' Her breath caught as more tears came.

Charlie looked at Donia, and then at the chain, but he caught the desperation in the old man's eyes. Charlie went quickly to the other side of the bed before putting the cup to his lips. The old man gulped at the water, his arms not moving, as if he was too weak. As he leaned forward for the cup, Charlie saw his skeletal physique. The sharp edges of his collarbone, the rack of his ribs. They were starving him.

'We'll come back for you,' Charlie whispered to him, and as the old man nodded, his eyes closing, Charlie went back to Donia and tried to work out how to get her free. The bedstead seemed the easiest way. Then her eyes went wide. 'Someone's coming.'

Charlie turned back to the door. He heard them too. Footsteps. Excited voices.

He looked around the room. It was sparsely furnished, with just a dresser in one corner. There was only one place to go.

He went to the floor and pulled himself under the bed.

He closed his eyes and tried not to gag as he got underneath. The smell of shit was overpowering now. His eyes watered, his mouth filled with saliva.

The door opened. Charlie peered along his body and saw heavy boots appear in the room. Steel-toecapped, covered in mud. He pulled his feet up to make sure he wasn't seen.

Charlie lay still, trying not to breathe, hoping that he could trust the old man not to give him away.

The footsteps were loud and they clomped slowly towards Donia. She shrank back, obvious from the rattle of the bed and the way one foot crossed onto the other. Was it a ringleader? If he took him by surprise, would it give him a chance with the others?

But what if he got it wrong? Donia was secured in the room. He could mess it up for her. He had seen what they could do. If they were still waiting for him, perhaps she still had a chance, as long as he didn't give himself away.

The feet stopped in front of Donia. The bedstead clanged as Donia pushed herself against it, in an effort to get away. Charlie's stomach rolled and he gripped the bedsprings so that they cut into his knuckles.

'Please, don't,' Donia said. He closed his eyes. He could hear the fear in her voice.

There was a chuckle, low and mean, and then the rip of cloth. 'I just want to see what you've got,' the voice said.

Charlie heard a slap. Donia cried out and then whimpered a small sob. 'You've got some time. I won't kill you without having a party with you first.'

Even though Charlie's eyes were still closed, the scene was all too vivid. He could hear the shuffle of the man's feet as he got closer to Donia, his breaths quickening, Donia's panic rising. He felt impotent, unsure what to do. When she cried out, Charlie knew he had no choice.

He started to slide out from under the bed, on the other side, so that the man would have to move away from Donia to get to him. Charlie's hands gripped the springs underneath as he pulled himself across the floor, and then when he was free of the bed, he got ready to spring up and surprise him. Charlie knew he would have to fight, there was no choice, because he was trapped and he knew what the group could do.

Then he stopped. There was the sound of running feet outside, excited voices. Something was happening.

Charlie pulled himself back under the bed and heard someone burst into the room.

'They'll be here soon,' a voice said, a young woman.

A pause and then, 'Who?'

'The police. They are bound to be on their way. If Ted Kenyon was here, he must have told people where he was. We need to get ready, we've got a fight ahead. And we need to get Dawn in the ground, and Ted Kenyon.'

Charlie closed his eyes. Why did you do it, Ted?

The silence stretched too long, and then the heavy boots left the room. Charlie could hear excited shouting outside.

He slid out quickly. He knew he didn't have much time.

Donia was against the wall, her arms covering her chest, exposed by the rip of her clothes. There was a swelling under her eye and blood on her mouth.

Charlie tried to control his anger, because it wouldn't help. He had to work a way out of this.

He looked again at the padlock. It was too solid to break. His eyes went to the bedstead. The chain at the other end was around a metal strut. Perhaps that was the weak point.

The old man was lying underneath where the chain was fastened. Charlie didn't want to hurt him, and so he ran to the other side of the bed and pulled at his arm, so that he was dragged away from the chain. Despite his frailness, the old man seemed heavy, as if he was wet. Moving him displaced some of the bedcovers as they wrapped around his body, and Charlie dry-heaved as the sheets were exposed. They were moisture stains on the edge of the sheets and the cloth was smeared in shit. Some of it old and dry, some of it fresher. The backs of his legs were sore and red, with blisters running towards his soiled pants.

'Do they just leave you?' Charlie said, his teeth gritted against the smell and what he could see.

The old man grimaced slightly but then nodded, his eyes closing. Charlie felt his shame.

'I'm sorry,' Charlie said to him, and then ran back to Donia. He rested his foot against the strut, to make sure he could reach it. Donia pulled her body away, her arm outstretched, the metal padlock at the top of the strut.

Charlie slammed his foot against the strut. It rattled in the frame but didn't bend. He grimaced and kicked it again, except this time the strut didn't rattle; the frame did. There was some distortion.

Charlie kicked it once more, and then he saw a bend in it.

He felt a surge of inner strength, the knowledge that he could do it, but he had to move quickly. Charlie gritted his teeth as he kicked the strut hard, each blow denting it a little further. The old man was trying to shield his face and Donia was grimacing.

He was stamping out with his foot, the bedstead banging against the wall. The strut bent in even more. There was shouting coming from outside. He had to go quicker. Perspiration popped onto his forehead He hit it twice more, and then he heard the metal strut clink against the wall, the top of it popped out of the frame.

Donia pulled the handcuff up the strut so that it came loose at the top, the metal chain hanging down from her wrist. But she was free. She gathered the chain in her arms and walked towards the door.

The old man groaned something.

Charlie looked round. He was nodding towards his drawers. 'Clothes,' Charlie said.

He went to the drawers and rummaged through. He found a jumper that might fit her. He threw it to Donia, who looked down at herself and then pulled it on, pulling the chain through the sleeve. She smiled her thanks to the old man.

'We can't leave him,' she said, looking at the bed.

The old man gave a shake of his head and looked towards the door. He made a sound that seemed urgent, as if he was telling them to go.

'We've no choice,' Charlie said, and as he grabbed Donia's arm and pulled her towards the door the old man put his head back. Charlie thought he saw a smile.

Charlie put his head out of the door. He looked along the corridor that led to the outside, felt the freshness of the breeze. He could see the group. Some were digging another hole alongside the one that was already there, working hard with a pickaxe and some spades. Others just stood around, watching. Charlie recognised the figure lying on the ground. Ted Kenyon.

Charlie put his head down and tried to fight off the guilt. He knew he was going to leave Ted there, but he and Ted had made their lives. Donia had a right to make hers.

He pulled Donia quickly towards the room at the end of the hallway. He didn't think that he could go through the front without being seen a second time, but there had to be a back door. From his memory of the layout, it would take them towards the dark hills, where there would be places to hide and they could stay until the morning came around.

Donia's hand felt small in his and Charlie felt her fear through the tight grip of her fingers. They moved through the room, careful not to dislodge anything, to make a noise. There were more shouts from outside but they didn't look. The way had to be forward.

They ended up in the tiled corridor that led to an external door. No one had interrupted them. They were almost there.

He reached out for the door handle, sturdy and reassuring, one push to freedom.

He pressed down slowly with his hand, and he gave Donia's hand a squeeze of reassurance. Then he pulled on the door.

It didn't move. It was stuck in the frame. Charlie pulled on the door again, but it just rattled.

It was locked.

Chapter Sixty-One

Charlie whirled round. There were voices getting closer.

'They're coming back inside,' he hissed, and grabbed Donia. He pulled her into the shadow of an alcove opposite the locked door, shielded by coats hung from hooks on the wall. His nose filled with the smell of dirty clothes, of cigarettes, wood-smoke and oil. He could hear Donia's panicky breathing, her hand clasped around his arm. The chain around her other wrist dragged against his leg. He reached round to give her fingers another squeeze, and her head leaned against him.

'What do we do now?' she said. 'They will kill us if they catch us.'

Charlie looked around to find a way out, but he couldn't see one. The door was locked and too sturdy to kick through. If he tried, it would just give away their position. There was barbed wire draped around the windows and grilles on the other side. It wasn't impassable, but it would take time. They didn't have that.

'I don't know,' he said, frustration creeping into his voice.

The sounds of people filled the house. They sounded agitated, excited jabbering.

'We can't stay here and hide,' Donia said. 'They'll see that I'm not in the old man's room and come looking.'

'We might have to run for it,' Charlie said. 'If we just bolt for the door, people might be shocked enough not to stop us. Just go for the front door and hope it's open. Get out there and run as hard as you can.'

'And if they do stop us?'

Charlie didn't respond to that.

Her hand squeezed his arm again. 'Are you a quick runner?' she said.

He closed his eyes for a moment. 'As long as you are, that's all that matters.'

Charlie tried to stop the tremble in his hand. He realised what he had just said, that he would be the slower prey that would allow the younger one to get away. It was the law of nature, except that he didn't feel ready for the sacrifice. He wanted to spend time with Donia, but that was selfish talk.

He opened his eyes to peer around the coats. There were shadows in the hallway. They would see at any moment that Donia wasn't there.

'Wait until they see that you're missing,' he whispered. 'They'll split up to look for you. That might be our best chance.'

'Okay,' she said, although Charlie heard the tremor in her voice.

Charlie sucked in some air and tried to calm his nerves. 'I'll go first. I might be able to knock some of them out of the way. Just tuck right in behind me.' He looked round, and there was uncertainty in her eyes. He tried a smile. 'Just run hard and fast and hope they move first.'

She smiled in return, but it didn't get near her eyes. They were filled with fear, and Charlie felt the sudden weight of responsibility. This wasn't just about him. He had to get Donia away.

Charlie watched the shadows get closer. It was three young

women, heading for the living room, walking past where the old man slept, and lived. They hadn't looked. They were animated, talking quickly. He heard the word *police*.

Then one of them turned to the old man. There was a shout.

Charlie gripped Donia's hand.

More people came running. Footsteps, shouts. They looked into the room and then split up, suddenly frantic. People ran upstairs, some outside. And then three came through the living room, heading towards them.

'Now!' Charlie hissed at Donia, and then he burst out of their hiding place, heading for the living room, for the people coming towards them. All he thought of was the open door to the field outside.

The women in front of him screamed as he charged. He gritted his teeth, flared his nostrils, and led with his shoulder. He hit the first one hard, who cried out and then fell backwards, taking the other two to the ground with her.

It slowed him down. He stumbled over them, could hear Donia behind him, her hand on his back, the chain around her wrist jangling. There was a man ahead of him now, in a tight vest, with a goatee beard twirled into a tail, muscles taut in his arms. He whirled round as Charlie ran.

Charlie couldn't stop, he knew that. He could see into the hallway, the open door at the end, artificial light spilling onto the grass. Donia was pushing at him, urging him on, panic in her voice.

He tried to run faster, just hoping that if he could get Donia into the open, her youth and fear would do the rest. He shouted out, his teeth bared in a snarl. The man in the vest spread his arms. Mistake. He was going for the grab, not for strength. Momentum was on Charlie's side. Hit him hard and pump with the legs, that was the key.

Charlie put his shoulder into the man's chest, whose head went backwards as he fell, arms flailing, but Charlie was still running, heading for the door. He scrambled over the man on the floor, was able to push away from him with his legs, and then the cold air hit his cheeks. He was outside, no one in front of him, just the dark shapes of the valley ahead, lit by the moon. There was grass under his feet, and shouts from behind him.

Charlie was about to start running when he realised that Donia wasn't pushing at him anymore. There was a scream, a shout for help.

Charlie turned around and then stopped. Donia was on the floor, and the man in the vest was holding on to her legs. Other people were pulling at her, taking her back inside.

They had her.

Chapter Sixty-Two

Charlie hung his head and sucked in gulps of air.

The group had pulled Donia all the way back inside, so the last Charlie had seen of her was her legs kicking out. There had been too many of them, and so it was always a fight she was going to lose. He could still hear her though, fighting against them, screaming.

A man appeared in the door. It was the small man with dark hair and piercingly bright eyes he had seen in Oulton, in a scruffy denim shirt. Charlie knew him now as Henry.

'So you didn't bring it?' Henry said, and Charlie detected some amusement in his voice, as if this was all part of the game.

'Let her go,' Charlie snarled at him.

Henry shook his head. 'That's not going to happen, you know that.'

'If you touch her, I'll kill you.'

'Did you think you could outsmart me?' Henry said. 'You know I want the original tape, but you haven't brought it, so you're just surplus now, a threat to our group.' He tutted. 'That isn't a good thing to be, a threat, because you know how we deal with that,' and Henry glanced towards the stones.

Charlie followed the gaze. He took in the naked woman first, dumped into a hole in the ground her skin pale under the moonlight, spoiled by dark streaks that he knew were blood. Then he saw Ted, face down, rolled into a more shallow grave, soil and grass sods piled up next to him.

He was transfixed for a moment, his mind working a few seconds behind his eyes, terrified by the knowledge that the same people who were now holding Donia had killed them both.

Some women appeared behind Henry, watching Charlie, smiling, enjoying the moment.

Henry spoke again.

'And something else has occurred to me,' he said. 'You've come a long way to rescue your office girl, but we know that she's more than just an office girl, because she told us everything on the way up in the van. People do that when they are frightened. So I wonder how she is feeling right now? So off you go, Charlie Barker, I don't mind. Run as fast as you can, I won't chase you. I'll be too busy enjoying myself in there with your beautiful young assistant. She's very pretty. It's such a shame.' Henry began to laugh, although his eyes remained mean, his brow creased. Then he turned to one of the women behind him. 'Get me a mask.'

Henry didn't take his gaze from Charlie as a plain white mask was given to him. He just smiled and let the mask dangle from his finger.

Charlie wanted to rush him, to wrap his hands around his throat. He faltered, knowing that going in there wouldn't guarantee Donia's safety. It might even condemn her. Both of them. But Charlie knew that he couldn't leave her, and so he walked towards the house. He held on to some vain hope that he might be able to grab Donia and make another run for it, but when he went into the hallway, Donia was at the other end, each arm splayed out, people holding on to her, the man in the vest holding a knife to her throat.

Adrenaline made his hands shake and his stomach turned cartwheels. There was a push to his back and he stumbled towards Donia, whose eyes had filled with tears.

They were outside the old man's doorway and he heard a moan, but Charlie ignored it.

'So what now?' Charlie said.

'What do you think, Arni?' Henry said.

The man in the vest grinned. 'A bit of fun,' he said, squeezing Donia's breast. She squirmed away, but Arni seemed to like that, his grin turning into a laugh.

Henry sidled up behind Charlie and whispered into his ear. 'What do you think, Daddy?' His breath was fetid. Poor diet and bad hygiene. 'Are you going to let Arni enjoy himself with little Donia first, just to buy you some time, or shall we end it now?'

Henry threw the mask at Arni, who caught it with one hand and pressed it against Donia's face. Her features were gone, rendered expressionless, a shop dummy, except for the whites of her eyes staring through the mask. Arni took the knife from her neck and pressed it against Donia's forehead, the blade pushing in the skin, ready to make a perfect line along the top of the mask.

Charlie closed his eyes as the image of Amelia came back to him, her face gone. He knew now how it had happened. He couldn't let it happen again.

Arni started to run the knife across her skin. A red line appeared as small flecks that jumped onto the white of the mask. Donia thrashed against her captors and screamed, but it was no good.

Charlie started towards them, unsure what he intended to do but knowing he had to stop it. Then there was another moan from the old man, louder this time. Charlie looked, just for a second, instinctively. When he saw what the old man was doing, he turned his gaze back to Donia, and saw Arni's grin filled with spite.

Charlie had seen what the old man was doing. He tried to work out how it would end up, his mind working quickly, driven by panic. It could go really badly, but his chances were running out. Anything unusual was the only chance he had.

The old man had somehow moved himself to the edge of the bed nearest the window, where the petrol bombs were stored. His arm was hanging out of the bed, so that it almost trailed on the floor, limp and useless. Except that it wasn't wholly useless. There was a cigarette lighter in his hand, and his thumb was flicking weakly at the wheel. Charlie's eyes had caught a spark, a yellow flash, and it was right underneath one of the petrol-soaked cloths hanging from one of the bottles.

'Stop now,' Charlie said, stepping in front of Arni, keeping the focus on him. He had to stop the group looking into the bedroom. 'If you think that Henry is your hero, then you've been smoking too much of what I've seen in your ashtrays.' He raised his voice so that everyone knew that he was addressing the whole group.

'Don't think we will make it quicker if you annoy us, to make the pain shorter,' Henry said.

'It?' Charlie said, and then looked at the rest of the group. 'You mean torture, murder? Congratulations everyone, I hope you enjoy your brave new world, if this is what you want. I prefer the one we've got now.'

At the periphery of his vision, he could see the old man's thumb flicking at the cigarette lighter again, with just the occasional spark as the result. Charlie willed him on, as the red line grew longer along Donia's forehead.

'You won't have your world for much longer,' Henry

whispered in Charlie's ear. 'Come with us, Mr Barker. You might enjoy it.'

Charlie didn't answer, because he knew that if Henry enjoyed their capture, he would prolong it.

Then the old man produced a flame.

His hand shook with the lighter as he held it under the cloth for a few seconds. The flames seemed to just dance around the rag at first, and the old man let out a long moan. Charlie didn't know if it was from exertion or satisfaction. Then the flame seemed to almost jump from the lighter to the cloth.

Fire shot upwards, streaking towards the neck of the bottle. The sudden brightness made everyone turn towards the room. Someone gasped. The glass bottle exploded, shooting fuel and flames onto the floor.

There was a scream. The fire spread through the room, the petrol on the floor making a churning sea of flames, setting light to the other petrol-soaked rags and then rippling towards the peeling wallpaper, like fingers edging their way forward.

The curtains were soon alight, disintegrating quickly, sending burning embers towards the bed. The view was becoming obscured by smoke, but as Charlie looked, he thought he saw the old man smiling.

Chapter Sixty-Three

Sheldon sat in the back of the marked police car, commandeered from two uniformed officers who were now walking the streets rather than staying warm in their car. Lowther was driving. The blue lights bounced from the windows of the town centre, transforming the quiet streets into a stroboscope. As the shops faded, there were curtain twitches from the houses they passed.

Soon they were into open countryside, and the headlights became a beacon across the open fields.

'So tell me about this group,' Tracey said, turning round from the front.

Sheldon leaned forward so that he was perched between the seats. 'Do you remember how Billy Privett's friends said they didn't get invited to the parties anymore?'

Tracey nodded.

'Billy got involved with this group. Or rather, the group got involved with him. They wanted his money. They were involved in Alice's death, and it seemed that Billy thought they were going after him, so he recorded a video, like a confession, and they found out. So they killed him. It's as simple as that, except they didn't know that the video was only to be made public if Billy died.'

'What about Amelia?'

'She made the video. Henry Mason was just getting rid of the witnesses.'

'But why cut the faces off?'

Sheldon sighed. 'Like most sick killers, Henry just likes the attention.'

'Is that it?'

'Can you think of a different reason? This group are attention seekers. You've seen them on the riot footage, those in white shop-dummy masks.'

Tracey shook her head. 'I've seen them, but I didn't think they were capable of that.' Then she raised her eyebrows, shock on her face.

'What is it?'

'The masks,' she said. 'Remember how neatly the faces were cut away?'

'A template,' Sheldon said.

'That's what I was thinking, that they put a mask on Billy and Amelia and then cut around it.'

'That will help in proving they did it though.'

'DNA?' Tracey said.

'That's right,' Sheldon said. 'If we can find Billy or Amelia's DNA on a mask, we can prove their involvement.'

'But we won't know which of them took part.'

'Arrest all of them. Separate them. One of them will give in and talk, because as much fun as it might be to be free in the hills, the thought of prison loosens tongues.'

Lowther pressed a little harder on the accelerator as they turned towards Jackson Heights. There were more cars coming behind them.

'Let's just hope we get there in time,' Lowther said. 'And I know something else too.' He looked at Sheldon in the rear view mirror. 'If what they did to Billy and Amelia is a sign, they are not going to come willingly.'

That made Sheldon sit back in his seat, because the hills were going to be dark, and they might be outnumbered. But he knew one thing; they were going to stop them, whatever it cost.

The group rushed towards the old man's room, but they all pulled away as the flames crackled through the room, the heat becoming more intense. Those holding on to Donia had let go of her. Arni had dropped the mask and was holding on to the chain around her wrist, his knuckles white as she struggled against him, blood streaming down her face. Arni stared at the doorway, the orange flickers reflected in his eyes, smoke belching out of the top of the frame.

'Get some water,' someone shouted.

Charlie looked into the room one last time, saw the figure of the old man, sitting up in bed, blackened by the flames.

He stepped back. The heat made his cheeks smart. Henry was no longer behind him. Charlie leaned away and started to cough. His eyes hurt from the smoke and the heat had become painful. Everything about him felt like it was searing. His skin, his face, his clothes.

People ran past, buffeting Charlie, holding cups of water. It was futile, like scattering ashes into a gale. He darted forward and grabbed Donia's hand, tried to pull her towards him. It seemed to jolt Arni out of his trance, because he pushed Charlie and yanked Donia back into the room. She tried to twist out of Arni's grip, but he was too strong. Arni was distracted though, his eyes darting from the flames to Charlie.

Someone shouted, 'Henry!' A young woman, a hysterical voice, and then there was a rush of air, fanning the flames onto the peeling wallpaper outside the bedroom. Charlie whirled around. Henry wasn't there anymore. There was no one there. And the front door was closed.

Charlie ran to it, just for an escape route, Donia screaming behind him, but when he pulled at the door, it was locked. He kicked at it, and then banged on it with his fists. 'Henry, Henry. What are you doing?'

No reply. It was getting harder to hear anything though. The flames were roaring now, and there were shouts and screams from everyone inside, with the occasional pop of a bottle from inside the room.

Charlie turned back to Donia. He had to shield his face, the heat was too strong. Arni's spare arm was over his head, curled over, coughing. Donia was hitting him, trying to get him to let go, pulling on the chain. She was coughing too, and so when the chain slipped out of Arni's hand, she fell to her knees, spluttering.

Arni crawled across the floor, eyes streaming, heading for the kitchen. Charlie guessed he was looking for a bucket, or maybe even a way out. The stream of people vainly throwing water at the flames had gone now, and they were backed into the corner of the living room.

The flames were peeling off the wallpaper in the hall, so that the fire ripped up the walls and spread across the ceiling, making an arch of flame. Donia was shrinking back, scared. The heat over Charlie's head was intense beating him back towards the door.

There was some movement near the living room window, the sound of smashing glass as someone tried to make an exit through a window, but the inward rush of air seemed to make the flames burn faster, long licks of orange and black, the crackle of destruction.

'He's left you,' Charlie cried. 'Save yourself. Forget him. Find a way out.'

The group was a huddle now, coughing, apart from one person trying to squeeze through the barbed wire, heading for the broken window, but stopped by the grille outside.

'Donia!' Charlie shouted. 'Come to me. Quickly.'

He had no plan, but he knew he had to get her away from the group, because they weren't helping themselves.

She started to crawl forwards, but then Arni's hand reached and grabbed her hair, pulling her so that she was at his feet.

Charlie knew he was going to have to get her.

Chapter Sixty-Four

There were just seconds left, Charlie knew that. It was time to gamble. If he got it wrong, he would die, along with Donia. Except that there was a good chance they would all die anyway.

The door to the front of the cottage was locked so there was only one way out, and that was up. Everyone was retreating into the living room, huddling closer together away from the window.

Charlie ran for the cluster of petrol bombs still lined up below the living room window. Arni went to grab him, but he was too busy holding on to Donia.

Charlie retreated back to the doorway, so that the flames were roaring just behind him. He had a bottle in his hand. It was hot and his skin felt like it was about to blister away from his cheekbones.

'Let her go,' Charlie shouted. 'Let her come to me, or else I light this and throw it at you all.'

Arni shook his head. 'You wouldn't dare.'

'It's over. Just let her go. Concentrate on yourself.'

'We're finished. She dies with us.'

Donia coughed and struggled, as she looked at Charlie, her eyes streaming. He nodded at her, tried to give her a cue with his eyes, that she had to be ready, but she wasn't focusing on him.

It was a simple plan, but if it didn't work, they would all die. It was a distraction, nothing more. It would make it more dangerous, spread the fire, but it might just give him that vital second to grab her.

'Donia!'

She looked up, and then gave him a small nod back. Do it.

Charlie closed his eyes for a second, but he knew there was no option.

He raised the bottle to the flames. The cloth caught fire, the flame running quickly along the material, towards the fuel. He didn't look at the people in the other room, didn't want to think of what he was about to do to them.

He threw the missile towards the bottles under the window, like a bowling ball at the tenpins. There was a smash, a clatter, and glass and fuel scattered over the floor and the walls. It was like slow motion, as the spread of blue fire grew over the floor, like a blanket thrown over the room. There was a scream, some shouts, quick movement, and then the entire room went up in a whoosh of flame.

John was thrown back against the wall, the group pushing against him, cowering from the flames. Someone went for the back door, but it was locked. It was always locked, because it would give someone a way in through a dark courtyard. The frantic rattle of the door and the shouts mixed in with the crackles of the fire. There was a scream. He couldn't tell if it was fear or pain. The heat was too hot on him.

Donia was struggling and thrashing around in Arni's grip, arms flailing, trying to pull away from the flames that arched over the doorway. He could get to the window, but he himself had fastened metal grilles to it and covered it in barbed wire. There was still a route through, up the stairs, but he couldn't push the group. They were pinning him back.

He reached for Gemma, so that he could feel the comfort of her hand, but she shrugged him off. She was trying to get past the flames, but the heat was too intense.

'Gemma!' he shouted. 'Go on, run. Save yourself.'

Hearing John's shout, Arni went to grab her, but she pulled away, trying to get nearer to the doorway. The heat beat her back each time.

He started to push, to force his way through, but then there was movement ahead.

There were shouts, a scream, and then there was a flash, more flames. The group pressed against him. Someone was sobbing. Jennifer, he thought.

He put his head back and watched as the flames licked the ceiling. He was going to die, he knew that now. He reached for Gemma again, but he couldn't find her.

Chapter Sixty-Five

Charlie turned away as the flames rushed towards him. He felt them scorch across his skin and his nose filled with the smell of burning hair, but the fireball retreated, instead turning into flames that started to eat up the wallpaper, the chairs, the cushions. He couldn't see Donia, and he thought then that he had misjudged it, but then there was movement of someone running towards him. It was Donia, screaming, her hands over her head, and someone else just behind her, running, pushing Donia forward.

Donia's jumper was on fire, smoke billowing from her hair, but Charlie dragged her along the hall, towards the stairs, the only part where the fire hadn't reached, and held her tightly to put out the flames. The smashed living room window pulled the flames towards it although the smoke was billowing upwards. He looked into the room again. The initial rush of fire had died down but was taking hold of everything in the room. A woman ran for the window and then stumbled away, her clothes on fire, screaming. The rest of them were huddled in the corner, hugging each other, one tight circle. Charlie turned away. He couldn't look. Arni was looking towards him, but he was in shock, staring through the flames.

Charlie ripped off his shirt and tore it into three pieces. He held out a piece for Donia and the other woman.

'Don't stop me,' Charlie warned.

'Just get me out,' she said, her voice scared.

He wrapped some of the cloth around his face, Donia and the other woman following. Then he bolted for the stairs.

The smoke was drying out his throat, like a tight grip, so that his coughs came in dry hacks, even behind the rag. His eyes were stinging and the view ahead seemed blurred, but survival was driving him. Donia stumbled behind him. He had no time to assess the situation. It was act now or perish.

'Windows?' Donia shouted, pointing.

Charlie looked into one of the rooms. There were metal grilles on those too.

'Too long,' he said. 'No time.'

'The roof!' Donia said, and pointed.

Charlie looked up. There was a wooden square in the ceiling above the landing. The entrance to the loft space. They could block out the smoke, give them time to break through.

He leapt onto the banister rail, balancing carefully, and then launched himself upwards at the square, at what he hoped was just a simple loft hatch. It moved when he hit it, but he hadn't fully dislodged it. He landed on the floor with a thump. He needed to get higher.

There were noises coming from below. Sobs, cries, the desperate whimpers of fear.

'Hurry,' the other woman pleaded.

Charlie went to his knees and put his head between Donia's legs, his back straining as he stood upright, her hands gripping his hair to get balanced. Once he was stood up, Donia was able to push at the board in the loft hatch, throwing it to one side. She turned away as the smoke rushed upwards.

'Get up there,' he shouted, coughing. 'I'll follow.'

Donia's legs kicked and thrashed and banged on the edges

of the hole, and then she was up there, scrambling into the roof space.

'Charlie, come up now,' she shouted.

He turned to the woman. 'You first.'

Her eyes watered and she nodded.

'Just go,' he said, and bent his back again so that she could get on his shoulders.

It was harder this time, his back straining as he pushed, coughing from the smoke, but eventually he straightened himself, his legs aching, jostled as she used his shoulders to get to her knees, her bony shins scraping on his shoulder blades. But then she was up there, Donia pulling her up.

There was a roar from below as something crashed to the floor in the old man's room, spewing out more smoke and flames into the hallway. The whimpers turned into screams.

'Charlie, Charlie!' Donia yelled, her arm hanging through the loft hatch, the chain hanging down, voice muffled by the shirt over her face.

Charlie was trying not to take any breaths, knowing that the next big one would just fill his lungs with smoke.

He tried to steady himself, but each second of delay just made it worse. Donia spluttered above him. He had to move quicker.

Charlie stepped onto the banister rail again, surrounded by black smoke, and pushed backwards towards the open loft hatch. He flailed against an empty space for a second, and then he felt it. Thick wood, splintered. His palm slapped against it and he swung forward as if on monkey bars. Thin hands grabbed at his wrist and so he reached with his other hand and tried to find the edge, to stop the swing before his arm gave up on him. He felt the reassurance of the wooden frame and paused for a moment.

Those years avoiding the gym worked against him, but

determination drove him on. Hands grabbed at him, and not just Donia's. There were two hands on each of his forearms, and he could hear their strains. Then his elbows were on the edge and he could start to pull himself up. His teeth were gritted with effort, sweat streamed into his eyes, but he made it. He flopped across the ceiling beams. They were sturdy oak. They would hold themselves up well.

'Keep going,' Donia said, pulling at him.

There were shouts from below, and as Charlie took one last look through the smoke billowing into the roof space, he saw Arni rushing for the stairs, hair ablaze, embers flying in his wake, snarling with rage.

Charlie needed the light from the flames to see where he was going, but smoke and Arni were greater enemies than darkness. He put the wooden hatch back into its slot, throwing the space into blackness, and started to shuffle along the roof beams. He needed to get under the sloping roof, so that he could try and break through. Charlie closed his eyes for a moment as he heard the sound of smashing glass from downstairs, and then screams of desperation and pain. He had to shut it out.

Charlie scrambled to his feet and straddled the space between the beams, coughing as he got higher, the smoke curling around his face. He could feel it in his hair, his eyes, in the way his lungs gasped for clean air. Donia and the woman were just behind him, shuffling, coughing, sometimes replaced by soft gasps of fear. His head touched the roof felt, and he was relieved that it was thin and ragged. His eyes stung, his head swirling, but he was working on touch. He closed his eyes and ran his hands down the roof felt, looking for a rip or a tear. It was rough on his fingertips, but as he probed and scoured, he found a gap, wet on the edges, only the roof tiles keeping out the rain.

He kicked it, then tore at it, tried to make the hole bigger. His hands were wet, with blood on his knuckles and his fingertips, but still he tried to make the gap bigger. There were crashing noises coming from below, and then a bang on the ceiling hatch. Arni was trying to make his way upwards.

Charlie pulled harder at the roof felt, and then he felt it: the cold slate of the roof tiles. He was through.

He reached into the roof felt and yanked it down, pulling it away from the supporting beams. It was old and damp, and once he had created a space big enough to crawl through, he kicked out at the roof tiles.

He felt them give way, but still the hole wasn't big enough, and so he kicked again, knowing that time was running out. Then he felt the clean fresh air on his ankle and heard the rattle of a roof tile as it slid down the roof towards the gutter.

The smoke rushed for the new exit. He moved to one side, his head down, spluttering through the cloth, becoming dizzy. Then he punched out some more tiles, the sound of them clattering towards the guttering like loud cracks. Once the space was big enough to get his shoulders through, he ripped off the cloth and took a lungful of night air, let his vision clear, the opaque light of the smoke-filled loft space replaced by the twinkle of the stars, beautiful and bright. Then he felt hands tugging at his leg.

He dropped back down into the loft and shuffled along the roof beams, making the way clear for Donia. Arni was still banging on the loft hatch, jumping up and trying to dislodge it. He grabbed Donia by her jumper and pulled her towards the hole. The chain around her wrist dragged along the beam.

'Be careful getting down,' Charlie whispered. 'Don't stop. Get to the corner and find a drainpipe. Jump if you have to, but just get off the roof.'

She nodded and paused for a moment, but then there was another bang at the ceiling hatch and this time it flew to one side, bringing light and then smoke back into the roof space. And Arni.

'Go,' he said, and shoved Donia towards the hole in the roof. As she wriggled through, he grabbed the other woman. 'This is for my conscience only. Don't let me down.'

'I'm Gemma,' she said.

'I don't care,' he said, and once Donia's feet were through and she was skidding down the roof, Gemma followed. She was agile, and soon he heard them talking on the corner, shouting for the best way down.

Charlie looked around, and he saw Arni climbing into the space, his head appearing slowly, hauling himself up, except that he had the muscles to climb up unaided.

Charlie got his shoulders through the roof again and used his hands against the tiles to clamber up, waiting for one of the rows to give way and make him falter. Arni was screeching with effort behind him. With a grunt of effort, Charlie found himself on the roof, the tiles cold against his back, taking deep breaths as the stars swirled and swam above him.

The sound of Arni's footsteps on the roof beams in the loft space made him move. Arni was moving quicker than Charlie had, because Arni had the light from the moon to give him a target, half the work done for him already. Charlie looked towards the corner of the roof and saw Donia easing herself over the edge, her hands on the gutter, the young woman holding on to Donia's jumper, still on the roof. They were not going to get down before Arni made it up there.

Charlie gestured towards them to keep going and then he scrambled to the ridge, sliding slowly to the other side.

He peered over the top, finding a groove between two ridge tiles. Donia was out of sight now, just Gemma following.

He could hear noises coming from the roof space. Coughs and grunts of pain.

Charlie put his head to the tiles and tried to suck in some more air. His lungs felt dirty. He could taste the smoke and could feel the fire on the redness of his skin. He turned over for a moment and let the fresh air cool his brow. The stars still seemed to be moving, but they were glowing at him too, small pulses of light. He could hear the crackle of the fire. There were no more screams though. He glanced down and saw the orange glow as the flames burst through the windows. Someone must see it soon. The view ahead was all darkness, no other buildings visible, so the cottage would stand out like a beacon.

There was a crash from inside, and he wondered about the walls. He couldn't stay up there all night. The house would collapse in on itself soon.

He turned back around and looked down the roof. Gemma was still clambering over the edge. Then Arni's head appeared, and her fear turned to terror. She wanted to rush but Donia was below her, edging down the wall on the drainpipe.

Arni started to scramble out of the hole in the roof, snarling, knocking more tiles off so that they slid down towards the gutter, rattles in the night. Some flew right off, and the smash on the floor below seemed to take a long time.

Charlie got to his knees and then stayed poised, cat-like, his fingers splayed on the ridge tiles, just waiting for Arni to appear fully onto the roof.

Gemma disappeared over the edge as Arni scrambled onto the roof, up on his haunches, not fazed by the height.

Charlie shouted, to give himself courage, to create a distraction. Arni turned towards him. Charlie leaped over the ridge tiles and ran down the other side, not thinking about himself, focused only on one thing; hitting Arni.

Charlie jumped over the hole in the roof, his feet high and forward. Arni had no time to react as he was hit square in the chest by Charlie's feet, his breath rushing out as Charlie's momentum carried him forward. Arni's feet slid on the roof tiles, and then he was falling backwards, his arms flailing. He hit the tiles hard when he fell. Some of them cracked and joined him in his fall, momentum making him slide towards the edge.

Charlie couldn't stop his own slide. The stars rushed past him now, his head filled with the crack and rattle of the tiles, his feet pushing against Arni. The field ahead accelerated towards him, and Charlie's arms were out, palms pressed against the roof, but it didn't seem to slow him. Arni looked shocked, and as he went, Charlie saw something else in his eyes; fear. He didn't know when the roof was going to end.

Arni's mouth opened to scream as the noise of the tiles under him stopped, and there was a second of silence as he seemed to hang there, realisation in his eyes that he was falling to the ground. As he disappeared out of sight, the only sound was that of Charlie's fight to stop his own slide, until there was the sound of the melon smash, the crack of Arni's skull on the ground.

Charlie slapped at the tiles, but he was still going, had hit Arni with too much force. He could see where the black sheen of the roof stopped, more of the silvery-green of the grass coming at him, the standing stones coming into view. There was silence as Charlie's feet stopped kicking out at the tiles and flailed in the air, just the sheer drop beneath him.

Chapter Sixty-Six

Charlie's hands found the guttering as he slid down the roof, his feet swinging in the air.

'Dad!'

It was Donia, from below. The word seemed alien, but he didn't have time to take it in. He glanced down. All he could see were his legs bathed in a flickering orange light as his body swung in front of one of the upstairs windows. The fire must have taken hold upstairs.

He grimaced as the aches in his arms got worse. It was too far to drop but he couldn't fight the urge to let go, because he wasn't strong enough to hold on. He looked across to the drainpipe. Donia wasn't there anymore. She must be on the ground, looking up at him. Gemma was scrambling down. He had to make it across to the drainpipe.

His arms felt like they were being pulled out of his shoulders. He knew he couldn't hold on much longer, but he tried to shuffle along the gutter.

Then there was the crack of glass, and a shatter, and unbearable heat ripped across his legs. The window had broken, flames roaring out in a rush. His fingers let go of the gutter, from instinct, to get away from the heat. He was falling swiftly, to the sound of a scream from Donia.

His feet hit the ground, hard, and then his body kept on

travelling, so that his knees twisted and his shoulder slammed against the grass. Shards of pain shot up his leg and then the night fell still.

Charlie was breathing heavily, agony making him splutter and grit his teeth. He looked around for Donia, and saw Arni, his eyes closed, his body splayed unnaturally. He heard the pound of footsteps running towards him, vibrations in the grass getting louder, and he tried to turn over, but his leg complained, making him shout out. He looked at it. At least his foot was pointing in the right direction. He flopped back onto the grass.

Donia went to her knees and wrapped her arms around him, squeezing his neck. There were tears running down her cheeks. 'Oh God, you're all right. Thank you, thank you.'

He let out a small laugh and then winced.

'Are you okay?' she said.

'It's my leg.' It was too painful to say much.

'We need to get away,' Donia said. 'That house isn't going to last much longer.'

Charlie looked over Donia's shoulder. There were flames coming from every window, smoke billowing out of the hole in the roof, so that the grass was lit up as if it was daylight, the heat too strong.

He gritted his teeth and started to haul himself up, using Donia for support, until he was standing, one leg in the air, trying not to put any weight on it.

It felt like someone was twisting a knife blade into his knee as he started to move, but he had no choice but to keep going.

'I don't think it's broken,' Charlie said, as he let go of Donia and tried to make his way on his own. He winced and gasped as he hobbled. 'The police will be here soon. We need to sit down and wait.'

There was a noise behind him, like a low laugh. He turned and saw the familiar twists of dark hair as Henry emerged from the shadows of the woods.

'Henry!' Gemma shouted. She had been spluttering and coughing on the grass, keeping away from Charlie.

Henry grinned. 'I'm glad one of us could make it out. But you know that I'm not going to allow witnesses. I died in that fire, that will be the message.'

Charlie stood straight, ready to get through the pain.

'It's over, Henry.'

Henry shook his head. 'It is for you,' he said, and then said, 'Gemma, grab her,' pointing to Donia.

Gemma hesitated and looked at Charlie, and then at Donia.

'Gemma, now,' Henry said, anger in his voice.

Charlie looked at Gemma. Tears were in her eyes. She was looking at Donia and shaking her head.

'I can't do it anymore,' Gemma said, her voice breaking. 'You left us in there to die, just so that you could get away. You said we had to be loyal, but that isn't true. You lied. You locked the door and shut us in. You saved yourself. Why, Henry, why?'

Henry ground his teeth for a few seconds as he looked at Gemma, and then said, 'Because I could. Now, I told you to get her.'

'That isn't good enough,' Gemma wailed. 'We believed in you. You lied.'

Henry stared at her, his jaw clenching, visible under the beard, his hands bunching into fists.

'So that was it?' Charlie said. 'You did it all just to show that you could? You sick, crazy bastard.'

Henry shrugged his shoulders, mocking Charlie, walking round him so that Charlie had to turn on his injured leg to keep him in view. 'A few years ago, crazy meant something,' Henry said. 'Now, everyone's crazy. Take the girl behind you.' He pointed at Gemma. 'She liked it too. So is she crazy, because I didn't make her like that?'

Henry began to walk towards Gemma but she backed off. Charlie turned so that he could keep track, but his knee sent messages of pain shooting upwards again.

'Don't you feel any remorse?' Charlie said. 'For Alice Kenyon? For Amelia? For the people in that house, or that poor woman on the stone?' Charlie flicked a hand towards them.

'Remorse? For what? You people have done everything in the world to me. Doesn't that give me equal right?'

'That's twisted,' Charlie said. 'You can't justify what you have done by self-pity.'

'Why not?' he said. 'We're all our own prison. We've each got our own guards and we do our own time.' He moved closer to Gemma, to Donia next to him, who recoiled. 'We get stuck in our own trips, act as our own judges – because I can't be a judge for anyone else, and so I try and be a judge for myself. I can do that and live with myself. Can *you* do that, Mr Barker?'

Henry came at him in a blur. His hands went around his throat, and then they were falling backwards, Henry on top of him, the ground rushing to meet him once more.

Henry's grip stayed around his throat, his weight bearing down.

'Get her!' Henry shouted at Gemma, looking towards Donia. 'Get rid of the witnesses. It's your only chance.'

Charlie's face was covered in Henry's spittle as he gripped and snarled. Charlie threw a punch, expected Henry to flinch or more, but he didn't. He just kept on squeezing, pushing down. Charlie started to flail. Henry was cut, Charlie's fist splitting one of his eyebrows, but it didn't stop him.

'Gemma, get her,' Henry shouted, teeth bared, panting with exertion.

Charlie couldn't see what was going on, and as he struggled to breathe, he thought of Donia, hoped that she was safe, that she was running across the field, Gemma nowhere near her. There was desperation in Henry's voice, that Gemma wasn't doing as she was told, but Henry's voice was getting fainter. Charlie's chest became tight as he tried to pull in air, but he couldn't find any, so that his body strained. His vision started to fade, and the stars started to swirl once more, the sky spinning.

Then he heard a scream, loud in his ear, the pound of rushing footsteps, and then some movement in his vision. There was the swing of something yellow, a jolt, then a crack, like an axe through kindling. Henry stiffened on him, but his hands relaxed around Charlie's neck.

Charlie sucked in some air and grimaced. His throat hurt. He pushed at Henry, who groaned, sounding in pain, then gasping for air.

Charlie pushed him again, and this time Henry fell back onto the floor. As he looked, Charlie saw Donia standing there, a pickaxe in her hand, the pointed end wet and glistening. And as Charlie looked over to Henry, he saw a growing patch of red under his shirt. Henry's hand was on the wound, and his fingers looked sticky and wet.

'Thank you,' he said to Donia, taking in deep lungfuls of air.

Henry started to shuffle backwards, one hand on the ground, the other on his body. Donia had got him between the ribs and pierced his side. He was groaning in pain.

'Don't let him get away,' Donia said, moving towards Henry, the pickaxe raised again.

Charlie pointed to the gnarled old tree at the edge of the

field, the one he had hidden behind before. 'Tie him to that,' he said. 'He can watch his commune burn as we wait for the police.'

'What with?'

Charlie grabbed Henry's collar to pull him along the ground towards the tree. 'Look around, find something,' he shouted.

Henry wheezed and then gasped in pain. His eyes were closed.

Donia ran towards the house, her arm over her head as she got near to the flames spewing out of the windows, the metal grilles now glowing orange. She went to the outbuildings at the side, using the flames for light. Gemma hung back, her arms across her chest, hugging herself. Charlie carried on dragging Henry, who wasn't offering much resistance, just his feet kicking against the ground. Charlie gritted his teeth against the pain in his leg, and as he got to the dead tree, gripped Henry by the shirt collar and hoisted him to his feet.

Henry slumped back against the tree, his head back. His eyes were getting glassy. Blood was running from the wound in his side and soaking his jeans. Charlie held him there, his arm outstretched.

'The police are coming, Henry,' he said. 'It's over.'

Henry tried to grin, but it turned into a groan and a grimace.

There were footsteps behind him. It was Donia. She was holding a length of barbed wire. The look in her eyes was pure hatred.

'Tie him up with this,' she said.

Charlie was about to say no, that it would be cruel, but then he thought of how close they had come to dying. 'Okay,' he said. 'Wrap it tight.'

Henry shook his head, moaning, but Charlie just pushed him harder against the tree.

Donia grabbed a piece of the wire that had no barbs on it, and bent it back and forth until it snapped. Then she did it again, until she had two long pieces.

Charlie let go of Henry's shirt and grabbed his arms instead, stretched them both along the two dead branches. 'Put the wire around his wrists. Make it tight, so he can't move.'

He held Henry up as Donia did that, moans escaping from him as his weight made the barbed wire dig into his wrists, one loose end trailing towards the floor, the other curling upwards, so that it caught in Henry's hair. When both wrists were bound, Charlie hobbled backwards.

Henry's outstretched arms made his head slump forward, his bearded chin touching his chest, blood pumping out of the wound in his side, the barbs on the wire in his hair standing out as a silhouette against the moon.

Charlie slumped to the ground. As Donia went to him, her arms around him, he rested his head. Gemma joined them, but she was looking at Henry, transfixed.

The night sky began to flicker with blue lights. Charlie closed his eyes. It was over.

Chapter Sixty-Seven

Charlie stepped back into the road to admire the window. He winced as his knee twisted on the cobbles, sending a jab of pain up his body. It had been a month since the confrontation at the farmhouse and his knee was still strapped up. He had twisted it badly, damaged some ligaments, but it would mend, he knew that.

It wasn't the pain in his knee that kept him awake though. It was the image of Amelia, dead in her living room. And Donia, tied up in that cottage. He had worked in criminal law for many years, but he realised now that he had only ever skirted the fringes of criminality. The true horror of the human psyche had visited him now, and it was raw and ugly.

Henry Mason was safe from everyone now, locked up in prison waiting for his trial. He didn't have a lawyer, and was fighting against judges who wanted him to have one. He knew his fate would be prison for life, and so he was settling for what he liked best: notoriety. He still had supporters, those who had become hooked on his message, spread along the internet, on forums and blogs, just looking for excuses for their lives. They peddled Henry's flawed logic and gave him the fame he had always craved.

He felt an arm come around him. It was Donia.

'I like it,' she said.

Charlie smiled. 'Yes, me too.'

Barker and Diaz was written in gold leaf across his office window. Henry Mason might have murdered his business partner, but that didn't mean that he had to forget her. It was only a name, he knew that, but he wanted to keep it going, just his way of saying thank you.

It had been a tough month, Amelia's funeral the most painful part. Her English relatives had cried and mourned, but they had tried to hold in their grief to maintain something they thought of as dignity. Her Spanish relatives had been much different. It was as raw to them as it was to the English, but they had let it out, sobbing loudly, wailing sometimes, words coming out that he couldn't understand. Charlie had felt himself crack a little.

Donia had been there for him, holding his hand, both of them still bearing the scars of what they had been through. Charlie had hobbled his way into church, with Donia's face bruised and scratched. Amelia had been murdered, but the scars on Donia were living reminders of how brutal her death had been. The hug Charlie had received from Amelia's father had been tight and long. He had helped to catch her killer. That was enough.

It was at that moment that Charlie had decided to keep Amelia's name alive, which meant that whatever thoughts he'd had of giving up on the law ended then. To keep Amelia's memory alive, he had to keep the practice going.

'Are you going to keep your promise?' Donia said.

He smiled. 'For as long as I'm working with you, will I have a choice?'

Donia returned the smile. 'I'll keep an eye on you.'

'You'll leave, when you get a better offer.'

'Is there a better offer than working with your father?'

Charlie couldn't answer that one, although he was going to keep his promise.

It had been Donia's idea. Act for the innocent. She thought he had become jaded because he had become sick of peddling lies and excuses. It was time to get a conscience. He would represent only the people who were telling the truth. If they wanted to admit their guilt, he would help them, but the spin would stop. No more of the 'his life is at a crossroads' speech, the mitigation-by-numbers bullshit that most lawyers use. If Charlie had to say that the client wants to change, the client would have to show it. Get a job, apply for rehab, go to college.

The not guilty cases would be the tough ones, he knew that. It would make him judge and jury even before the cases started, because unless he was convinced by their innocence, he wouldn't be interested. No more 'no comment, *you* prove it'. That just acquits the guilty. No, this was the new way. Take a moral stance. Let people like Henry Mason squirm around with someone else's help.

Charlie had liked the idea as soon as Donia said it. It had a certain innocence, like youthful hope, where everything is painted in stark colours, and nothing has been smudged into dull grey by cynicism and experience.

'So when do we open for business?' Donia said. 'My student bills will need paying soon.'

Charlie laughed. 'I'll work you hard, you know that?'

'Work me all you want. This is my route to qualification. My fees are expensive. I need this job to fund my studies.'

'It beats serving pints and pizzas, I suppose.'

Donia grinned.

Sheldon Brown came out of the doorway, holding a piece of red ribbon and a pair of scissors.

'So have we decided which will be my room?' Sheldon said.

'Amelia's old room,' Charlie said. 'I still want to keep some of my old ways.'

Sheldon nodded that he understood and then joined Charlie in the road, to take in the new lettering on the window.

Sheldon had taken early retirement from the police. They had decided on it pretty quickly, unsure about what he might do if they let him stay. Chief Inspector Dixon hadn't been quite so lucky. She had interfered too much to keep her daughter out of trouble, and so she was heading for a court appearance of her own soon.

Charlie felt some remorse for her, because he knew that she had done what she had to protect her daughter, that her motherly instincts had overridden everything else. Charlie could understand a fraction of that, because of the protective feelings he had for Donia, and he knew his emotions must be a long way short of what Dixon must have felt. She had given birth to Gemma, nurtured her. She wasn't some absent father trying to take up the reins too late, when all the hard work had been done.

At least Dixon still had her daughter though, although it would be a few decades before Gemma would be free from prison. Family visits would be done in communal rooms, with Gemma wearing a sweatshirt and a red bib. She had promised to give evidence against Henry, which would help her get an earlier release date. Marie Cuffy hadn't been so lucky, and now her parents knew that she hadn't been on the run, but had died at Billy Privett's house, bleeding out onto his floor after Arni had slashed her throat and then buried in a field, just a stone to mark her grave.

Of course, Marie's wasn't the only body they found at the

house, and Gemma had done her best to tell the police who had been buried there, along with providing names for the charred corpses they found inside the house, John Abbott included.

Charlie watched as Sheldon went to the door to the office, between the tattooist and the kebab shop. He held out the ribbon for Donia, who skipped across.

Charlie smiled. He had offered Sheldon the job as his legal clerk, a non-qualified helper. He hadn't been interested at first, but the thoughts of the empty days ahead made him change his mind.

Donia took the ribbon from Sheldon and stretched it across the doorway. She was grinning, jumping up and down excitedly.

'Cut the ribbon,' she said.

Charlie stepped up and took the scissors from Sheldon.

'Are you going to make a speech?' Sheldon said.

Charlie thought about that. 'How about "this will be interesting"?'

Donia laughed. Sheldon pursed his lips, he had expected more than that, but then a smile broke across his face.

'That will do,' Sheldon said. 'This will be interesting.'

'It certainly will,' Charlie said, and he snipped the ribbon.

They were open for business.

Neil White's Writing Tips

I have been writing crime fiction for eighteen years now, although only as a published author for the last six of them. The twelve years before then were all about trial and error, submission and rejection, along with the occasional fallow year when I just got on with living my life.

I do not pretend to be any kind of an expert on the craft of writing. All I do is give it my best shot and hope for the best. With that in mind, I have been asked to give my top five writing tips, and so here goes.

I'm not going to tell you anything about how to write your prose. If you have got this far you are a reader, and so you know what you like to read and this should be reflected in what you want to write. Neither am I going to talk of environment, and how you should find your special writing space, like there is some kind of literary feng shui. I write on an oak desk with the stereo playing BBC Radio 6 Music, in a room where the Playstation 3 tempts me to be distracted, but that is only because I've been able to negotiate a private space in my house, like a nerdy version of a garden shed. My writing space has been all sorts of things: a cupboard under the stairs, the dining room table, a table on a train. I've written on holiday and in my car during the lunch break in my day job. The environment has never affected my writing, provided I had some peace and quiet.

I'm not saying I would like to write a whole book on a laptop in the front seat of my car, but the important thing is the ability to think, not the quality of the space in which you think.

My writing tips relate to the discipline of being a writer. These hints and tips might not work for everyone, as writers work differently, but these are the guidelines I set for myself.

1. *Accept it won't be good at the beginning and keep going*

Like a morning jog, the hardest part of writing is setting off. All that stands before you is 100,000 words and you do not know what they will be. So you can turn off the computer and do something else, or else you can plant that first word on the page and keep going.

One of the problems I have, whenever I start a book, is that the last piece of writing I have seen of mine was a completed manuscript that had been rewritten and reshaped countless times, and so it represented my very best effort. When I start something new, it is back to unpolished, and so it is too easy to think that it just isn't good enough. It is the same for new writers, where you set out with grand designs of the next great novel of our time, but then stall through lack of confidence after a read-through of the first couple of chapters.

Break through that and keep going. The later parts of the book will be easier to write than the opening chapters, where you will find your style and your rhythm. I rewrite my opening few chapters more than any other part. Just accept that and keep going.

2. *Write it how you like it*

I set out with one goal whenever I start a book, and that is to write something I like. It might be that your ambition is to write for fun, not to be published, but whatever your motivation, there is no point if you don't like what you have written. Write what you want to read, not what you think other people want to read.

So don't follow trends or piggyback other ideas. Don't write about a boy wizard who goes to wizard school just because Harry Potter was very popular. Write it only if you like it. A story written by someone whose heart wasn't in it will be just a book without heart.

If you write what you like, all you can hope for is that other people like it too, and even if they don't, at least you can be happy that you think it is a worthy piece of work. You can hardly expect other people to like it if you don't like it either.

3. *Be prepared to cut out things you like*

One of the hardest things about rewriting is editing out passages or phrases you like, because they sound good or convey a certain message. To put it bluntly, if something doesn't add to the story or character, get rid of it.

Not one reviewer will say, 'Poor story, but it was worth reading the whole book for that second paragraph on page thirty-seven.' If it is a good story, the removal of irrelevant passages, however well written, will enhance it, rather than detract from it. On the other hand, if you can only write one good paragraph, stick to the day job.

If you really like the passage or turn of phrase, save it and use it in later books.

4. *Know your ending*

My journey as a writer started on holiday in 1994, when I decided that sunbathing wasn't my thing, and that my time would be better spent scribbling in a notebook. I wrote four pages during that holiday. I thought it was great. When I got home, I bought a typewriter and set off on the journey. It was the start of something big.

It was important to keep going, I thought, and that the story should evolve naturally, an organic experience. So I did that. Four hundred pages followed, where the plot just unfolded in front of me.

Well, I say unfolded. It just sort of tumbled out. It was rubbish. From start to finish a jumbled and confused mess, with no narrative thread. It took me three years to arrive at that realisation.

I started again, a new plot, a new idea, except that this time I planned it. I wrote a summary, which expanded into four parts, and then each part expanded into smaller segments, so I ended up with chapters, which I broke down into scenes. Most importantly, I knew what the story was about.

If you know the ending, and a few key points in between, it helps you to write the story because you know what will become important later on. You may not follow your plan, I meandered my way through mine, but you can take a detour if you know where it has to end up again. The book I planned became my third book, *Last Rites.*

5. *Finish it*

One of the hardest disciplines is accepting that your work is as good as it is ever going to be.

Writing your first book is filled with dreams and aspirations. Publishing deals, book tours, awards: they all lie ahead. You've told your friends that you are writing a book, and it sounds great for a while, except that your friends start to ask, 'So where's this book then?'

You can get away with delays for a while, blame it on reshapes and rewrites, but eventually it becomes clear that the great work isn't finished because you are stuck in the rewriting loop, convinced that it needs just one more edit, some final tweaks.

I am no different. I rewrite and edit continually but I have deadlines, and so they get me out of the rewriting loop, because there comes a time when I have to attach the book to an email and send it off.

Stop avoiding the end. Give yourself a deadline. Two years. Live your life at the same time, but finish it. Believe that it will be good enough and do something with it. Editors are proud of the work they do, and so there isn't an editor in the land who will say, 'You know what, there is no way I can improve on that.' And improve on them they do. Every book I have submitted has been a much rougher version of what eventually hits the shelves. Don't expect perfection first time, and you can over-edit something so that your work loses its voice and becomes sterile, stripped of its soul.

You will get rejections, lots of them, but you have to finish it to get any chance of an acceptance. You could even publish it yourself, but you can't do that until you have put down that final full stop and raised a glass to your finished work. Until then your great first novel will stay as a pile of paper next to your chair that always needs just one more rewrite.